REGRET - The Price of Truth

Everhide Rockstar Romance Series – Book 4
by
Tania Joyce

EVERHIDE
ROCKSTAR ROMANCE

For lovers of dreams.

Chapter 1

LEXI

I tilted my head back and let the cool night air brush my skin. With too much vodka buzzing through my veins, I swayed and strolled beside my roommate, Hayden Moore. As we headed toward our West Village apartment, my ears hummed, still fuzzy from Everhide's deafening rock concert and the loud music at the after-party. Our best friends were the biggest rock band in the world for a reason. They were born entertainers. Truly talented stars. They'd put on a show that I was truly grateful to witness.

"That was the best concert ever. Gem was amazing," I hollered into the night to dull the unrelenting turmoil tumbling around inside my head. After Gemma's horrific kidnapping two months ago, I'd wanted to forget how close I'd come to losing my closest girlfriend. Vodka had helped, but it wasn't enough. It hadn't erased the nightmares, the fear, the anxiety that someone close had wanted to hurt her. It hadn't numbed yesterday's news of Dad announcing he wanted to remarry. It hadn't deadened today's draining effort dealing with my mom's manic mood swings during lunch. If I could make it through Thanksgiving tomorrow and survive Christmas without any more drama, the new year had to be better than the past few months of hell. "It was so good to see her back onstage with Kyle and Hunt."

"They were freaking awesome." Hayden hooked his arm over my shoulders. "They put on an incredible show."

Grabbing my hand, he twirled me around like a ballerina. The heel of my boot caught on the edge of a crack in the uneven sidewalk. I tripped, stumbled, and wobbled forward a few steps. I burst out laughing, so loud it echoed off the surrounding buildings in the narrow street.

Hayden chuckled and caught my arm to keep me upright. "Are you okay?"

"Absolutely." Still giggling, I drew my shoulders back and straightened my woolen coat. "I could've broken my ankle."

"You shouldn't wear such high-heeled boots." Beneath the lone streetlight, Hayden's steel-gray eyes shimmered with shards of silver, his grin totally contagious.

I leaned against his shoulder. I raised my foot and wriggled and circled my stiletto boot out in front of me. "They are a bit of a health hazard, aren't they? But they're fabulous, and . . . I can't afford new ones." I might live in the West Village with Hayden, but our place was one of the cheapest apartments, on one of the worst streets. Our close group of friends were famous rockstars, stylists, models, and actors, but our own make-it-rich-in-New York dreams hadn't yet come true.

"I'll buy you a pair for Christmas," he said with an assurance that caught me off-guard.

What? He didn't need to buy me anything. "Don't be silly."

I went to step away, but Hayden hooked his fingers through my coat belt and pulled me back toward him. "Hey."

"What?" Laughing, I spun my head around, sending my curls flying, and met him eye to eye. But the intensity of his gaze made me freeze. He took a step closer. His eyes narrowed. A stormy darkness swirled in their depths. Just like in the Maroon 5 song, I found it harder and harder to breathe. Why was he looking at me like that? He *shouldn't* be looking at me like that. All daring, fevered, sexy and smoldering.

Shit! I knew that look. I'd hooked up with enough guys to know what he wanted. And wanting *that* with *me* wasn't an option. My list of fuck-ups was lifelong—from being my parents' mistake of a third child, to causing their divorce, to wasting three years at college studying photography, to always falling for the wrong guy. I wasn't about to destroy the best thing in my life. Hayden's friendship was the one thing I wouldn't risk.

His dark-brown hair flopped forward. Rubbing his hand over my coat sleeve, he let out a slow breath. "Lexi?"

My heartbeat hammered faster. Faster. Faster.

I was too drunk. Way too drunk. So was he.

I wanted to run, but some magnetic force glued my feet to the ground. I eased my arm free. "What are you doing?"

A smile quivered across his mouth. He cupped the side of my face. "Something I should have done a long time ago."

"Hayd—"

But it was too late. His lips crushed against mine. Clenching my fists, every muscle in my body tensed. Every cell screamed. He was my best friend, and had been since our first year at NYU. We'd been roommates for seven years. We gave each other shit. We were each other's wing person, sidekick, plus one, shoulder to cry on, and friend to call on when needed. Hanging out together was as natural as breathing. We could talk for hours, sit in silence, or dump our dramas on each other. We'd often set each other up on dates and divulged every detail—the good, the bad, and all about the sex. We told each other everything. But we weren't into each other. We'd never kissed.

Kissing was off-limits.

My hands shot up, and I shoved him back a step. My eyes stung as I shook my head. It hurt to draw breath. "Don't do this. You promised."

"Shh." He slid his hands around my hips and shuffled me back a couple of steps until I connected with the building's brick wall. His jeans brushed against mine. His body pressed into me. A devilish grin curled the corner of his mouth. "I promised many things when we first moved in together. I promised not to tease you about the guys you brought home. Not to clean up your mess. Not to eat your mango ice cream. I've broken every one of those rules. And now I'm breaking one more."

My eyes dropped to his lips and flicked back to his gaze. His broad shoulders formed a barrier, blocking my escape. This was dangerous territory, a path I'd sworn never to go down.

He dipped his head. His mouth hovered an inch from mine. "Kiss me."

Kiss him?

What the hell?

I wanted to laugh, scream, cry, run. Placing my hand on his chest, I had every intention of pushing him away. *Every* intention. But vodka-infused adrenaline spiked through my veins. My head spun from the intoxicating smell of beer on his breath and the hypnotic scent of his Prada cologne—a mix of sandalwood, cedarwood, and every bit Hayden.

"Lex." My name, rumbling deep in his throat, sent a jolt of electricity straight between my legs. Caressing the side of my neck, he leaned closer. "Please?"

I closed my eyes.

This was a bad idea.

A huge mistake.

This was trouble.

He touched his warm lips to mine. I dared not draw breath, dared my heart not to beat. But with a flick of his tongue, he deepened the kiss . . . and sent me into a spell-induced trance.

Heat surged through my veins like steam through a fissure. Threading my fingers through his thick hair, I craved to taste him. To kiss him harder. Longer. Deeper. Each lick raised my body temperature. Every breath tapped against my troubled heart. Each touch of his lips sent heat rushing to my core, fueling my want and dampening my panties.

Crap.

So, so good . . . but so, so wrong.

Driving his hips forward, he nudged his hardness against my crotch. His jeans couldn't hide the effect our kiss had on him.

Shit! I squeezed my eyes shut and clutched his short hair. This kiss had gone too far. This was just some drunken foolery between friends. There was nothing to it . . . *right?* We'd laugh about it tomorrow over our morning coffee.

This kiss had to stop . . . in a moment.

"Get a room," some guy walking on the other side of the street yelled.

My pulse skidded to a halt like tires on asphalt. *A room? Shit.* Yep. Stop. *Stop. Stop. Stop.*

But oh . . . sweet mercy.

Why couldn't I pull away or utter any words?

"Ignore him." Hayden's voice, hot and heavy, brushed across my mouth. He smiled, swayed, and kissed me again.

Each touch of his lips erased any logical, reasonable thought. Light as a feather, he glided his fingertips down my cheek, my throat and slipped them underneath my open coat. My pulse quickened as he skimmed his hand across my knit top and stopped beneath my breast. *Tease.* In tantalizing strokes, he circled his thumb over my nipple, hardening it into a peak. *Why does that have to feel so good?* My head spun as it fell back against the wall. *We really should stop . . . Yes, we should . . . We must . . . In another second . . . or two.*

His lips never left mine as he melted against me, molding to my curves. My heart raced too fast. My body betrayed me, wanting him closer. More of his touch. More fire.

"I love you, Lex," he whispered over our kisses. "So goddamn much."

What the fuck?

No. No. No.

The spell obliterated.

I fell back to earth with a crash. I shoved against his chest, forcing him back two steps. Tears prickled my eyes, and I shook my head. He couldn't have fallen for me. No way. I'd made it clear from the day we'd moved in together. I never wanted to fall in love.

Love destroyed you.

It corroded your soul until there was nothing left but an empty shell. Like what had happened to me when my ex, Quintin, had left. Like what had happened to my mother. And my father. Divorce hadn't healed their broken hearts. Time hadn't healed mine.

Love sucked. Love died. Love wasn't for me.

Love wasn't worth the pain.

"No. You don't love me," I whimpered. "Don't be stupid."

He shuffled forward. He caught one of my spiral curls between his fingertips, pulled it straight and let it go. It sprang back into place. "It's not stupid. It's the truth. Do you honestly feel nothing for me?"

The agony carved into his voice was a crushing vise around my heart. I clutched his hands. "Of course I do. You're my best friend."

"I want more." His eyes searched my face as if hoping to find a lifeline.

I had no rope to throw. "I'm sorry. I don't feel that way about you. I'll never feel that way about you."

Pain rippled across his face, drilling a deep furrow into his brow. He lowered his chin and nodded. "I had to know. Had to find out."

"By kissing me? You could've just asked." Too much heat flushed my cheeks. The chill in the air made them hurt. I wanted the remnants of our kiss gone.

"Where's the fun in that?" He smiled, but no humor touched his eyes. "I was hoping for a different outcome."

"I feel terrible," I uttered as a cab zoomed down the street.

"No. Don't." He shook his head. "But are you one hundred percent sure?" He peered at me from underneath his thick eyelashes. "Have you ever wondered, thought about, had any remote curiosity to see if we could be something more?"

I searched deep within my heart. The place I'd reserved for him could never be more than friendship. I wouldn't fall in love again. I didn't have the strength to face loss or loneliness, or to have life leached out of my body. There was no way I'd end up like my mother. "No, I haven't."

He stuffed his hands into his duffel coat pockets, and flicked his hair back. "You can't keep people at a distance forever, Lex. We've all been hurt. It doesn't stop us from trying again."

"Hayds, it's not that." It so was, but I needed to erase his disappointment.

"I know you." He splayed his palm across his chest. "It was stupid of me. I'm sorry. I should've known I wouldn't be the one to win you over. If you're certain, it makes my decision easier."

Confusion swam through my head. "What decision?"

"I'm gonna move out."

The pain in my chest tripled, ripping and clawing at my ribs. "What?" I screeched. "Are you joking?"

He shook his head slowly. "Nope."

"But you can't."

"I have to." His breath misted in the chilly morning air. "The guys and I got a gig in Boston. We start at the end of January."

"Boston?" My knees buckled. Luckily the wall was behind me, or I would've fallen to the ground. "No. No. No. Not Boston." He'd been the drummer in his band, The Saylors, for six years, working local gigs and events. They'd had one Top 100 hit three years ago but hadn't capitalized on its success. *Shit.* "What about your work here?"

He shrugged his shoulder. "I'll miss the studio. And Broadway. They've kept me sane and helped pay the rent. But the guys and I are tired of chasing gigs, waiting for another break. Nothing has happened. It's too competitive in New York. Too hard to get our demos heard. One hit has meant shit." He scuffed a boot against the concrete. "Kyle, Hunt, and Gem have helped promote us, but we're not as good as they are. We haven't captured the interest of any record company, so we've gotta do it on our own. In Boston, we'll earn some decent money. We'll save up and record another album. We've landed a decent booking agent, and we'll hit the festival season next summer."

My vision blurred as I stared at the taillights of a car cruising by, its wheels splashing through a puddle from the earlier rain. *'Boston'* kept drumming in my ears; nothing would drown it out. "But your dream was to make it here. Not in Boston. You hate half your band."

"We're fine." His gaze hit the ground.

Yeah . . . I didn't believe him.

"The move will be good for us. Make us stronger. I just want to play drums every day for the rest of my life."

"You do that here." I clutched and pulled my scarf.

"We need to try something different." He lowered his voice. I could barely hear him over my crying heart. He toyed with a toggle on my coat. "I wanted you to come with me, and take a chance on being more than friends."

"Go with you?" A lone tear escaped, catching on my cheek. "I can't. My life is here. My job is here. I'm in the running for a promotion." The opportunity to further my career at *The Gourmet Reviewer* magazine—move from restaurant reviewer and blogger to senior editor—was within my grasp. I'd worked hard for it. I didn't want to miss the chance.

He shot an icy glare at me, pinning me to the wall. His jaw tensed like a tightrope. "Why do you even want it? I know the money would be great. You write brilliant reviews. But it's not what you want to do." Frustration cut deeper into his raspy voice. "When are you going to pursue your photography? If you get that promo, you won't touch a camera." He placed his hand over his heart. "I'm going after my dream. When are you going after yours?"

I puffed out a short breath over my callous laugh. "Umm . . . never. There's no money in photography. I loved shooting Kyle and Gemma's wedding, but I don't want to do that kind of photography full-time. I love my weekends too much. I hate sports. I don't travel. Fashion is too competitive. Freelancing is unreliable. I've submitted my portfolio to nearly every goddamn gallery in Manhattan only to be rejected time and time again. I can't see MoMA wanting me to exhibit my work anytime in the future . . . or ever. If I climb my way up the ranks at the magazine, it might get me a foot in the door at some other publication . . . maybe something home or lifestyle-oriented."

He threw his hands up in the air. "Oh . . . kill me now. I'm all for career changes, but that's not you. What happened to working for *Bazaar*, *Elle*, or *Rolling Stone*?"

Ouch. That hurt. My photography had become a hobby, not a career. "Reality hit. Dreams have to change. I'll never make a living through photography."

"You can. Come to Boston with me. I'll cover costs until you find a job."

"No. I don't want you looking after me. Not ever."

"Why not? We'll stay with the guys. Once you get work we'll move into our own place. Start fresh. Be together."

"No . . . I don't want—"

"Shh . . . I'm sorry." He closed the gap between us and cupped my face again, his touch toasty warm. "I don't want to fight." Regret loomed in his voice. "I have to move, Lex. Music is who I am. It's gonna hurt like hell not having you around." He stroked my cheek, pressed his forehead against mine. "I'm gonna miss you like fucking crazy."

Did he just reach into my chest and rip out my heart? I couldn't draw breath. "You can't leave. You promised we'd be friends forever."

"We will be. We'll still see each other. You can come visit, and vice versa."

I clutched his forearms, dug my fingers in hard to steady myself, to stop my knees from buckling. "You're my best friend. I can't lose you."

"You won't." His breath, heavy with alcohol, teased my face. "I can't make you love me, Lex. If you wanted to take a chance on us, I would've begged you to come with me, done long-distance, or given up everything to stay. But you don't. So it's time for me to move on."

I pressed my palms against his unshaven cheeks and squished them. "I do love you . . . just not in a romantic-relationship way."

He smiled a sad smile; crinkles formed at the edges of his eyes. He sighed and drew my hands away. "Got it. But you've stopped letting people get close to you for so long you've failed to see what's right in front of you."

I jabbed my finger against his chest. "You shouldn't be such a fool to put your faith in love."

He staggered back a step and took my hands in his. "I have to believe there is someone out there who will love me for me. I thought that was you. We've had the best fun together, partying hard, going out and hooking up with different people. But in the last few months, you're the only one I wanted to be with."

"No . . . That's crazy talk." Sirens wailed in my heart like the ambulances zooming past the end of our street. But what if I had deeper feelings for Hayden? Denied them? *No. No. No . . .* now I was being loco. "We need each other's friendship, not love. This crush you have will pass. We'll laugh this off, put it behind us and go back to being just friends. Go back to normal."

He play-punched my arm. "We're far from normal, Lex."

So true. "What are you going to do about your mom?"

That snuffed out the light in his eyes. "I'm four hours away. If she relapses, I can be here soon enough. You don't have to worry about her."

"Please don't go." I clutched the lapels of his coat and gave him a shake. "Just when I was looking forward to the new year, you've gone and destroyed everything."

He caught my hands, wrapped them around his waist, and pulled me into a hug. "No, Lex. It's time for a change. New adventures." He caressed the back of my head and gave it a soothing rub. "Once I've settled in, you can come see me play. You'll always have a VIP backstage pass. I promise."

I sobbed against his shoulder. *No. No. No.* I didn't want passes to his shows. I wanted him here. I didn't want this to be one of our last hugs. Losing him would break what was left of my tattered heart. "What will I do without you?"

"Don't be upset." He rested his head against mine. "We have two months until I move. So let's make the most of the time we have left together. Let's do all the crazy things we've always wanted to do. Lots of first-time fun. Lots of last-time adventures. Lots of good times to be had."

I closed my eyes and held him closer. "I don't know if I can do that. I don't have the strength to say goodbye."

"You do. I know you do."

"No promises."

Toward the end of January, he'd be gone. Every bone in my

body ached. My heart tried to crawl out of my chest. It crippled me. I'd never contemplated Hayden leaving, and now it stared me in the face. What would I do without him? We had such a short time left to make new memories, ones that would last a lifetime.

But I liked his plan.

We'd work through our bucket list. I'd send him off with a bang. *Oh crap.* I couldn't breathe. I never wanted to say goodbye. Why did the news of his leaving hurt so goddamn much?

Chapter 2

LEXI

After Thanksgiving dinner, I joined my girlfriends on the balcony at Hunter and Kara's penthouse. The bright city lights of Tribeca and the view south filled the night sky. Curling up on the comfy outdoor sofa next to Gemma, with Kara sitting opposite, I drew a throw rug over my legs and savored the warmth emanating from the nearby gas heater. My head still spun from Hayden's confession last night. I still hadn't processed his move to Boston. The news had hurt even more when he'd told our friends during dinner. The ache that had sprouted deep inside my chest hadn't gone away.

My life had been turned upside down.

What would I do without him?

I wanted to kick myself for not seeing the signs Hayden loved me. We'd always flirted, had a lot of fun, and had an unwavering friendship. I couldn't pinpoint the time when things changed. When had the way he looked at me, the way he touched me and each suggestive innuendo altered? When had normal not become normal? For me? . . . Since last night. Being in the same room was now awkward. All day, I'd walked around on eggshells and had watched what I'd said and done.

I didn't want anything between us to change. But it had.

Gemma sipped her JD and flipped through the folder of proofs for the hundredth time, checking each photo I'd taken at her wedding in Belize last month. "It'll be hard to pick one for the wall. They're all awesome."

"Um . . . thanks." My voice deadpanned. My vision blurred as I stared at the scented candle burning on the coffee table.

Gemma snapped the folder shut and placed it on the sofa beside her. "Lex, what's wrong? You've been acting weird all night. Is it because Hayden's leaving?"

I puffed at a stray curl dangling down my forehead and stared into my wine. Ever since I'd walked home with Hayden last night, my mind, body, and soul had seized. No amount of grease could get my cogs turning. Living with Hayden had an expiration date. A date I'd never wanted to face. As I swiveled the stem of my wineglass between my fingertips, I wished the cold air would penetrate deep into my skin, freeze the pang in my chest and ice over the mess that had been stewing inside my head since he'd kissed me.

It was more than his leaving. I was afraid of the depth of his feelings toward me. Afraid of the *never-want-to-let-you-go* soft spot I had for him. But letting that evolve into something more wasn't an option. Love wasn't worth the risk. And I'd never stand in the way of his dreams.

Gemma placed her hand on my knee and gave it a gentle nudge. "Something's got your panties in a knot. Did you and Hayds have a fight?" She jerked her head toward the doors behind us. "He's probably in there telling Hunter and Kyle about whatever's bothering you, so out with it."

"Gem's right." Kara grabbed the bottle of wine to refill our glasses. "The sooner you tell us, the sooner you'll feel better. It can't be that bad."

The joy of having tight-knit friends. There were no secrets.

I glanced toward the kitchen. Hayden stood at the counter drying a dinner plate. I caught his gaze. My heart sank, fluttered, raced, faltered. It was like it didn't know how to beat correctly anymore. Everything between us had changed.

He smiled, but sorrow had replaced the normal vibrance in

his eyes. My stomach sank to the floor. If I told the girls what had happened, I'd have to relive last night. But all I wanted to do was forget. Forget the walk home from the after-party. Forget his kiss. Forget his whispered words.

I swallowed the lump in my throat. The pounding in my head grew louder and louder. But with Hayden leaving . . . I needed Kara and Gemma's support in the coming weeks. "It's worse than bad." Nausea bubbled up my throat. I closed my eyes and drew in a shaky, shallow breath. "We kissed. In a make-out kinda way."

Gemma shot forward, choked and spluttered on a mouthful of JD. It snorted out her nose. Kara froze; her wine glass suspended halfway to her mouth. Their eyes, wide and white, bulged in the soft light.

Gemma thumped her fist against her chest, coughed and cleared her throat. "You. Did. What?"

"But-but-but—" Kara's words came out as fast as a clicking camera. Her fair skin turned even paler. "I didn't think you liked him that way."

"I don't. He started it. We were drunk and got carried away." My shoulders slumped two inches. How could I have crossed the line? "But it gets worse." My grip on my glass tightened so much I was afraid it might shatter. My heart ached with every single beat. "He said he *loved* me."

"Holy shit." Kara's hand shot over her heart. "Hayds loves you? Since when?"

It was good to see they were as shocked by the news as I was when those words had slipped from his mouth.

"He said things had changed over the past couple months. He wants me to be his girlfriend."

"So, are you together now?" Excitement lilted in Gemma's voice.

I couldn't shake my head fast enough. "No."

Gemma twisted toward me. She propped her elbow on the back of the sofa and rested her head against her hand. Bewilderment was still etched on her face. "Is that what's troubling you? You have feelings for Hayds but you turned him down?"

"No. I don't feel that way about him." Ignoring the unease swaying through my stomach, I wriggled and squirmed on the seat. I couldn't have deeper sentiments for Hayden. That would only lead to another smorgasbord of problems.

"Are you sure about that?" Kara tucked her model-length legs beneath her; worry darkened her deep blue eyes.

The niggle at the base of my neck twisted tighter and tighter. "Yes. Don't be stupid. You know me better than that. I don't want a boyfriend. Been there, done that. I'm twenty-five and in the prime of my life. I love being single and hooking up with hot guys. I won't mess with our friendship." I'd sworn never to fall for anyone again, especially a musician. We'd been madly in love. Had thought we'd survive anything. But my relationship with Quintin had died a slow, painful death when he'd left to work on a cruise ship in the Caribbean. Long-distance had destroyed our love. The heartbreak had scarred my soul for life. "Kissing Hayds was a mistake, some drunken foolery. I can get over that. But not the whole *I-love-you-and-I'm-leaving-you* thing. We had a deal. No love. Never leave each other. Now he's done both."

Gemma clutched and squeezed my hand. "I'm sorry, Lex. I always thought you and Hayds would end up together."

"What? No." I yanked my hand free. Frustrated, I stared into my wine. "Music is his number-one priority—always will be. No girlfriend of his has lasted because of it. We're just good friends who have a great time together."

As Gemma poured another JD, smugness quirked across her mouth. "Yeah—but *just friends* don't make out. Take it from me, one kiss can change everything."

I shook my head. "It won't." I didn't want to unpack what had happened between Hayden and me any further. Not now. Not ever. I needed to lock it away and shove it into the back of my mind like a jar of old spices in the pantry. "I want to forget what he said. Forget what happened."

I had to deliver two months of fun and good times before he moved, and make sure our friendship stayed intact.

But would spending more time together make things worse?

I didn't want him to fall more in love with me. I didn't want to break his heart or be cruel.

After placing my glass down, I pressed my palms against my eyes. I wanted to erase the vision of him kissing me that had been permanently etched into my brain. We could never be more than friends. I wasn't like Gemma, who'd found love with her best friend and fellow bandmate, Kyle. I wasn't like Kara, who'd found love with Hunter after they'd shared a traumatic experience. My girlfriends had found happiness . . . for now. I was stoked for them. I prayed their relationships lasted. But the reality was they wouldn't. Love always ends in broken hearts. One day they'd come pounding on my door and I'd be their shoulder to cry on.

Gemma swirled the JD around in her glass and stared at the amber liquid. "I can't believe he's moving. I'll miss jamming with him."

Fighting the sting in my eyes, I sniffled and rubbed the tip of my nose. "He asked me to go with him. But I said no. I can't. I have a career. I have to keep an eye on Mom."

Gemma peered over the rim of her glass. "You totally rejected him, didn't you? But Lex, are you being honest with yourself? Hayds has always been there for you. You two are inseparable. On top of everything else, he's freaking hot. Are you sure there is nothing between you?"

I feigned a laugh; it overruled the tremor in my heart. "I'm not blind. I know he's good-looking." I'd taken more than a million photographs of him. Pictures, especially the black and white ones I loved taking, had never lied. But now, the smoldering shimmer in his eyes when he'd looked at the camera had taken on a different meaning. *Damn it.* I'd thought he was just photogenic. A beautiful soul. My friend. If he'd developed deeper feelings for me, then that was his problem. Not mine. He just had to get over them. "Hayds is the best roommate, awesome to hang out with, and has helped me through some shitty times. But I can't change the way I feel. I've known him for too long."

If I wanted a relationship, I'd need a guy with more than good looks and laughter. Security, stability, and someone who put me first—before music or whatever career they had—would be at the top of my list. Hayden was as unstable as corn kernels on a hot plate. He'd drummed his way from his part-time sessional work at an indie recording studio to occasionally filling in at Broadway musicals like *Wicked* or *Aladdin* when someone was sick, to local gig after local gig. Nothing was regular or consistent. I didn't know how he survived, but he did.

A devilish glint flared in Gemma's eyes. "Is he still a great kisser? Did he cop a feel? Did he get you off?"

I grabbed a cushion and threw it at her. "You're not helping. You can trip down Memory Lane, but I don't want to think about kissing him again." Not his hot lips, or his tantalizing tongue, or his roaming hands. *Nope. Nope. Nope.*

But since making out with Hayden, the ache between my legs hadn't subsided. It had coiled so tight I was like a pressure cooker about to explode. No attempt at self-preservation had relieved the symptoms. Last night, when I'd finally crawled into bed, I'd tried to masturbate, picturing Liam Hemsworth doing wicked things to my body . . . but Hayden had popped into my head. Like being doused with a bucket of ice, my efforts had come to an abrupt end. I couldn't . . . or didn't want to . . . get off to him.

I was unsatisfied. Frustrated. In need of a good fuck. *Damn you, Hayden.*

I grabbed my wine and took a sip. I swirled the rich red around in my mouth and swallowed hard. "To answer your question, no, I didn't get off. Being around Hayds has turned awkward. There's this tension in the air. Every time I look at him, his eyes are filled with disappointment and hurt. I feel terrible. I've tried to avoid him today, but it was near impossible with him rehearsing at home. I want to spend as much time with him as I can before he leaves, but I can't think straight anymore." When he was near, all I wanted to do was run away. Hide. His very presence made my breath hitch, my pulse jump, and my heart pound like I'd run a marathon. Heat had flushed my cheeks. My body was not listening to my brain. This had to stop. "I'd love a few days away to put the kiss behind us, to process he's leaving and to come up with a game plan."

"Just don't shut him out." Gemma shook her head slowly. "He won't handle that."

"I won't." No, I could never do that. We'd been through too much. But a few days apart wouldn't hurt.

Kara sat two inches taller and flicked her long golden-brown ponytail over her shoulder. "I have the perfect solution. Come with us to LA." Her gaze jumped to Gemma. Since Kara worked as Everhide's stylist, she no doubt sought approval. She'd gotten no objections from Gemma . . . but from me?

"Whoa. Whoa. Whoa." I held up my palm. "I had a week off last month for the wedding. A long weekend before that for Gem's bachelorette party in Vegas. I can't afford more time away from work. I'm not irreplaceable."

I didn't want to upset my boss. I didn't need to be next in the firing line.

But some time away from Hayden would be nice. Petty, but nice.

For the next few weeks, Gemma, and the guys would flit across the country to attend and perform at music award celebrations, Christmas shows, and gala events. Kara, as part of their entourage, would travel with them. A wave of jealousy crawled beneath my skin. I'd love to travel, but I couldn't be away from home for more than a few days. I needed to check in on my mother. She'd been diagnosed with bipolar disorder when I was ten. She often forgot to take her meds and eat, and some days couldn't get out of bed. There was no one else around to help. Aunt Nora was useless. My two brothers were deployed in the army. The responsibility of looking after her had fallen on me.

I was terrified I'd share the same fate as Mom. That I'd end up depressed. Lonely. Lost. I'd never want to rely on someone to look after me.

Gemma slapped my thigh. "Your boss loves you." She flashed her rock-star-goddess smile. Her emerald eyes shimmered in the soft light. "Haven't you got a stash of articles and restaurant reviews that have never run in the magazine? Just use them." She bounced on her seat like she always did when excited. "Please come with us. We fly out Monday morning and will be gone for two weeks. We have plenty of room in our new house. I'll get you into some after-parties. We'll have some crazy fun."

I pursed my lips to contain my smile. Gemma never hesitated to include Hayden and me in their outings. Nothing was ever an inconvenience. And I did like flying on Everhide's chartered jets. A dash of excitement eased the stress constricting my veins. A getaway was what I needed. Could I get the time off?

"It sounds perfect. But my boss is a creep." The thought of meeting with Chase sent chills scurrying down my spine. "To get approval means I have to talk to him, and I'd much rather not be in a room alone with him. He makes Harvey Weinstein look like a saint."

"Why? What's he done?" Kara's brow furrowed beneath her bangs.

The wine in my stomach curdled like sour milk. "At the Halloween party last month, he was really drunk and touched my ass when he introduced me to a board member. It made my skin crawl. I'm not sure if he did it on purpose or if it was a genuine mishap."

"What?" Gemma's voice pitched high. "You didn't tell us?"

"No." I brushed Gemma's concern aside. "You were away on your honeymoon, then busy with rehearsals."

Worry flickered through Kara's eyes. "You need to report him to HR."

"No." I jerked my chin back. "I won't jeopardize my promotion. Chase is just a fucktard. No one likes him."

"Don't let him get away with anything." Gemma waggled her finger. "If he puts a hair out of place, you let me know. I'll kick his ass to the curb for you. I have an exceptional lawyer."

"Thank you, beautiful." Gemma had always had my back. And I hers. We'd been friends since she'd moved in with Kyle and Hunter into the same apartment building after they'd signed their first record deal. Everhide had moved on to luxurious penthouses in Tribeca. Hayden and I were still stuck in the same shabby two-bedroom, one-bathroom, sometimes-cockroach-infested apartment. But I loved it. It was the first place that had felt like a home—no parents arguing and no brothers fighting. I clutched Gemma's hand and hoped I never needed to take up Gemma's offer of help. "I love how you look out for me."

"Always." Gemma's smile radiated warmth. "But seriously . . . " She took a sip of her JD. "I'd love you to come to LA. The guys and I have rehearsals and shows, but you could chillax, take photos, avoid your boss, aaaannnnd . . . have a couple weeks away from Hayden."

I glanced toward the kitchen. Hayden leaned against the counter as he talked to the guys. My heartbeat fluttered toward my throat, then flopped to the pit of my stomach. Dryness crept into my mouth. A sip of wine offered no relief. I wanted to savor every second we had together, but avoid him at all costs. *Ergh!* I didn't want to feel like this around him. Time away, a quick break, was what I needed.

I could do this.

I'd meet with Chase and pitch the idea to review restaurants in LA. He'd wanted fresh ideas at the team meeting last week. Millions of people would travel over the Christmas and New Year period. New Yorkers needed to know where to eat when visiting the City of Angels. This could work. It had to. "I think I have an idea Chase might buy." Zest-filled tingles zipped across my skin. My chest felt lighter. "Girls, I'm in."

Kara clapped. "Yay. We're going to have so much fun."

Some Californian sunshine would be as good as therapy. Getting several photos of the sunset over the ocean and around the city would look spectacular in my portfolio. Not that I'd ever need it. My hobby had never turned into a full-time profession. I'd accepted that a long time ago. The perfect balance between doing something I loved sprinkled with travel, excitement, and earning a decent income didn't exist.

But jumping at the offer to go with my friends was a no-brainer.

I slapped my leg. "You've got me pumped. Time in LA will be

perfect." Away from the cold. Away from work. Away from Hayden.

Hayden wanted to experience things we hadn't done before, so I was about to throw him a first. A huge curveball. I would avoid him. Just for two weeks. Allow the storm he'd created to settle.

I wanted to spend time with the girls. Feel the ocean breeze on my face when I walked along the Santa Monica Pier. Fill my lungs with fresh air as I rode a bike down Venice Beach. I wanted to fill my heart with the rapture of the sunset over the Pacific Ocean. And most of all, I didn't want to think about, see, or hear the tiniest tap of a drumbeat from Hayden. I had to prepare for his send-off. Prepare for life without him.

"I'm in. Even if I can swindle time off without pay, I'll do it. I'll come to LA. It's exactly what I need."

Chapter 3

HAYDEN

After helping Kyle and Hunter clean up after Thanksgiving dinner, I grabbed a six-pack from the fridge. Time to jam with the guys in Hunter's home studio. The three of us hadn't played together in over eighteen months thanks to Everhide's grueling tour schedule, surviving some horrific ordeals and celebrating Kyle and Gemma's wedding.

I needed a good session. This would be one of the last chances I'd get to play with them. But, more importantly, I needed to thrash out the crushing pain in my heart.

Lexi's rejection had hurt more than I'd ever expected. I'd never thought it would cut so deep. It stung that she'd avoided me since we'd kissed. I was adamant there was something magical between us. We could be something great. I wanted my two loves—music and Lexi—to meld. I'd taken a gamble . . . but had lost. Big time.

The only way to extinguish the fire that had ignited in the pit of my belly a couple of months ago was music. Would that be enough? No breakup with a girl had ever crushed me this much . . . and Lexi wasn't even my girlfriend. When I moved to Boston, it would be weird not having her around every day, but if she didn't feel the same way about me as I did for her, it was time to move on.

Crossing the living room, I glimpsed the girls sitting outside, laughing, chatting, and drinking. My heart lurched against my ribs. *Fuck.* I shouldn't have told Lexi I loved her. It was the stupidest thing I'd ever done.

Idiot.

No matter how much I'd apologized for kissing her, she'd avoided me for most of the day. It was killing me. I charged down the hallway and followed the guys into the music room. I needed beer and music to beat out the dents in my heart.

Taking a deep breath, I scanned the room. Hunter's home studio rivaled Cannon's, the indie recording studio where I worked part-time, or anything my band and I had. It was fully decked out with state-of-the-art soundboards, computer equipment, racks of guitars, a digital piano, and microphones. *Fuck.* The value of the equipment in this room was more than I'd earn in ten lifetimes.

Taking a seat behind the Pearl drum kit, I downed a mouthful of my Budweiser. The guys grabbed their guitars. Hunter sat on a nearby stool; his fingers glided slowly over the steel strings. Kyle pulled up a chair next to him, propped his bass on his lap and positioned his fingers, ready to play. He homed in on the chords and notes Hunter struck. It didn't take Kyle long to pick up the rhythm. A tune formed. I puffed out a quick breath. My friends were just too talented. I'd never reach their level.

But playing drums was what I was born to do. It was in my blood. I'd picked up a set of sticks at my first foster home when I was ten, and I'd never looked back. Being a drummer was all I'd ever wanted to do.

I put my beer on the floor, picked up the sticks, pumped my foot against the pedal, and struck the snare. The room's acoustics were perfect, but the quick beat matched the constant clamoring inside my head: *you-idiot-you-idiot-you-idiot.* At dinner, Lexi had sat diagonally across from me, next to Kara, not beside me. She hadn't joked with me—hadn't even looked at me. Weren't friends supposed to forgive each other? Laugh mistakes off? Be there for each other no matter what?

Zwwwiip. Hunter's fingers slipped over the fretboard and stilled his strings. He threw me an *enough-with-your-bullshit* stare. "Hayds, it sucks you're leaving. It won't be the same without you around. But there's something else up your ass. What is it?"

"Nothing." I grabbed my beer, took a sip, and set it back on the floor.

"There sure is." Kyle didn't look up from playing his bass. "The way you were at dinner, I assume it has something to do with Lexi. You two have a fight?"

"No." I jerked my chin back. "What makes you think that?"

"Shit, man." Hunter flicked his shoulder-length brown hair off his face. "Even I can tell there's something going on. And I usually don't notice anything or give a fuck about anyone."

That made me grin. Hunter was right about that.

Kyle and Hunter were my best friends. I got on better with them than anyone in my band . . . except for Lewis, he was on par. But the three of *us* had supported each other through good times and the bad, successes, and knock-backs. These two guys were my inspiration, but serious girl talk hadn't been our strong point. Probably because I'd never been serious about a girl before. "It's nothing."

"Bullshit." Kyle rested his arm on top of his bass and jutted his chin toward me. "Out with it. Or we'll just get you drunk until you puke your guts up and tell us. Shall I get the JD?"

The last thing I needed was to get drunk around Lexi again. I didn't want to get into an argument with her, or make matters worse by trying to kiss her again. "Fuck, guys. Can't we just play?"

Kyle ruffled his fingers through his dirty blond hair and rubbed his undercut. "So, it is about the Lexster?"

I twirled a drumstick in my hand and whacked it against the floor tom. "Why do you think it's about her?"

Kyle half-grinned. "I've seen the way you look at her."

I grimaced. *Fuck.* I didn't think my feelings for Lexi were that obvious. When these guys were away for months on end, I spent my spare time with Lexi, going to MoMA—her favorite place on earth—riding bikes around the city, going to live music gigs, and letting her photograph me wherever she wanted to. My feelings for her had crept up on me . . . and then had gotten the better of me. "Yeah, well, there's no *look* anymore. I fucked up. We kissed. She rejected me. I told her I was leaving. Now she won't fucking talk to me."

"Holy shit." Hunter's laugh burst across the room. He struck his guitar strings hard. The lingering reverberation hummed through the air. "You kissed her?" He tilted his head to the side, arching one eyebrow. "What kind of kiss? Was it a touch on the lips? You slip in the tongue? Or totally fucking made out like rabid dogs?"

I chuckled, but regret punched my guts. "We made out, but not like rabid dogs. The minute things heated up between us, she stopped." There was no way I'd tell them I'd said I loved her.

"I didn't think you liked Lex that way," Hunter said, still wide-eyed.

"I didn't until a couple months ago." I let my head fall back, and I stared at the ceiling. "I had to find out if there was something between us. But I went about it the wrong way. Now she's avoiding me."

How could I have hurt her? Not talked to her about my feelings first to see if she felt the same way? Instead, I'd dived in and stuck my tongue down her throat, hoping for a positive outcome. Major. Epic. Fail.

I clutched the sticks and pummeled the hell out of the drum kit—snare drum, the tom-toms, the cymbals, and back again. Again and again. Harder and harder. Each strike triggered memories. Each beat snagged my heart. Kissing her had been amazing . . . for the couple of seconds it had lasted. Her lips had tasted of vodka and lime. Her tongue had explored my mouth just as much as I had explored hers. Her body had molded to mine when I'd held her close. She'd moaned against my mouth, tugged me closer, grabbed my hair. She'd set me on fire. Touching her, tasting her, teasing her had me come undone. I wanted her. Wanted her bad. But when I'd slid my hand underneath her coat, touched her boob, and told her how I felt, I'd killed the vibe.

Dickhead.

Pounding at the drums, I couldn't get rid of my anger. My disappointment. My regret. Lexi was my light in my darkness. She kept me grounded, and I'd gone and blown her trust. Damaged our friendship. I struck the hi-hat hard. *You stupid moron. You complete shithead.* Thumping the bass, my heart screamed. *Shithead. Shithead. Shithead.* Snare. Tom-tom, Cymbal. Bass. Snare. Tom-tom. Cymbal. Bass. *Fuuuuck!*

Panting and puffing, I stopped. The clang of the cymbal filled the air. I looked up. Kyle and Hunter stared at me with eyes widened to the size of bagels. I smirked and wiped my sweaty brow on my shirtsleeve. "What?"

"What . . . the fuck?" Kyle's voice rocked with disbelief. "When did you learn to play like that?"

I sucked air deep into my heaving lungs and gave a half-hearted shrug. It didn't matter how much I practiced or tried to perfect my skills; I was just an average drummer. My mom's shrieks still rang through my head. *'You're useless. You'll never make it to the big time.'* My heart twisted, still tainted by her words. But music was all I knew. "That was nothing. You guys have been away for over eighteen months. I worked with some really cool, crazy-assed indie bands that came through the studio this past year. I learned a heap of new stuff and corrected some of my techniques for their recordings."

"Bud." Hunter pointed his guitar pick at me. "That was freaking amazing."

"Yeah, right." I stretched my neck from side to side. "I don't know what that was. Just random hammering." It had felt good, though. Therapeutic. Just what I'd needed.

"No way." Kyle waggled his finger at me. "That was brilliant."

"Thanks." But why were they still looking at me weirdly? *Ugh!* I swatted the air, brushing their compliments aside. "Stop trying to make me feel better. It won't work. And don't ask me to repeat it as I have no idea what I just played."

Kyle slapped his thigh. "Damn, I wish we'd recorded it."

"Don't waste your time," I mumbled under my breath.

I'd auditioned for my friends once, before I'd joined The Saylors. But their management team and record company opted for more talent than I'd possessed. I'd respected that. I wasn't cut out for the major leagues. But a love of music had formed a bond between us I'd treasure forever.

Kyle leaned forward. His gaze drilled into me. "So was that slay on the kit because you're bummed about moving to Boston, or fucked up over Lexi?"

Both, but mainly Lexi. I wriggled on the stool. "The move is fine—it'll be good for the band. But . . . yeah. I'm having a hard time handling Lex being upset." Deep down, I was scared that she was now uncomfortable around me. That she didn't want anything to do with me. She'd be conscious of my feelings, and wouldn't want to cause me any more grief. But shutting me out and keeping me at a distance was worse than not being around her.

"She'd be devastated you're leaving," Kyle said. "We all are."

I wiped my hand over my face, wishing it would erase my fear of losing Lexi and my friends. "I know. But the guys and I need to do this. Playing at Kilt's dad's new hotel is the right step for our career, giving us something permanent." The new nightlife venue in a vibrant part of Boston would help establish The Saylors' name. We needed stability and a decent income to help us take another step toward the big time.

"Do you want to be an in-house band?" Hunter grimaced as he picked up his beer and took a swig.

"Yeah." I shrugged my shoulder. "It's regular work and part of the bigger plan. We'll lay down an album and hit the road next year."

"Why don't you record at Cannon's?" Hunter asked.

"I wish." I fidgeted with my drumsticks and swiveled on the stool. "It's too expensive and booked for months. We'll make it happen in Boston."

Hunter shook his head and scratched his chest. "Fuck, man. It sucks you're jumping cities."

"I know. I'm gonna miss you guys." The move to Boston had to work. I didn't want the fighting in my band to continue. Could we keep our shit together for long enough to write a new album, tour, and become popular? Fuck, I hoped so. I wanted a bond with my bandmates like Everhide had formed. It was vital for success.

Lexi had been my escape from my band's bickering over music styles, gigs, and creative direction. She was my security blanket I'd never wanted to give up. But it was time to make the break. I couldn't live with her forever if there was no chance of evolving into something more than friends. "I don't know what to do about Lex, though. I've apologized, but nothing's worked."

Hunter's mouth morphed into a grin as he peered over the rim of his beer. "You know the best way to get over some chick is to get another one underneath you. You need to go out, hook up, and get laid. Do you have a night off before we leave for LA? We'll go out somewhere."

I wasn't in the mood for picking up a girl, but a night out sounded perfect. "Absolutely. We could go out this Saturday after my gig." I twirled a drumstick around in the air and caught it. "Maybe after that, I'll take a couple days off and go away somewhere. I'll give Lex a moment to come to terms with my moving."

Kyle's brow furrowed. "Is that what you want to do? Aren't you going to try to change her mind about being together?"

My leg jiggled. I had a better chance of winning the lottery than of winning Lexi's heart. "Why waste my time? She's not interested."

Why did one kiss and three little words have to ruin everything? *Fuck it!*

"I don't know about that. Sometimes it pays to be patient." Kyle smirked. "Worked for me."

I didn't possess patience like Kyle and didn't possess any panty-dropping charm like Hunter. If Lexi didn't want me after living together for seven years, there was nothing I could do to change her mind. There was only so much rejection a guy could take.

I brushed Kyle's suggestion aside. "You know Lex—she's out for fun. I was wrong to think otherwise." I knew her better than anyone else. She hadn't had a serious boyfriend since Quintin two years ago. It would take someone, no one short of a god, to break her out of her ongoing, never-ending dating game. Good luck to them. I stretched my arms above my head. "Rejection's a bitch. But

I'll be fine. I just need Lex to get over what happened." To forgive me. To forget I said I loved her. To move on.

"Sorry? What's that? Rejection?" Grinning a goofy grin, Hunter placed his empty bottle on the floor. "I don't know what that is."

Laughing, I threw a drumstick at him, hitting him on the arm.

"Ow." Hunter clutched his bicep. "What was that for?"

"Made me feel better," I chuckled.

But the more I thought about moving to Boston, the more excitement flickered to life in my veins. My big break was coming. I could feel it in my bones.

Kyle wiped his hand over his thigh. His skinny black jeans with ripped knees had seen better days. "Well, you can't sit around here and sulk."

I shook my head. "I won't."

Since last night, I'd felt like I'd severed what Lexi and I had. It was my fault. I was the only one to blame. But I wouldn't waste my last two months in New York waiting for her to come around. I had my bucket list of things to complete, with or without Lexi.

I grabbed a spare drumstick from the canister beside my stool, twirled it around and tapped away on the tom-toms again. *Thrum. Diddy. Thrum. Diddy. Thrum.*

Kyle snorted and chuckled. "Hayds, I know how fucked up you can get over a girl. Gem certainly made me jump through hoops. But if you want to take a few days off, have some space to clear your head and some more time to let things smooth over with Lexi, why not come to LA with us? We've got a crazy schedule, but we'll have some time to hang out. Gem won't mind. You cool if Hayds comes, Hunt?" Kyle kicked Hunter's boot with his foot.

"Absolutely fine by me." Hunter scratched the tip of his chin. "We need to christen your new house with a good party or two."

"Fuck yeah." Excitement glinted in Kyle's eyes as he nodded.

"Why did you and Gem buy a house in LA?" I asked him.

"We spend so much time there. It beats staying in hotels." Kyle strummed a low beat on his bass. "It's in Pacific Palisades and has a great view of the ocean. We'll get a few friends over, have some drinks and help you forget all about Lex."

"Thanks." My gaze fell to the floor. I didn't want to forget about Lexi. I wanted things to be right. But having a few days away from her, maybe even a week or two, might do us a world of good. Oh, Kilt—my band's lead vocalist—would love this. *Not.* But I didn't care. The world didn't revolve around him like he thought it did. I'd get his brother, Basil, to fill in for me for our gigs. I'd easily get time off from the recording studio. I hadn't told them I was leaving yet. I'd do that when I got back. There were other drummers available if needed on Broadway. I had all my bases covered.

I had nothing to lose. I needed to reset. Put my mistakes behind me. Give Lexi the space she needed to forgive me. "If Gem's okay with it, I'd love to come. Some time in LA will be good." No Lexi. No drama. No hassles. "Count me in."

Chapter 4

LEXI

I lost track of time. Dancing at the nightclub on Saturday night had at some point segued into Sunday morning. Music blared. Bodies gyrated around me. A night away from my continued awkwardness around Hayden had been perfect. Burning up the dance floor with Kara and Gemma was just what I'd needed ... but the guy with his hands around my waist, trying to get friendly? Not so much. Mr. Handsy, who'd yelled his name 'Zac' into my ear three times, had been fun to dance with. Now, I'd had enough. I'd made excuses—*'It's girls' night,' 'I'm here with friends,'* and *'I'm not interested'*—but he wasn't taking no for an answer. Not getting the message, we were done. *Dickhead.* I'd been nice, but my manners had worn thin. So much for being in the VIP section. Creeps existed everywhere.

"Thanks for the dance." I eased out of Zac's hold. "But I'm going for a break with my friends." I waved at Kara and Gemma dancing nearby, and thumbed toward our booth. "Let's go." But Zac caught my hand, pulling me back to his side.

"Hey, hey, hey." He slithered closer. "I'll come with you. Let me buy you a drink."

"No, thank you." I snatched my hand free.

Zac tilted his head and smiled, his eyes glassy from too much alcohol. He had that sexy, suave Jared Leto thing going on—the long hair, stunning blue eyes, and groomed beard. "Give me a kiss before you leave. Or are you gonna promise to come back and have another dance?"

Ugh! He was the clingy type of guy who'd want to stick around, go on dates, get to know me. Not what I wanted. Kissing Hayden and the turmoil of awkward emotions it had created had reaffirmed my pledge to the single life. I wanted no drama. No commitments. No fuss. I was much better off alone. "Sorry Zac. No promises. No kiss. Gotta go." I linked arms with Kara and Gemma and headed for our booth.

The usual *'Oh wow. It's Gemma. From Everhide.'* rippled through the crowd as we jostled our way off the dance floor. There were flashes from cell phones, a lot of starry-eyed ogles, but no one stopped us. Thank goodness, because tonight *was* girls' night and time to celebrate. Chase had approved my trip to LA. He'd been impressed with my pitch, commended me with a slap on the back—or was it a rub? *Ew . . . Don't go there.*

Chester and Giles—Kara and Gemma's bodyguards—stood on either side of our booth. They faced the crowd with *don't-mess-with-me* looks chiseled onto their faces. Gemma shuffled past them and slid into the middle of our circular booth.

"You want another drink?" I hollered at the girls as I waved at the cocktail waitress decked out in a gold-logoed *Lennon's Nightclub* midriff top.

"Absolutely." Gemma drummed out a rapid beat on the table with her palms. "The night is still young. Let's par-ty."

After ordering a round of drinks, I scanned the bobbing crowd. Disco lights flashed off faces, reflected off shiny clothes, and sparkled on rhinestones and bling. I sank deeper into the comfy cushioned seat, excited to be here with my girls . . . and even more thrilled to be heading to LA with them on Monday. I hadn't been to California in ten years. I couldn't wait to see the beaches and the vibrant city, and experience that Hollywood charm again. Even better to capture it through my lens.

Bernie, the waitress, returned with our drinks—champagne,

JD, and vodka. We grabbed our glasses and clinked them together.

"Here's to LA," I toasted, holding my vodka, lime, and soda in the air. "Away from Hayden for two weeks, some fun work, and a mini vacation. Woohoo!"

But guilt smacked me in the back of the head. I had to leave Mom in the hands of Aunt Nora. She thought lunching with friends was more important than checking on her own sister. And . . . I shouldn't be away from Hayden for so long. Not when our time left together was limited. But now I could blame work, not the weirdness that had lingered between us since we'd kissed.

Kara's champagne didn't make it to her lips. Her eyes widened, and she pointed toward the door. "Not sure you'll avoid him tonight though. The guys are here."

Fuck! My throat ran dry. My grip on my glass tightened. *Why are they here?*

Hunter, Kyle, and Hayden, followed by Mick and Sam, Everhide's security guards, made their way through the crowd, ignoring the *ohhs*, *aahs*, and *OMGs* from girls in the club.

Hunter made a straight line for our booth, people parting as if he were a king. But it wasn't Hunter who held my attention. It was Hayden. His long gait made him look like he was gliding in slow motion across the floor. His half-grin, steel-gray eyes, olive skin and messed-up hair screamed *damn-I'm-sexy-and-cool*. His slim, black jeans and button-down shirt molded perfectly to his toned, ripped body. A wave of heat surged through my veins and pooled low in my belly. *Shit.* I hated that since he'd kissed me, I'd become *hyper-aware* of him—from his good looks to his very presence. I didn't want to feel like this. Or react like this. The trip to LA couldn't come quickly enough.

Hunter slid onto the seat next to Kara and laid one kiss on her lips, then another and another.

Kyle stepped onto the seat beside me, strode over my legs and plonked next to Gemma. He hooked his arm around her neck. "Hey, babe."

She crawled onto his lap and kissed him.

I rolled my eyes and sipped my drink. I'd seen my friends make out often enough not to be fazed. But Hayden's stare stopped me short. His face held no expression, no smirk, no sparkle in his eyes, no furrows in his brow. I couldn't read him anymore. Did he think I wanted to make out with him? *No chance.*

But my gaze drifted to his mouth. *Oh, those lips.* My pulse jumped a notch—maybe three. Kissing him slammed to the forefront of my mind. Us, up against the wall. His hands caressed my face. His hot mouth on mine. The taste of his tongue. And, oh my, his body crushed against me.

Fuck!

Heat crept up my neck and turned into a feverish flush by the time it reached my cheeks. *Is it hot in here?* I wriggled on my seat, peered around the burly bodies of Everhide's security, and searched for an escape.

Hunter pulled away from sucking Kara's face. His azure eyes caught the nightclub's lights, and an *I'm-a-fucking-rock-star-and-will-do-what-I-want* grin lit his face. Kara's cheeks blazed bright red, but the biggest smile curled across her mouth. Hunter leaned forward, resting his elbows on the table. "Sorry to intrude on your girls' night out." He jutted his chin toward Kyle. "He's still in the honeymoon phase. It's pathetic. After Hayden's gig and a few drinks, he had to come see Gem."

Still on Kyle's lap, Gemma twisted to face Hunter. "Oh, pa-leeease. He did not." Her voice rolled with a *you're-so-full-of-shit* tone. Turning back to Kyle, she cupped his face and rocked her hips against his. "But I'm not complaining."

Kyle groaned and grinned. He rested his head back against the padded booth and circled his hands over Gemma's ass. "Neither am I."

Hayden glanced at me. He placed his hands on the edge of the table and swayed. By the smell of his breath, and the fumes radiating off Kyle, the guys had been into the JD.

Great. They were drunk.

Hayden narrowed his eyes. They gleamed, dark and predatory, like a lion's. I couldn't tell whether he wanted to pounce on me or feed me to the pride.

"How was your gig?" Ignoring the flutter in my stomach, I fumbled to put my straw in my mouth. *Klutz.* I took a big drink, downing the rest of my vodka in one massive slurp.

"It was okay." Hayden's lopsided grin softened and widened.

"Okay?" Kyle butted in. "Dude, you nailed it." He clicked his fingers at Bernie. She came running, and he ordered a bottle of JD for the table.

"He's exaggerating." Hayden chuckled and leaned forward, way too close for my liking. With a flick of his wrist, he pointed at the vacant seat beside me. "Can I?"

Hmm. Squished in a booth next to him. Legs touching. Arms brushing. *Nope.* Not good. I needed space. "Sure can." I slid off the seat and straightened my short party dress. His simmering gaze traveled down my legs and back up again, dragging spiraling tingles up my spine. He shouldn't look at me like that—all smoldering and seductive. I shouldn't react like this—all hot and bothered. *Breathe. Just breathe.* "You can have it. I'm gonna dance. By myself." I waved at the girls to stay. "Have fun. See ya."

I spun on my toes and headed toward the dance floor, but I felt his eyes drilling into my back.

"You can't avoid me forever." Hayden's voice trailed after me.

"Bye." I twinkled my fingers over my shoulder. My heart rate eased a fraction with each step I took away from him. So much better.

Jostling my way onto the middle of the dance floor, I closed my eyes. Absorbing the vibe from the crowd and letting the DJ's music into my soul, I held my hands in the air and danced to the beat.

It took less than half a minute for creepy hands to span my waist. I spun around. Zac staggered before me. He was even more intoxicated than he had been twenty minutes ago. He leaned closer. His breath reeked of rum. "You've returned."

"To dance. But not with you." I took a step back, bumping into someone behind me.

"Don't lie," Zac hollered over the loud, throbbing music. Drunken confidence smeared his face. "You came back for me."

My laugh came out as a snort. "No. I didn't."

I went to leave, but he grabbed my hand, hooked his arm around my waist, and tried to drunk-waltz with me.

Placing my hands on his shoulders, I pushed back hard. "Let go of me." If he didn't, there'd be trouble. As a close friend of Gemma's, Everhide's security team had given me some basic self-defense training, and I wasn't afraid to use it or call on them if needed.

"One dance." Zac swayed his hips and cocked an eyebrow.

Oh my God! Was he giving me the sexy eye?

He leaned in.

Ew! Was he trying to kiss me?

I shoved against Zac's chest, but his grip was a vise.

Should I knee him in the groin?

Maybe a good slap would set him straight. I gathered my wits, clenched my teeth, and looked Zac square in the eye. I tensed my hand, ready to strike. But over his shoulder, movement caught my attention. Hayden stormed through the partygoers. He slapped Zac on the arm and spun him around. "Hey buddy, thanks for looking after my girl, but I'll take over from here."

"Dude, fuck off." Zac flicked Hayden's hand away. "She's dancing with me."

"Um . . . She's my girlfriend. So please let her go."

I threw Hayden a stern *I-don't-need-your-help* glare. I didn't want him fighting my battles.

His jaw tensed and ticked. His eyes narrowed. He'd gotten the message. He nodded once and turned to leave, but in a flash, I grabbed his arm. What had I been thinking? His help was exactly what I needed. My brain had to stop malfunctioning around him. I slid into his embrace and forced myself to smile. "Honey, you're here. What took you so long?"

We'd played this wingman, *save-you-from-the-clutches-of-intoxicated-leeches* part often over the years. It was second nature.

He pulled me close, hard against his side. His posture was rigid and cold. But within one breath, he relaxed and rubbed his hand up and down my arm. "Sorry, angel. I got held up at work."

Heat swirled beneath his warm touch and crept across my

skin. *What the hell?* I wriggled to ease away, but his hold remained unrelenting and in place.

Fine.

He wanted to role-play. I could do that. Sucking in a deep breath, I placed my hand on his chest and fiddled with a button on his shirt. "That's okay, honey. Zac was just being a gentleman and having a dance."

Hayden gave Zac a curt nod. "Thanks, dude. But your services are no longer required."

Zac grunted, held up his hands and backed away. "Your girl's a fucking prick-tease. I'd watch her if I were you."

Hayden stepped toward Zac and got up in his face. "What did you call her?"

Fire flared in Zac's eyes. "She's been all over me tonight."

Hayden eyed Zac up and down; his lip curled at the corner. "Doubt it. She's mine. Now beat it. Or I'll have my security throw you out." He jerked his head toward Everhide's bodyguards standing with their arms folded by our booth. They were watching intently, ready to intervene.

I pursed my lips and tried not to giggle. *Wow.* Hayden had never taken charge like this before. He'd never risk getting into a fight, especially over me. Was it wrong that I liked it?

Zac threw a dagger-filled glare at me. "Bitch." He stormed toward his buddies sitting at a bar table just off the other side of the dance floor.

Hayden turned to me; a victory grin lit his face.

Resisting his infectious smile, I jammed my hands on my hips. "Thank you, but I didn't need your help. I had everything under control."

"Yep. You sure did." Taking my hand, he drew me close and placed his palms on my hips.

My breath hitched and got stuck in my throat. Arching my back, I pushed against his chest, attempting to break free like Penelope Pussycat escaping Pepé Le Pew, but I had no luck. "What are you doing?"

"Better dance with me so Zackie-boy gets a clear message."

Shit. Zac stood by his table, glaring at me like he wanted to murder me. *Fuck. Shit. Fuck . . . But dance with Hayden? . . . I can do that.* There was nothing to it. Right? "Um . . . okay."

I hooked my trembling hands around his neck. His grip on my hips tightened, and we stepped from side to side in time to the music. Two nervous, virginal teenagers would have looked more comfortable. I did my best to keep an arm's width between us, but Hayden slid his hand onto the small of my back and pulled me against his chest.

I closed my eyes, afraid to meet his gaze. But I felt him everywhere. His hips were flush against mine. His thighs nudged into mine. His heart beat in sync with mine. His whiskey breath on my face made my knees wobble like Jell-O.

"Lexi." Hayden's voice rumbled low and soft near my ear. "Please stop avoiding me. How many times do I have to say sorry for kissing you?"

I licked my dry lips and found my voice. "At least one hundred more."

"I'm-sorry-I'm-sorry-I'm-sorry—"

A giggle escaped me as I put my hand over his mouth. "Stop. You goose." But my smile lasted less than a second, wiped away by the ache flaring inside my heart. I placed my hands on his chest, glided them upward, and linked my fingers behind his neck. "I'm not worried about the kiss . . . well . . . I've tried not to think about it. But something's changed between us, and it's scaring me."

"Lex, I had to tell you how I felt." He cupped the side of my head. "You're my best friend. I love you. I wanted to see if we could be more, but you said no. I'm disappointed, but I'll be okay. I'll get over it. Stop worrying about me."

Something in his tone was off. Was he lying about being okay? "I will always worry."

"I'm sure you're just upset I'm moving."

"It's more than that." I softened my tone. "I'm sorry you thought we had a chance at a relationship. You know I don't want to fall for anyone ever again."

"Stupid of me, wasn't it?" A playful glint shimmered in his

eyes. He guided me toward a less crowded spot on the dance floor. "But if you don't feel anything for me, why can't you look at me? Why are you playing with the back of my hair?"

Shit. My fingers froze. I'd been running my fingernails through his hair without even knowing. "Sorry. It's just that every time I'm around you now, I feel awkward."

He took my hand, twirled me around, and stepped in close, my back against his chest. He rested his chin on my shoulder. "What can I do to prove to you we're good so there'll be no more weirdness between us?"

His hot breath on my neck sent goosebumps shooting down my arms. He might be good, but I wasn't. He wrapped his arms around my waist, and thousands of soda bubbles popped inside my stomach. This felt familiar, like my shattered memories of Quintin, only the buzz was stronger. It terrified me. I couldn't develop stronger feelings for Hayden. Not ever. It would only end in heartache.

His lips hovered near my ear. "Unless . . . you're not being honest with me. Do you have feelings for me?"

No. No. No. No. NO!

I closed my eyes and dug my fingers into his forearms. "I told you. I don't."

"Good. So let's dance."

He spun me around to face him. Letting go of my waist, he jigged to the music. It took me a second to clear the haze from my mind. Hayden jumped, clapped his hands, and boogied to the beat. The smile on his face lit up the entire club. He knocked his hip against mine and pulled a crazy face. I laughed. I missed this. Spending time with him, goofing around. Hayden wasn't the one with the problem—I was. Had he put a crack in the hard shell around my heart?

Hell no. No way. Baste that bitch back up.

The DJ's mix changed to a slow, sexy beat.

"Yeah," I scoffed and shook my head. "I'm not dancing to this."

I turned to head off the dance floor, but Hayden's waggling finger was like a lasso, roping me in, drawing me closer. A smoldering, playful smile slid across his mouth. "You're not going anywhere. Dance with me."

I fidgeted with the neckline of my dress. I didn't close-dance with Hayden just for the fun. The boundaries of our platonic friendship had to remain secure and intact.

But he wasn't taking no for an answer. He eased toward me and slid his hands around my hips. In my pumps, I was only an inch shorter than him.

"Lex." His voice, a deep baritone over the music, rumbled through my veins. His steel-gray eyes shimmered in the swirling lights.

"Mmm?" My throat ran dry. My heart raced crazy-fast.

The crowd pushed against us, forcing us closer. Groin. Legs. Knees. Arms . . . heartbeat. His body touching me . . . everywhere.

I dragged my gaze away from his. "What are you doing?"

"Dancing."

No. Not like this. Too close. Too, too, too close.

My head spun. My pulse whooshed in my ears. "Please. I can't . . . can't—"

I placed my hands on his shoulders to push away, but a cold shudder ran up my spine. It pooled at the base of my neck. Crawled across my skin. Zac hadn't moved. He stood staring at me, his eyes icy spears. He pointed from himself to me, then grabbed his crotch. He made a *V* with his fingers over his mouth and slithered out his tongue.

Panic seized my throat and pushed me into a tight corner. I clutched the back of Hayden's head and drew his lips to mine.

Crap.

What the hell was I doing?

I could've called security to get rid of Zac rather than throwing myself at Hayden.

Hayden's body turned rigid; his fingers dug into my waist. Music pounded in my ears. Lights swirled before my eyes. This kiss had to stop. *Now.* But Hayden sucked in a deep breath, relaxed his shoulders, and moaned against my mouth. *Holy shit.* A jolt of electricity shot through my core. *Damn it . . . stop.* This was just a kiss to piss off Zac.

Hayden snaked his arms around me and slid his hands up my bare back. *Not the night to wear a backless dress!* I squeezed my eyes shut. Kept my lips tensed. My heart jackhammered like a tappet against my ribs. *No. Hayds. No. Just play along. Don't read anything into this.*

But holy fucking wow!

The taste of the JD on his lips and the touch of his strong hands set fire to every cell in my body and weakened my knees. I wriggled in his arms, ignoring the growing want between my legs. Tilting his head, he opened his mouth and flicked his tongue to deepen the kiss.

No.

I ripped my lips away, the crush in my chest excruciating. "I'm sorry . . . for kissing you. Zac's watching." *I'm such a fool.* "I panicked."

I yanked out of Hayden's hold and dashed toward our booth.

He grabbed my arm before I reached the edge of the dance floor and pulled me to a halt. "Lexi." The fire in his eyes singed my soul. "Wait."

I ripped my arm free and splayed my hands by my face. "I'm sorry." I waved in Zac's direction. "Zac was making rude gestures. I didn't think things through."

Hayden drove his fingers through his hair, leaving tousled tracks in their wake. "What the hell is going on?"

His tone hammered my head. I wished I knew. "I don't know. Why did you try to stick your tongue down my throat?"

"Me? It's just the way I kiss."

Oh . . . I remembered the fiery flicks and taste of his tongue. My pussy ached with jealousy. *Fuuuck.* I had to get Hayden out of my head.

His stormy gaze unnerved me and did strange things to my pulse. Just as well I was going away. I'd be able to put this nonsense to rest. Now was as good a time as any to tell him. "Hayds . . . so much has happened in the past few days. I need some time to get my head together. Time to reset. My boss has approved an assignment for me . . . in LA. I'm gonna stay with Gem for the next two weeks."

"What?" The color drained from his face. "No. You can't."

"Why not?"

"Because that's what I'm doing. The guys asked *me* to go to LA."

"Since when?" I screeched.

"Since Thursday night at Thanksgiving. I organized leave from the studio yesterday."

"And you didn't tell me?" Why didn't Gemma say anything? Was this part of some twisted matchmaking plan? *Not. Going. To work.*

"Well . . . we haven't really seen or talked to each other. You've been avoiding me. Remember?"

Oh, yeah. *That.* "What about your band?"

He shrugged. "They're pissed that I'm taking off with Everhide again, but that's nothing new." He closed his eyes. When he opened them, they flooded with hurt. "But . . . do you think we need a break? From each other?"

I fidgeted with my curls. "No . . . yes. I don't want things between us to be awkward anymore. I want to put this mess behind us."

"Mess?" He flicked his hand toward the dance floor. "Was that what that kiss was? It felt pretty good to me."

"It was nothing."

"Nothing?" His nostrils flared. "So why are you running to LA?"

"Because I don't know what's wrong with me. With us. I want to fix it. I'm afraid of what you said to me. I don't want you to be in love with me. I don't want to lose you."

"Lex, you'll never lose me. We're friends first. I'm not crazy in love with you. Get over it."

I rubbed my forehead to ease the throbbing tension. "I'm trying."

"Can we please stop this bullshit and be sensible?" Frustration etched deep into his face. "We can both go to LA. Some time away from home might do us some good."

"It better." For my sanity.

"It will. I promise." He pulled me in for a hug, and I rested my cheek on his shoulder. I closed my eyes and inhaled the sandalwood scent of his Prada *L'Homme for Men* cologne. The scent I loved. It reminded me of summer holidays at the lake with my parents, watching the starry sky from the end of the jetty. But just like vacation, like marriage, like love, it had all come to an end.

I brushed my nose across his shirt and took a long breath. I couldn't slip up again. I had to keep a line drawn with Hayden. It couldn't be crossed. I didn't want to confuse him, hurt him, or lead him on.

Instead of space and distance, I'd be stuck in a house with him in LA. *Crap.* I'd have to drown myself in work, busy myself with my photography, and hang out with the girls when they had free time.

"You're right. LA will be fun." Doubt lingered in my voice as I stepped out of his embrace and straightened the waistline of my dress. I didn't want to think about his hands gliding over my body, searing my flesh . . . or that kiss. "It'll be like a vacation. Maybe we can do some of the things on our bucket list."

But like I'd done here in New York, I'd find as many excuses as possible to steer clear of Hayden in LA. I needed to sort myself out. Was that even possible when I didn't know what was wrong?

Fuck. Fuck. Fuck.

I headed back to the booth where our friends were downing JD. Hayden trailed behind me.

I grabbed a spare glass, poured a shot and knocked it down. So much for time away from Hayden. I wouldn't even get one night. I couldn't believe my lack of luck. Couldn't believe I was going to LA with Hayden.

Fuck!

I couldn't believe I'd spend two weeks with the one man I'd tried to avoid.

Chapter 5

HAYDEN

I loped down the stairs. Blazing Los Angeles daylight speared my eyes and drilled into my head. The glow streaming through the massive expanse of bi-fold doors that led out to the pool glistened off the glossy floor tiles. I needed sunglasses. Gemma and Kyle's second home was too white and bright. The sectional sofa, dining table, kitchen, and walls were all *white*, only intermittently toned down by royal blue and charcoal-colored decorations, cushions, and artwork. I rubbed my tired eyes. The joys of having a hangover . . . everything hurt.

I'd arrived in California with Everhide, their entourage, and Lexi yesterday morning. Last night's housewarming party had turned into a crazy gathering of about sixty people. Scanning the mess left on every surface, I shuddered. My blood ran cold in my constricting veins. *Mess.* Childhood memories of living in squalor pummeled my head. My parents preferred to spend their dimes on drugs rather than on me, on basic things like food and clothing or having a comfortable home to live in.

I clenched and unclenched my hands and blocked the nightmares from my mind. But for my sanity, I had to get this place in order.

Ambling around, I picked up empty beer bottles, crushed

packets of chips and pizza boxes, and threw them in the trash. I grabbed a used glass off the coffee table and stilled, holding it in my hands. *Lexi's.* Her pink lipstick stained the rim. Jealousy rocked and rolled in my gut. Last night, she'd flirted with Flint Glover, one of Everhide's rising rockstar friends. Unable to watch, I'd downed too many beers and stormed off to bed around two in the morning. I glanced up the staircase. Had she hooked up with Flint?

I scratched at the ache in my chest. Fuck, this sucked.

Being in love with someone who didn't feel the same way was shit. I had to lock away my feelings for her, pound them to smithereens. I hadn't done so yet, but I would once I moved to Boston. Until then, I could pretend everything was normal.

As I loaded the dishwasher with a stash of dirty glasses, soft, loping footsteps padded on the stairs. *Lexi.* I looked up and my heart skipped a beat. In her black flannel pajamas covered in daisies, with her hair a wild mass of unkempt blonde curls and her brown eyes smudged with makeup, she was a vision, totally adorable. I raked in a deep breath and scanned the stairs behind her. There was no sign of Flint. *Thank fuck!*

"Morning." I grabbed a glass out of a kitchen cupboard, filled it with cold water and handed it to her.

"Thanks." She took the drink and gulped it down. "What a night." She scanned the room. "I think we can successfully say Kyle and Gem's place is well and truly christened."

"Yep. I've cleaned up half the mess." I pointed to the overflowing trash can. The stench of stale alcohol lingered in the air, even with the bi-folds open. "There's still more to do." The huge white table was covered in bottles of liquor. Outside there were beer bottles and cans scattered by the pool and sun loungers, and the kitchen was a mayhem of used bowls and plates.

Lexi put her glass down and wrapped her arms around my waist. "It's okay, Hayds. You don't have to do it."

She'd been to my parents' house often enough to know why I liked order. The home I'd lived in until I was ten, before I went into foster care, was always strewn with filth. The stench of pot and chemicals still infested the air every time I visited. I could handle being around alcohol; I loved a good party and drinking, but never drugs. Living with addicts had scarred my soul, permanently.

Lexi circled her hand over the back of my sweatshirt. "You're an angel sent from heaven. Gem and Kyle will love you for cleaning up. But I'm sure they have a housekeeper."

"I know. I just wanted to help." Squeezing her close, I shut my eyes and inhaled the scent of her gardenia shampoo. The clean, fresh fragrance soothed my mind. I'd miss morning hugs when I moved to Boston. I had to savor every one between now and then.

But all too soon, she jerked out of my embrace. "Sorry."

"What for?" My arms froze, still posing in hug mode. Did I hold her too tight?

"Are hugs okay?" She grimaced and scratched the side of her neck.

"Why wouldn't they be?" My hands fell to my sides. "We hug all the time."

She fumbled with the neckline of her pajamas. "I know. But last night, you kept glaring at me. Are you still pissed at me for kissing you?"

"At the club? No."

"Is it because I talked to Flint last night?"

I clenched my hands, punching down the ball of jealousy festering in my gut. A short, sharp laugh burst from my mouth. "For the record, you weren't just *talking* to Flint. You were putting on the moves. You were nudging his arm." I faked a chuckle as I mimicked her actions from last night. "You were touching his knee. You ruffled your fingers through your hair when you giggled at his jokes. I know your pickup moves. You were on fire."

Her eyes widened. Her mouth fell open. Her cheeks flushed. "I was not."

"Oh. Yes. You. Were." I kept my tone teasing and playful, but my hands twitched, wanting to break a wall . . . or Flint's good-looking face. Jealousy was something new. I didn't want to be like this around Lexi. "Did it work? Is he upstairs?"

"No, he's not." She lowered her gaze. Resting her hip against the counter, she folded her arms. "Did you hook up with Julz?"

"Julz?" I jerked my chin back. Confusion swirled through my sore head. "We talked. I haven't seen her in two years."

"But you had a thing for her."

"Yes. A long time ago." In New York. Three years ago. She'd been a damn hot summer fling. That was it.

"I never liked her." Lexi's brows pinched together. "She's not good enough for you."

I shook my head. Julz, who'd scored a lead role in a Netflix series, wasn't good enough for me. *Fuck.* "Who is then, Lex? Why should me talking to someone other than you be a problem?"

No girl I'd ever dated had survived Lexi's ruthless screening process . . . or was it sabotage? Lexi happily pointed out my good and bad points to whoever I'd brought home before I'd made them a morning coffee—the main one being my music would always be my number-one priority. But hey, there was nothing wrong with that, right? Girls often got weirded out by my friendship with Lexi—the way we joked around, hung out together, did everything together. That had never sat well with any of them. *Fuck.* We were like an old married couple. "Were you jealous, Lex?"

"No. Not at all." But the tension in her face told a different story. That was new. "But when I was talking to Flint, you kept glaring at me. When you took off upstairs, I felt terrible. If I liked . . . or loved someone—" she winced, "—and saw them talking, or hooking up or flirting with another person in front of me, it would hurt. So, I'm sorry. I should've been more considerate of your feelings. I'll make you a promise. I won't hook up with anyone in our last two months together."

I puffed through my nostrils and wiped my hand over my face. That was Lexi. She had so much compassion and consideration for others it blew my mind. But I wasn't a fragile egg. "You don't have to do that. I'm not broken."

"I know." She put a few plates into the dishwasher. "It's okay."

That made me laugh out loud. After grabbing a dishwasher tablet, I popped it into the machine and turned it on. "You're going to go two months without getting laid?"

A ripple of doubt flicked through her eyes before defiance

burned bright. She straightened her shoulders and nodded. "Yep. Easy."

"Yeah, well . . ." I grabbed a dishcloth and wiped the countertop clean. "Maybe I should join your pact. I haven't gotten laid since Vegas."

"What?" Disbelief shot through her voice. "Since Kyle's bachelor party? In September?" She blinked several times. "Wow. That's why I haven't seen or heard you bring anyone home lately."

I shrugged. "I got mixed up over you, Lex. Shit happens." I'd jerked off thinking about her more times than I cared to admit. But it was best if I kept those details to myself. "We've been busy with the wedding, dealing with Gem's kidnapping, and my band making changes. The lack of sex hasn't bothered me." *Liar.* It was sending me fucking insane. I was tonguing for a good fuck. But the only one I wanted in my bed was standing in front of me.

Shit. I needed a cold shower. Maybe I should take Hunter's advice while I was here in California. I should go out and sample some of the local talent, not mull over Lexi.

She stretched her neck. "No sex for weeks will possibly kill me. Tinder may call to make sure I'm still alive. But I can do this. No hook-ups until you move." She sucked in a deep breath like she was stapling that statement in big, bold print onto her memory board. She clutched onto my forearm. "Our pact is to have fun, right? Many firsts, lasts and good times. But right now, I need food. Let's eat." She swung around and opened the fridge. Scanning the contents, she bent over to look on the lower shelves.

Damn . . . she had a fine ass. I'd love to take hold of her by the hips and—

She straightened and turned around. Her arms were overloaded with bacon, eggs, and wraps. But by the *don't-even-think-about-it* gleam in her eyes, I could tell she'd read my mind.

What was I supposed to do? She had a great ass. And yes, I wanted to fuck her.

She dove back into the fridge and grabbed the tomatoes. "What are your plans after breakfast?"

I rubbed my pounding forehead. She was right; I needed food.

Greasy food—even better. "Um . . . Gem and the guys asked me to watch their rehearsal this afternoon." Our friends were not early risers. "I'll practice this morning." I waved toward the stairs that led to the lower level. "Have you checked out their home studio? It's freaking insane. Kyle's bought another wicked set of drums. Other than that, I don't have anything on. You?"

She dumped her load of ingredients onto the rear kitchen counter. "I'm going with the girls to Gem's dress fittings later this morning. Then she's getting her hair cut before she meets up with the guys. This afternoon, I'll have to work before I go to my first restaurant to review tonight."

After searching through several cupboards and drawers, I found two fry pans and a mixing bowl in the massive walk-in pantry. I turned on the cooktop and stared at the heating element. The knot in my chest tightened. A night at home in this huge house by myself didn't sound like fun. Everhide had a function on, and I didn't want to venture out on the town without friends in tow. "You want some company tonight for dinner?"

We could dine together. I'd gone out on her reviews many times. We were just friends having a meal and having fun. This was an opportunity to reset. Be normal. Just like now, cooking breakfast. We worked like clockwork.

She grabbed flippers and tongs and an egg whisk from the cutlery drawer. "Um . . . sure. Company would be nice."

I drummed my palms on the white granite countertop. "The Haydster and the Lexster. Out on the town. It's a date."

Her gaze cut through me like a sharpened knife; concern swirled in the depths of her dark brown eyes. "It's not a date. It's work."

I slapped her butt with the flipper. "Lex. Chill. It's a joke."

"Fine." She jabbed her hip against mine as she cracked eggs into the bowl. "I don't want you to get the wrong idea."

My heart lurched and sank, still longing for her. I couldn't switch it off. But I'd live with it. I threw several bacon rashers into the hot fry pan. Sizzle and smell filled the air. "There is no misunderstanding. I got your message loud and clear."

Heat coiled up my spine. I glanced sideways at Lexi. She held the bowl steady and whisked the eggs slowly. Her gaze raked over my body, from my feet up to my head.

My heart fist-pumped my ribs. I liked her looking at me like that. It did all crazy things to my insides. Maybe being truthful about my feelings had affected her. Maybe she wasn't being honest with me. Or was that wishful thinking? Probably. "Something wrong?"

"Yes." She poured the egg mixture into the other fry pan. "I'm not sure if it's you that smells or if it's me."

I chuckled. *Nice diversion, Lex.* "It must be you. I smell like fucking roses." I sniffed my T-shirt I'd worn last night and winced. It stank of beer. I should've grabbed a fresh shirt, not picked up this one off the floor this morning. "Okay, maybe not. I'll shower after practice."

"You're such a goose." She giggled, nudging her elbow against my arm.

Yeah, a real goose, for falling for a girl who doesn't feel the same way about me.

Together, we cooked the food—the bacon crisp and crunchy, the eggs smooth and creamy, the tomatoes grilled to perfection. There was enough left warming in the oven for the others when they dragged themselves out of bed.

After eating our much-needed greasy breakfast wraps at the dining table, Lexi glanced at the wall clock. "Shit. I better wake the girls. We're supposed to leave in thirty minutes."

"Don't worry about your plate. I'll clean up." Greasy food had had the desired effect. I didn't feel hungover anymore.

"Thank you." She stood and rubbed the back of my shoulders but was quick to withdraw her hand. "So . . . for tonight, be ready by seven-thirty." She pushed her chair in and strummed her fingers on the back of it. "I've booked a car service. We're going to a swanky French restaurant, so wear something nice. Did you bring something better than jeans?"

"Yes, I did."

"Awesome." She clicked her fingers and pointed at me. "Let's go spend my boss's money on expensive fine dining."

I hooked my arm behind her, drew her against my side, and rubbed my hand up and down her thigh. "See, that's one of the reasons I love you."

She froze, clutching and pulling on my hair.

"Ow! Sorry." I held up my palms. "Slip of the tongue. I should've said, 'Dinner on your boss. Fuck yeah'. Is that better?"

"Hmm . . . for now." A playful glint shimmered in her narrowed eyes.

Did I have to watch what I said around her? No, I wouldn't do that. She knew me better than anyone else. Not every comment that came out of my mouth was about my love for her. She shouldn't be reacting like this—like she wanted to run and hide after everything I said or did. I'd rattled the ground beneath her feet by admitting my feelings. But something more serious was going on with her, and I had to get to the bottom of it.

She'd gotten jealous seeing me with Julz. She wasn't going to hook up with anyone while I was around. She was being mindful, considerate, compassionate. She cared about me. I knew that. I knew she feared falling for someone again. But did her feelings for me run deeper than she wanted to admit? Was there any way to dig into them further? I didn't know where to start. Should I take her on a date? Or just fill our days with activities we'd always promised to do?

Whatever happened over the coming weeks, I had to ensure my heart remained intact. Lexi really might not feel the same way as I did. But I had to find out. It was risky. A challenge. But maybe . . . just maybe . . . I needed to rattle Lexi a bit more.

Chapter 6

HAYDEN

Stepping out of the car at the Sur La Mer Restaurant in Marina Del Rey, I burned the back of Lexi's head with my I'm-over-this-shit gaze. She'd hardly looked at me since we'd left the house. She'd sat as far away from me as possible in the car and stared out the window. She'd scanned her phone and ignored me. It'd fucking irked me. A lot. If she didn't want me here, why didn't she say something?

I'd hoped the tension that had lingered since we'd kissed and the jealousy that had flared at the party last night had ended. Clearly not. Something was still bothering her. But now wasn't the time to push her buttons. She had a review to do. I was here for support and as a friend. Tonight was about her job—not the touchy subject of *us*.

I sucked in a deep breath to clear my head. I straightened my tie, buttoned my dinner jacket, and followed her inside. After not eating at Everhide's rehearsal this afternoon, I was starving.

"Welcome, Monsieur-Dame." The pristine-suited maître d, Marcy, greeted us and took Lexi's coat. "Please follow me." With the menus tucked under her arm, she led us toward the back of the bustling restaurant.

I inhaled the delicious, rich aromas that wafted from the

kitchen, adding to my hunger pains. Being near Lexi didn't help either. She exacerbated my cravings. My gaze slid down to her ass, over her sexy legs, her high heels and back up again. I was certain I'd left my simmering feelings for her back at the house, right beside the bottle of Budweiser I'd drunk while waiting for her to get ready.

No such luck.

She looked good enough to devour. Her knee-length ruby dress clung to her sexy curves. The low neckline emphasized her decent rack of cleavage. *Yep, it will be hard not to look at that all night.* Her flawless makeup accentuated her gorgeous brown eyes, and her red lipstick matched the color of her dress. Her blonde curls, pinned into a high bun, highlighted the fine curves of her neck. How had I not fallen for her sooner when she was everything I wanted in a woman? Beauty and brains, brazen and breathtaking.

But, unlike every guy she'd dated and dumped quicker than a techno-beat, I'd never captured her interest. Never been more than a friend. I was still banking on changing her opinion. Just not tonight.

As we took our seats, Marcy introduced us to Dion, our waiter for the evening. With a dip of her head, she glided off to attend to other guests.

"Good evening." Dion said as he picked up the white linen napkins, flapped them open and placed them on our laps. He poured glasses of sparkling water and ran through the dinner specials. "I shall give you a few minutes to browse the menu and return shortly for your order." He bowed and disappeared.

I drummed my fingers on the table and jerked my chin toward the kitchen. "They don't know you're a reviewer, do they?"

"No, not tonight." Lexi tugged on one of her dangling tasseled earrings. "I'm incognito."

"Good." I'd been on plenty of reviews with her before. When the restaurant knew who she was, the waiters groveled around her, and chefs offered her complimentary dishes, desserts, and delicacies. When they were clueless, it was a much more relaxed outing.

But Lexi was far from chilled. She fiddled with her hairdo, fidgeted with her cutlery, fussed with the roses in the center of the table. Surely she wasn't nervous about her first LA review. I could picture her article now . . . *"Every table has a spectacular view of the marina, but not from where I sat behind a pillar. The dark walnut furniture, deep red drapes, velvet-covered chairs, and Moulin Rouge inspired artwork gave the place a cozy boudoir feel, but paper tablecloths over linen lost me."*

I half-grinned, puffed air through my nose and leaned back in my chair. Lexi scanned the restaurant, the guests, and the waitstaff. She looked everywhere but at me. My presence had made her edgy. *Hmm.* Maybe she was fighting her burning want for me. Maybe I should kiss her again, just to give her something to be flustered about. Anything would be better than this silent treatment. It was killing me. I'd had enough. "Lex, what's wrong?"

"Nothing." She smoothed her hands over the tablecloth. "I'm fine."

"Are you worried about your review?"

"Nope."

"Is it your mom? Did she call this afternoon?"

Her jaw tensed as her shoulders sank an inch. "Yep . . . same old sob story. I ruined her life. So did my dad and their marriage. Oh . . . and I got a bonus rundown, complete with Instagram photos of every cup, saucer, and dish she's made in the past few days. So . . . she's great."

Lexi's pained smile was like a punch to the stomach. "You think she's off her meds?"

It was never a good sign when Celina rattled on about her divorce and made copious amounts of pottery. It usually meant she was on one of her manic highs. I prayed Nora would do the right thing and check on her while Lexi was away.

Lexi scratched her fingernail across her eyebrow, a visible tremor in her wrist. "She says she's taking them."

Good. So why couldn't Lexi sit still? I quirked the corner of my mouth. "If it's not your mom, is it me?"

"What makes you think that?"

"You haven't sat still for one second. You know we're cool, right? The party . . . the kisses . . . they're behind us. Forgotten."

A ridge formed between her brows, and she flopped her hands onto her lap. "I know. I'm sorry. I'm being silly. It's not you."

I wasn't convinced. I'd affected her, hopefully in a good way. Just the thought of making her pulse race sent a hum through my veins. "Good." I pursed my lips, suppressing my smile. "Then stop fidgeting. You look beautiful." *Stunning.*

"Thank you." She blushed and played with a curl that had escaped her bun.

I should give her more complements and make her feel good about herself more often. I made a mental note to do so. But before she turned as pink as a peach, I needed to take the edge off. She needed to relax. She had a job to do—her review. I picked up the wine list and handed it to her. "I don't know about you, but I need a drink. Would you kindly do the honors?"

"Absolutely." She snatched the wine list from me, scanned it in record time, and waved to Dion. She ordered a bottle of Moët & Chandon. Dion bowed and rushed off toward the bar.

I gave her a quizzical look. "Are we celebrating something?"

"Yes . . . no . . . maybe." She leaned over to smell the two miniature red roses in the vase. "I guess we need to celebrate your big move." She sat upright and glanced around the dimly lit restaurant. "But . . . more than anything . . . I'm gonna miss going to places like this with you."

A pang struck my heartstrings. The sadness in her eyes tore me in two. So that was what was bothering her? She wasn't crushing on me. She was upset that this would be one of the last times we went out together for her work. Another reality I didn't want to face. I caught her hand and curled my fingers around hers. I wished I could hold on to her forever. "Yeah. Me too."

I stroked my thumb over her smooth skin. Her pulse on the inside of her wrist thrummed beneath my touch. I'd love to take her out to fancy restaurants like this when she wasn't on the clock. But between her work and my gigs, we rarely had an evening free. I wanted to give her the world, the lifestyle she deserved, but that dream had to die. I couldn't wine and dine her from Boston. No point in any long-distance effort if she doesn't reciprocate my feelings. I glanced around the busy restaurant, but there was no sign of Dion. Where was that drink when you needed it?

Her hand quivered in mine. She tugged it free and picked up her menu. "You want me to order for you?"

"Yes, please." I pushed my menu aside—didn't even bother to open it. "I'll eat anything." She always ordered the dishes she wanted to review. I was happy to try anything.

Dion returned with the champagne, filled our flutes, and put the bottle on ice. He took our dinner order and headed toward the kitchen.

The second Dion was out of earshot, I rested my arms on the table and leaned forward. "Lex, what did you order?" She'd spoken so fast to Dion, and in French, I hadn't understood what she'd said.

"Appetizers of quail, flammekueche, and oysters with prosecco mignonette. And entrees of poulet à la diable and beef bourguignon."

"You ordered oysters?" I arched my eyebrow.

The slightest smile quivered across her lips. "You afraid they're an aphrodisiac?"

Hmm . . . I could only hope. The only slippery thing I wanted in my mouth was her tongue, and that wasn't going to happen. I swiped up my glass and tilted the flute toward her. "For your sake, I hope they're not." I downed a mouthful of champagne. "But I'll be happy to help you out if needed."

She lowered her lashes and shrugged her shoulders. "That won't be necessary. They don't affect me."

"If you say so." Turning the volume down on my voice, I summoned my best suave, French accent. "And what the hell is *poulet à la diable*?"

Her giggle was like a flicker of candlelight. Its warmth swelled inside my chest.

"You goose." She kicked my leg . . . well it was more of a rub of her calf against mine. It sent a shiver up my shin and the hairs on my leg jumped to attention. I'd be happy if she touched me under the table the whole night, but she was quick to pull her foot away. "It's chicken in a mustard sauce."

"*Terrifiant.*" I chugged two mouthfuls of champagne. The quicker the alcohol dulled my senses, the better.

But a waiter rushing by knocked my elbow. My champagne spilled down my shirt, jacket and onto my suit pants.

"Oh, *monsieur. Pardon.*" The waiter whipped out his napkin, ready to wipe up the spill.

"It's fine. Don't worry about it." I grabbed the cloth, dabbed myself dry and sent the waiter on his way. There hadn't been much champagne left in the flute to worry about. I didn't drop the glass.

Lexi giggled again. That was the Lexi I wanted to see. My smiling, happy, beautiful angel.

But as Dion returned and refreshed our drinks, the sparkle in her eyes faded. She stared at my chest. She always got like this when a tug-of-war went on in her mind. I hoped she contemplated how good we could be together. That she'd made a mistake and wanted to be with me. But whatever had zoned her out disappeared when she blinked. She sucked in a deep breath and pasted on a reassuring smile. She raised her flute. "To us. To friendship. May ours last forever." Her soft voice stabbed me in the center of the chest.

Fuck. What the hell was I doing?

Holding out for her feelings to change?

Praying for a sweet miracle?

She only wanted to be friends.

I had to get my feelings under control before I lost my mind.

Stop wasting my fucking time.

I could do this. I picked up my glass and dipped my chin. "Friends forever. I promise." I clinked my flute against hers. The reverberations hit low and hard in my gut. I was a fool to think I could sway her mind. But if she wanted to be friends, what would it take for her to look at me the same way as she had before we'd kissed? How could I look at her and not always want more? *Fuck.* If I could undo the damage I'd caused, I would. Or would this ache inside my chest always remain?

She downed her champagne like she was in a beer-guzzling competition. Placing her flute on the table, she licked her lips. The '*mmm*' sound humming in her throat sent a jolt of electricity straight into my dick. *Damn.* I stretched my neck from side to side and loosened my tie. Coming out to dinner with her had been a bad idea. I'd thought I could handle it, but my body had a mind of its own.

I needed more alcohol.

I grabbed the bottle and refilled our glasses. Fuck waiting for the waiter.

Drinking would either turn the night to shit, or . . . it would loosen us up and we'd have a great time. I prayed for the latter.

It took only one more glass for Lexi's cheeks to turn rosy and her genuine smile to return. By the time we'd gotten halfway through the third glass, the alcohol had eased the knots between my shoulder blades, and Lexi no longer sat ramrod straight. *Thank fuck.*

I leaned back in my chair. With the flute nestled between my fingers, I wiped the condensation off the side of it with my fingertip. "We didn't catch up this afternoon. How was your morning with the girls?"

Resting her elbow on the table, she cupped her chin in her hand. "I don't know how Gem does it. She tried on, hmm . . . twenty dresses. Kara fussed over every outfit. Bec took notes, placed orders and was constantly on the phone scheduling travel and appointments. I was exhausted watching them."

I grinned. Yep, alcohol had loosened her tongue. I loved it when she rambled. It took my mind off my problems—my band, the move . . . being in love with her.

She dug into her clutch and pulled out her cell phone. "I got some great photos. I've uploaded them from my camera. Here . . . check them out."

I flicked through the images she'd taken of Gemma joking around, dressing up, laughing, and pulling faces. They were stunning. Gemma shone in front of the camera, but it wasn't Gemma that I admired—it was Lexi's talent. She'd captured

Gemma's vibrant personality, just like she'd done at the wedding. "Lex, these are incredible. Has Gem seen these?"

"Nah." She put her cell phone back in her clutch. "I was just goofing around."

"You need to show her. And Kate. They're brilliant." Everhide's publicist would love those shots. So would their fans.

She tucked a flyaway hair behind her ear. "You really think I should?"

"Yes." Her photos were better than most of the professional shots I'd seen of my friends.

"I don't know." She slumped her shoulders. "Maybe. If I get the chance. They're so busy. I don't want to interfere with their crazy schedule."

"Do it."

"Nah." She swatted her hand as if there was a bug flying around. "Forget it."

Nope. There was no way I was going to let it go. Not this time. I'd make sure Gemma saw those shots.

We'd polished off the entire bottle of Moët and were into a glass each of Sauvignon Blanc before our appetizers arrived. Lexi took a couple of quick photos of the dishes before we dug in.

She spooned the prosecco mignonette onto an oyster, held the shell up to her mouth and devoured the slippery mollusk. "Oh my God. These are sensational."

My dick twitched. *So not good.* Somehow, I dragged my eyes away from her blissed-out face and slid an oyster into my mouth. The second the acidic sauce hit my tongue, I winced, struggling to swallow the horrid, rubbery little fucker. "Hmm. Not for me. You can have the last two. I'll pass."

"You're crazy." She covered her mouth as she spoke. "They're delicious." She swallowed another, then dabbed the sauce from her lips.

The pleasure rippling across her face made my cock throb even more. God, I'd love to see that look on her face when we were naked, in bed, fucking each other senseless.

Stop thinking with your dick. Idiot!

But it was hard not to when she licked her lips and moaned after every mouthful. It did all kinds of strange things to the depths of my stomach and sent my blood rushing south. She grabbed her cell and typed notes, her fingers flying across the screen. She winked at me over the top of her phone.

Yep . . . more alcohol was required . . . And food.

I picked up the fork and loaded our plates with the other appetizers. *Gotta keep my wits about me. She's just doing her job.* I grabbed my glass and gulped down two large mouthfuls of Sauv Blanc before we polished off the oniony *flammekueche* and herby, creamy stuffed quail.

"Are you satisfied?" she pouted with a saucy glint in her eye.

Kill me now. "Not even close." I chuckled, placing my cutlery on my empty plate. "I'm still starving." *For more food and you.* "But if you are, that's all that matters."

"Food *always* satisfies me."

Alcohol had definitely gotten to her. At least she'd slipped back into our normal mode of teasing. Some progress was better than none.

I was saved by our meals arriving. My mouth watered as Dion placed steaming dishes in front of us. After Lexi took her photos, I dug into my chicken, and Lexi, her beef bourguignon . . . whatever the hell that was. It looked like fucking stew.

"Hmm." As she chewed, she furrowed her brow, tilted her head from side to side, and pushed the meat around the dish.

I'd seen that stern, analytical seriousness on her face many times before—her reviewer mode. She'd be contemplating presentation, texture, and balance of flavor.

She finished her mouthful and swallowed. Cute wrinkles formed on the bridge of her nose. "The beef is chewy and dry. And the sauce is too salty."

I reached over, spiked a cube of meat from her dish, and popped it into my mouth. "Tastes good to me, but I'm no critique." I chewed the mouthful; her beef was definitely more flavorsome than my chicken.

She waved her fork at my plate. "Can I have a bite?"

"Sure." I cut a piece of chicken for her and waved it in front of her mouth. "But it will cost you."

Her eyes chiseled into me. She raised one fine eyebrow and glowed with sexiness. "How much?"

Yep . . . more alcohol required. "A bottle of wine. Something heavy, not too sweet."

She stole the meat off my fork. After her mouthful, she nodded. "Done." She waved down the waiter and ordered a bottle of Pinot Noir.

I ignored the stuffy diners sitting at the table next to us. They peered down their noses at us for being uncouth. I didn't care if it was rude eating food off each other's plates; we'd always done it. I wouldn't stop doing that for anyone.

The dessert of flaming Grand Marnier crepes with fresh berries and sorbet topped off the meal. It was the best thing I'd eaten all night. Light and fluffy crepes, decadent rich sauce and tangy sorbet were a decadent combination. My stomach was full to the brim.

Lexi arched back and rubbed her tummy. "Delicious. Let's finish the bottle and head home."

I'd be happy sitting here all night talking to her now that she'd lightened up, but she emptied her glass in record time. I tossed back my last mouthful. "Let's go."

I held out my hand and helped her to her feet. I caught her tiny smile—one of the many things I'd miss about her. After she finalized our bill, including a generous tip, and collected her coat, I wrapped my arm around her shoulders. We staggered out of the restaurant to meet our car.

But as we zoomed up the highway toward the hills and the city lights flashed by, a low thrum hovered between us. Every touch, every glance, every smile ignited the air. Sparks shimmered. The vibe was electric enough to power Downtown LA. As I stared ahead, I felt her gaze slide over me. When I stole a sideways glance, she quickly turned away. The moment I dragged my eyes off her, she did it again.

"You okay?" I gripped the door handle and closed my eyes to

steady my overactive, fuzzy mind . . . it didn't help much.

"Yeah. I think so," she whispered.

We'd had a great night out, just like old times. We'd drunk too much, like always. I didn't want either of us to do or say something we'd regret. Now wasn't the time to be stupid and question her feelings for me again.

I wanted to, but tonight was not the night.

After fucking things up by kissing her when I was drunk, I didn't want to do that again. I wanted to end the evening on a good note. I needed to sober up. Go to bed. *By myself.*

I dug my fingers into my thigh and stared out the city lights.

Yep. I've got this.

I'm. In. Control.

Go home. Go to bed. End of story.

Chapter 7

HAYDEN

I ripped off my tie and threw my dinner jacket onto the table. The rich, French dinner had been delicious. The wine and champagne, sensational. The company, always good even if awkward at first. I needed to drink a ton of water before hitting bed. *Bed. Go straight to bed.* But as I headed into the kitchen, Lexi stood in front of the wine fridge holding up her favorite bottle.

Shit. Too much wicked temptation.

I wiped my hand down my face and took a long, slow breath. She certainly knew how to torture me.

"Have one more drink with me?" She pouted and pleaded. "Now I'm not working, I want to chill for a while."

Chill mode was not what my body temperature was set to. I shouldn't drink any more. Each drop made it harder and harder not to do something stupid . . . like kiss her. But these were the nights I loved spending with her, where we'd often stay awake until the wee hours talking about anything and everything. These were the nights I'd miss. Rubbing my forehead, I checked my willpower was intact and ignored the warm buzz lurking through my veins.

One glass. That's it. Then bed.

"Sure. I'll grab the glasses."

We headed over to the living room, turned on the gas fireplace and sank into the sectional sofa. Side by side, we stared out the huge windows, down the hills, toward the ocean. The view was incredible. Not as incredible as Lexi, but still good. As she cracked open the red wine, I rubbed my palms against my eyes. *One drink. I can do this.*

She handed me a glass and curled in beside me. Her knees rested against my thigh. Her shoulder touched mine. I barely had time to draw a breath before she sank back into the cushions and talked about work. Slowly my tension dissipated. Spending time with her was as easy as a four-on-the-floor drumbeat.

We reminisced about some of her reviews gone wrong, places where the food had been terrible, to the extreme opposites, where we'd been treated like royalty and spoiled with exquisite delicacies. We laughed so much my stomach muscles ached. One glass led to finishing the entire bottle.

It was near one a.m., and our friends still weren't home. My head spun from too much alcohol. Time to call it a night. Holding out my hand, I dragged Lexi to her feet. Giggling and wobbling, we stumbled our way upstairs.

"Night." Lexi waved to me from halfway down the hall. At the main bathroom, she reached out for the handle, missed it, and crashed headfirst into the door. "Ow! Motherfucker!"

"Are you okay?" I rocked on my feet. Genuine concern for her wellbeing sloshed around inside my brain.

"I hit the door." She rubbed her forehead, pouted, and swayed on her feet.

"Yes, you did." I rushed toward her and opened it for her. "You need some help?"

"No. I'm fine." She stepped onto the bathroom tiles in her high heels and slipped, crashing to the floor. "Oh, shit." She burst out laughing, despite being close to doing the splits. "Did you see that?"

"Fuck, Lex. Are you alright?" I held out my hand to help her up. As I swayed and staggered, my leather soles slipped and slid. I wasn't much use.

"I'm fine." She clambered to her feet. "I need to take my shoes off." She bent over and fumbled with the straps, swaying like a tree in the breeze. "Buckles. I can do buckles."

I shook my head. "Let me do that. Sit." I waved toward the closed toilet, but she slid her ass onto the bathroom counter.

Leaning back against the mirror, she held up her ankle. "You're so sweet. You know that?"

"Yep. Sweet as." *Hmm.* I slid my hands around her calf, then hooked them underneath her foot. I rested her shoe against my thigh. Damn, she had sexy ankles. And arches. And cute little toes. Was it wrong I wanted to suck them? I knew that would ignite the ache between her legs. Turn her on.

Nope. Not going to happen. I unclipped the tiny buckle and eased off her stiletto. I put her foot down and repeated the process on her other shoe.

She rolled her ankles, pointed and stretched her toes. "Thank you."

Leaning forward, I placed my hands on either side of her hips. "You good?"

She pulled one hairpin out of her updo and then another. Then another. "Yep. I'm tooootally fine."

Her curls fell around her shoulders. My fingers twitched, wanting to touch her golden skin. I scanned across her shoulder, along her fine collarbone, and up the length of her throat to her mouth. Her lips . . . her deep pink lips . . . Damn it . . . *Don't look at her lips.*

"Crap." She winced and straightened. "I. Can't. Get. These. Stupid. Pins. Out . . . *Ow!*"

I chuckled and eased a fraction closer. "Here. Let me help." I hooked my hands behind her head and dug through her mass of hair for the pins. She tried to assist, but I slapped her fingers away. "I got it. Don't move."

Her hands fell to my hips as she rested her forehead against my shoulder. She spread her knees and drew me forward. *No . . . focus.* But my body temperature turned feverish beneath her touch. Massaging my fingers through her hair, I concentrated on searching for more pins, not her dress riding up her thighs or her breath on my neck. Slowly, I pulled one pin out and slid it down the length of a curl until it popped off the end. Then another . . . then another and another. Her hair was so beautiful and soft and . . . I inhaled deeply . . . it smelled like gardenias, smelled of her. Finding no more pins, I smoothed my hand over the silky strands and rubbed the base of her neck. "All done."

She lifted her head. An intoxicating smile curled across her lips. "Thank you."

"What for?"

"For being you."

With her less than a foot away, my pulse strummed an erratic beat. I should go, leaving her to get ready for bed.

But she didn't seem to be intent on moving.

Neither was I. I was afraid if I moved, the charge hurtling through my bloodstream would burn me.

She caught her bottom lip between her teeth. Gold shards flickered in the depths of her dark brown eyes.

Fuck, I wanted to kiss her.

My heart pummeled my ribs, trying to escape, begging my control to lapse. I clung to it by a fraying thin thread. "You okay, Lex?"

She shook her head slowly. Her fingers tightened on my hips. *Shit.*

"What's wrong?" I swallowed hard, my throat dry as dirt. "You going to be sick?"

"No." She tipped her head to the side and rubbed her hands up and down my sides. "Wanna do something stupid?"

I wanted to do many things to Lexi, but kissing her was at the top of the list. *Moisture.* My mouth needed moisture. I licked my lips. *Breathe.* "Maaaaybe. Like what?"

"I don't want to hurt you." Hooking her fingers into my belt loops, she tugged me forward another inch.

"What are you talking about?" My head spun faster than a DJ's turntable. I placed my hands on the granite counter beside her hips. Being this close to her, feeling her breath on my face, was entering the danger zone.

She glided her hands up my chest and rested them on my shoulders. "You know how you said you want us to have many first and last experiences before you leave?"

"Yes." *Sweet Jesus. Keep it together.*

She licked her lips. A sheen shimmered in the wake. She lifted her chin and leaned forward a fraction. "I want to kiss you."

My knees buckled, striking the cabinet door. *Ow!* My heart drummed out a double-bass beat. *She what? Fuuuuck!* "Lex, you're drunk." She'd never kiss me when sober. "I'd love to kiss you, but I don't think we should."

She linked her fingers behind my neck and shuffled toward the edge of the counter. "Just once. For fun."

Is it hot in here?

Why is it so hard to breathe?

Shit. Shit. Shit.

She spread her legs wider. Her skirt rose higher. *Don't look down. Don't look down.* But the zipper on my suit pants skimmed dangerously close to her panties. A piece of paper could barely fit between us. My dick twitched, desperate for connection.

Fuck, she was killing me.

"You want to kiss me?" It was impossible to steady my heartbeat. Hearing those words from her lips was like heaven, but it was wrong. Afraid to move, afraid of wanting her too much, I cemented my feet to the floor. The burn inside my leg muscles was brutal. "It's not a smart thing to do."

She floated her hand down my cheek, her touch light as a feather. Her gaze reached into the depths of my soul. Being with her felt like home, like somewhere I belonged. But I was just being stupid, because how the fuck would I know how it felt to have a loving home?

"I know it's crazy." Her voice was low, soft, and melted my bones. "I'm curious to know what it'd be like." She brushed her thumb across the top of my mouth, tickling my shaven skin. "One kiss. Without being caught off-guard or trying to get away from some loser. But if you don't want to, I understand. I know you have feelings for me. I don't want you to get the wrong idea. It's just that—"

I placed a finger over her lips. I'd wanted to rattle her more, but now she was rattling me. "Shh." Blue flames of blazing alcohol scorched all my logic and reason. Leaning in, I snaked my hand underneath her hair and cupped the back of her neck. "I can assure you my feelings are totally under control."

Like hell.

My hips sank between her legs. Her knees hugged my sides. Her breasts, teasing against my chest, sent shockwaves through my system.

"Okay." Her gaze locked onto mine. Her voice was barely audible, too breathy over our thundering heartbeats. "I don't want to cause more problems."

Oh, this was causing so many problems I didn't know where to begin. But I liked the want in her eyes, and the hot flush creeping up her neck.

"No. That wouldn't be good." I tilted my head to the side and breathed her in. The room temperature soared higher and higher. "Things between us are weird enough."

"You're right. It'd be a big mistake." She clutched onto my collar, tugged me forward, but I resisted . . . *just.*

"It'd be a huge one." There was less than an inch between our lips. Not to mention the gap between my crotch and her panties had disappeared.

"Uh-huh."

I brushed the tip of my nose along the edge of hers. "Want to stop?"

"No."

I could do this. Just one kiss. Another taste. Another memory to add to my dreams about her. *Shit.* The sweet scent of wine on her mouth was like an addictive drug, and I wanted to take a hit. *Just one.*

Closing my eyes, I pressed my lips to hers. Lightly. Gently. Softly. I lingered . . . for just a few seconds.

Then . . . I pulled away.

Lord, send me to Hell now. I'll die a happy man.

"How was that?" I murmured low and raspy.

She nodded, smiled, and then shook her head. "It was terrible. Try again."

Before I could blink, she crushed her mouth against mine. Dizziness swam through my head. My pulse drummed as loud as a Chinese drum in my ears. This time, there was no tension in her lips, no rigid posture. Just soft, full, delicious kisses. I didn't want to rush this. I'd go at her pace. Respond to her lead. But my body didn't want to listen. It craved more.

Parting my lips, I flicked my tongue, teasing her open mouth. There was no hesitation from her, no resistance. She kissed me back, hot, fiery, and fierce. A guttural moan growled deep in my throat. Now this was how I'd wanted our first kiss to be. I slid my arm behind her back, drew her against me, and kissed her harder.

"Hayden," she whispered against my lips.

"Yeah?"

"More." She wrapped her legs around my hips and drew my body flush with hers. Her dress rode higher and higher. She wriggled, driving the zipper of my suit pants and my growing hard-on against her exposed panties.

Holy fuck. This was way more than I'd anticipated. But after last time, I wouldn't fuck this up. Just kiss her. *But damn* . . . I tilted my groin, pressed into her. I wanted more friction. More fire. More of her.

No. Idiot. Don't blow it.

She moaned, and a jolt of electricity surged through my dick. I trailed a line of kisses down her neck. Her skin blazed beneath my mouth. Her floral perfume filled my head. After she'd said she didn't have feelings for me, I'd never dreamed I'd end up here, kissing her like this. I glided my hands up her bare thighs, so silky and smooth. I clutched a fistful of her skirt, scrunching it around her hips. My fingers twitched, wanting to rub over her panties and slip underneath the fabric. No . . . I wanted to tear the fucking things off. I wanted to touch her. Feel her hot sleekness. Make her lose control.

But I didn't want to go too far too fast. This agonizing heaven was bliss. I clutched her ass and tugged her forward.

She drove her hips against mine.

"So good." She panted over our kisses as she pulsed and rocked her pussy against my suit pants, and dug her nails into my shoulders.

My dick ached and throbbed. Her heat seeped through my pants. I wasn't complaining. But if we didn't slow down, if we didn't put this fire out, I'd come in my pants like a teenager . . . or rip off her panties and fuck her hard and fast on the counter.

Fuuuuck!

Stop. Now . . . Soon . . .

Shit!

Kissing, sucking, and tasting her top lip, bottom lip, and licking into her mouth, I savored every touch. It was hard to stay in control when her tongue lashed against mine, begging for more. The sweetness of the wine we'd drunk fueled the buzz surging to every extremity of my body.

Her hands roamed over my shoulders, drove through my hair, and snaked around my waist. She slipped them underneath my shirt and dug her fingers into my lower back. Her touch was an ice pack to my fevered skin. Closing my eyes, I drove my hard-on against her. God, I wanted to get naked and bury myself inside her. It took all my willpower not to strip off her clothes.

She moaned against my mouth. My heart hammered harder and faster. Her legs gripped around me tighter. Her breath panted, entwining with mine. She pulsed and rocked against me.

Fuck.

She shuddered in my embrace. A whimper escaped her lips.

Shit. Had I gone too far?

She shoved against my shoulders, forcing me back a step.

"Lex? What?"

Her eyes widened. The color drained from her face. "Fuck!" Her eyes welled with tears. Her hand shot over her mouth as she shook her head. "I'm so sorry. Fuck. I'm so sorry." She leaped off the counter and rushed from the bathroom.

"Lexi." I dashed after her. But she ran down the hallway and slammed the bedroom door in my face. "Wait." I slapped my palm against the timber over and over again. I tried the handle, but it was locked. "What's wrong?"

"Please, Hayds," she sobbed. "Leave me alone."

"No. This was my fault. I'm sorry. I shouldn't have kissed you." I thumped my forehead against the door. "Please? Let me in. Can we talk? Please?"

"Go away." Her muffled cry ripped through my ribs. "Just go."

My heart screamed. *What the fuck?* Another kiss had gone wrong. But it'd felt so right. So good. *Too* good. My raging hard-on proved it. Was that what was wrong with Lexi? She wanted more and was too afraid to let go? Or reality had struck and she'd thought our kiss was a mistake?

Fuck, she was doing my head in.

I leaned forward and banged my forehead against the door again. "Lex, please forgive me. It was just a kiss."

Alcohol blurred my vision. I clutched my dick to ease the aching tension. My suit pants were damp . . . but that wasn't from me. She'd been so turned on. *So hot.* And that shudder. *Oh shit . . .* had she orgasmed?

Damn!

I half-grinned and shook my head. I'd never dry-humped anyone to an orgasm. That was a first. *Wow!* "Lex, please don't be upset about what happened."

"Go. Away."

"Are you sure?"

"Yes."

"Okay." Before my balls exploded, I needed to take a shower. "I'll be in my room if you need me. We're cool, I promise."

Adjusting the bulge in my pants, I staggered down the hallway to my bedroom. That kiss had been no normal kiss. Her body had craved my touch, my dick. That had been freaking hot. *Too hot.*

But I'd gone too far. I'd upset her.

Idiot.

When was I going to learn?

Kissing her had been another mistake. I'd rattled her too

fucking much.

How the hell would I fix this fucked-up mess?

Chapter 8

LEXI

After waking late the following morning, I dressed in sweatpants and a hoodie and slipped on a pair of fluffy socks. Clutching my cell phone against my chest, I held my breath and tiptoed past the open door to Hayden's bedroom.

Please don't be awake. Please don't be in there. I'm not ready to talk about last night.

I snuck a peek inside. His bed was empty. *Phew!* I could breathe more easily . . . for now. I didn't have to face him . . . *yet.*

As I headed downstairs to the kitchen, soft muffled music—guitars, keys, bass, and drums—drifted up from the home studio on the lower level. Gemma and the guys were jamming. At ten o'clock? That was early, considering I'd heard them walk through the door at three-thirty a.m. Hayden would be with them. *Good.* It gave me more time to make sense of last night. How could I ever look him in the eyes again?

At the restaurant, it had taken a couple of drinks to flush away the flurry of emotions tearing at my insides every time I'd looked at him, and had helped me not to dwell on his move to Boston. We'd had a great dinner. Everything was like old times—the teasing, the banter, the laughs. A bottle of champagne. A few bottles of wine . . . and then we'd kissed. *Again.*

Fuck.

It'd been my mistake.

Would he accept my plea of temporary insanity?

But *that kiss.*

Curiosity to see if there *was* something between us had gotten out of control.

I couldn't remember the last time I'd kissed someone like that, where the impact had lingered. It scared the crap out of me. Since Quintin had left, I'd avoided affection. Being with a man was always purely physical, with no emotional connection. But Hayden had melted my insides like chocolate fondue.

I pressed my thighs together. My pussy clenched and ached. Resting my palms on the kitchen counter, I closed my eyes. I'd gotten off grinding against Hayden's dick. What the fuck was wrong with me?

This was a whole new level of humiliation.

I shouldn't have drunk so much. When he'd stood before me, undoing my hair, a fiery rush had struck every nerve in my body. I'd wanted to kiss him. Needed to kiss him. I'd never desired him before. Not ever. It was like he'd known exactly how to kiss me, hold me, drive me crazy. But things had gone too far. My lack of sex lately hadn't helped. But *fuck. I'd orgasmed! Fully clothed!*

Mortification plagued me. Was there any chance he hadn't noticed? Would he think my feelings toward him had changed? They had . . . but not in a good way. The cocktail of shame and sentiment, regret, and regard, concern, and curiosity that Hayden had shaken and stirred petrified me. I couldn't let my guard down. I needed to stay strong and focused. I refused to break the vacuum seal around my heart for Hayden. Not when he was leaving. Not even if he stayed.

My cell phone vibrated on the countertop. I glanced at the caller ID. It was my boss. *Ugh.* I swiped the screen. "Hello Chase, what's up?"

"Alexandra." Chase cleared his throat. "I'm glad you made it to LA safely."

"Um . . . Yes, thank you." I rubbed my forehead trying to erase my mild hangover. "I did my first review last night. You'll have my article by close of business tomorrow."

"I know I can always count on you." His subtle, flirtatious tone sent a shudder down my spine. "I don't want you to enjoy that warm winter sunshine too much or take too many sunset strolls along the beach."

"I'm not. I have three other reviews already booked. I'll make more reservations today." *Crap.* I really needed to pull my finger out. I'd gotten sidetracked with Gemma yesterday, taking photos. Work had taken a back seat.

"That won't be necessary. I'm sorry to do this, but please cancel your plans. I need you back here to report on this weekend's Bryant Park Food and Wine Festival. Fallon was supposed to review the event, but she's become ill. I'd like you to take her place. We'll go to the gala dinner, the food-stall sampling, and the wine-tasting events."

Go with Chase? No, thanks. "I'm not a senior editor. Why not take Lanie or Diego?"

"They're on assignment. The other editors are on publication deadlines. This festival will be a great experience for you. I'll book your return flight for today so you're here, rested up, and ready for the first function on Friday night."

"But I've only been here a couple days. What happened to two weeks? I've got a review this Friday. I've got plans this weekend with my friends." *Shit.* I shouldn't have told my boss I'd be socializing when I should be working.

"You can hang out with your friends anytime, but you work for me. I need you back here ASAP."

I wiped my bleary eyes. The potential promotion lobbed me in the back of my head. I shouldn't argue with Chase. I needed that new job so I wouldn't have to find a new roommate.

Although I hated my trip being cut short, it had its advantages. I'd have a week and a half to myself. Time away from Hayden, like I'd originally planned. Time alone. My stomach cinched. The empty ache lingering deep inside was new. Whenever Everhide and Kara had traveled, Hayden was always at home with me. Soon, he wouldn't be around. I had to get used to living by myself. No new roommate could ever replace him. This early return home would be a great practice run for when he moved to Boston. It'd give me the opportunity to pull my ridiculous emotions into check. They'd grown too overwhelming and crazy since we'd first kissed. Friends didn't fuck each other around.

Friends didn't make out.

Well . . . what was one orgasm between friends?

So. Not. Good.

"Lexi?" Chase dragged me from my thoughts. "You there?"

"Yes, I am. I'm good," I mumbled. "Book a flight for mid-afternoon."

"Done," Chase said. "I'll get the girls in admin to email through your itinerary."

"Thanks." I hung up and stared across the dining area out toward the pool.

Crap. I had no time to dwell. I had to cancel my restaurant reservations and pack. I'd better go tell my friends I had to leave. While I was at it, I'd shoot one last round of photos.

I looked around for my camera. I swore I'd left it on the dining table. Staggering around the table, I searched the chairs. *Not here.* I headed across the room and found it on the sofa. I didn't remember putting it there.

Taking the Canon out of its bag, I headed down to the studio. The muffle of guitars, piano, and the steady beat of the drums filled the air. I walked up to the heavy wooden door and peered through the glass panel. Gemma sat cross-legged on the floor with her electric guitar in her lap. She sang, but I couldn't make out the lyrics. Kyle stood beside her, plucking his bass. Hunter sat at the keyboard, his fingers gliding over the ivory keys. Hayden was on the drums. I couldn't see any sign of Kara; she was probably out shopping.

Total contentment lit Hayden's face as he struck the tom-toms at speed. He never looked that happy and relaxed playing with his band, not for months.

I hated interrupting their session and really didn't want to confront Hayden.

Would he cause a scene in front of our friends? Tease me?

If he did, I deserved it.

I snuck in the door and pointed my camera at Gemma. She smiled and kept strumming her guitar. These were the shots I loved taking of my friends. When they were playing, being natural, being themselves. When there was no media or millions of fans watching them. I took photo after photo of Gemma, Hunter, and Kyle. Then I turned to Hayden.

He stared through the lens. A frenzy of butterflies swirled above the thick pool of unease lurking at the bottom of my stomach. I took a deep breath and focused. The viewfinder grid framed his face. The happiness that had lit his eyes moments ago disappeared, replaced by gray clouds of concern.

Kissing him flickered through my mind, replaying every second in high-speed sports mode. The Canon trembled in my hands. My palms turned clammy. My cheeks felt as hot as a teppanyaki grill.

With drumsticks in hand, he half-rose from his stool. "Are you okay?"

"Uh-huh." My voice squeaked as I held up my palm. "Don't get up."

He lowered onto the stool; a deep furrow etched his brow.

Gemma ripped out a killer riff on her guitar, then stilled her strings. "Lex, what's up?"

I lowered my camera and slumped my shoulders. "I'm sorry to interrupt. My boss called. He wants me to cover the Bryant Park Food and Wine Festival this weekend. Fallon's sick, and the other editors are on assignment. So, I have to go home. I've gotta leave in a few hours."

"Fuck. That sucks." Gemma ruffled her fingers through her long dark hair. "We have two free days, and I wanted to hang out."

"Me too." I switched off my camera and replaced the lens cap.

"Surely there's someone else who can review the festival." Hayden wiped his hand over his face. Desperation swirled in his eyes. "You've only been here a couple days. You have reviews to do here."

"I know." Lowering my chin, I let my hair curtain my face. Anything to avoid looking at him. "But with a promotion on the line, I need to stay in Chase's good books."

Gemma jumped to her feet and gave me a hug. "I feel bad that we haven't spent much time together." She leaned in to whisper in my ear, "How are things with Hayds working out?"

"Not good," I murmured, tears burned the back of my eyes. "It's more fucked up than ever." I didn't have time to tell her about last night. I'd call and spill later.

"It'll be okay." Gemma rubbed my arm. "Hey." Her voice jumped up a scale. "Hayds showed me the photos you took yesterday at the fitting."

I glared at him. So that was why my camera hadn't been on the table. I turned back to Gemma and shrugged my shoulder. "Oh . . . they're nothing."

"Nothing? Are you kidding?" Gemma's voice swung with the same level of excitement she'd had when she saw the wedding photos I'd taken. "Can you send them to me? I want to show Kate."

"Really?" I wrinkled my nose. Kate—Everhide's publicist— was the gatekeeper, dictator, and freakishly amazing manager of their public image. Excluding the gossipmongers and paparazzi, nothing went to the media, no interview was given, no official photo was taken, and no word was written about Everhide without her approval.

"Yeah." Gemma play-punched my arm. "I'd love to use some of them, post them to our social accounts."

As I hooked the camera strap over my arm, my eyes widened. "You want to post *my* photos? To your fans?"

"Yes. Your shots are awesome." Gemma pointed to the camera hanging by my side. "Must be that beast you bought to use for our wedding. You make us look good, and I love that."

That wasn't hard to do. Gemma, Kyle, and Hunter were extremely good-looking, very photogenic and loved being in front of the lens. Just like Hayden.

"O-kay." My heartbeat danced in circles. "I'll email you the link." *Wow.* I'd be stoked if Gemma selected one of my photos to post. In the years I'd known her, she'd never asked me to send my shots to Kate. Gemma and the guys had shared my photos on their private accounts but had never released them publicly. Every image they published on their main socials was always strategically and carefully controlled—a marketing tactic or something to please the fans. *Damn.* Maybe this new camera had been worth the six-thousand-dollar investment.

Hayden folded his arms and let out a puff. "Told you they were good."

I shot him a quick glare. Any longer, and last night's flustered memories would consume me.

Catching Gemma's hand, I gave it a gentle shake. "I'm so sorry I can't stay longer. Make sure you kick ass at your shows. And don't party too hard without me. I'll see you at home at the end of next week." I hooked the camera strap higher on my shoulder and stepped back toward the door. "I've gotta go pack. I'll let you play. Whatever you were working on sounded awesome. Guaranteed next hit."

"Um . . . it's already a hit." Gemma laughed and struck her guitar strings. The electric reverberation hummed through the amp. "We were playing 'Escape.'"

That was what I wanted to do. *Escape.* Get out of that room. *Now.* Hayden's eyes were drilling into me, making me break out in a cold sweat. "Oops. Sorry. Let's have lunch together before I head off. Gotta go." I turned and reached for the doorknob.

"Wait." Hayden leaped from the stool, rushed over, and grabbed the back of my hoodie. "We need to talk."

Shit. So close to escaping.

I spun around and straightened my shoulders. Tension throbbed in my temples. My headache pounded my skull.

"Do you really have to go to New York?" A muscle ticked in his taut jaw. "Or are you running away from me like you did last night?"

Gemma struck, then stilled her guitar strings. "What happened last night?"

Prickles darted across my skin. I wasn't ready to discuss what had happened. I didn't want to admit my mistake. After losing Quintin, I'd sworn not to be erratic, intense, and compulsive. But last night, I'd relapsed. I didn't want to mess around with Hayden's feelings. Didn't want to keep fucking up like I had.

"I'm not running away," I snapped at Hayden in a hushed whisper. "I have to leave for work."

"Not before we talk." He didn't lower his voice, not even by a fraction of a microbar.

"Talk about what?" Gemma hollered.

Hayden's intense gaze nailed my feet to the floor. He sucked in a deep breath, puffed out his chest, then blurted to our friends, "Our kiss last night."

I squeezed my eyes shut, wanting to melt through the floor and disappear.

"'Bout time," Hunter mumbled, tinkering on the piano keys. "Now go fuck and be done with it."

I threw Hunter my most evil glare. "Shut up. It wasn't like that." Spinning back to Hayden, I spoke through clenched teeth. "There's nothing to talk about."

"Oh, yes there is. Let's go. Now." He grabbed my hand and led me up to my bedroom. He slammed the door shut behind us. In the middle of the room, he drew me close and smoothed his hands over my curls. "Lex . . . last night?"

A crippling pain shuddered through my chest as I lowered his hands. "It was a crazy bit of fun. I told you not to get the wrong idea."

"Are you serious?" The cutting edge in his tone sliced and scored my heart. "That was no ordinary kiss, and you know it."

I lowered my chin, unable to meet his challenging gaze. There had been nothing ordinary in my behavior last night. The kissing. The grinding. The madness. All a mistake. *Alcohol.* Could I blame the alcohol?

"For fuck's sake, Lexi."

I closed my eyes. Heat burned my cheeks. Did he know what had happened? My core clenched, still aching from having his dick against me. "It was a nice kiss. That's it." I wouldn't allow myself to draw any other conclusion.

"A *nice* kiss. Is that what you think?" He shook his head and took two steps back. "You're such a liar."

My heart bled. I had to stop hurting him or I'd drive him away. "You were right. We shouldn't have kissed."

"You started it." He closed the gap between us and cupped my face. His eyes turned to molten metal. "I know what happened. I *felt* you shudder. I want to throw you onto that bed and make you orgasm again and again and again."

"Stop." I yanked free of his hold. "Stop saying things like that."

"Stop fighting this. Stop fighting and admit you have feelings for me."

"No. I don't." I covered my eyes with my hands. I didn't want to feel anything.

He drew them away. "Stop being afraid. Let me in."

"No." I shook my head. He was already in my heart, but I couldn't give him any more of it. I was too damaged. Too broken. Too dead inside. My tears threatened to fall. "You're moving to Boston. You have your career. I have mine. Don't ruin what we have."

"We could be happy."

"No, we'd end in disaster."

"You don't know that."

"Yes, I do. Long distance never works."

"I'm not Quintin. You won't know that unless we try."

I covered my ears to block the optimism in his voice. "Just stop. We're not going to turn into some screwed-up, friends-with-benefits fiasco."

"I don't want it to." He lifted my chin with the tip of his finger and met me square in the eye. "I want you to be mine."

Fuck. No. Don't say that.

My defenses shot up—spikes and wire and spears guarded my aching heart. "Stop. Please. I don't feel that way about you."

The cold steel in his eyes tore through my chest. "Fine." He clenched his jaw and hissed. "You win." The frost in his voice cut through my skin. "You can stay locked in your stupid bubble, Lex.

Miss out on seeing if we could be good together. I care for you too fucking much to keep pushing you. So, no more games. You know how I feel about you, but I don't want to lose you. I'll back the fuck off . . . after this." He clasped the back of my head and crushed his lips to mine.

His scent filled my head. My body melted against his. Fire ignited my heart, threatening to burn down the walls.

No. No. No.

I clutched his arms to push him away. But . . . there was something in his kiss—the tension, the desperation, the longing. It struck a chord in my heart, and weakened my knees.

A whimper escaped my lips.

He ripped his mouth off mine. Our breaths panted. Resting his forehead against my brow, he massaged the back of my neck. "I love you, but I don't want to hurt you anymore. I don't want to play games, and I don't want to wait for you to feel something that you don't. So . . . that's it. I'm done. No more kisses. I promise." He turned and headed for the door; he didn't glance back. "I'll see you at home next week."

He walked out of the room and slammed the door. I stared at it. Shock rattled every bone in my body, right down to the marrow. A tear caught on the tip of my cheek.

What the fuck?

I sank onto the bed and sobbed. What happened to having fun in these last few weeks together? What happened to just being friends? This bedlam of emotions was not part of the plan. I didn't want every moment I spent with him to end in hurt. If it felt this bad now, how much worse would it be when he left?

Fuck. This. Shit.

I had to set things right.

He was the one who'd messed things up. But I'd made them worse.

I grabbed my suitcase, tossed my belongings into it, and zipped it shut.

I couldn't get out of LA fast enough.

I needed the week at home without him. I needed to get him

out of my head.

And most of all, I had to stop him chiseling his way deeper and deeper into my heart.

Chapter 9

HAYDEN

I stretched out my legs on the lawn by the pool and tipped my head back, enjoying the rays on my face. My friends lazed around me—Kara and Hunter lay on a blanket, her head rested against his stomach; stretched out on her tummy, Gemma kept humming, singing and scribbling lyrics onto her notepad; Kyle sat opposite me, playing Gemma's acoustic guitar. Only one vital person was missing. *Lexi.* She'd headed home to New York yesterday afternoon. She'd left another gaping hole in my chest.

I tugged my baseball cap lower and straightened my sunglasses. I couldn't comprehend that our steamy bathroom kiss had meant nothing more to her than some drunken fun. I'd sworn we had a connection. Our kiss had blown me away. But . . . *fuck*. I couldn't torture myself anymore. It was time to let go of the idea of us. Of being more than friends. Yep, I was done.

Kara grabbed her cell phone and checked the screen. "Hayds? Gem? Have you heard from Lexi? I've tried calling and texting her, but she hasn't replied."

Gemma stopped humming and glanced at her cell phone. "Nope. Nothing."

I leaned back on my hands and stared at my sneakers. I didn't need to look at my cell phone; I'd checked it more than one hundred times since her flight had landed in New York. "I'm the last person she wants to talk to right now."

I'd downloaded the details of our bathroom encounter to my friends over dinner last night. They'd laughed, teased, and joked but had also been confused and concerned. Everyone except Hunter held on to hope, convinced we were a good thing. But I knew better than that. Lexi and I were a lost cause.

Kyle plucked the strings and bobbed his head. "She'll come around. Trust me."

Hunter lowered his arm over his eyes. "Don't bet on it."

Gemma didn't look up from her writing. "Leave Lex alone. Hayds, she's after that promo at work. You're moving to Boston and doing nothing but causing her grief."

"What?" I snapped. "She kissed me. I had no intention of repeating the first time... or the second one at the club." *Shit!* We'd kissed three times in the past week. *Damn!*

Hunter coughed into his hand. "Bullshit."

"Okay . . . I'd kiss Lexi anytime, but she's said no to being something more. So that's it. I just want to put the past several days behind me. Forget we kissed and move on. I'm gonna focus on my music and the move to Boston. Nothing else."

I'd been trying to do that, but something kept drawing me back into Lexi's atmosphere. I couldn't exit her orbit.

Kara grabbed gloss from her hoodie pocket and smeared it across her lips. "Hayds, I have some packing boxes when you need them."

"Thanks." I scratched my stubble. So much had changed in the past few months. Hunter and Kara had moved in together. Kyle and Gemma had gotten married. I was about to move to a new city. "I'm not looking forward to packing. Lex and I have bought so much shit together. I don't know what's mine or what's hers."

Hunter chuckled and kicked my foot. "You two have been in a relationship without the fucking benefits, dipshit. Now you've gotta get divorced."

I picked at the short grass. I furrowed my brow. The truth hurt like a bitch.

Gemma scribbled faster and faster. Her hum grew louder and louder. Concentration chiseled her face. Kyle leaned toward her, adjusted his aviator sunglasses, and picked up on her tune. He struck the strings, played and fumbled with different chords and notes. Hunter's fingers strummed against his thigh.

They fell into sync. Playing. Tapping. Humming.

I fell mesmerized, witnessing them in action. They were a few months away from recording their next album. Any time we'd hung out like this or jammed, they'd jot down lines and lyrics, record licks, and riffs, sing tunes that popped into their heads onto their phones. They feed off each other to create magic. I didn't have that dynamic with Kilt. My band's lead singer wrote and composed most of our music. We didn't vibe the same way as Everhide did. But when we played gigs, we had a lot of fun. I couldn't wait to work on new material and hammer out some fresh, wicked beats. I itched to make another album. If Kilt kept his short fuse under control, everything would be fine.

Moving to Boston was such a huge step for my band. I'd miss working at the indie studio more than filling in occasionally on Broadway. But leaving those jobs was easy compared to leaving Lexi.

After fucking up so much, I just wanted my best friend back. For things to go back to normal. Was that even possible? I had no idea.

Gemma stared at her page. The tone of her hum changed. It dialed down from light and airy to low, drawn-out . . . and sad.

It hit too close to home, making my chest ache. I reached out and slapped her on the ass. "What's up with you? That sounds morbid."

She jabbed her pen against my shoe, then peered over the rim of her sunglasses. "I'm picking up your moody vibe. What's going on in your head?"

I picked up a dead leaf and ripped it into pieces. Lexi was in my head. Every time I thought about her, I came to the same tangled web of crossroads. "Confusion."

Kara rolled onto her side. "About Lexi? I think she is too. She cares about you a lot."

"I know she does." I grunted. "Just thought after our kiss—."

Hunter groaned. "Get the fuck over it. She's just not that into you. Maybe she doesn't want to fucking settle down." He smirked and clicked his fingers. "You gotta love her . . . what's that dating game she goes on about—the Five Fs?"

"Oh yeah." Kara giggled and counted down her fingers. "Find 'em, flirt with 'em, feed 'em, fuck 'em, flick 'em. It's brilliant . . . for a single girl not looking for love. She certainly keeps her dating apps busy."

"I've never needed an app." Cockiness swung through Hunter's tone. "I need security to keep the girls off me."

"Same." Kyle half-grinned, not looking up from his playing.

"Same . . . only guys, not girls . . . actually both." A cheeky smile crept across Gemma's lips. "But I don't miss being single. Not one bit." She leaned over and kissed Kyle on the knee.

He bent forward and kissed the top of her head. "Love you."

I couldn't summon a smile. I'd had that *meant-to-be-together* inclination about Lexi. Being with her was as natural as breathing oxygen. Our connection went beyond friendship. But she didn't see it that way.

We weren't meant to be.

So fuck it.

Gemma chewed on the end of her pen. "With Lex, would you have done anything differently?"

I closed my eyes and absorbed the warm winter sunshine. The past week flashed through my mind—walking home from the concert, the nightclub, kissing her in the bathroom . . . her pushing me away every time. "Everything. I regret kissing her. Regret telling her how I feel. Regret hurting her. She's my best friend. I don't want to lose her over what's happened."

"Don't ever regret being honest." Kyle strummed quietly. "Better to know how she feels than not."

"True." I half-heartedly nodded. He had a valid point.

Gemma put pen to paper. "That's it."

"What is *it*?" I asked, dazed.

"I think I've got a song." She hummed the tune, tapping the pen slowly against her pages. Kyle played some chords. Gemma lowered her voice and sang.

> *Just wait . . .*
> *Don't walk away*
> *I'm standing right here*
> *Struggling to find the words to say*
> *Sorry, I hurt you*
> *I'll regret it for the rest of my days*
> *My heart is bleeding on the floor*
> *I want you forever more*
> *Love is messy, love is blind*
> *If I could, I'd wind back time*
> *All I know is I want you to stay*
> *All I want is for you to be my babe*
> *My love for you grows stronger every day*
> *All I need you to do is . . . stay*

My heart cinched. The mellow tune seeped into my bones. Gemma had tapped into my emotions with the stroke of her pen and her freakish talent. I grabbed and chugged my soda. It took a moment to regain my composure. "Thanks, talented bitch. That just makes unrequited love feel so much better." Sarcasm swayed through my tone.

A smart smile tugged at one corner of her mouth. "I'll be your therapist anytime."

"Don't need one. I've got my drums."

"Thank God for music," Hunter hollered.

"So true." Kyle ripped out a riff on his guitar, then stilled his strings. "Hayds, are you sure moving to Boston is the right thing to do? I know you've been with The Saylors for years, but sometimes you've gotta look out for yourself. Do you want us to put the word out to our friends again? See if anyone is looking for a new drummer, for touring or full-time? You've gotten really good."

"Thanks. But I'm good. Unless Slade plans on quitting." I joked, but I was half-serious. The drummer in Everhide's backup band was a legend. I didn't think I'd ever reach that status.

"Nope. Sorry." Kyle shook his head. "But I don't want to see you waste your talent."

"I won't. I promise." I just prayed that my band grew closer when we moved to Boston, and that another big break came our way, and we wrote another hit, or twenty. "Just don't forget me. Come visit when you can."

"We'll do better than that." Kyle rested his arm on top of the guitar. "We want to come to your first show."

"Yes." Kara clapped; her voice pitched with excitement. "We'll be your groupies in the front row."

That brought a grin to my face. "That'd be cool."

My cell phone rang. I grabbed it off the grass, hoping it would be Lexi. But it wasn't. I recognized the number. The blood drained from my face. Nausea pooled in my stomach. *Fuck.* My fingers shook as I swiped the screen to answer. "Hello."

"Is this Mr. Hayden Moore?"

"Yes." I closed my eyes, waiting with bated breath. How bad would it be this time?

"This is Nurse Davies from Glen Cove Hospital."

Air leaked from my lungs. Familiar dread crawled beneath my skin. "Hey Ruth." Was it bad that I knew the staff at the emergency department on a first-name basis?

"Hayden, your mother has been admitted to emergency again. The doctors have stabilized her."

Slipping my hand underneath my sunglasses, I wiped the sting from my eyes. "Heroin or cocaine?"

Gemma stopped writing. Kyle stopped strumming. Hunter stopped playing with Kara's hair. They'd know what had happened. They'd witnessed these calls before.

"Heroin," Ruth said. "The paramedics brought her in. The report said her employer called the police because she hadn't turned up for work for two days. They found her at home, unconscious in bed."

I pinched the bridge of my nose. Frank—her sponsor and local Foodmart owner—did so much for the community, helping recovering addicts get back on their feet. But the thing was . . . my mother *was* an addict. She didn't want to recover.

"How bad is she?" My legs wobbled as I stood and walked over to the edge of the retaining wall. I looked down the canyon toward the ocean. My mind morphed into meltdown. What the fuck was wrong with my mother? Why couldn't she fucking stop? I'd begged and pleaded and implored her a million times. Nothing got through. I wasn't a good enough reason for her to stop. Dad wasn't worth it either. But my father was the reason she was like this. He fed her addiction.

No amount of rehab or support fixed her. She continually relapsed. Every time I'd helped her, she'd push me away. She'd yell and cry and remind me how pathetic and useless I was. She'd kick me out the door. But I could never stay away. She was my mom, regardless of how fucked up she was.

I paced the lawn. I'd locked away my emotions for my mother ever since I'd come home from school and found her unconscious with a needle stuck in her arm. I'd been nine. That had been her first OD. Her second trip to the emergency room was when I was ten.

The third time my neighbors had helped me because Dad wasn't around.

But every time she'd been admitted, she'd yelled, '*You're a worthless heap of shit*' or '*I hate you*' at me from her hospital bed.

There'd been more times since.

I fought the tears burning at the backs of my eyes. Mom had never gotten better, only worse. My parents had never shed a tear or fought for me when I went into foster care. I'd never had a place to call home. I'd never belonged anywhere . . . until I moved in with Lexi. But I'd gotten that wrong too.

Fuck.

I rubbed my eyes again and refocused on the call. I knew the answer before I asked the question. "Did you get in touch with my dad?"

"No." Ruth's voice swung with sorrow. "We haven't been able to contact him. Is he on the road again?"

"I don't know where he is. I haven't heard from him in months." That was nothing unusual. Dad spent his days and nights driving long-haul trucks, snorting cocaine, and popping pills to stay awake. Then he'd hit the booze and heroin whenever he was at home with Mom. *Dick.*

"Okay," Ruth said softly. "Your mom will be fine by the morning. Do you want us to start the paperwork to have her submitted into the program? She was court-ordered to go if she OD'd again."

"Sure. Seventh time could be the charm." Bitterness tainted my tone. I didn't want to deal with my mother. I had enough on my plate with Lexi.

"I know this is hard." Ruth's voice was full of compassion and care. "But everything will be okay. You're doing a great job just being around to support and help her."

Help? Mom didn't want help. Nothing could fix her. *Maybe I don't want to take care of her anymore. Maybe I just want Mom to OD and be gone for good . . . Shit.* I shuddered, and my heart splintered. I didn't want that. I wanted her to get better. I shook the *I-m-so-over-this-crap* thoughts from my head. "Thanks, Ruth. It's just tough sometimes."

"I know." She paused. "Can you come and get her?"

I clenched my fists. Cold blood meandered at a snail's pace through my veins. *Fuck.* "I'm in LA. I'll get a flight and be there by morning." I wanted to slam my fist through a wall, or into a punching bag, or into my dad's face. *Fuck. This. Shit.*

I ended the call, and Gemma rushed to my side. She wrapped her arms around my waist and hugged me tight.

"I have to go home," I murmured against her hair. All I wanted was Lexi. Gemma's hug, although appreciated, just didn't feel the same.

"Gathered as much." Gemma looked up at me. Tears pooled in her eyes. "I'll call Bec to book you a flight home. ASAP, right?"

"Yeah. Thanks." We walked back to the others.

Kyle put down the guitar. "Your mom fall off the wagon again?"

"Yeah." I rubbed the back of my head. "She's gotta go into another program. I need to take her there."

"Fuck, Hayds." Lying on the blanket, Hunter flopped his arms wide. "That's shit."

"Family. Who fucking needs 'em?" I grunted.

"We're your family." Gemma grabbed my shoulder and gave me a gentle shake. "Remember that. You won't ever get rid of us."

Meeting these people had changed my life. Our different levels of success didn't matter. Our friendship had kept me sane. They made me feel more worthy than my band. Yet . . . I still felt like an outsider.

"I'd better go pack." I waved toward the house.

Kara sat upright and clutched my hand. "You've got this. Your mom's gonna be okay. Let us know if you need anything."

"Thanks. Will do." I dragged my feet up to my room and stuffed my belongings into my suitcase—T-shirts, jeans, underwear, and the suit I'd worn to dinner with Lexi. I sank onto the bed, buried my face in my hands, and wiped my tired eyes.

Fuck. This would be the first time in years I had to deal with Mom without Lexi by my side. She'd never asked or complained or hesitated. She just went with me to the hospital or to my parents' house and helped me deal with a lot of shit.

I rubbed at the hollow ache in my chest. I wasn't sure how to handle this on my own. Should I call her? No, no, I couldn't do that. I didn't want to look needy. I could do this by myself.

Yep. I've got this.

Alone.

Ten minutes later, a text came through from Bec. My flight was confirmed for midnight. Everhide's PA was a treasure. I was one lucky bastard to have such great friends. That they looked out for me. If that luck could strike my music career, make Mom better and help me sort out my mess with Lexi, wouldn't life be great?

But I wouldn't sit around and wait for things to happen. I had to chase my dreams, and let the ones involving Lexi go.

She'd preoccupied my thoughts for long enough. No girl was worth this shit. Dragging my mother back to rehab and getting her to stay there would be a breeze compared to locking my feelings away for Lexi.

But resetting them had to wait.

I had other pressing concerns and worries.

Right now, I had to go deal with my screwed up, fucked up mother.

Chapter 10

LEXI

Rushing through the doors of Glen Cove Hospital, my heart pounded. Hayden sat in the waiting room, leaning forward with his elbows resting on his knees. His suitcase stood beside him. His brown hair was a disheveled mess, and a coffee cup dangled between his fingertips. He looked tired, like he hadn't slept in days. I pushed my hurt aside that he hadn't called me. But I was here. For him. Always would be.

I undid my scarf, pulled off my gloves and scuttled down the short hallway. I called to him softly, "Hayds?"

He leaped to his feet. Bewilderment flashed in his eyes. "Lex? What are you doing here?"

I wrapped my arms around him and held him tight. His black duffel coat warmed my cold cheek. "Gem called. She told me what happened and that you'd be here. Is your mom okay?"

"Yeah. Just another OD." He slid his hands across my back, held me against his chest for a couple of seconds, then pushed out of my embrace. His voice scraped just above a whisper. "Sorry . . . I didn't want you to worry."

I grabbed and squeezed his hand. "You goose. I'm here for you. No matter what." The craziness of the past week couldn't unravel seven years of friendship.

Taking a step back, he pulled his hand free and stuffed it into his coat pocket. "You didn't have to come. I can do this on my own."

I shook my head. Why was he pushing me away? "But you don't have to. I'll always support you through thick and thin. You don't have to do this by yourself. Not ever."

An ocean of troubled dark water swam through his beautiful steel-gray eyes. He turned his head to hide the welling tears. "Thank you." His voice wobbled as he nodded. "You're an angel. Come on." He held out his bent elbow. I curled my arm around his, and he led me over to the seats.

After undoing the buttons on my woolen coat, I sat beside him. Half-heartedly, he flicked his hand toward the nurses' station. "I'm waiting for some paperwork to sign, and then I have to go via Mom's house and grab her some things. Mom's bad, Lex. They thought she'd be alright by this morning, but she's not well. I can't drive her to rehab. They're sedating her to transport her to the center via an ambulance."

My heart lurched. Celina's comedowns from heroin were never good. She'd often get angry, violently sick, and irrational.

I clutched his hand. "She going in for ninety days?"

"Yeah. Unless she checks herself out again."

"I'll drive you."

He lowered his chin and rubbed the back of his neck. "You don't have to. I'll be fine."

"I know. But I want to. You're always there for me and my crazy mom. I'm not going anywhere." I glanced around the waiting area. It hadn't changed since the last time I was here with Hayden six months ago. Same pale gray floors and walls, and a small flat-screen TV scrolling through the hospital's services. "How did you get here from the airport?"

"I caught an Uber. I called Lewis, but he and the guys were bent, so none of them could drive."

I liked Lewis, The Saylors' bassist. He liked to party hard and was fun to hang out with. But Reg and Kilt often rubbed me the wrong way. "You should've called me."

The distance in his eyes tore at my soul. I hated seeing him like this. I'd only added to his pain lately, and I didn't want to do that anymore. I cared about him too much.

He glanced at his watch and frowned. "Aren't you supposed to be at work? It's eleven a.m."

I threaded the tassels of my scarf through my fingers, setting the motion on repeat. "I've got the food festival tonight, so I have some flexibility today."

"I'm sorry." He reached over and squeezed my hand. The gratitude in his touch enveloped my heart. "Thank you for coming."

"Anytime."

After Hayden signed the paperwork, I drove him to his mom's house on the outskirts of Glen Cove. It wasn't far from my mom's home in Sea Cliff. Funny how we'd grown up in the same area but had never met before college.

Near noon, I pulled into the driveway. I followed Hayden through the overgrown grass, stepping carefully from one broken paver to the next, up to the front door. Pale blue paint peeled in flakes off the walls, and broken timber framed the old cottage's picture windows. Hayden grabbed the key from under a dead potted plant and opened the house.

The stench that hit us made me gag. "What is that?" I covered my mouth with my gloved hand.

Hayden clutched his nose. "Oh . . . that's disgusting."

We stepped inside, and my eyes widened. I'd never seen this place this bad before. Clothes, dirty plates, old takeaway, overflowing ashtrays, foil, used needles, and trash covered every surface. Nausea flooded my stomach. I dry-retched at the chemical odor in the air.

Hayden stormed into the living room and threw open every window and the back door. He halted in the middle of the floor. He clenched his jaw, his fists, his brow. Tears welled in his eyes. "Fuck this shit."

My heart cried. I rushed toward him and rubbed his arms. "It's okay. We'll clean the place up."

He sniffled, lowered his bloodshot eyes and nodded.

Glancing around the room, I wasn't sure where to start. "Let's do it."

We peeled off our coats and gloves and left them on the console table by the front door. It was the only clean spot. Weaving around the furniture, I screwed up my nose as I grabbed piles of dirty clothes and threw them into the washing machine. Hayden found trash bags and filled three with wrappers, takeout boxes, rotting food and empty bottles. He flushed the drugs down the toilet and disposed of the needles and pipes. I grabbed the plates congealed with sauces and remnants of food, and tossed them into the sink. "I'll wash up. You go pack a bag for your mom."

His furrowed brow hooded his eyes. Taking a deep breath, he turned and headed down the hallway toward the bedrooms.

Digging around in the cabinet beneath the sink, I found the pair of rubber gloves I'd brought last time we were here. I grabbed cleaning cloths, spray, and dishwashing liquid. I yanked up my sleeves, pulled on my gloves and turned on the faucet.

Thuds and thumps came from the bedroom.

"Fucking bullshit." Hayden's cursing drifted down the hallway as he slammed cupboard doors and drawers. "I don't need to deal with this crap . . . you heaps of shit."

A tear slipped down my cheek. I wiped it off on my sleeve and kept on scrubbing.

How could his parents live like this?

There was no love in this house.

Love had done nothing but destroy this family and break Hayden's heart. His parents' love of drugs was stronger than their love for him. They were selfish and cruel. After filling the sink with glasses, I washed and rinsed each one. I clenched my teeth. I was more of a family to Hayden than they'd ever be.

He was the kindest and most caring person I'd ever known. Hayden deserved so much better. He deserved to be loved by . . .? By whom? Who would ever be worthy of someone so wonderful and funny and selfless?

I snatched up a dinner plate caked with egg yolk and scrubbed and scrubbed and scrubbed. Whoever came into his life, fell in love with him, had better be fucking incredible. Or they'd have to deal with me.

My heart rattled like a chain in my chest. The thought of Hayden with someone new when he moved to Boston punched me low in the gut.

Someday . . . I'd be replaced, overruled, discarded.

Shit. I grabbed the cleaning spray, squirted it onto every surface, and wiped them down. Wipe. Rinse. Wipe.

What would I do without him? I sniffed, fighting back my tears. My girlfriends—Gemma and Kara—were always jet-setting around the globe. I didn't have any other close friends. Hayden was it. Without him around, I'd be . . . alone. I'd never been alone. Living by myself no longer had appeal.

Hayden walked into the living room and dropped a small suitcase onto the wooden floor. He rushed over to the sink and hooked his finger under my chin. "You crying?" He pulled me into a hug. "Please don't. Mom's not worth it."

"I'm fine. Just the smell got to me." *Yep . . . lying was good.* "Is the place clean enough?"

"Yes. Thank you." He kissed my forehead. "You're my angel."

"Come on." I pulled off my gloves and stashed the cleaning products away. "Let's get out of here and go see your mom."

On the drive to the center, Hayden stared out the window. With his ankle hooked over his opposite knee, he drummed his fingers against his leg. I put my hand on his thigh and gave it a gentle rub. He covered my palm with his and entwined our fingers. My heart skipped a beat. Why did it do that? I kept my eyes on the road, driving one-handed.

Thirty minutes later, I pulled into the rehab center and killed the engine. I lingered by Hayden's side at the reception as he filled out more paperwork. We listened to the administrator rattle off the procedures and program details. Hayden could repeat the drill off by heart, and so could I.

While Hayden was inside the room talking to his mom, I waited on a lone chair outside the closed door. I hugged my purse against my chest and cringed as Hayden and his mom's voices got louder and louder.

The door flung open, and out he strode. I jumped to my feet. Stone had cemented his jaw. Ice had set in his steel-gray eyes. Steam shot out of every pore.

I peered into the room. My breath hitched. His mom shook her scraggly brown hair. Her gray, sickly skin hung like limp leather over her thin frame. She gnashed her yellow teeth and rattled her cuff restraints and screamed. "Hayden. You fucking worthless heap of shit. How dare you put me back in here? I won't stay. You can't fucking make me stay."

"I can't. But your court-order will. Get better, Mom." His hand trembled as he shut the door. He closed his eyes and took a deep breath. "Fuck. Let's get out of here." He hooked his arm around my shoulders, leaning on me like he needed me to help him stand upright.

Back at our apartment, he dropped his suitcase by his bedroom door, grabbed a beer from the fridge and collapsed on the sofa. Dark shadows circled his eyes. "What a fucked day."

"Are you going to be okay?" I stood in front of him and ruffled my fingers through his hair.

"Yeah." His smile didn't touch his eyes. "Thank you."

"Anytime." I glanced at the wall clock in the kitchen. "I have to get ready for this function tonight. You want to come?"

"No." He rested his head back on the sofa. "I'm exhausted after the flight and dealing with Mom."

"Okay." I went to turn away, but he caught the hem of my coat.

"Hey." His eyes flooded with so much pain that my ribs ached. I wanted to crawl onto the sofa next to him and take his worries away. "I'm sorry. For everything. For LA. For fucking us up."

"Me too. Let's forget about it. I'll always be here for you." I stepped in and kissed the top of his head. "Always." I turned on my heels and headed into my room.

Today had been a reality check. We'd always been there for each other. I never wanted that to change. It was my wake-up call to stop hiding from him and pushing him away. Time to stop making stupid mistakes. I had to savor every moment we had left together. He was the most incredible, remarkable man I'd ever known.

Oh shit . . .

Was there something deeper between us?

No. There couldn't be. Don't be stupid.

The past week had proven how much we cared for each other.

I wouldn't let a few crazy kisses twist our friendship into something it wasn't.

No matter where he went or whomever he ended up with, I would always be a part of his life.

The problem was . . . I didn't want him to be with anyone else.

Whoa . . . I couldn't unpack that notion right now. I had to go to work.

I tightened the chain around my heart. After the long ,emotional day, I wasn't thinking straight. I didn't want Hayden fermenting my brain.

Lock him out. Lock him out. Lock him out.

But it was futile. I closed my eyes and clutched my chest. Thoughts of him flooded my mind. His smile. His hugs. His lips . . . Our kisses.

Shit. Fuck. Shit.

It wasn't possible . . . was it?

There was no way I could be in love with Hayden.

No-no-no-no. NO!

No. Fucking. Way.

Chapter 11

LEXI

Standing in the icy rain, with my umbrella in one hand and clasping my coat to my chest with the other, I shivered. Once the pedestrian light turned green, I dashed across the road and down the street toward Bryant Park. My high-heeled boots clicked against the sidewalk. I was late. Super late.

Winter had hit New York with a vengeance. Christmas decorations lined the streets. Drizzle fell in misty waves across the avenues. After the daunting day dealing with Hayden's mother, the weather matched my mood—dreary and irritable. The chill had exacerbated my fatigue.

But I had to push my exhaustion aside and whisk up some cheer for the festival. The promotion at work was to be announced before Christmas. And I wanted it. It was mine.

"Alexandra. I'm glad you've made it." My boss greeted me at the coat-checking area with a quick kiss on the cheek. *Ugh!* He'd never done that before. His breath reeked of alcohol, and the night hadn't even begun.

I slid back a step, quick to put distance between us. "Sorry I'm late. It's been a crazy day." I tugged off my gloves and put them in my purse. "My roommate's mom—"

He swayed, leaned toward my head, and inhaled deeply. "Hmm

. . . you smell good. Nice perfume."

"Okay . . ." I held up my hand. Fire shot through my tone. "You did not just smell my hair, right?"

"No." Chase frowned. "I was just paying you a compliment."

"Right." A knot twisted in the base of my neck. After my harrowing day, now I had to put up with this? *Great . . . not!* "Um . . . okay . . . thanks. But it's unnecessary. Anyway, I was late because my roommate—"

Chase handed me an orange lanyard press pass. "I'm not interested in hearing about your problems. We're here to enjoy the festival." With his silver-fox hair and shiny gray suit, Chase looked older than his forty-two years. His smile held too much arrogance as he jutted his chin toward the inner depths of the huge outdoor event tent. "Let's go."

I sighed. The weight on my shoulders grew heavier. I wanted to download the dramas of my day onto somebody. But Chase was right. He wasn't that person. Hayden was the one I'd always talked to, even if it was about his mom. Every day that drew closer to his leaving, the more I worried about missing him.

Damn it. Stop. Tonight I wouldn't think about Hayden.

I hooked my purse over my shoulder and smoothed my hands over my black knit dress. Time to focus on work. I had the festival and food to review.

After an hour of drifting around inside the tent, watching food demonstrations, tasting rich Indian curries, spicy Moroccan salads, and juicy American fusion cuisines, I had scheduled five restaurant reviews and gathered several business cards from places to follow up. My stomach was full, and I still had to sit through the main dinner.

At eight o'clock, we headed to the far end of the tent. Round tables, decorated with white cloths and tall cylindrical vases filled with holly, faced the stage, ready for the guest speakers. Chase placed his hand on the small of my back and guided me toward our table. His hand slipped too close to my ass. My skin prickled, and a shudder crept up my spine. I didn't want him touching me. Stepping a foot to the side, I flashed him a glare full of warning.

"Please don't."

Chase smirked and pulled out my chair. "I'm just being a gentleman." He swayed, waving his hand for me to sit. He took the chair beside me. I hadn't drunk a drop of alcohol tonight, but Chase had sampled every wine on offer and had often gone back for seconds.

"I'm more than capable." I clutched my purse to my lap. Maybe I was overreacting. Maybe he was just being nice. But still, some distance would be good.

"I'm sure you are." Chase winked at me, then called over the waiter to pour the wine. I declined a glass. Chase chugged his down in a few gulps and leaned closer. "That's what I like about you, Alexandra. You're full of spirit."

I conjured a smile, but a throbbing ache swelled behind my eyebrow. Was I getting a migraine? Being this close to Chase made me uncomfortable. Should I make my excuses and leave, or could I ignore him and make small talk with the other guests at the table?

I didn't get the chance to do either. Chase leaned against my arm and gave me a gentle nudge. "Thank you for cutting your time in LA to come here on short notice."

I moved my chair away from him and dug my fingernails into the soft leather of my purse. *Be polite. Be polite. Be polite.* "Thank you for the opportunity. It's been an amazing evening." But even to my ears, my voice sounded strangled.

As the waiter attended to the other guests at our table, Chase's gaze lingered on me. "The office wasn't the same without you."

Sirens went off in my head. I tucked my hair behind my ear and didn't look at him. "I doubt it. I was only gone for a few days."

"I know." He placed his arm along the back of my chair. His round eyes narrowed and held way too much twinkle for my liking. "But you were in Belize in October. In Vegas before that. I notice when you're gone."

"Please stop." I arched away from the back of the chair and put as much distance between us as possible. He'd only noticed I was gone because I worked my damn ass off and had never missed deadlines. I did my job, put in long hours, and never complained.

But I had my rules and boundaries . . . and Chase was crossing them.

I glanced at the other guests at my table. They were engaged in their own heavy conversations. No one sensed my discomfort.

I had to leave.

"We're just talking, Alexandra. Relax." He eased away from me. *Thank fuck.* He grabbed the wine the waiter had left on the table, topped up his glass and waved the bottle toward me. "Come on. Have a drink."

I covered the top of my glass with my hand. "No. Thank you. I'm working." I needed to keep a clear head; otherwise, under the influence of alcohol, Chase would feel the full force of what *don't-fucking-touch-me* meant.

A slimy smile slid across his face. "It's part of your job to experience every aspect of good food and wine, dear Alexandra. One drink won't hurt." He waved the bottle like a pendulum at me. "The night is still young. Let's have some fun."

My palms turned clammy, and I scratched my neck. Every time I got nervous, I broke out in a rash. My skin turned red and blotchy. "No, thank you."

"Alexandra, you look . . . so . . . lovely, tonight." His eyes dropped to my cleavage and meandered slowly back up to my face.

God, I was going to be sick.

He looked like he wanted to eat me. I wasn't on the fucking menu.

My skin crawled with spiders. My pulse raced as fast as a chef's knife chopping chives. I had to get out of there. "Excuse me. I need the restroom."

I leaped from my chair and rushed toward the portable restroom trailers outside the tent. I dashed into a stall and shut the door behind me. Struggling to catch my breath, I hung my purse on the hook and closed my eyes. *Asshole. Chase is a fucking asshole.*

What was I going to do? Leave? Where was my wingman when I needed him? My eyes stung. I couldn't rely on Hayden anymore. I had to stand on my own two feet. Be strong. Be professional. *Yep.*

I've got this. I could deal with a creep like Chase. Taking a few deep breaths, I pulled myself together.

That's it. Good. Everything is fine.

I'd just get my coat and go home.

I might have imagined things. Chase might be harmless. But I wouldn't take any chances.

I walked down the restroom trailer stairs and jolted to a halt. Chase stood by the row of tall potted plants with his hands buried in his trouser pockets. The rain might have stopped, but my heartbeat rattled like thunder. I looked around. This area at the back end of the library was dimly lit. The plants shielded us from the main entrance to the tent. The guest speaker was on stage; his voice hummed through the speakers. Guests would be seated, listening to him. Hardly anyone was around. And I had no plan to stick around either. I went to charge past Chase, but he stepped in front of me.

"Alexandra," he slurred. His cheeks blazed red, flushed from alcohol and the cold night air.

"Yes?" I tried to remain aloof and keep my distance. The back end of the portable restrooms loomed behind me.

"You know . . . " He smoothed his hand over his tie as he staggered a step closer. "I've been thinking."

"About what?" My blood turned to ice. My voice caught in my throat.

"I could open up so many opportunities for you at the magazine if you impress me." He undressed me with his eyes.

Nausea pooled in my stomach. I glanced around, searching for security. No one was in sight.

"It's cold, Chase." My breath misted, despite the nearby gas heater. "I'm going home."

I took a step sideways, and so did he.

"Wait." He licked his lips.

Ew!

"For what?" I glared at him, trying to remain calm. "What do you want, Chase?" My voice sliced through my teeth. I wasn't stupid. I knew what he wanted. But there was no way in hell that would happen.

He tilted his head and raked his sleazy eyes over my dress again. "I know you want the senior editor's role. My recommendation to the board is everything. So how about you prove to me you're worthy of the promotion?" He ran his fingers up my arm and gave it a gentle squeeze.

I yanked my shoulder back, breaking away from his touch. "Chase, enough. You're making me uncomfortable."

He ignored me. "Please don't be like that, Alexandra. You're a talented woman. I have the power to fast-track your career. Let me help you."

"We can talk about it in the office, with HR present, thank you." I went to step around him, but he blocked my escape again.

"That won't be necessary." He edged forward, leaving only a foot of space between us. "I've seen the way you look at me. We could both benefit from this situation."

Anger scalded my veins. *Asshole.* "You're married," I hissed through my clenched teeth. "With three kids. What the hell? I'm not interested in you. I never have been. Never will be. There is no *look.*"

"Think of your career." He licked his lips like a salivating serpent. One hand slid around my waist and clutched my ass. The other hand groped my breast. He dipped his head and tried to kiss me.

"Stop!" I slapped him across the face so hard my palm stung.

But he hardly flinched. He pulled my body against his. "No. You want me."

Fear and shock hurtled through me, but self-defense kicked in. "No. I. Don't." I drove two fingers into the hollow at the base of his throat, hard, forcing him backward. Then, with all my might, I kneed him in the groin.

"You bitch." He bent over, clutching his balls.

My eyes prickled. My heart slammed against my ribs. "Don't fucking touch me, ASSHOLE."

People near the entrance turned. A man and a woman rushed to my side.

The man towering over Chase yanked him aside and shoved him against the wall.

The woman draped her arm around my shoulders and drew me several feet toward the entrance. "I've got you. You're safe. Are you okay?"

"No." I shook all over—hands, legs, breath. Tears escaped. "Chase, my boss, tried to hurt me."

Chase hissed, unable to break free from my rescuer's hold. "Get off me. That whore wanted it."

"Doesn't look like it." The man built like a tree slammed Chase against the wall again.

Others came to my aid. They tracked down security and dragged Chase back inside the tent. The lady wrapped her shawl around my shoulders, and we followed the men into the security section by the coat-check.

The next hour was a cloudy haze. Security called the police, I filed a report, and the two witnesses gave statements. Shaken by what had happened, I shivered all over. Was this why the other girls at work had quit? I'd had my suspicions. What was I going to do? Leave? How could I work in the office with Chase there? It was inconceivable. But there was no way I'd let him get away with what he'd done.

I stared at the floor. I didn't know where to start.

Where was Hayden when I needed him?

Oh . . . Hayden.

Without him, I was lost.

The female police officer offered to drive me home. I accepted the kind gesture, grabbed my coat, and drove to my apartment.

As I fell through my front door, the shock of the evening took hold. My breath seesawed in my lungs. My heart raced. My head spun. I slammed the door shut.

Shit. Shit. Shit.

I dumped my purse and keys onto the tiny dining table. Tears spilled from my eyes.

"Lex?" Hayden came out of his bedroom wearing his long navy pajamas and rubbed his bedhead hair.

I sobbed and he rushed to my side.

"Lex, what's happened? You're home early."

I shook my head and fell against his chest. He wrapped his arms around me and held me tight. Stroking my hair, he let me cry. My tears soaked into the fabric of his soft shirt.

"You're scaring me, Lex. What's happened? Are you hurt?"

I struggled to draw breath. "Ch-Ch-Chase," I stuttered. "He cornered me by the restrooms, and . . . and tried to kiss me. Tried to touch me. Tried to . . ." I didn't want to think about Chase's hands on my ass or on any part of my body. Oh God, I was going to be sick.

Hayden stiffened, sucking in a hard breath. "Did he hurt you?"

"No." I sniffled. "I've never flirted with him, never bantered with him, never given him cause or reason to make a pass at me."

"I'll kill him." Hayden's voice growled like he was a hound ready to hunt.

I clutched onto him tighter and shook my head. "No. Don't go near him. He's a fucking prick."

"You call HR first thing on Monday. You report this son of a bitch."

"I've already done that. I sent a message to Amelia." I rested my chin on his shoulder. "Security called the police, and I've filed a report. There were witnesses too."

"Good." His voice was clipped. "Take that bastard down. The board should fire him."

"I don't want to be there anymore. It won't ever be the same."

He rubbed his hands in slow circles across my back. Why was it that the only place in the world I'd ever felt safe was with Hayden? He always looked out for me, protected me. Never questioned me when I needed his comfort and often gave it without hesitation.

He rested his head against mine. "Quit and come to Boston with me."

I clutched onto a handful of his shirt and squeezed my eyes shut. "Please, don't. I don't want to think about anything right now."

"Shh. Okay. I'm sorry." He kneaded the back of my neck,

soothing out the tension. "You want a coffee? Hot chocolate? Something to eat?"

"No. I'm fine." I slumped and slid out of his embrace. "I need a shower." My skin still crawled with Chase's touch. I needed to be rid of it.

Hayden pinned me with his gaze. His jaw tensed and ticked. "You swear Chase didn't hurt you?"

"He didn't hurt me." I wrapped my arms around myself and swayed on my feet. "I hurt him though. I kneed him hard in the groin."

"Prick deserved it."

Oh shit. The blood drained from my face. "But what if this backfires on me and he accuses me of assault?"

"He won't. You have witnesses, and I'll testify for you. This isn't the first time something's happened."

I didn't want to remember the office Halloween party. My chin quivered as I shivered. "Hayds, I was so scared."

"Oh, angel." He caught my shoulders. "I'm so sorry. I should've been there with you tonight."

"No. It's not your fault."

He cupped the side of my neck. "But I'm here now. For whatever you need. You know that, right?"

I nodded, flicking the tears from my cheeks. *Here for now, but not forever.* I'd leaned on him for support for so long, and now he was leaving. The tiny opening in my heart snapped shut. Sealed tight.

"I'll go start the shower for you." He wiped his thumb across my damp cheek, his touch so soft and delicate. "In this cold weather, you know it takes five minutes to warm up."

I sniffed and rubbed my nose. "Thank you. I'll go get my PJs."

"Okay." Worry clouded his eyes. "Are you sure you're all right?"

"Yes, but no."

He smiled, but it didn't touch his eyes. "Just holler if you need anything. I'll come check on you after you've finished."

"'Kay."

After showering, I didn't feel much better. I climbed into my bed and curled into a ball underneath the quilt and blankets. Clutching my pillow, I couldn't get Chase out of my head. His breath. His hands. His voice. I shivered, and tears slipped down my cheeks again.

Hayden knocked on my door and eased it open. "Lex?"

"Yeah?"

"Can I come in?"

"Yeah." I sniffled.

He glided to the edge of the bed. "You okay?"

"No." I didn't want to be alone.

"Need another hug?"

"Yeah."

"Move over." He tapped my legs. "Let me in. It's cold."

I lifted the covers, and he slid in beside me. It had been months since I'd fallen asleep next to him. I'd often drift off leaning against him while we watched TV or sat up late, drunk talking, or when I was too tired to make it to my bed. He gave the best hugs, and right now, I needed a million of them.

I needed my friend.

I curled into his embrace and rested my head against his shoulder.

He pulled the bed coverings over us and held me close. As he stroked my hair, he kissed my forehead. "I got you. Always."

Closing my eyes, I breathed him in. His woody scent calmed and soothed my troubled mind. His warmth seeped into my bones. His touch made me feel safe.

"Yeah," I whispered. "For seven more weeks."

"Yeah. Seven more weeks."

I fought the sting in my eyes. Fought the pain in my heart. Why did everything have to change? Rip us apart? I didn't want him to move to Boston. I needed him more than I cared to admit. But he needed to follow his true love . . . music.

Saying goodbye to him would be the hardest thing I'd ever had to do.

Chapter 12

HAYDEN

While I set up my drums in the Mercury Lounge for tonight's show, Lewis plugged in his bass and worked with Jordan, the venue's sound technician, to balance the sound. As I screwed in the last of my cymbals, I cursed myself for the millionth time for not going with Lexi to the food and wine festival last week. Guilt had eaten into every pore of my skin. Lexi had been frightened and shaken by being harassed by Chase. She still hadn't recovered. That had hit me hard. I should've been with her. Been there to protect her. Not wallowing at home over my pathetic mother.

Since that night, Lexi hadn't been the same. She was anxious and quiet. She'd wanted me to go with her everywhere—walk her to work, meet her for lunch, and take her to the grocery store. She'd said she was fine, but I knew she wasn't.

I'd gone with her every day to meet with her human resources manager and the company's legal team. I was with her as she documented the incident against Chase. I was there to give her the courage and strength she needed. After Lexi made her formal complaint against her boss, two other women came forward with allegations. I hoped he went to jail and never walked the streets again.

I thanked God Lexi hadn't been hurt. I'd never forgive myself if she had been. She was an angel not to be messed with.

I sat behind my drum kit, picked up my sticks and hammered out a beat. It was time to focus on our gig and not be consumed by thoughts of Lexi for a few hours. I needed to bring my A-game.

As Lewis and I ran through a song, Kilt, and Reg charged into the venue, slamming the door behind them.

Kilt stormed toward the stage. His spiky red hair matched his bloodshot eyes. He had the build of a lanky Scotsman but was as American as McDonald's. He flicked his hand at Reg. "I'm fucking sick of singing 'Highway.' Swap it for 'Feeling High.'"

"But it's our hit single. We can't cut it." Reg struggled on his short legs to keep up with Kilt's long stride. "The fans love it. If you change that, we have to change the whole intro."

I ground my teeth and struck the crash cymbal hard. Why the fuck couldn't Kilt and Reg stop arguing? It did my head in. "Guys, stop," I yelled. "We're not changing the set list hours out from a show. Pull your fucking heads in."

Three sets of eyes stared at me. Mouths gaped. I rarely got fired up about anything. I usually went with the flow. But not anymore. I'd had enough of their crap. We were moving to Boston. This bullshit bickering had to end.

Kilt's lip twitched into a snicker. "What's eating you?"

"You." I pointed my stick at him. "You're late. Hurry up so we can finish sound check."

"Yes, Your Highness." Kilt bowed, scaled the steps, and grabbed his mic.

Reg sighed and mouthed *"thank you"* in my direction, and strode across the stage. He picked up his Gibson and hooked the strap over his head. He struck the strings and played the intro to our song "Reckless".

"Reg, dude, please tune your fucking guitar." I grimaced at the pitched sound coming through my ear monitors.

"There's nothing wrong with it." Reg's shred sounded more like a shriek. "Just shut up and play the drums."

"Gladly." I rolled my shoulders to release the tension twisting through my shoulder blades. With a spin of my sticks, I broke into a speed-defying gallop across the snare and rack tom.

It took one song and the wicked beat to kickstart our energy and for us to find our rhythm. This was what I needed. My band. Music. The stage. When we played, we melded as one. All the drama disappeared.

Moving to Boston was the right decision. Lexi would be okay without me. If she needed me, I wouldn't be far away.

Fifteen minutes into sound check, the main doors flung open. In walked Hunter and Kyle, flanked by their security. They headed straight toward the stage.

I halted my sticks. My band stopped playing, grumbling at the interruption. Pulling out my ear monitors, I leaped from my stool and stuffed my sticks into my back pocket. I stepped around my drums, over cables, and dodged a speaker to reach the front of the stage. "Hey guys." I squatted and threw them a questioning look. "What are you doing here?"

Kyle tucked his sunglasses into the pocket of his leather jacket. "Sorry to interrupt. You got a few minutes?"

I glanced over my shoulder. Lewis, strumming low and slow on his bass, eye-fucked Kyle like he did every time they were in the same room. Reg grabbed a sip of water from his bottle, unfazed by the disruption. Kilt gripped his mic and sneered at Hunter. There was no love lost between those two.

"Um . . . sure." I wiped sweat from my brow with my sleeve and waved toward the bar. "I'll meet you back there in a sec." I stood and repositioned the drumsticks wedged into my back pocket so they wouldn't fall out. "Won't be long," I said to my band and scooted down the stage steps.

"Better fucking not be," Kilt called out after me, his voice a low, disgruntled growl.

I pulled up a stool beside Kyle and Hunter and ordered the guys a beer. Sam and Mick, their bodyguards, sat at the end of the counter and opted for a soda. Taking a sip of my drink, I turned to Kyle. "So, what's up? Everything okay?"

"Yeah." Kyle rested his wrists on the bar and fidgeted with a coaster. "We just came from seeing Lex. Gem and Kara are still with her."

A chill shuddered through my veins. "Is there something wrong? Has something else happened?" *Shit!* I'd done everything for Lexi this week. Had I missed something? Was she more fucked up by what had happened with Chase than she'd let on?

"She's still shaken but fired up to take that fucker down." Kyle tapped the coaster against the counter.

"Yeah. That's Lex." Throughout the past week, she'd paced our apartment cursing, and had sworn justice would be done. Then, in other moments, she'd cried and trembled in my arms. She was tough, but not that tough. It twisted my gut that she'd have to face more legal proceedings in the coming months without me. But I couldn't postpone moving; my band had signed a contract with the venue. I was committed to our new gig, but I didn't want to leave Lexi. I hated being torn in two.

Damn it. Stop.

"I hope her boss rots in hell." Hunter smirked and tilted his head toward their bodyguards. "Anytime you want Sam and Mick to give Chase a touch-up, just say the word."

Sam folded his burly arms, narrowed his eyes, and shook his head. Keeping Everhide safe from crazed fans was their job, not roughing up assholes like Chase. But I wouldn't mind if they came across him and permanently rearranged his face.

Kyle downed half his beer. '*Ahh,*' escaped his lips as he placed the glass on the counter. "Actually, Hayds, we're here to ask a huge favor."

"Sure. You'll know I'll do anything for Lex."

"No. This isn't about Lexi. This is something we'd like from you." Kyle folded his arms and leaned back on his stool. "Slade's first baby arrives next Friday. His girlfriend's cesarean has been brought forward. We have a show on Saturday, the Jingle Ball, down in Washington and were wondering if you could fill in for him."

I choked on a mouthful of beer. Froth flew up my nose. "You want me to *what?*"

"Come play for us. Please?" Hunter gave me a quick slap on

the back.

My eyes widened. My heart rate jumped so fast my head spun, and I swayed on the stool. "Are you fucking serious?"

"Um . . . yeah." Kyle grinned and nodded.

Holy fuck! My pulse whooshed in my ears. "But I have a show."

Crap. My band will play at The Bowery Ballroom. It'd be our biggest gig in months.

"Fuck," Kyle muttered. He wiped his hand across his chin as he stared at the wall of liquor behind the bar. "That's okay. Sophie will find someone. We have a few guys around town or out in LA that can fill in for Slade. Thought we'd ask you first."

Me? Wow!

Everhide's show would be huge. A once in a lifetime opportunity. Panic, fear, nerves, self-doubt, and excitement clutched my heart. I'd be crazy to let this chance pass me by. "Wait . . . You really think I could do it? That I'm good enough?" I hadn't been before. Why now?

"Yeah, we do." Kyle bobbed his head. "You've always been brilliant, Hayds, but over the past year while we were away on tour, you've gotten even better. You know half the songs we'll be playing. We'll rehearse every day next week. You'll nail it. It's eight songs, man. Not a whole two-hour fucking concert."

My vision blurred. My brain throbbed. It took weeks, if not months, to rehearse set lists and perfect transitions, to learn each other's signals and signs and set the pace of a show. They wanted me to do that in a week? Could I do it? *Fuck yeah.* "Shit. I'm sorry . . . I'm in shock. You've never asked me to play before."

Hunter downed a mouthful of beer, then licked the froth from his lips. "You know we had no say in anything when we were at SureHaven."

My friends had been tied to a ruthless contract. SureHaven Records had controlled every aspect of their career—their songs, their image, their lives. When Everhide signed with a new label, Slade had contacted them. Kyle, Hunter, and Gemma had been smart. They didn't let talent like Slade go.

"Now we have control." Unwavering confidence set in Hunter's voice. "We make every decision. We choose who plays, stays, and goes. We love you, bud. We want you. So are you sure you can't make it?"

My mind spun like a cassette on fast forward. I wanted to play for them, but I had a show. Could I get out of it? Kilt's brother, Basil, would hopefully fill in for me like he'd done when I'd gone to Vegas, and Belize and LA. *Shit!* My band wouldn't be happy about me missing another gig, but this was an opportunity I couldn't turn down. "Fuck, I'll make it. I want to do this. Is it okay if we post on socials that I'm filling in for Slade? That way, I can drop my band's name a few times?" We needed all the publicity we could get.

"Absolutely." Kyle knocked back the last of his beer. "We can do that."

My chest swelled. Fuck, I loved these guys. But then my stomach knotted. I winced and glanced over my shoulder. I had to tell my guys I was ditching them for another show, spending more time with Everhide. *Crap.* That wouldn't go down well. "I'd better go tell them."

"Can I?" A huge grin inched across Hunter's face. "It will give me great pleasure to piss off Kilt."

"Thanks, but I'd better break the news." I stood, fidgeted with my sticks in my back pocket, and headed toward the stage. Kyle and Hunter followed.

Kilt put his foot on the speaker in front of his mic and leaned forward, resting his arm on his knee. "Take long enough?"

"Yep." I glanced from Kyle to Hunter, then up at my band on the stage. I stuffed my hands into my front pockets to steady my shaky hands. I doubted whether any of my band members would be excited as I was. "These guys want me to play for them next Saturday in Washington."

"You?" Lewis's eyes lit up as he swung his bass back over his shoulder. "Play for Everhide? That's fucking awesome."

Okay. Lewis got me. We'd been good friends for a long time. He'd kept me sane.

"But we're playing The Ballroom," Kilt snapped. Straightening, he pulled his shoulders back and crossed his arms. "It's a big gig for us. We come first."

"That's not fair. You know you do." I was committed to my band, heart and soul. I'd always supported everyone's different ventures and interests; why couldn't Kilt support mine? "We didn't stop you from releasing solo material during our downtime two years ago. And Reg . . . " I flicked my hand at our guitarist. "He often plays for another band. And Lewis . . . " I pointed at our bassist. "He's always DJing with his boyfriend at nightclubs. Everyone has other lives. So do I. I want to play with these guys for one night, so don't be a prick about it."

I was still bewildered. Playing for Everhide would be freaking awesome. I couldn't wait to tell Lexi. She'd be ecstatic. She'd dance around the room, jump on our sofa, shriek at the top of her lungs.

Shit! I closed my eyes and swayed on my feet. My heart sank into my stomach. Soon, I'd miss coming home to her, miss her excitement over good news, miss her face lighting up and her sparkling, big brown eyes. I'd miss her contagious energy and support. *Crap!* That was hard to contemplate. But I'd decided to move, and I had to live with the consequences. I had to stop loving her so fucking much and get on with my life.

"We're not being pricks." Kilt sneered, snorting air through his nose. "You're being a flake, running off with Everhide again."

Determination set in my jaw. This opportunity *was* for my band, for our new start in Boston. "This isn't for a vacation or a wedding. This gig *is* for us. We'll post on socials that I'm playing for them and help get our name out there."

Kilt shook his head. "Don't be delusional. You're a temporary fix in the backup band. No one gives a fuck about the drummer."

What was wrong with him? If the tables were turned, Kilt wouldn't hesitate to fill in for a big band. Was he envious? Threatened? Afraid I'd leave? Or was his ego just clashing with Hunter's? Their icy glares cut through the air like daggers. I couldn't see Kilt sharing a stage with Hunter anytime soon . . . or ever.

Kyle chuckled and sat on the edge of the stage. "You should tell that to Slade. He has a huge following."

"But he's a legend." Kilt scraped his fingers through his spiky hair. There was so much gel in it, each strand stood back upright. "He's been drumming for fifteen years, and for some of the biggest artists on the planet."

Yeah, I know. Two of those years were with Everhide.

"Kilt. Enough." Reg cut in, tugging on his ear-monitor cords. "This will be a fucking incredible experience for Hayds. You can't deny that. We'll get some social posts out of it. It'll be great. Basil can fill in for Hayden."

"No," Kilt's eyes bulged and his nostrils flared at Reg. "Hayden's our fucking drummer. It's us or them."

I clenched my fists so tight my knuckles ached. "You're my band. Don't ever question that." I was leaving Lexi for them. Chasing my dreams with them. I wasn't fucking going anywhere.

"Kilt, don't be a dick." Hunter folded his arms and widened his stance. In his sleek black designer T-shirt and jeans, and with his fierce blue eyes blazing, he radiated a John Wick *don't-fuck-with-me* attitude. "Are you worried that it's Hayden drawing your crowds, not you? He's certainly far better looking than you, and way more talented, ass-face."

"Fuck you." Kilt stabbed his finger at Hunter. Fire flickered in his eyes.

Hunter didn't flinch. "Is it the money you're worried about? Let's take that out of the equation." Hunter scratched his cheek, furrowing his brow in concentration. "So . . . at The Ballroom, you'd be taking a full percentage of ticket sales . . . The venue holds . . . what . . . five hundred people? You'd be charging around thirty dollars a ticket. That's . . . fifteen grand for the night." He lifted his chin toward my band. "I'll pay each of you thirty-five hundred on top of next weekend's takings if you give us Hayden for the night."

Kyle's mouth fell open, but then he shook his head and laughed.

My breath caught in my chest. I didn't know what to think. But Hunter bribing my band was entertaining.

"Don't patronize me, you asshole." Kilt's voice dripped with spite. "Don't flash your cash at me."

"I'm happy not to pay you a fucking cent and still have Hayds play for us." Hunter grinned as he slapped Hayden's shoulder. "Take it or leave it."

Kilt's lips curled into a snarl. Money had always been a factor behind Kilt's dislike of Everhide. Kilt wanted fame, fortune, and attention. He hated I'd gotten to experience the high life with my friends. But I didn't care about Kilt's petty hang-ups. This chance to play with a huge band like Everhide might never come again. I had to do it. To prove to myself that I was talented, that I wasn't a loser like my parents had said, and that I was on track to make something of my life.

I'd take Lexi with me. She'd love to see me play live with Everhide.

I took a step forward. "Kilt, I'll make this work, for us."

Kilt paced in front of his mic and mumbled under his breath. I could almost see the steam coming out of his ears. Stretching his neck from side to side, Kilt jerked to a halt. "Fine." He jabbed his finger at Hunter. "You better fucking pay up. I'm holding you to your word." Then Kilt glared at me. His eyes flashed with warning. "Once and once only. You hear me? The sooner we move to Boston and you get away from this heap of shit, the better." Kilt jerked his chin toward Hunter.

I whispered sideways to Hunter, "Why does Kilt hate you so much? Did you sleep with his girlfriend or something?"

Hunter shrugged his shoulder. "Possibly. I don't know half the names of the girls I slept with before Kara. I didn't care if they had partners or husbands. I just fucked 'em and sent 'em on their way."

I chuckled. "You *are* an asshole."

"Totally." His face lit with a shit-eating grin as he nudged my arm. "But it looks like we have our drummer for next weekend. I'm fucking stoked."

Kyle stood and gave me a quick hug. "Bud, we're going to have so much fun. Gem will be stoked. We'll call the rest of the backup band, and schedule rehearsal times."

I ran my fingers through my hair. Dizziness swirled through my head. I couldn't believe what had just happened. I'd play for

Everhide. *Whoa-fucking-yeah!* "Thanks. I'll be there. But right now, I better get ready for tonight."

"Absolutely. But thanks, Hayds. You're a lifesaver." Kyle patted my shoulder. "We'll come watch you play tonight, so we'll see you soon."

"Thanks. I'd love that."

Kyle dipped his chin, slipped on his sunglasses, and headed out the door with Hunter and their bodyguards.

I turned to my band. Excitement skipped through my veins. Kilt should be happy for me, like Lewis and Reg were. His attitude wouldn't kill my high. Of all the drummers available, Kyle and Hunter had chosen me to play for them. *How freaking cool!* I scaled the steps and scooted across the stage to my drums. Shaking off Kilt's icy glare, I ripped out the sticks from my back pocket. "Let's finish sound check. Tonight's gonna rock!"

Reg stuffed in his ear monitors and struck his strings. Lewis gave me a big grin and a thumbs-up. Kilt sipped from his water bottle, sneered at me, then turned his back.

Fuck. I twirled my sticks. I didn't need more issues with my band. I was trying to bring us closer, not to create a bigger rift.

I wouldn't allow that to happen.

Kyle, Gemma, and Hunter wanted me to succeed. They believed in me.

It was my decision to play for Everhide. I wouldn't let them down.

Clutching my drumsticks, I played hard.

Playing at The Jingle Ball would be good for The Saylors. It'd give us new publicity. Bring new fans. Find new followers.

Lexi would see my hard work had paid off. I'd practiced, upped my skills, and kept pursuing my dreams. I'd never quit. She might finally see the man I've become, the man she could want, the man she could depend on.

I wanted to inspire her to chase her dreams. She had a gift for photography; I didn't want that to go to waste.

But reality hit me like static in a speaker.

Not all dreams come true.

She'd given up on having a career behind the camera.

Her wanting me wasn't likely to come to fruition.

That didn't matter. I'd always love her. I'd always have my music.

Some things could never die.

Some things I could never let go of.

Lexi and music. Music and Lexi.

No . . . just Lexi.

Chapter 13

LEXI

At Everhide's rehearsal space in Brooklyn, music boomed from speakers, vibrated across the floor, and rattled the old studio's windows. I darted around my friends taking photos as they ran through their set list for tomorrow night's Jingle Ball. Dodging the crew, the band, equipment, and cables, I snapped shots of everyone—not just Hayden at the drums.

As I took a picture of Kyle singing at his mic from behind, I shuffled backward, tripped over a guitar stand and stumbled into Hayden's kit.

"You okay?" Hayden half-rose from his stool, grabbing the cymbal before it fell over.

"Sure am." I laughed at my clumsiness. "Sorry. I've a hazardous hobby." I found my feet, took a few shots of him, and stepped clear of the drums.

With a huge grin, he shook his head and continued to play. His sticks flew across the drums. He mouthed the lyrics. He bobbed, rocked, and swayed to the rhythm. *Damn!* My heart *thud, thud, thudded* in time with his beat. There was a raw fire in his eyes. His vibe was electric. I couldn't drag myself away from him. Hayden was a brilliant drummer. Our friends had given him an incredible opportunity. I was so happy for him. His career was moving forward. Mine had hit a stalemate.

After what Chase had done to me—and to other women in the office—my job at *The Gourmet Reviewer* would never be the same. Just when a promotion was within my reach, the icing had been stripped off my cake. I'd worked so hard for a job I now didn't want. Chase had been stood down while the lawyers dealt with the case being built against him. I counted my lucky stars I hadn't been harmed. But others weren't so lucky. His absence from the office had offered some mental reprieve. But I couldn't leave. I had no other job prospects, bills to pay, and rent was due. I had to stay put . . . For now.

As I snapped shots of Gemma playing her guitar, every beat from the band ignited my soul. I'd love a job where this vitality hummed through my veins every day. Gemma, Kyle, and Hunter were so vibrant, captivating, and charismatic, even at practice. Put them on stage in front of a live audience, and they were even more exhilarating. They were living the dream. Hayden was following his. Mine had to be rewritten. I didn't know what I wanted to do anymore. I'd re-evaluate my options in the new year. Until then, I just wanted to have some fun.

At the end of their song, Gemma spun around and hollered at the band, "Let's run through the last two tracks again and then we'll call it quits." She held her hand high in the air and counted down on her fingers. "From the top. One. Two. Three. Four."

Hayden's drumming filled the room. The heavy bass, the thumping snare, tom-toms, and crashing cymbals reverberated in my chest. Hayden was on fire—his talent, his speed, his magic— there for everyone to see. He was all toned muscle, hot grit, and pure stamina. I pointed my lens at him again. I floated toward him, taking shot after shot after shot. Sweat flew from his hair, trickled down his face, and molded his T-shirt to his torso. My palms sweated. The camera shook in my hand. *Damn . . . he's hot.*

But my chest ached. After this show, I wouldn't have many opportunities to see him play. His band only had a couple of gigs lined up before they moved to Boston.

Why did he have to move so far away? I didn't want him to

leave.

"That's a wrap." Gemma strummed her electric strings so hard the entire room reverberated. "Yeah! Well done, guys." She clapped at the band as a rocking smile lit her face.

Sophie, Everhide's manager, pumped her fist and whistled. "Brilliant job, everyone."

"Hayds, you nailed it." Kyle gave him a thumbs-up, then placed his bass on the rack. "Adam, Joey, Link—great work as always."

Everyone put down their gear and headed over to a table to grab a bottle of water.

I stepped in beside Hayden and gave him a high-five. "You were awesome."

He draped his arm around my neck and pulled me into a headlock. He was hot and sweaty, and smelled all manly . . . all Hayden. "Thank *you* for not breaking the drums."

"Or my ankle." I pushed out of his hold to reel in my rising body temperature.

Hunter mopped sweat from his brow with a towel and threw a spare one at Hayden. "Play like that tomorrow night and you'll have nothing to worry about. Great job."

"I'll do my best." Hayden dragged the towel over his face and rubbed the back of his neck.

I play-punched his arm. My heart filled my chest. "You're a rockstar!"

"And it feels fucking great." He chuckled, his smile as big as Broadway.

"Guys?" Hunter waved at their backup band. "Awesome work. We'll see you tomorrow." He swiped his bag off the floor. "Kyle, Gem, let's get showered and changed. We've got a meeting to get to."

"Yep. . . but give me a few minutes." Gemma peeled the sweaty strands of hair off her face and retied her ponytail. "I need a quick word with Lex."

"About the thing?" Kyle waggled his eyebrows and winked. He clearly knew what Gemma was talking about.

"Yes. About the thing." She kissed Kyle on the cheek and

swiped her water off the table. "I won't be long."

"What thing?" I straightened, wrapping the carry strap around my camera lens and placing it on a chair. "What do we need to talk about?"

Hayden hooked his towel around his neck and stretched his arms over his head. "Do you want me to stick around, Lex? If not, I might grab a beer with Adam and the guys."

My gaze raked over his arms as he bent from side to side. Stretching. Warming down. But my body temperature had other ideas. It rose as his muscles flexed, sweat dripped from his hair, and his abs peeked out from underneath the bottom of his T-shirt. *So ripped. So cut. So . . . hmmm.* My mouth ran dry. I swallowed hard. *Shit!*

I needed a shower. And an icy cold one at that.

Hayden flicked his towel at me, snapping me out of my daze. "Lex?" The glint in his eyes made my toes curl. *Crap.* "Beer? With the guys?"

He wanted to hang out with Everhide's backup band. He'd be away with our friends for the weekend. Jealousy played my insides like a harpsichord. With Christmas next week, our time together was slipping by too quickly. But I didn't want to dampen his high. I had no claim over him. "Sure. Go. I'll see you at home later."

The guys waved and headed to change. Sophie, Bec and Kate fell into conversation with the security team about the Jingle Ball. Gemma grabbed me by the hand and dragged me toward a couple of equipment trunks, away from her team, engineers, and stagehands packing up gear for tomorrow night's show. We sat on two large boxes opposite each other.

"What's up?" I tucked a curl behind my ear.

Gemma took a mouthful of water, then wiped the corners of her mouth with her fingertips. "Did you notice there were twenty people in the room, or did you only have eyes for Hayden?"

My mouth fell open. My eyes widened. I fidgeted with the neckline of my top. "What? No. I took photos of everyone." Maybe not the lighting technician, but I'd gotten everyone else.

Gemma leaned forward, pinning me to my seat with her bright

emerald eyes. "What's going on with you two?"

"Nothing. I've told you that a million times."

"Then stop eye-fucking him."

"I'm not." *Shit!* I totally had been. I needed to get my head examined.

"Yeah, you were. Do I have to intervene?"

"Intervene? Why?"

Gemma puffed air through her nose and shook her head. "Come on, Lex. Enough with the bullshit. You're into him. Admit it."

Into Hayden? I rubbed at the dull ache in my brow. I certainly was confused, pressured on all sides by him and my friends. Being encouraged to look at him as something more than a friend wasn't as easy as flicking a switch. I'd been adamant about avoiding love; now, it twisted my mind and messed with my heart. I didn't know which way was up or down. Checking him out and getting flustered around him had added more complications to my life than there are colors in the spectrum. Even his smile now affected me. What was with that? I cared for him deeply. But was I into him? Did I want something more? I had no clear answer. And one factor was a major issue. "He's moving to Boston."

"So? Go with him."

"What?" *To Boston?* The ache in my brow turned into a hard throb.

Hayden wanted more than friendship. I couldn't give him false hope. My feelings were in shambles. If I moved, I'd have no income, didn't have a lot of money saved and had no job prospects. There was no way I could toss away my career and rely on him to support me until I found a job. I never wanted to be a burden to anyone. The idea of moving was pointless. "No. New York is my home. I still have a job. I need to be here for Mom."

"No, you don't. Your mom suffers from depression. She's not incapacitated. Get your brothers and aunt to pitch in and hire help. Boston isn't that far away." She placed her hand over her heart. "I love you. I can see it in your eyes you're fighting your feelings for Hayds every time you look at him." A smile tweaked the corner of her mouth. "I told you; one kiss can change everything. So, what's it gonna take for you to give him a chance?"

I clenched my jaw and stared at the floorboards. "I can't."

"You can." Exasperation snapped in Gemma's tone. "He loves you so hard. He'd do anything for you."

I closed my eyes. The ache in my chest puffed up like a soufflé then sank like someone had ripped open the oven door and the whole eggy dish had flopped. I couldn't rely on chance. When life got difficult, he'd grow to resent me, like my parents resented each other. My track record ensured we were destined for failure. "How can I do that when I've fucked-up every relationship, from my parents to Quintin? I won't fuck up my friendship with Hayden."

"You won't." Gemma squeezed my hand. "We've all been hurt, broken, rejected, fucked up by our parents, or screwed over by someone, but those things should never stop you from trying again. You deserve to be happy. You're beautiful, talented, ambitious and one of my best friends. I don't want you to regret not tapping the hell out of the chemistry the rest of us see between the two of you."

I wiped a tear from my eyelashes and sniffled. "I thought Kara was the motherly one. Not you."

Smug satisfaction slid through her smile. "She totally is, but we agreed you needed a clip over the head."

"Are the two of you ganging up on me?" I didn't want to trouble my friends. I loved that they cared about me, but Hayden was not an area for their concern.

"Four of us, actually. Hunt and Kyle agree. I know Hayden's leaving is hard on you. We'll miss him like fucking crazy. But you need to do yourself a favor. Sift through all the drama rattling around in your head and listen to your heart."

"I have. I've tried. I care about him." Digging my fingernails into my jeans distracted me from the ache looming inside my chest. "But I'm confused. I don't know what to think, or feel, or do. This talk isn't helping." Gemma was supposed to support me, not add extra ingredients into my chaotic mix of emotions.

"Yeah . . . it is. You're not in total denial anymore, so we've made progress." Gemma gave me a *my-bad* smile and took another sip of water. I wanted to wipe the grin off her face. "He's a great guy. Don't lose him because you're afraid to try."

As I stared at a nail in the floorboard, my pulse droned in my temples like a song stuck on slow motion. Was Gemma right? If there was something more than friendship between Hayden and me, I'd be foolish not to find out. We'd hurt each other so much since we'd kissed. But it would be unbearable if we didn't work out, and I lost him.

There was too much at risk.

His future was at stake.

My heart wasn't ready to take the leap.

"Gem, stop. Hayds and I are friends. That's all there is to it." Yep, I was chickenshit. I couldn't risk breaking his heart. Didn't want to be a burden on his career, his happiness, his dreams. There was no us. I had to be sensible and realistic. Risk aversion was key.

"Okay." Gemma held up her hands in surrender. "I won't say another thing. But there is something else I'd like to discuss . . . tomorrow's show."

She pursed her lips and tapped her feet together. The sparkle in her eyes glittered. An electric vibe skipped through the air.

Whenever Gemma was like this, she'd come out with some wild plan or ecstatic news. I wasn't sure I was in the mood for either.

Placing her hands on the trunk, she rocked forward. "I talked to Kyle, Hunt, and Kate. I'm sorry, but you can't come to the show tomorrow night as our guest . . . Instead, we want you there as our photographer."

My chin hit the floor. My heart resumed beating; it had temporarily stopped when Gemma had said I couldn't go. "You want . . . *what?*"

Excitement jumped in Gemma's every word. "Please, Lex? We've loved the shots you took at rehearsals this week. The fans have gone crazy over the posts. Your work impressed Kate. We want you."

My heart stumbled against my ribs. *Holy fuck!* "But this is a big event. Not just playing around."

"Yeah, we know." Gemma's face shone with her vibrant smile. "You're so good. Please shoot the night for us."

"Oh, wow!" I splayed my hand across my chest. Stars swirled before my eyes. Gemma wanted to hire me again? Like she'd done for her wedding? This was huge. A professional gig.

How could I ever thank Hayden for showing my photos to Gemma? This would never have come about if it hadn't been for him. "Oh my God, yes. I can't believe you want me to do this. But I'm so yours."

"Awesome." Gemma clapped her hands on her thighs. "Oh . . ." She held up her finger. "But there's one small, tiny, minor condition. It's the weekend before Christmas and Bec can't get more rooms in the hotel. So . . . you have to share with Hayden."

"Oh . . ."

"Is that a problem?" Gemma's perfectly fine eyebrows arched skyward. "You've never had issues sharing before."

I glared at her. Too much pleasure twinkled in her goddamn eyes. *Nice try, Gem. Your matchmaking won't work.* I drew my shoulders back and injected confidence into my voice. "Not at all. That'll be fine."

But shit. A night in the same hotel room with Hayden? Warmth crept into my cheeks, and butterflies stirred in my belly. I sucked in a deep breath but found no inner calm.

"Relax." Gemma laughed and slapped my knee. "I'm kidding. You'll have to share with Carla. Is that okay?"

"Oh. Yes. Absolutely." *Phew!*

"Cool. We're gonna have so much fun." Gemma slid onto her feet, held out her hand and dragged me off my equipment trunk. She gave me a big hug. "I can't wait."

Excitement skittered across my skin. Taking photos for Everhide would be totally surreal. It was a chance to get my name in front of some industry professionals. That'd be incredible. "Thank you." I slipped out of Gemma's embrace and wiped my trembling hands on my jeans. "You do so much for Hayden and me. You're an angel. I wish there were some way I could repay you."

She caught my hands in hers. "You're my best friend. I don't need anything in return. I wish there were more I could do to help."

"Letting me shoot tomorrow is more than enough."

Oh, wow! I had to tell Hayden. He'd be so excited. He'd pick me up, twirl me around until my head grew dizzy, and take me out to celebrate.

Oh . . . wait.

He wasn't here.

He'd gone for a drink with the guys. He was always the first one I wanted to break any news to. Not my mom, not my dad, not my girlfriends—it was always him. Always Hayden.

Crap.

Damn you, Gemma, for getting inside my head.

Gemma squeezed my arm. "I gotta go. Bec will email you the schedule. "Do you want to come with us, go on the bus with everyone else, or catch the train to D.C.?"

My mind was still stuck on Hayden, but I answered. "Um . . . I'll have to drive. I'll have to leave early on Sunday to get to Mom's for her birthday."

"Okay. We have to be there by eleven for the dress rehearsal. Don't be late." She turned to go but spun back around to face me. Seriousness set in her tone. "And think about what I said regarding Hayds. The key is honesty. And even if the two of you don't work out as a couple, your friendship will survive. You've got a connection with him like I have with Kyle and Hunt. Nothing can destroy it—not even each other."

I tugged on the cuffs of my sweater and folded my arms. I didn't know whether to laugh or cry; this conversation was too confronting. "Don't you have to be somewhere?"

Gemma fluttered her eyelashes. "Yep. Love you. Bye." She flicked her hair over her shoulder, gave a saucy Betty Boop wink, and scooted out of the room.

Left standing by the equipment trunks, I stared at the door Gemma had closed. Memories of Hayden bombarded my mind. The day we'd met drinking at a bar near the university. He'd challenged me to a game of beer pong and I'd won. A few weeks later, we'd moved in together. We'd never argued over who'd gotten what room, or where items had belonged. We'd never argued about bathroom time, or cooking dinner, or cleaning. His OCD took care of that. He'd often go with me to check on Mom. He had such a soul-warming laugh. A good heart. He gave the best hugs. But the reality was his gigs were random, his income irregular, and music ruled his life. I'd often covered his half of the rent and bills and often had to buy the groceries because he couldn't afford them. And his razors were always blunt when I needed to shave my legs.

But somehow things always worked out.

We'd been inseparable friends for seven years.

My heart rattled in its cage. How could I place my feelings for Hayden onto a set of scales and see which way they'd tip? It would be easier to sort a cup of sugar grains by size and shape than sift through years of emotions and memories.

But I didn't want to think about Hayden anymore.

I'd deal with him after the show.

Right now, I wanted to prepare for tomorrow night and make sure my gear was ready.

I grabbed my bags, said my goodbyes to Everhide's team, and headed outside to catch an Uber. Hugging my camera bag against my chest, I shivered in the icy breeze. Glancing toward the Manhattan skyline, I breathed in the city that inspired me. I wanted to let the high of working for Everhide take over my mind. I needed to go somewhere where I could put Hayden out of my thoughts and let creativity fill my head. I wanted to relax and get lost in the world of art. *Yes.* That's it. After dashing via home to drop off my gear, I'd head to the Museum of Modern Art. My favorite place on earth.

Somewhere I could be alone. By myself. Bliss!

MoMA, here I come.

Chapter 14

LEXI

With my hands stuffed into my coat pockets, I meandered through the latest photography exhibition on Level 3 at MoMA. But the silence was far from calming. This was supposed to be my sanctuary, my source of creativity, but thanks to Gemma, Hayden had intruded into every thought. So much for preparing for tomorrow night. Throughout the museum, wall after wall, room after room of paintings, pictures, and sculptures, culture, history, artistic interpretations of light, sound, and movement, and Manhattan's magic, captured in so many beautiful forms, had evoked so many emotions . . . about Hayden. All the color, depth, and detail . . . had reminded me of Hayden.

Shit!

I'd taken my time to read each plaque about the artist, the story behind their creation, and absorb each image—the lighting, the filters, the angles. But it'd been pointless. Chaos had reigned inside my head. It made a Pollock painting look like nothing but a bunch of straight lines.

Fuck.

I had to straighten out my maddening feelings for Hayden, and tap into my truth so the way forward was clear. I couldn't go on like this. Was the answer within these walls?

After another hour of wandering around the floors and avoiding other museum visitors, I took a seat on the cushioned bench by the wall of windows, overlooking the sculpture garden below. I leaned against the glass and stared at the black-and-white photo across from me. A lone, beautiful woman in a flowing couture gown ran down a vast dirt road toward distant mountains. Her long, dark hair, and skirt billowed behind her. Heavy broken chains hung from her wrists. The shot depicted strength, courage, beauty, freedom, burden . . . loneliness. I'd end up alone if I didn't do something about it. I had great friends and a good life. But without Hayden, it held no appeal.

What was I going to do?

I turned toward the garden. A few brave souls stood talking in the late afternoon chill, holding steaming drinks in their hands. The trees were bare. The fountain, empty. As I rested my head against the window, my breath misted the glass. I dragged my fingertips through the condensation, leaving streaks on the pane.

I needed to unpack my feelings for Hayden.

Closing my eyes, he flickered through my mind like a video playing at one thousand frames per second. We'd been through everything together. We knew each other's baggage and deepest secrets. Taking a chance to see if we were more than friends terrified me. I couldn't lose him. I clutched at my chest. The rims of my eyes stung.

Why wasn't this easy?

The long, cushioned seat puffed up with a rush of air as some douchebag sat beside me, too close to my back. What happened to personal space? I grimaced and turned to leave. I'd find another place to sit. But my heart hit my skull. My mouth gaped like a fair clown. *Hayden.* My brain scrambled to find words. "What . . . what are you doing here?"

Dimples embedded into the grooves by his mouth as he tried not to smile. "When you texted you'd be here, I had to come. This is our place, remember?"

Oh yeah . . . *that.*

"You alright?" He pulled off his beanie and stuffed it in his coat pocket. "Are you upset about something? Do you want to talk about it?"

"No, I'm okay. I just wanted some timeout." I rubbed the threatening tears from my eyes. When did I start lying to him? "How're you holding up?"

Hayden picked at his thumbnail. His leg jiggled like crazy. "I'm freaking out about playing tomorrow night. I have to hold the entire set together. I don't want to let Everhide down. I'm terrified I'll fuck up. Gem will eat me alive."

"Maybe . . . Nah. She loves you." I tucked my hair behind my ear, but my heart still hadn't calmed down. He was here. In our treasured spot.

"She terrifies me sometimes."

"Why?" I giggled.

"She's just so fucking good at what she does."

"True. The three of them didn't make it to the big time by being sweet and submissive."

"I know." He drummed his fingers against his thigh. "I'm gonna run through the set a few more times when I get home, just so I've got it drilled permanently into my head."

"Hayds." I placed my hand over his to still his jitters. "You've done that. You were amazing today. You're as good as Slade."

He puffed out a doubt-filled breath. "Now I know you're lying. But thanks."

"What are friends for? But trust me, you'll nail it."

"I hope so." He entwined his fingers with mine. I stared at our hands resting on his lap. His touch had always felt good. Comforting. Natural. It was something so simple and something we'd always done. Was there more to it?

His eyes glinted as he elbowed my arm. "Kyle told me they loved your photos. It's so cool that you'll be shooting tomorrow night."

I held out my free, shaky hand, palm facing down. "I'm still trembling."

"You're so talented, Lex. I wish you could find a job in photography."

"I wish you and your band wrote another ten hits."

He chuckled and nodded. "Yeah. Me too."

I wanted Hayden to have the same success as Everhide. It should've happened by now, but that break had still eluded him.

He clutched my hand tighter. "Things will be good in Boston."

"It'd be better if you stayed." *Shit. That slipped out.* But it was the truth.

He didn't say anything—he just leaned into me and rested his head against mine. I snuggled against his arm, soaked in his warmth, and stared at the black-and-white photo again. It crushed my heart knowing the next chapter in our lives would pull us apart.

Hayden pointed at the photograph. "I like that. It captures freedom. Fear. Courage. Risk. The unknown. That sometimes new roads must be faced alone. It might be hard and scary, but if you don't try, you'll never know what you can achieve."

I closed my eyes. We were so in tune. "I thought almost the same things." My voice came out barely above a whisper.

"It's like us, isn't it? We're about to take different paths and head into the unknown." Sadness hovered in his soft voice. We sat in silence for a minute, staring at the photo. "You take better pictures than that."

"I wish." The image was under-exposed, but I liked the depth the darkness added. "One day I'd love to have my photos exhibited here."

I doubted that would ever happen. My best chance of finding a new job would be at another magazine in the hospitality industry. I had more than enough blogging and editing experience. With Hayden leaving, my weekends would be free. I wouldn't be going to all his gigs. Maybe I could do some freelance photography. I could shoot weddings and functions. Adding tomorrow night's event to my portfolio would do wonders for my name. Hopefully, I'd pick up some more professional gigs after talking to other artists and their managers at the show.

But whatever I did, I needed full-time work. I couldn't survive on random, unreliable income. I needed stability and free time to visit Hayden in Boston. I couldn't handle not seeing him occasionally . . . often . . . a lot. *Fuck . . . oh fuck!*

I drew in a deep breath and turned toward him. I studied his beautiful face. I'd taken more than a million photos of him, but it was like seeing him for the first time—his perfect olive skin, manly but boyish charm, eyes that swept you into the depths of their steely-gray ocean.

Warmth stirred low in my stomach. Butterflies took flight. My pulse quickened.

I couldn't deny it any longer.

I liked him. I *really* liked him . . . in an *I-want-you-to-be-more-than-a-friend* kind of way. But with so much history between us, when I knew everything about him, how could I cross the line to see if we could be more than friends without the risk of getting hurt? As our eyes locked, it was like my fingers hovered over the button on my camera. I wanted to press down, but was too afraid to take the shot.

But Hayden lowered his chin. He fidgeted with my hand, swiveling my dress ring around my finger. Trouble furrowed his brow.

"Hayd? What's wrong?"

He cleared his throat. "Kilt called. His dad wants us to move to Boston earlier. In mid-January. That means moving in three weeks, not five."

My heart leaked out of my body and trickled across the floor. My whole body drooped like the melting clocks in the Salvador Dali painting. "No. Not earlier. You can't."

I couldn't work out what we could be in that timeframe, could I?

He squeezed my hand. "I have to, Lex."

I threw my arms around his shoulders and held him tight. Tears burned my eyes. "No. I'm not ready for you to go."

"Me either. But it'll be okay."

Shit. "No. That means we have less time together." My whole body ached like it missed him already, and he hadn't even left yet.

I'd wasted too much time avoiding him, and lost too many hours mulling over kisses and feelings that had knocked at the walls around my heart. I'd been shaken by the incident with my boss and had worried about my job. But none of those things mattered anymore. My dial switched to panic mode. We had so many things to do together before he left. We had to spend every moment with each other.

Sadness filled Hayden's smile. "There's no point in delaying the inevitable. It might make leaving easier."

"I doubt it." I wouldn't squander another second. Leaping to my feet, I hauled him up. "There's no time to waste. We have to get through our bucket list. We start now. There's one thing I've always wanted to do with you." I grabbed his beanie from his coat pocket and jammed it onto his head, tied his scarf, and buttoned his coat. After putting on my gloves, I grabbed his hand. "Let's go."

We rushed down the stairs. At a run, I led him along Fifth Avenue, weaving around workers, tourists, and shoppers laden with Christmas bags and gifts. At the Rockefeller Center, I slowed to a walk, panting in the cool evening air.

Underneath the trees lit with twinkle lights, I drew to a halt by the ice rink. "Wait here." I giggled at Hayden, pointing toward the ground for him to stay.

"What are we doing?" He puffed; his cheeks flushed from running.

"You'll see." I waved over my shoulder as I disappeared into the crowd.

Five minutes later, I returned and held up my hands. The blades of the skates clinked together.

Hayden laughed a big belly laugh. "You're kidding, right? Ice skating?"

"Yes." Excitement zipped through my veins. "I've walked past here a gazillion times and seen it in the movies. I've always wanted to do this. So lace up."

He grabbed the boots and chuckled as we headed down the stairs to the rink. "I better not fucking break a leg . . . or an arm. Gem and the guys *will* kill me if I can't play tomorrow night."

"Nah. We can skate like champs. If you're worried about your balance, hold my hand. I won't let you fall."

"I'll hold you to that." He nudged his arm against mine as we tied up our laces.

Butterflies fluttered like snowflakes in my stomach as we took to the ice. After a couple of laps to find our feet, we hit cruise mode. Hayden's gloved hand slipped into mine. Warmth from his touch seeped through to my skin. Gliding around the rink, avoiding collisions with kids and beginner skaters, I couldn't drag my gaze away from him. The cool breeze caught the ends of his hair that peeked out from his beanie. His eyes twinkled like the Christmas lights. His contagious smile was hypnotizing.

He pulled me to a halt in the center of the rink. Mischief curled through his smile. "Race you. Two laps. On the count of three."

Oh, it was on.

I flicked my scarf behind my shoulders, dug the edge of my blade into the ice, and bent down, ready to take off.

He pulled his beanie on tighter, clapped his gloves together. "Ready? One . . . two . . . three. Go."

I pushed off, but he caught the back of my coat and swung me around. "Ha-hah." He whooped and took off through the crowd.

"You cheat." I raced after him. Zipping around people, I caught up with him. "That was mean." I pushed him on the shoulder hard and sent him wobbling on his feet.

"Whoa. Shit." He swung his arms wide. His feet backpedaled and scraped the ice. He twisted sideways. Slid in a circle. Dug his blade into the ice and stood upright. "Fuck, that was close. No leg breaking, remember?" As he straightened his coat, his laughter filled the rink. But revenge flared in his eyes.

Oh no. Shrieking, I took off. He sped after me, but I was too quick.

After a full lap at top speed, I skidded to a halt in front of the golden Prometheus statue to catch my breath. Seconds later, Hayden crashed into me. He wrapped his arms around my waist and spun me in a circle. My head swirled with a dizzy high. I grabbed onto the lapels of his duffel coat and gave him a shake. "You didn't play fair."

He caught me around my hips and pulled me closer. My

skates slipped on the ice, and I smacked into his chest. His eyes glimmered with cheekiness. "Me? What about you? You pushed me in front of some kid."

"My bad." I ran my fingers up to his collar and tugged on the edge. *Hmm.* "I'm the winner."

"No. You're a troublemaker."

"Yeah?" My voice hinted at sauciness. "What are you going to do about it?"

His gaze fell to my lips and drifted slowly back up. My pulse quickened. The air between us grew so hot I was sure the ice would melt.

We were so close. Skates, knees, thighs, and hips pressed together. My heart no longer raced from the exertion of skating but from the way he looked at me with molten eyes. His lips curled at one corner. Our breaths collided.

"Lex?" He swallowed hard. "You make it so fucking hard for me not to break the rules."

My heart skidded toward uncharted territory. The boundaries of our friendship blurred. *Fuck it.* "You don't have to break them. I will."

I grabbed him by the scarf and yanked him forward. I pressed my lips to his, and time stopped. Afraid to breathe, I stood there with his mouth hot against mine. *Holy crap.* My pulse thundered like a jumbo jet in my eardrums. Shivers shot up my spine. He sucked in a deep breath and dug his fingers into my hips. As he tilted his head, he parted his lips. His warm, delicious tongue flicked out to meet mine. We tasted each other. Savored each touch. Sparks shot through my veins as he deepened our kiss.

I moaned against his mouth.

His hands wrapped around my back, and he crushed my body into his. My heartbeat hit the Top of the Rock. *Wow.* Each nip and lick melted my insides, sent heat rushing to the tips of my fingers and toes, and oh . . . my core.

This was good. This was hot. This was . . .

"Ew gross. Kissing." Some bratty girl zooming past shrieked and smacked me on the arm.

The world around me returned. Music boomed through the rink's speakers, people skated past, and the clock chimed the top of the hour. But my head still lingered in the clouds.

Hayden's hands fell to my waist, and he pressed his forehead against mine. A sexy grin curled across his lips. "Was that on your bucket list too?"

"No. Just a bonus."

"Come on. Let's go home." Taking my hand in his, we glided over to the edge of the rink.

We couldn't stop giggling, nudging each other, or grinning on the subway ride home. There were no nerves or awkwardness or *shit-I-shouldn't-have-done-that* unease in the air.

That kiss on the rink had uncovered something new. It hadn't been like our other kisses. There was no drunken foolery to blame. It had been pure want and surrender. I'd let down my guard for the first time in years, and it scared me. Was this the first step toward seeing if there was something between us? *Yes . . . No . . . maybe . . . Yes.*

But as we ate pizza for dinner, Hayden sat as far away from me as possible on the sofa. He grew quieter and quieter. My blood had grown thicker with worry. He didn't touch me or attempt to kiss me. He cleaned up, did the dishes, and took out the trash. He acted as if nothing had happened. How could he do that? I was going crazy and my insides burned. Was that his game plan? To taunt me? After everything that had happened, I'd thought he'd be all over me.

Shit. Fuck.

Oh no.

Had kissing him been a mistake?

Surely not.

"Can we talk?" I wanted to discuss what had happened, make sense of it all, and find out what was going on in his head.

He held up his finger and shook his hair. "Nope. Later."

Stuffing my leftover pizza crust into his mouth, he took to his drums. He put on his headphones and switched on his music, no doubt the songs for tomorrow night. The heavy drum mute pads muffled the thuds, thumps, and clangs as he played.

The silent treatment hurt my chest. The show was more important to him than I was. Music was more important. He didn't give me a second thought. I wasn't a priority. Splinters shot through my heart. Our kiss had meant nothing to him.

He was lost in the music, focused on the songs. He didn't even glance my way.

Fine. I can handle this. Yep. Absolutely.

Stretching out on our old leather sofa, I grabbed my phone and Kindle off the side table, stuffed in my earbuds, and turned on Spotify. But as I read my ebook, I couldn't concentrate. I couldn't get kissing Hayden out of my mind. The taste of his lips was still fresh. The heat swirling low and deep in my core wouldn't dissipate. I tugged the blanket high under my chin. Hayden and I had to talk. But maybe it was best to wait until after the show. By then, I'd know what to do about these unlocked feelings. With the ache growing between my legs, I knew exactly where I wanted to take things. But judging by his reaction, maybe he didn't feel the same way anymore. He didn't want me anymore. I'd rejected him too often, and he'd given up on me.

I couldn't blame him.

This was why I didn't do relationships; they caused nothing but emotional torture. I'd wanted to sort out my feeling for Hayden, not make them worse. I should put the lid back on them and forget we'd ever kissed.

He was moving to Boston. I wasn't.

I needed to protect his heart and mine. Our kiss tonight was just a hiccup. Another mistake. Yep.

Forget his lips.

Forget his touch.

Forget the sparks.

There was nothing else to contemplate.

Chapter 15

LEXI

My hands quivered like bow strings as I checked my camera and accessories for the thousandth time in the dressing room at Washington D.C.'s Capital One Arena. Three spare batteries, five spare flash cards, two spare lenses, chargers, and my old SLR in case my new DSLR failed. Everything was in order. But I checked my bag again just to be sure. Everything was working. Except my brain. I worried about Hayden. He'd taken off at dawn with Everhide. I'd never seen him so nervous about a show. But that was no reason to shut me down. No reason not to talk to me. Our kiss may have been a mistake, but I was still his best friend.

I glanced around the bustling room. Everhide stood surrounded by their hair and makeup crew doing final touchups. Kara fussed with their outfits. Three members of their backup band sat on a sofa drinking beer, looking relaxed and ready to go. But Hayden paced the floor. Dressed in skinny black jeans, a T-shirt, and combat boots, and with his hair styled back perfectly, he exuded a sleek, sexy suaveness even though his cheeks were pale and his gaze was distant. He mumbled under his breath as he tapped his favorite drumsticks against his palm. He was no doubt running through the set list on repeat. Wiping his brow on his shirtsleeve, he looked like he was about to throw up.

He needed some calm reassurance and a confidence boost. I drew my shoulders back and walked over to him. I adjusted the focus on my camera to take a picture, but he covered the lens with his hand. "Please don't."

As I lowered the camera, my chest ached. Regardless of what had happened last night, I was here to support him. "Hayds, you'll be fine. You know this set backwards." I gave him a quick kiss on the cheek, but my lips lingered on his skin. My heart dipped and danced. He smelled so good, all woodsy and sweet. *Hmm, so nice.* Tearing myself away from him, I pasted on an encouraging smile. "You've got this."

He just lowered his head, turned and resumed pacing.

This was ridiculous. He'd never shunned me before. "Hayds?" I caught his arm. "Are you okay?"

His nod was quick and shaky. "I'm just nervous."

Liar. There was more on his mind than the show. I couldn't handle that he was upset. I couldn't hold my tongue any longer. "Hayds, about last night, our kiss—"

He held up his finger and closed his eyes. His jaw ticked. "Not now, Lex. I need to focus."

I opened my mouth to protest, but he shook his head.

"Okay." I eased back a step. "I just want you to know I'm sorry. For everything."

Anguish burned in his eyes. I hated that I'd caused it. But right now, I had a job to do. I wrapped my camera strap around my hand tightly and refocused. I took a deep breath, glanced at Gemma and the guys, and absorbed the heightening pre-performance energy. I wouldn't let this night be dampened by anything, not even Hayden. "We've been to so many shows before, but working for our friends is so different. This is so fucking cool."

"Yeah, but I'm onstage." He waved toward the dressing room door. "I'm about to play in front of twelve thousand people. This is my biggest gig ever." He brushed his hand down his blanched face, then ripped his fingers through his hair. "I'm peaking out."

"Hayds. Breath." I placed my hand on his chest and softened my voice. "Just breath. Deep breath in. Deep breath out."

He closed his eyes, clenched his jaw, and shook his head. "Fuck. Please. Just stop."

My heart hurt. My head ached. He'd put up a wall after last night. He wasn't just nervous . . . he was pissed . . . at me.

Nice one, Lex. You idiot.

Torment swirled like a tornado in his eyes. This wasn't part of the plan. Not that I had one. But I hadn't meant to upset him. *Crap.* I needed to get out of there before I said something I'd regret. "Fine. Go break a leg."

Turning, I couldn't get away from him fast enough. I rushed toward the restrooms on the far side of the dressing area. I needed a moment to clear my head . . . and to pee.

I was here to take shots of Everhide. My nerves kicked to life. Since I'd arrived just before lunch, I'd taken photos of them at their dress rehearsal, and at the meet and greet with fans this evening. The images I'd taken so far had turned out amazing. But I'd never taken many photos of them onstage, under flashing lights, washes, and lasers, not to mention the huge, bright projector screens playing behind them. I prayed they'd come out great.

Fifteen minutes until showtime.

After drying my hands, I hooked my camera over my shoulder and headed out of the restroom. But as I stepped outside, Hayden stood in the short corridor, leaning against the wall, tapping his fingers against his thigh.

"You waiting for someone?" I jammed my hands onto my hips.

"Yeah. You." He grabbed me around the waist, pulled me against his chest, and kissed me. Hard. Deep. Full-on, melt-my-panties tongue.

Stars swirled behind my eyelids. Air shot from my lungs. I clung onto his shoulders to keep upright because I'd lost the use of my knees.

"*Mmm*," I groaned, pulling back from him. I struggled to find my breath. My heart thundered against my ribs. "What was that for?"

"Luck." He winked at me, turned and walked off.

What the fuck?

I fell against the wall. I closed my eyes and took a couple of deep breaths. Was that kiss a good thing? That things between us were okay? *Ugh!* I had no idea. Hayden had done my head in. But I touched my lips and smiled a small smile. They still tingled from his kiss. He'd followed me. Kissed me. That had to mean something.

"Ten minutes," Sophie's voice hollered from the center of the dressing room.

Crap. Photo time.

I raced over to Everhide, peered through my camera, and clicked some shots. Carla hot-ironed last-minute curls into Gemma's long hair and teased them out. Kara threaded Hunter's ear-monitor cords through his silky button-down shirt, and Sophie helped Kyle with his transmitter, clipping it onto his belt. As I circled in front of them, my friends jumped together, struck a pose, and made peace signs in the air. They all rocked black leather pants. Gemma wore a sexy, snug leather vest, and the guys wore black patterned button-downs. They screamed, "Rock on."

Gemma stepped toward me and gave me a big hug. "Are you having fun?"

"Yeah." I bobbed my head. My adrenaline stepped up a rung. "This is awesome."

Kyle untangled his ear-monitor cords and hung them over his shoulders. "Did you see Hayds? Is he doing okay?"

"He's nervous as hell." I glanced toward the door. He stood with the backup band, ready to head to the stage. With a deep breath, I sent him all the good-luck vibes I possessed.

"Hayds will be great. Remember to take lots of photos. Especially of me." Hunter flashed me his pearly whites as he caught Kara's hand, stopping her from doing up his shirt. He popped open the top three buttons and kissed Kara on the cheek. "I like it open. It gets too hot . . . and it makes the girls scream."

"You're such a showoff." She cupped his chin and kissed him on the lips.

I raised my camera and snapped a photo of them. *Too cute.* But fuck . . . It'd be ugly if he ever broke her heart.

"We'd better warm up." Kyle hooked his arm around Gemma's shoulders and headed over to the side of the room to run through their vocal exercises with Hunter.

I jumped up on a chair beside them and took some incredible shots.

***

As the host of the Jingle Ball captivated the audience with stories and jokes, the stage was reset for Everhide to close out the show.

I stood offstage. My fingers trembled as I checked my camera one last time—battery fully charged, spare in my pocket, settings all good. My heart beat as loudly as the people hollered in the auditorium, *'Everhide! Everhide!'* Holding my camera ready, my palms sweated. The lights dimmed. The crowd shrieked.

Hayden's bass drum filled the air.

Shivers darted across my skin.

A lone stage light hit him, and my heart careened toward exploding. His steel-gray eyes shimmered in the lights. His sticks pummeled the drums. Every beat stole my breath. He was pure perfection. I'd never fully appreciated his deep drive, ambition, and dedication to honing his craft—from musicals, to the studio, to his band. He'd worked hard, had made something of himself, and deserved every success. He was a true inspiration. So talented. I was so proud. I prayed tonight led him toward a bigger and brighter future.

I raised my camera and took dozens of photos of him before the rest of the backup band joined in the overture. His bass drum thudded through my chest. More lights blazed to life. Then Everhide ran onstage, and I reluctantly turned my lens toward them.

Chapter 16

LEXI

Taking a seat at the bar after the Jingle Ball, I ordered a glass of champagne while I waited for Everhide to arrive. They'd been whisked away by security from the concert venue, along with the band, and hadn't turned up to the after-party yet. My night was far from over. I still had photos to take, but one drink wouldn't hurt.

As I kept my eyes on the door, my foot jiggled against the footrest. My stomach flipped like a flapjack tossed in the air. I couldn't wait to see my friends but I was even more excited to see Hayden. He'd nailed the performance. I wanted to congratulate him. Celebrate. This was his night, and he deserved his moment to relish the spotlight. But his pre-show kiss flickered through my mind. I desperately wanted to sort out what was going on between us before my head exploded. This wasn't the place to talk, though. I'd have to wait until after the party.

I glanced around the crowded room to make sure I hadn't missed him come in. Sophie mingled with the other artists. Kara chatted to celebrity guests demolishing the free-flowing alcohol and hors d'oeuvres. Bec and Kate talked to the radio station crew and media representatives.

I twitched my booted toe against the kickboard and glanced at the door again. *Chill.* Hayden will be here soon.

"Mind if I join you?"

I spun around on my stool. A bald man in his forties with thick-rimmed glasses slipped onto the seat beside me. The hairs on my arms spiked like a porcupine caught in a trap. I knew this guy—Gerard Rivers from *Entertainment On-Show*, one of the biggest entertainment TV and Internet news sites in the country. Gerard had caused my rockstar friends nothing but grief.

"Sorry, I was just leaving." I gulped down the remains of my glass and slid off my stool, but he held out his hand, stopping my escape.

"I'm Gerard Rivers."

"I know who you are." Picking up my camera bag, I refused to shake his excessively manicured claw. "I'm working, so please excuse me."

"I won't take more than two minutes of your time." A slimy grin slid across his face. "I know who you are, too. I'd like to talk business."

I blinked several times. "With me?" I was a nobody. Why was I on his radar?

"Yes. Alexandra Mitchell. But your friends call you Lexi. You work at *The Gourmet Reviewer*. Live with Hayden Moore. You're best friends with Kara Knight and Gemma Lonsdale."

What the hell? What did he want with me? "How do you know who I am?"

"You're friends with Everhide. I'm a journalist. I've done my research." He waved down the waiter and ordered a beer. "Let me get you a drink."

"No, thank you. I'm fine." I untangled my hair from underneath my bag strap and flicked it over my shoulder.

"I'm interested in your photography." He took a sip of his beer and then dabbed his lips with a napkin.

I drew back my shoulders. *Really?* My heart beat with caution. No one outside my friends had ever been interested in my photography. My ass reconnected with the edge of my stool. "What did you say?"

"I've seen your recent images of Everhide on their social

media accounts." Gerard's beady eyes were as round as a mole's. "I've read your review articles. I like your style. You write with a sassy attitude."

"Are you interested in my photography, my journalism skills, or my friends?"

He half-smiled. "I like you, so I'll get straight to the point. You could make a fortune photographing celebrities. You go to a lot of VIP parties. They trust you. I'd be willing to pay top dollar for your photos, especially if they were of a *newsworthy* nature, if you know what I mean?" His voice, while smooth and innocent, was back-loaded with double entendre.

He wanted compromising photos of my friends? *Prick.* No fucking way.

I clutched my shoulder strap tightly so I wouldn't punch him in the face. Fire licked through my veins. "I thought EOS was a reputable news site. I didn't think they lowered themselves to trashy gossip."

"Oh, EOS is." He straightened his tie. "But I'm interested in your talent for another company EOS owns . . . Gossipline."

A loud ringing exploded in my ears. I couldn't believe what I'd heard. "The tabloid gossip site? No. Absolutely not." For the tiniest, smallest fraction of a second, I'd gotten my hopes up at the prospect of entering entertainment journalism. *Stupid me.* I stood and straightened my camera bag. "This conversation is over."

He held up his palm. "Think about it. You could earn thousands of dollars a week freelancing." His voice held no emotion, yet it sent a chill down my spine.

I got up in his face and sneered. "I'm not interested."

Was this how EOS and Gossipline got their headline stories? They bought and bribed the friends of celebrities? I'd been approached years ago by some jerk on the street offering to buy photos from me just because I knew Kyle, Hunter, and Gemma. No matter how badly I wanted a job in photography and to further my career, I'd never betray the people I loved and cared about. Not ever. "There's not enough money on the planet for you to sway me. I love and respect my friends and will do anything to protect them.

Go to hell."

He chuckled, seeming undeterred by my disgust. He dug into his inside jacket pocket and held out his business card. "If you change your mind, call me."

I met him square in the eye and shook my head. I snatched the card from his fingertips, ripped it up and dropped it into his beer. "There's nothing to think about. Leave me alone. Leave my friends alone."

"Got it." Gerard nodded and stood. "The offer is always open. Nice talking to you, Miss Mitchell." Looking pleased with himself, he disappeared into the crowd.

Asshole.

Swiping a wayward curl off my face, I headed to the tables reserved for Everhide. I flashed my pass at security and dumped my gear on a chair. Disappointment sat like a grease trap in my gut. Gerard wasn't interested in my skills—only gossip. My hopes of finding a better job had been extinguished as quickly as they were ignited. But money wasn't everything. I wanted a new job and craved a better salary, but I'd never compromise my self-respect and integrity. In the past two weeks, my boss had sexually harassed me, and one jackass journalist had wanted me to sell my soul. Where were the decent men in the world?

My gaze drifted to the commotion at the entrance. My heart leaped into my throat. Behind the media frenzy and Everhide, Hayden walked into the room.

I splayed my hand across my stomach to settle the butterflies. Hayden was a good guy—decent and kind to the core. So were Hunter and Kyle, but it was Hayden who'd broken another chain from around my heart.

But wow. His smile lit the room. Tonight, his music career had gotten the boost it'd deserved. Publicity would raise awareness of his band. They'd get more gigs, more fans, more online streams. They had to take advantage of that. *Shit.* My shoulders sank an inch. Boston was the right move for them. Hayden was destined to be a star. Exploring the spark between us was a stupid idea. He didn't need to be tied down to me. A relationship with him wasn't worth capturing on film, processing it in a dark room, and seeing what it developed into. It'd be a waste of time. I'd locked away my feelings for so long, I could do it again.

Shoving my heart back into its cage, I kicked into best-friend mode. It was so much easier. Less stressful. Less complicated. I rushed over to Hayden and threw my arms around his neck. He picked me up, and I shrieked as he spun me around twice, and placed me back on my feet.

"You were amazing," I yelled over the noisy guests.

"Oh, Lex." He clutched my arms. "It was soooo incredible!" The excitement in his voice lifted my spirits. "Did you see me nail 'Forever?' That song is so hard to play. I did it. I freaking did it. And the crowd . . . Wow! It was so fucking awesome."

His electric energy filled the room. As he drew me in for another hug, people gathered around us and squished us closer together. Eager voices and hustling bodies wanted to chat to Everhide and the backup band . . . specifically Hayden. I slipped out of his embrace and squeezed his hand. "Go. Enjoy the night. I'll take some more photos and catch up with you soon."

But he didn't drop my hand. It was like he didn't want to let me go. My chest ached. I was so happy for him. He was going places, moving on to better things . . . I wasn't. But we were good, always would be. I smiled and tugged my hand free. The crowd waving cell phones and snapping pictures jostled around him, and he disappeared from view.

Gemma bounced over to me on her post-performance high. "Let's get these photos done."

"I'm at your service." I grabbed my camera off the table and followed Gemma, Kyle, and Hunter over to a designated area set aside for their Jingle Ball photos with guests. Between each shot, I searched the room for Hayden. He talked to the media, to managers, and to a bunch of other artists and friends. He belonged in this world. I prayed Boston made all his dreams come true.

Once my friends finished their promotional duties and no more photographs were required, I packed my camera away and stowed my gear on a spare chair at our table. With the excitement of the evening still zipping through my veins, it was time to party with my friends.

Gemma handed me a shot of JD. "Thanks for working with us tonight, Lex. I can't wait to see the photos."

"Of the thousands I took, I hope some are okay." I clinked glasses with everyone and knocked the shot down. "I've had an incredible time. Thank you."

It'd been an amazing experience. For the next couple of hours, the girls, the guys, and I danced, drank, and laughed. But by the time the clock struck midnight, the excitement, and adrenaline, and the rollercoaster of emotions slammed into me like I'd hit a brick wall. Exhaustion sank deep into my bones. As my friends and I returned to our table, I yawned. "Guys, I'm going to call it a night. I have to head off early in the morning to get to Mom's."

"Pussy." Hunter poured everyone another shot, but I declined.

Kara flashed him a *don't-be-mean* glare, then she reached across the table and clutched my hand. "It's okay. We understand. You have a great day with your mom. Please wish her a happy birthday from us. " She tapped my hand. "Will we see you tomorrow night or not? We head off early on Monday morning."

Shit. Christmas break. Hunter and Kara were off to Chicago to spend a few days with his parents. Kyle and Gemma were heading to his cousin's place in Seattle. Then, my friends were heading overseas to play a New Year's gig in Japan and do some promotional work. They were off traveling the world while I was stuck at home, going nowhere. "Um . . . I won't be home until late. I might not see you before you leave."

"Then, we'd better say goodbye now." Gemma sprang off her chair and gave me a big hug, squeezing me tight. "Send through some photos as soon as possible. Kate will want to post something online." She eased back and rubbed my arms. "Thank you for helping us out tonight. We had a blast. I love you heaps. Have a fabulous Christmas."

"Will do." I gave her another quick hug. "I love you. I'll see you in the new year."

After circling the table, hugging, and kissing my friends

goodbye, I reached Hayden. We weren't going anywhere for the break. I'd see him at home tomorrow. I held my arms wide. "Night."

"Nah. I'll come with you." Hayden downed his drink. "I think my adrenaline has run out, too."

Gemma nudged her hip against mine. "Go, you crazy kids. Don't do anything I wouldn't do." She winked. Her playful tone held too much suggestiveness.

I ignored her as Hunter and Kyle hugged Hayden, slapping him on the back.

"Thanks for playing tonight, man," Kyle play-punched Hayden's arm. "Loved sharing the stage with you."

"Same. But don't ever steal my spotlight." Hunter waggled a finger at Hayden, then smiled his trademark superstar smile.

"Wouldn't dream of it." Hayden laughed and grabbed his coat and my camera gear. I didn't need his help, but if he wanted to carry my heavy bag, I was happy for him to do so. He waved farewell. "See y'all. Merry Christmas, happy New Year, and all that jazz."

Arm in arm, Hayden and I scuttled down the street in the freezing cold. Light snowfall dusted our coats. My head ached; my feet ached. All I wanted to do was have a long, hot shower and go to bed.

In the hotel lobby, I dug into my purse for my room access card. *Fuck!* Not there. "Shit. I left my card in the room." I could picture it on the nightstand by my Kindle. I tilted my head back and groaned, then gave Hayden an *I'm-too-fucking-tired-to-deal-with-this-shit* look. "Carla's out clubbing. I'll grab another one from reception. Hold on."

Hayden hovered behind me as I dragged my feet over to the counter and smiled sweetly at Henrietta, the receptionist. "Hi. I'm Lexi Mitchell. I've left my key in my room. Room seven-two-one."

"I'm sorry, ma'am. I have no booking under that name."

"Is it under Carla Bonaris?"

The receptionist shook her head as she clicked her red fingernails on the keyboard. "No, sorry. I have no guests listed under that name either."

"I'm part of Everhide's entourage. Bec Arnold would have booked the room."

"Sorry, ma'am. Do you have a booking reference?"

Fuck. No. I'd just arrived and Carla had let me into our room.

"Look." I tried to keep my cool. "I'm tired. It's late. I just want to go to bed. Is the reservation under Gemma Lonsdale? Her booking name is Janis Daniels." I'd always loved Gemma's fake booking name. She'd combined one of her favorite artists—Janis Joplin—and her favorite drink—Jack Daniels. *Super clever.*

"Sorry, ma'am. For security reasons, I can't help you unless you have a booking number."

What bullshit. "Hold on. I'll call Bec and sort this out."

I dialed Bec, but there was no answer. I tried Gemma. It went straight to voicemail. I rang Carla—no response.

I hung up. *Shit.* Now what?

"Lex." Hayden tapped me on the shoulder and jerked his thumb toward the elevators. "You can crash in my room until Carla gets back."

My shoulders slumped. My purse weighed a ton. I didn't even have the energy to argue or refuse. "Are you sure? I'm so tired. Carla had better be home soon. I need sleep. I have to leave by seven to get back to New York." I had to pick up the catering for Mom's party before heading out to Sea Cliff.

"It'll be fine. Come on." He adjusted my camera bag on his shoulder and held out his elbow. He leaned in and lowered his voice. "I promise to keep my hands to myself."

He wasn't the one I was worried about. But I really was too tired to contemplate anything but sleep. We'd shared a room dozens of times before when we'd traveled with Everhide. This wasn't an issue. Talking about our kiss could wait until tomorrow night. Everything would be fine.

I threw the receptionist my best stink-eye glare, took Hayden's arm, and walked with him toward the escalators.

In his room, I fell onto the chair by the desk and peeled off my boots. *Bliss.* Wriggling my toes, I massaged my sore feet and eyed the inviting, *oh-my-God-it-had-my-name-on-it* king-sized bed.

"How come you get a room to yourself?"

"I'm in the band." Hayden's smirk oozed sexiness as he hung his coat in the closet.

I threw my boot at him and giggled. "You goose. Don't let the fame of one night go to your head."

"Never." He tossed it back to me and sat on the bed. Unlacing his boots, he looked up at me. Sincerity glowed in his warm gaze. "You'll always keep me grounded, Lex."

The hot honey in his deep voice did strange things to my pulse. I swallowed the dry desert in my mouth. "Yep. You're right about that." I'd hunt him down and slap him hard if he turned into a dick.

Dragging my eyes away from his, I grabbed my cell phone and sent Carla another message. "Hayds, I'm really sorry about this. I hope Carla won't be long."

"Don't worry about it." He placed his boots beside the bed. "You want to take a shower?"

I closed my eyes and dug my toes into the thick carpet. Hot water. Steam. The soothing, sweet smell of fresh soap. A shower would be perfect. "I'd love one. Is that okay?"

"Yeah. Go for it." He waved toward the bathroom. "Want the hotel bathrobe or a sweatshirt to wear?"

"A shirt would be nice if you have a spare."

"Sure do." He dug in his bag and handed me a white top. I held it up and sniffed it to make sure it was clean. It was . . . It smelled of him and fresh laundry. *Nice.*

I bit my lip to hide my smile and ducked into the bathroom. I locked the door. Being alone in a hotel room with him no longer felt innocent. Kissing him had scrambled my brain.

Just shower and go to sleep. Got it?

Yep.

Ten minutes later, I felt like a new woman. I used one of the hotel-supplied toothbrushes to brush my teeth, combed my hair, and slipped on Hayden's soft, cotton sweatshirt. I was just long enough to cover my butt.

After gathering my clothes, I walked out of the bathroom and dumped them on the desk. "Bathroom's all yours."

He grabbed his long pajama pants and T-shirt. "Thanks. Won't be long." He shuffled past me and disappeared to take a shower.

I glanced at the bed, then at the closed bathroom door. I pictured Hayden naked, in the shower, with water cascading down his sculpted body, lathering soap over his chest, his abs, his groin . . . *Shit. Don't go there. Just don't.* I squeezed my eyes shut. My body screamed for rest.

That notion won.

I pulled the bed covers back and crawled onto the mattress. The soft, silky sheets felt cool and luxurious against my bare legs. I didn't think I'd ever been in a bed this comfortable before. So warm and toasty and soft. I wriggled and tugged the pillow underneath my head. Exhaustion hit with a vengeance. If I just closed my eyes for fifteen minutes, then I'd be okay to stay awake and watch TV until Carla got back. A power nap was all I needed.

I was half asleep when Hayden came out of the bathroom. The mattress dipped as he crawled in beside me. With my back to him, I sensed him watching me. Felt his gaze scan over my body. My heart stirred, and I smiled a sleepy smile. *Crazy, stupid heart.* He switched off the light and snuggled beneath the quilt.

His slow, deep breath hovered in the air.

His body warmth enveloped me.

The scent of his freshly showered skin filled my head.

With him this close and the low hum strumming between us, was sleep even an option?

Chapter 17

HAYDEN

I brushed my fingertip across Lexi's brow, shifting a curl away from her eyes. In the dim lighting of the hotel room, I could make out the fine line of her cheeks, her cute nose, and gorgeous lips. With the buzz of the show still coursing through my veins, and Lexi beside me, I couldn't sleep, didn't want to sleep. If I did, I was terrified the high would come crashing down. I didn't want this rush to end.

Her hair fanned over the pillow like angel wings as she slept. Her breath was slow and deep. So much had changed in the past couple of weeks. At any point, if she'd said she loved me and had asked me to stay, I would've given up everything for her . . . my band, the move, my fresh start . . . everything. But she'd said nothing. Had said she didn't have feelings for me. That had made the decision to move to Boston easy . . . and necessary. But now I was torn in two. Something had changed between us, something hopefully for the better. But fuck . . . playing with Everhide, in front of a huge crowd, had made me even more determined for my band to succeed. It had been too long since we'd been on the charts. I wanted to be more than a one-hit wonder. But leaving Lexi seemed impossible. She was a part of me.

Resting my head on my hand, I could lie here all night watching her. She'd kicked off the covers and lay with her bare legs twisted toward me. My sweatshirt barely covered her panties. *So sexy.* I'd love to touch her, feel the warmth of her skin beneath my fingertips, trace every curve of her body.

Our recent kisses replayed in my mind. I was certain her feelings had changed towards me, and she was confused and scared and uncertain. So was I. I didn't want her to tell me that our kiss on the ice rink had been another mistake—not before the biggest show of my life. I'd wanted to savor that moment for as long as possible, afraid she'd knock me down . . . again. But I couldn't resist kissing her before the show. I was so nervous about the performance, she was the only thing that had calmed me.

I'd promised not to kiss her after LA. I'd failed. *Twice.* I'd tried to reset our friends-only status, but it'd been impossible. We were something; I just didn't know what. With three weeks until I left for Boston, how could I erase her doubts, her fears, and worries? Make her see we were meant to be together. If I'd misread the signs, I risked pushing her away and shattering our hearts. Oh . . . who was I kidding? Lexi already owned mine; it was hers to make or break. I'd said I wouldn't do anything foolish, but I guessed I hadn't learned from my mistakes. I prayed I didn't fuck things up. But each day, I fell for her more and more. I loved her so goddamn much.

She was so beautiful.

It was wrong to kiss her while she slept. *Wrong.* But fuck it . . . I had to taste her perfect lips.

I leaned forward and smelled her hair, inhaling the sweet smell of her gardenia shampoo. So heavenly, so Lexi.

Her eyelids fluttered. Her skin shimmered in the night light. Her mouth curved into a perfect arch as she breathed.

I lowered my head.

Just one kiss

One soft kiss.

I didn't want to wake her.

She wriggled.

I froze.

I held my breath. My lips hovered a few inches from hers.

She scratched her cheek, flopped her hand beside her head, but didn't wake.

She didn't stir again.

My teeth caught my smile.

My heart pounded.

I closed my eyes and pressed my lips to hers, light as a feather. Just a quick soft touch.

I pulled back.

Two glistening eyes peered up at me. I stilled as if a blade was held to my throat. My heartbeat slammed against my ribs.

Fuck.

But no sound passed her lips. No scream. No swearing.

She didn't thump me or push me away.

She just looked at me.

Silent.

Still.

I couldn't move and dared not breathe. The only disturbance was the soft hum of the warm air-conditioning and the electric vibe between us charging the air. Seconds passed—maybe an eternity.

"What are you doing?" she whispered.

"I was checking to make sure you were alive."

"Am I?" I could barely hear her soft voice.

"Yeah." My voice was as quiet as hers. "Sorry to wake you. Go back to sleep."

I moved to roll away, but her hand shot upward, flattening against my chest. *Shit.* My heart galloped as fast as a bolting mustang beneath her touch.

"Hayds?" Her voice quivered.

"Yeah?"

"I think you'd better check again. Make sure I'm alive."

I closed my eyes. *Fuck.* "Lex . . . if I kiss you, I won't want to stop."

She cupped the side of my cheek, drew her thumb over the stubble at the top of my lip. "Then don't."

My body tensed. Every part of me turned feverish. I wanted her. So much my balls ached. We weren't drunk. We weren't playing games. It was just us, here and now.

My pulse quickened as I touched my lips to her forehead, kissed one eyelid and then the other. I placed the lightest of kisses on the tip of her nose and each cheek. "Are you sure?"

She combed her fingers through my hair. "Yes. No regrets. I promise."

To hell if there are.

I kissed her sweet mouth. Heat surged through my veins and exploded in my heart. I wanted to explore and taste, lick, and kiss every inch of her body. But I didn't know where to start. I was terrified that if I moved too fast, she'd want to stop. That she'd disappear into thin air and I'd wake from the most incredible dream with empty arms.

But she knotted her fingers through my hair and pulled on the strands. My pulse thundered in my ears. This was no fucking dream . . . this was heaven. She moaned against my mouth, parted her lips, and flicked her tongue against mine. She kissed me hard and hot.

Every cell in my body hummed.

An inferno had ignited inside my soul.

I draped my arm over her waist and edged closer. Fumbling with the edge of her sweatshirt, I slipped my hand underneath it and brushed my cool fingertips against her fiery flesh. I wanted to touch all of her. Go fast. Go slow. Savor every inch of her body. I glided my palm over her hip, her ass, and bare thigh. I memorized every curve into my brain. There'd never be enough time in the world to explore her gorgeous body.

But I wouldn't waste a second.

I rolled on top of her and placed my forearms by her head. My lips never left hers. Having her beneath me was a fantasy come true. "You still okay?" I murmured over our kisses.

Wrapping her legs around me, she rocked her hips against mine. My dick grew even harder. "Yeah. This was on your bucket list, right?"

"Fuck yes," I chuckled as my breath entwined with hers. I kissed her mouth, her jaw, her neck, and grazed my teeth over her earlobe. "But I never expected it to happen."

"Me neither." She caught the bottom of my T-shirt and tugged it upward. "Take this off."

I reached behind my head, yanked it free, and tossed it on the floor. "Better?"

"Absolutely." Her gaze raked across my chest, over the tattooed bands on my arms, then back up to my face. A sheepish grin curled across her mouth. Little wrinkles formed on the bridge of her nose. "Do you just want to get naked?"

"Yep." I drove my hips forward, pressing my stiff cock against her crotch. "Would you like me to take your panties off with my teeth?"

She squirmed beneath me, grabbed the hemline of her sweatshirt, and pulled it over her head. "You can take my panties off, but you don't have to use your teeth."

Fuck. As I eyed Lexi's naked boobs, all my blood rushed south. "Well, now you've distracted me, you're going to have to wait."

I shuffled downward and took my time exploring each soft, silky, smooth breast. Trailing my fingers over her chest, I circled one nipple, then the other. With the gentlest of tweaks, I teased each bud until it was a hardened peak. Little goosebumps dotted her flesh.

She'd walked around our apartment in her bra and panties a gazillion times. I'd noticed her, but had never cared. But now, every time she was in the same room, want gripped every inch of my body. The ache for her burned as I lowered my head, flicked my tongue over her nipple, then licked it, taunted it and drew it into my mouth. I sucked one bud, then the other. The gentle groan that rumbled deep in her throat, and the arch in her back was all the coaxing I needed to do it again.

But I wanted more.

Kissing a trail down her stomach, I clutched the side of her panties. I tugged them down and slipped them off her feet. Her naked body stole my breath. *So beautiful.* I kissed her ankles, sucked her toes, and worked my way up, teasing the inside of her thighs. Her muscles quivered, and she moaned. *God, she'll be the death of me.* Her fingers combed and circled through my hair as I meandered my way up her legs. I wanted to pleasure her in every way but wasn't sure my cock would hold out for much longer.

Fuck. Condom. "One sec." I rolled off the bed, dashed to my bag and grabbed some condoms from my toiletry bag. I chucked them onto the nightstand, whisked off my pajama bottoms and left them on the floor.

As I crawled back onto the bed, the mattress dipped underneath my weight. Lexi's gaze fell to my hard-on. Her eyebrows shot upward. She hummed and licked her lips. A jolt of electricity surged through me. *Fuck.* I'd love her mouth on me, but not right now. I wanted to show her what she meant to me. Adore her. Make love to her until the sun came up.

"You still good?" I stretched out beside her, caressed her neck, and touched my lips to hers.

"Yeah. I'm not going anywhere." She hooked her leg over me and edged closer.

Her bare pussy pressing against my dick, and the scent of her freshly showered skin made my head spin. She was the best drug ever.

"Hayds." She nipped and sucked on my lower lip. "Lie back." She pushed gently against my chest, and my head connected with the pillow. Kicking the bed covers out of the way, she straddled my lap, trapping my dick beneath her. She pulsed and rocked her hips, sliding her hot, sleek pussy against me. Her eyes flashed with sexy wickedness. "You like that?"

I tensed and flinched beneath her torturous touch. "Don't be cruel."

Grabbing her hands, I pulled her forward. Hovering over me, she giggled. Scooping her hair back, I twisted it around my hand. I loved her hair, but I wanted to see her face, her eyes, not have her hide behind her curtain of curls. "You're so beautiful." My voice rumbled low and deep in my throat. I couldn't contain how I felt. "I lo—"

"Shh . . ." She placed her finger over my lips, then kissed me.

Maybe she didn't want to hear that I loved her. But she already knew it to be true.

Her hot breath rushed against mine as I teased her lips, dipped my tongue into her mouth, tasted her. I savored every touch and filled my soul with every kiss.

Sliding my hands up her thighs, I dug my fingers into her flesh. A playful smile inched across her lips as she shuffled back a fraction. Her eyes locked onto mine. She slid her pussy along the length of my cock again. Slowly. Seductively. Sexily. And groaned.

Holy. Fuck.

My dick thrummed to a sweet melody.

I tilted my head back, burying it deep in the pillow. Did she know she set my blood on fire? Made me lose my freaking mind? One slip and I'd enter her. The temperature in the room had hit dangerous levels. I needed to be sheathed. I'd self-combust if I didn't bury myself inside her. "Lex. Condom. Now."

I fumbled for the rubber, but she grabbed it before me.

"Stay." She smiled and pushed me back. The pillows puffed beneath my head.

She ripped the foil open, and my heart thundered against my ribs. *This is happening. This isn't a dream.* Fire engorged my cock as she rolled on the rubber. She fondled, rubbed, and stroked me. My vision blurred. I clutched onto the bedsheets to stop myself from exploding.

"Angel. Come here." I grabbed her hands and pulled her toward me. The heat blazing in her eyes sent shockwaves through my chest. I smoothed my hand over the back of her hair, cradled her head, and drew her lips to mine. Kissing her felt like home, completed my soul, filled me with light. I lifted my shoulders to roll over on top of her, but she pinned me down.

"Nuh-uh. I wanna be on top." Her sultry voice was music to my ears. "I haven't had sex in weeks. Let's do this."

An ache rippled through my chest. Was this just sex for her? Not an admission of having feelings for me? I wouldn't believe that. I'd never had a connection like this with anyone before. Not even my ex, Caroline.

Lexi read my body like she knew what I wanted and needed. We'd talked enough about our past encounters to know what we liked. Yeah, I fucking loved it when a girl rubbed their pussy against me. She loved being on top, liked being touched at the same time. *Oh, yeah . . . I could do that.* I wanted to pleasure her in every way.

But she rendered me useless as she rubbed against my cock. The cutest smile quivered across her mouth as she rolled her hips and teased the head against her clit. *Oh, my God!* My balls were about to erupt. Sliding my hands onto her hips, I sucked in a deep breath. I needed to be inside her. The agony, the anticipation, the ache burned hot in every muscle. Foreplay time was over.

I slid my hand between us, took hold of my dick, and nudged it against her. Hesitating, I gave her one last chance to stop. She didn't. I closed my eyes, thrust forward, and eased inside her. Slowly. Gently. Tenderly.

Oh. Fuck. Yes!

Her breath rushed from her lungs. Her eyes fluttered shut as she pulsed and rode and drove my cock into the depths of her pussy. The sweetest bliss shot up my spine. Everything around us melded into a world where only the two of us existed. I never wanted this to end.

"Wow." My voice came out breathless and desperate, but I didn't care. My body burned. I wanted her with every ounce of my being.

"Fuck, you feel good." Lexi rocked and pulsed her hips.

"So do you, angel."

Drawing her lips to mine, our bodies became one. She rode me steadily. I drove into her hard and deep. Our mouths tasted and savored sensual kisses. Our hands roamed over each other's bodies, touching every inch. I loved her with all I had. When the hot tension reached blazing point, I slipped my fingers between her legs. As I rubbed and circled her clit, she clenched around me.

New sounds rumbled from her throat. *'Mmm.'* New whispers. *'Hayds.'* New sighs. *'Ooh.'* New moans. *'Yeah.'*

I nearly came undone. "You feel amazing." I struggled to say anything comprehensible over our fervent kisses. Being inside her overruled my thoughts. "But I'm close."

"Same." Her breath quickened. She rode me harder. I thrust into her, rocking my hips in time with her rhythmic pace. I'd had so many dreams and fantasies about sleeping with Lexi, but none of them had been half as good as the reality. We connected perfectly. She'd touched me in all the right places. She'd made me feel everything everywhere.

Sweat licked our skin. Leaning forward, she grabbed the headboard and rocked against me. There was no wild, loud, or animalistic craziness—just slow, languid, *give-me-more-sweet-pleasure* pulses.

So intense. Electric. Profound.

Her breath neared a pant as I applied more pressure to her clit. Her eyes fluttered closed as she rubbed against my touch. I drove my dick into her deeper. "Hayds . . . there. Yes."

Her thighs tensed. Her insides clenched around me. With a jerk of her hips, she found her release. Quaking and quivering, she shuddered above me.

It was the most beautiful sight. My undoing.

With a body-arching moan, I came inside her. Pumping, throbbing, spilling into the condom. My chest heaved. My dick pulsed. The high of the night had gotten better and better. Every inch of my body buzzed with electricity and jolted with bliss. I wanted to scream *I love you, Lexi* from every rooftop in the city.

But a furrow formed between her eyebrows.

No-no-no-no-no.

"Hey." Stroking her hair, I kissed her sweet lips. "I've got you, angel. Come here."

I drew her down beside me. I grabbed some tissues off the nightstand for her to clean up and for me to discard the condom. After tossing them in the trash, I drew the bed coverings over us and held Lexi in my arms. I didn't want this moment to end. I kissed her on the forehead. "Why did we wait so long to do that?"

"Because I'd never wanted to," she whispered.

"I'm glad you changed your mind." I combed my fingers

through her hair and rubbed the back of her head.

"Everything's changed. I can't . . . I don't . . . "

"Lex, shh. Everything's good." I didn't want her to regret what we'd done. Yep, this may have tossed us into the center of a complicated pile of shit. I didn't know what step to take next. But we'd work it out . . . together. "That was incredible. Don't say anything unless it involves doing that again." Smiling, I kissed her on the temple. I'd be more than happy to have another round between the sheets . . . maybe in the shower.

But she drew tiny circles on my chest . . . and didn't say anything.

My heart constricted and ached. I never wanted to let her go. But with every second that passed, she grew distant. Quiet. Tense.

Fuck.

Tonight had been so perfect. We were good together. I didn't want her to think otherwise. We'd find a way to work. I lifted her chin and kissed her. "Lex, we've got this. I promise."

She cupped my cheek, gave me a distant smile, and whispered, "I need to get some sleep." She rolled onto her side, and I snuggled in behind her.

Shit. Had I already lost her? I wouldn't accept that. Not this time. "We'll talk before you leave in the morning."

"Okay."

So many ideas of how we could be together hurtled through my mind. Nothing would be easy, but I'd be willing to try anything. Being with Lexi was meant to be. We had to work things out. We had to.

After a long day, sleep finally took hold of me.

But when I woke late the next morning, Lexi was gone.

Shit.

There was no note. No trace. No text message.

My heart sank to the floor.

So much for talking things out.

Chapter 18

LEXI

I stomped the snow from my boots, shoved open Mom's front door with my shoulder, and stepped inside. I really needed to get the damn door fixed. The stupid thing always jammed. After dumping my purse on the console table, I hung up my coat and called out, "Mom? It's me."

I took a quick glance in the mirror to check my hair. *Shit!* My eyes were red from crying. During every unrelenting mile I'd driven from D.C. to Sea Cliff, I'd relived being with Hayden last night. I'd laughed, I'd cried, I'd blushed, and I'd panicked. *Oh God.* I'd slept with him. It hadn't made my feelings for him crystal clear. It hadn't presented a path forward. *Nope.* My brain was still a tangled mess. But I wouldn't lead Hayden on. Our time left together was too precious. Before I faced him again, I had to decide—to be with him and find a way to make it work or laugh it off and just be friends.

How to choose? I had no fucking idea.

"Mom?" I called out again as I straightened my tights and knit dress.

Still no answer.

Walking down the small hallway, I passed my old room that Mom had turned into her pottery studio, my brothers' twin bedroom that was still made up the same way as it was when they'd left fifteen years ago, and my mom's room opposite the bathroom. The hall walls struggled to stay upright under the weight of all the glory pictures of my army-jock brothers—their graduations, their military ceremonies, their send-offs. There was only one tiny frame of me at my high school graduation. I'd gone to university, had a decent job and worked hard, but my achievements didn't register on Mom's radar. I was never as good as my brothers.

But why was the house so dark?

In the living room, I pulled off my gloves and scarf. Every curtain was shut. The fire had gone out. The house was freezing cold. I flicked on the light.

Shit.

Mom, pale, and frail, sat in her armchair, staring out the tiny slit between the curtains. Was she staring at the boats bopping on the unsettled, gray ocean or was she lost in her own dark thoughts again?

I rushed over and squatted beside her. I clutched her bony hand; her skin was rough, leathery, and cold. "Mom? What are you doing?"

"Oh, Lexi." Mom blinked and pulled her yellow cardigan across her chest. With her sunken cheekbones, lackluster little eyes, and graying hair, she looked much older than her sixty years. "Hi. What time is it?"

"It's nearly noon." I patted her hand. "Did you take your meds today?"

"Noon? Oh, my." She fidgeted with her green beaded necklace. "Yes, yes, I took my medicine."

The jury was still out on that one. I rose and headed for the dining table where I'd left my mom's medication in a slotted pill box, marked with days and times. I opened the lid, and my heart faltered. *Shit.* She hadn't taken any meds for three days.

"Mom, you haven't. They're all here." I should've come and checked on her on Friday instead of hanging out with my friends, having fun at their rehearsal. I rushed into the kitchen, grabbed a glass of water, and took the pills over to her. "Here. Quick. Take these."

"Oh, no. I don't need them." She flicked her hand at me. "I'm feeling fine."

"Let's not have this discussion again, Mom." Fighting the sting in my eyes, I waved the pills and water in front of her. "The meds help you feel better. You can't stop taking them." I dropped the medication into her hand. "Hurry up. Take them. We have a party to get ready for."

My mother mumbled something incomprehensible, took the glass, and swallowed the pills. After placing the glass on the side table, she folded her arms and gazed out the window. "I don't want a party. I don't want to turn sixty."

I opened the curtains to let in the soft winter sunlight. The house instantly grew warmer. "Well tough, because today *is* your birthday, and everyone will be here soon. I've got the food in my car. So get up, go shower, get dressed. I'll light the fire and bring in the catering."

Mom didn't move. She twisted her necklace around her fingers. "Did you hear from Hank and Billy?" Her voice, soft and meek, quivered. "Are they coming?"

No, my brothers couldn't just leave deployment in Afghanistan, Iraq or wherever the hell they were to come to a party. "No, Mom. They can't make it. They'll be home in March. Remember?"

"Oh yes, yes, that's right." Mom glanced toward the front door. "What about Phillip? Is he going to drop by?"

I jammed my hands onto my hips. Dad hadn't been here in years—not since my twenty-first. "No, Mom. Dad won't be here either." He'd be gallivanting around the country somewhere with Tina, his new fiancée. His latest Facebook post came from Buffalo.

My mother shot forward and caught my hand. "Have you been crying? I hope it's not over some boy. Is everything alright?"

No, everything wasn't alright. Everything was shit. Dealing with Hayden and walking in here and finding Mom staring out the window and not taking her meds wasn't fun. Nothing was right. But I couldn't say anything, or Mom would get upset, judgey, and more depressed than she already was.

I pulled my hand free and headed over to the fireplace. On

my knees, I stacked kindling and logs in the grate and struck a match. Rubbing my hands together, I warmed them against the growing blaze. "I'm fine, Mom. I'm just tired after working in D.C. last night." *And from fucking Hayden and only getting four hours sleep. But I'll survive.* "I'm excited to be here to celebrate your big day. They're happy tears."

Mom pointed her finger at me. "You don't look happy. Did something happen at the show? Where's Hayden? I thought he was coming with you."

"No, he stayed with Gem and the guys." I sat back on my haunches. "Oh, Mom, you should've seen Hayden play last night." Just mentioning him caused my heart to swell. "He nailed it. I've never seen him play like that before. He was absolutely amazing." As I fought back my smile, warmth flooded my chest. His performance had been incredible . . . in and out of bed. *Tick, in favor of being with him.*

Hmmm.

Could I decide whether or not to be with him by tallying my ticks?

Could I just weigh up the basic pros and cons, and not over-analyze the depth of my true feelings like I'd tried to do. Would that work? *Maybe.*

"Did something happen between the two of you?" Mom's tone hardened with a cold edge.

"No. Why?" Could I get away with lying to my mother?

Mom shook her head slowly. "I've told you a thousand times, don't mess around with him. Don't go falling for a guy like that. He's a musician. Music is his life."

"I know." Mom was right. I'd never come first. *That was a cross against him.*

"Don't make the same mistakes I did." Anguish darkened her eyes. "Hayden's a sweet guy, a good friend. But he's like your father. He's a free spirit, likes his women. He'll disappear the moment something brighter and shinier and younger comes along."

Mom's words speared my heart. Hayden wasn't like that. He'd always been faithful and committed to his past girlfriends. The girls had always called it quits, not him. He'd never strayed from his music. He was truly dedicated and passionate. *Hmm.* I liked that about him. *Tick in his favor.*

"Mom, I love being single. I have no interest in having a boyfriend. I never want to get married." But my chest ached. One day . . . I wanted those things.

Mom's gaze sharpened. "Good. You're too young to worry about that nonsense. Don't go chasing after some guy. You'll end up pregnant and ruin your career like I did."

There it was. The nail in the coffin. The dig at me for being a mistake. It was always a highlight in many of our conversations. I grabbed another log, jammed it on the grate, and prodded the fire with the poker. "Thanks for the reminder."

"You'll thank me one day. You only need to look after yourself."

"Yes, Mom." *Got that message. Loud and clear.*

My parents' constant battle over money had always been a central theme in their arguments. After having me, Dad had wanted Mom to go back to her job in marketing. But she didn't. She'd blamed me for ruining her career. I was unplanned, born eight years after my youngest brother, Billy, and she'd taken too much time off work to care for me. Youthful, more qualified people had filled her position. Dad had kept pressuring her to find work, but she'd given up. So had he. It had fed their bitterness and resentment and killed their love. It didn't help that Mom's condition had worsened every year. The end result . . . divorce.

Dad had always wanted more out of life. Mom had no such drive.

That was another thing I had in common with Hayden. We were motivated, wanted more out of life and were hungry for success. *Tick in his favor.*

Shit. The scales were tipping in his favor. Was it this easy?

Was he great to live with? Yes. *Tick.*

Was he neat and tidy? Absolutely. *Tick.*

Did his drums take up too much space in our living room? Yes. *Cross.*

Would our careers tear us apart? Yep. *Cross.*

Nope. This wasn't easy.

"Lexi, dear? What's troubling you? You're not your happy self today."

Happy? I didn't know what that was anymore. I was happy until Hayden had kissed me, told me he loved me, and in the next breath had said he was leaving. *Cross against him.* I rose to my feet, glided over to the floral sofa, and sank into the cushions. I buried my face in my hands to wipe the sting from my eyes. The marrow in my bones ached. "Hayden moves to Boston in three weeks."

A deep *"hmm"* rumbled in my mother's throat. "So what's the problem?"

I sniffled and stared at the ceiling. I closed my eyes and shook my head.

"Oh, shit." My mother's hands fell into her lap. "You stupid girl. You're in love with him, aren't you?"

"*No.* No, I'm not." It wasn't love. Surely it wasn't love. But, fuck . . . I liked him a lot. "I'll just miss him."

"Did you expect to stay roommates forever? Don't be silly. It's time you two moved on. You're better off without him."

My breath shuddered through my chest. It would be best to let him go. But life without Hayden seemed dull and void. I rubbed my temples. My head hurt from too much thinking, too much crying, and too much emotional bullshit. I'd had enough. I'd deal with Hayden later. "You're right, Mom." I slapped my hands against my thighs and summoned a smile. "Today isn't about him. It's about you. Come on, we have a party to organize. Let's get ready."

I helped Mom to her feet and sent her off to change. Maybe I should pop one of her pills to relieve my anxiety. *No, don't go there. I'm not like Mom.*

I headed out to my car and unloaded the foil trays of baked vegetables, pasta salads, roast meats, and dessert treats, and placed them inside on the kitchen counter. As I put the last one down, I glanced out the window, across the snow-covered garden. Avery, Mom's best friend from next door, came through the open gate juggling two plates of food. "Yoo-hoo. Celina."

Trudging through the couple of inches of snow, Hayden rushed to assist her.

What? My heart hit panic mode. *What the fuck is he doing here?*

Chapter 19

My pulse rang in my ears like loud, clanging pots. I wasn't ready to see Hayden. Not yet. No. No. *No.* I hadn't processed last night or decided what to do about us.

How did he get here? Just inside the garden gate, he grabbed the dishes from Avery and headed toward the back door.

Before they passed the kitchen window, I ducked beneath the counter, sat, and slammed my back against the cabinet.

My mother came into the room and glared at me on the floor. "Lexi, what are you doing?"

I crawled across the tiles to the kitchen island. "Shh. I'm hiding."

"Who from?"

"Hayden."

"Oh. I thought you said he wasn't coming."

Heat rushed up the side of my neck and burned my cheeks. "I can't see him. Not now."

"Why not?"

Because I fucked him last night. Why do you think? My blood pressure spiked even higher when the door banged open and footsteps headed my way.

"Happy birthday, Cel." Avery hugged Mom.

"Hey, Celina." Hayden's deep voice filled the room. "Happy birthday."

"Thank you, dear." My mother sighed. "I'm feeling old as the hills in this cold weather."

I rolled my eyes as I curled into a ball behind the island, doing my best to avoid being seen. My mother was so overdramatic. *Says me, cowering behind the cabinet.*

"Lexi here?" he asked. The plates of food slid across the countertop. "Her car's out front."

Mom kicked my foot. "Yes. She is. She's right here on the floor."

Fuck. Thanks, Mom. *Not.*

I sprang to my feet, my heart thudding against my ribs. "Hi." I wiped my clammy palms on my dress. "What are you doing here?"

"We got back early." Hayden thumbed toward the front door. "Kyle loaned me his car. I went to see Mom, then came here."

"How is Anita?" I asked.

"Hating detox. Still in rehab, so that's a good thing. But . . . " Concern rippled through his eyes. "What were you doing on the floor?"

"Um . . . Mom dropped an earring." I said the first thing that popped into my head.

Hayden glanced at Mom. Two dangling red earrings hung from her earlobes. "Oooookaaaay. Did you find it?"

"No." I lifted my chin. "I'll look for it later."

He took a step toward me and lowered his voice. "Can we talk? Please?"

"I've gotta get the food ready."

"Don't be silly." My mom swatted at the air. "Avery and I can do that."

Hmm, her meds must've kicked in. She was way too cheerful.

"It's okay. I'll help." I reached for a tray to put in the oven, but she caught my arm and dialed down her volume. "I don't know what's happened between you two. I can only guess. So, go. Talk. And don't make any more foolish mistakes."

Thanks for the pep talk, Mom.

Hayden held out his hand. "Please?"

"Is there any way I can get out of this?"

"Nope." He shook his head.

"Fine." I stepped over to the sideboard, grabbed the stereo remote and turned the music on so Mom and Avery couldn't eavesdrop.

Taking Hayden by the hand, I dragged him down the hallway into my old bedroom—the pottery studio—and shut the door behind us. The smell of damp earth, paint, and turpentine filled the air. Old bedsheets lined the wooden floor, used paintbrushes stood in bottles of cleaning solution on the worktable, and blocks of clay sat on the shelves where I used to have hundreds of books.

As I ambled over to the desk by the window, where Mom's latest creations of vases and bowls sat on display, clay crumbled under my boots. My hand shot over my mouth. All the cups and saucers Mom had posted photos of two weeks ago were smashed to smithereens on the floor. No doubt the result of another one of her meltdowns. I reached for the broom behind the pottery wheel, but Hayden caught my shoulder.

"Lex, stop. We need to talk." He pulled off his scarf and coat and tossed them on the chair by the door.

"Why? You didn't talk to me after our kiss at the ice rink." I winced, pulling myself up on my sarcasm. I didn't want to be snarky. We needed to move forward. If he still wanted me—which was no doubt why he was here—I needed to make my choice. "I'm sorry. That came out wrong. We always talk. About everything. Can we *not* not talk?"

Furrowing his brow, he closed his eyes and nodded. "I was afraid you'd say our kiss was another mistake. I didn't want to hear that before the show."

My heart lurched like a shunting train. I used to read him, know what he was thinking, but I'd pushed him away one too many times. "Well, you should've." I added a pinch of sauciness into my tone. "We might've ended up in bed sooner."

"Really?" His voice cracked like a teenage boy's. "Damn." He rubbed the back of his head, ruffling his fingers through his messed-up hair. "Read that wrong, didn't I?"

"Yeah, you did."

He took a step closer and caught my hands. "And what about last night? Have I got that wrong? Please tell me it wasn't a mistake. I hated that you'd left this morning without talking or saying goodbye."

"I had to come here." I retreated a couple of feet, needing some distance between us. Why was being in the same room with him awkward again? So hot? I fanned my face and tugged on the neckline of my knit dress. My body temperature had jumped. I felt like I was wearing thermals in the middle of summer.

"I could've come with you." He eased a fraction forward.

"You'd said you wanted to stay with the band." I sidestepped to dart past him, but he caught my arm.

"Lexi . . . stop. Did being together change anything? Mean anything?" His stormy eyes searched my face as if looking for answers, but my brain was still a scrambled mess.

I lowered my chin. The rims of my eyes stung like acid. "Of course it meant something. It was amazing."

"But?"

"What do you want from me, Hayden? If it's for me to throw myself at you, say I love you, and race off to Boston with you, you'll be disappointed. I can't do that. I don't want to hurt you any more than I have. Last night was good . . . incredible . . . great. But as for the next step . . . I have no idea. I don't know how to sort out my feelings."

"Let me help you work them out." He cupped the side of my face and swept his thumb across my cheek. "Be mine. Let's find out if this is something."

No. Too close. Breathe.

"We have too much history." I ducked under his arm and stepped out of his reach. The hot rush from standing close to him still shimmered across my skin. I just needed a second to think clearly.

"That's why we'd be so good together." He stormed over to me near the bookshelf. "Stop running away from me. What's killing me is that you're not being honest with yourself."

"I am being honest. Why do you want things to change?"

"Because we could be so much more."

"We are everything."

"No, we're not." He grabbed and clasped my hands against his chest. His heart thudded hard and raw beneath my fingers as his gaze bore into mine. "You're so pigheaded. I'm not taking no for an answer. Not this time." Determination set in his jaw. "So . . . let's make a deal."

"A deal?" I jerked back my chin. I tried to tug my hands free, but he held them tight.

A small smile played across his lips. "We have three weeks. Give me the chance to convince you we belong together and prove you have deeper feelings for me. If I can't, I'll leave. No strings attached. We'll go back to being friends. But if this evolves into something more . . . fuck, wouldn't that be awesome? And maybe down the track, you can move to Boston."

I squeezed my eyes shut and shook my head, my curls flicking my face. "I can't move." A lone tear slid down my cheek. I pulled my hands free and waved toward the door. "I walked in here today and found Mom sitting in the dark. She hasn't taken her meds for days. Mom needs—"

"Lex." He placed his finger over my mouth. "I'm sorry you found her like that." Anguish swung in his voice and swirled through his eyes. "I should've been here with you." He hung his head for a quick second before he lifted his chin and met my gaze. "But stop using her as an excuse. We'll hire help. Stop closing yourself off and denying yourself the chance to find happiness. I hate seeing you like this." He wiped my tear away with the tip of his finger, then tucked my hair behind my ear.

"I was happy until you first kissed me," I whispered.

"Kissed you like this?" He cradled the back of my head and drew my lips to his.

I placed my hands on his chest, ready to push him away, but my body had other ideas. His lips were too perfect. His touch, too impossible to resist. Clutching onto his coat, I held him close, absorbing him into every cell. Stars and clouds swirled behind my eyelids. Was this what I wanted? *Him?* The fire igniting in my heart threatened to burn down my walls. Hayden wasn't making this easy.

I tore my lips from his and gasped for breath. "What are you doing?"

"Kissing you." He kissed me again and walked me backward to the desk by the window. He picked me up and placed me on top. The desk slid. The legs scraped against the wooden floor before it slammed against the wall. *Smash.* A cup from the batch Mom hadn't broken joined the others on the floor. *Oops.*

But Hayden's lips never left mine.

"Lexi?" Mom's voice drifted down the hall over the music. "Everything okay?"

Shit. My pulse spiked. Tugging on Hayden's hair, I ripped my lips from his. "Yeah, Mom. We'll be out soon."

Hayden's grin screamed, *"No chance."* He edged between my legs and kissed me, harder and hotter.

God, his mouth. Every part of me craved more of his touch. The heat rising between us was hot enough to melt the snow on the roof. But this was too much. Too soon. Too intense. *Was it? Fuck.*

With all my might, I pulled back and panted. "Hayden. Stop." My heart shuddered. My head spun. But as I flattened my palm on his chest and met his intense gaze, the air warped. He cared for me, loved me, wanted me. I'd be crazy not to give us a shot. I had to let go of my fears. "Do you think we can do this? Be together?"

"Yes. I honestly do."

Could I risk our hearts, our friendship, when I knew love died? The thought of losing him crushed me, but the thread of hope to see if we could be something more grew stronger every day. "I'm afraid."

He brushed his fingers down my cheek. "I am too." His voice was barely above a whisper. "But I promise to catch you if you fall."

"Do you think you can change me?"

"I don't ever want to change you, Lex." He grabbed my hips and tugged me forward on the desk. His gaze penetrated my soul. "I just want you to be happy. Give me the chance to make you happy."

I clutched onto his shoulders. I'd never seen him this adamant before, this determined, this fierce . . . about me. He was like this about his music, but he'd never been like this about any other girl.

"We can do this." The husky rumble in his voice and the want in his eyes sent fire rushing through my veins.

But reality squeezed my heart. "I don't want to move to Boston."

"Okay." He ran his hands up my arms and cupped my neck. "We'll cross that bridge when we come to it. We'll make it work."

I had to believe him. I trusted him with my life. I didn't want to end up lonely, depressed, and bitter like my mother. I didn't want him to be another Quintin.

Taking a shaky breath, I slid my gaze along the line of his chiseled jaw down to his mouth. I caught my bottom lip between my teeth. His sweet taste still lingered on my tongue. He'd woken something inside of me I'd ignored for too long. Something I'd refused to acknowledge. But now, I wanted to explore, excavate, and examine how deep my feelings were for Hayden, in every possible way.

"What do you propose?" I whispered. "Do you just want to fuck me for the next three weeks and see what happens?"

He groaned and drove his crotch against mine. *Fuck.* My insides were still hot from being with him last night. His lips twisted into a smile that was as delicious as a flambéed crepe. "If that's what I have to do, then yes." He touched his lips to mine. Just a tease. A quick taste. A promise. "But I want to do more than that, Lex. I know you. And you know me. I want you to be in this. To be mine. And to be one hundred percent honest with me."

Feverish waves rushed across my skin as the reverberations of his want-filled words hummed across my lips. *Three weeks.* Could I dive in and not drown in the process? *Hell*, I was already in too deep. "*If* we do this . . . " I ignored the flare of hope in his eyes. "We don't tell anyone, not even Gem, Kara, and the guys. Not until we know what this is. They're away until the first weekend in January, so it shouldn't be hard."

He slipped his hand beneath my curls, cupped my neck, and

nuzzled into the soft spot beneath my ear. "You know they have an uncanny way of finding shit out?"

"Yes, but hopefully they won't. I don't want the girls drilling me for details. I don't need Mom lecturing me about this being a mistake. Please . . . promise me.?"

"Lex, we're not a mistake." He looked me square in the eye. "But I warn you, if we do this, I'm not holding back. Once we get home, every second we're not at work, we're together. We're going to *be* together, go everywhere together, do everything together. Not as friends, but as lovers. Be prepared for sexy dates, dirty texts, and hot, hot fucks. Okay? If we're caught, tough."

My core clenched. My thighs squeezed his hips. Butterflies spiraled through my stomach. "Okay."

He bent his knees and peered up at me. "So, are we doing this?"

Losing him terrified me, but I'd regret it if I didn't find out if this was something special. *Were we doing this?* I clutched his shirt and nodded. "Yeah."

The brightness and warmth of his smile enveloped me and sent tingles skipping across my skin. I barely had time to draw a breath before his lips were on mine. As I wrapped my legs and arms around him, a canister of pencils hit the floor. *Crap.* We were making too much noise. I didn't care anymore. I kissed him back, flicked my tongue into his mouth and tasted his sweet lips. *Mmm,* he felt so good, and kissed like a fucking rockstar.

My mother's fresh words of warning swam around inside my head. My damaged heart pounded against my ribs. My doubts rattled through my brain. But . . . I'd decided.

I wanted to be with him.

I prayed I wouldn't regret my decision.

I prayed this wouldn't destroy us. If it did, I had no doubt I'd end up like my mother.

I'd put my faith in Hayden's hands. Trusted that this was right.

"So now what?" I whispered against his lips.

"Let's start with this." His voice rasped in his throat as he slid his hands down to my ankle, unzipped my boot and took it off.

He did the same to the other foot. With a wicked glint in his eyes, his hands disappeared underneath my dress and pulled down my tights and panties, eased them off my feet. He fell to his knees. Nudged my knees apart. Rendered me speechless as he kissed his way up my inner thigh. With a flick of his tongue, his mouth claimed me.

I stifled a moan. My head fell back.

Holy. Fuck!

Luckily, I was sitting down because my legs had turned to jelly. I clutched at his hair, pulsed against his tongue. My mind exploded like a fucking firework.

Oh, sweet Jesus!

What the hell had I gotten myself into?

Chapter 20

LEXI

Lying in my bed with my back against Hayden's chest, and his arm draped over my waist, I glided my fingernails over his forearm. The fine hairs tickled my fingertips. I hadn't had a boyfriend in so long I'd forgotten how cozy morning cuddles could be. Hayden had hugged and comforted me many times before, but never intimately. This was nice. Taking the plunge into a full-blown relationship still rattled my nerves. I didn't have my "Five Fs" dating game to fall back on. I had no wingman, no escape, and had to stop thinking we were doomed from the start. I had to trust this feeling swirling around in the depths of my stomach. I genuinely wanted to give us a real chance. I had to truly cross the friends-to-lovers line to open my heart. We'd had a magical moment in Washington, a heated moment at Mom's three days ago, but we hadn't spent any time together since then. He'd been called in to fill in on Broadway and had worked long hours at the studio. I'd had a hectic schedule reviewing Christmas specials at restaurants all over Manhattan and Brooklyn.

He'd crawled into bed at three a.m. after a late gig.

Today was Christmas. We had no set plans.

The anticipation of being with him again flickered inside me like a slow-burning flame. It tempted, teased, and taunted me. It triggered my anxiety. *Maybe I wasn't good enough. I hadn't met his expectations. He'd tired of me already.*

No. He was here. Right beside me.

"Morning." He nuzzled closer and kissed the back of my shoulder through my flannel pajamas.

"Hey," I whispered, afraid to move. Had my overactive thoughts somehow woken him?

"Hmm." He hugged me tighter. "Waking up next to you is the best Christmas present ever."

"You didn't ask Santa for a Ferrari?"

"Nah. I can't fit my drums in a sports car." He rolled on top of me and propped himself up on his hands. "I need a big-assed Griswold station wagon."

"Ooh . . . such a sexy machine." Giggling, I curled my legs over his.

He rocked his hips forward. Through his pajamas, his morning hard-on pressed against my crotch. Heat touched my cheeks. I covered my eyes with my hands and wrinkled my nose. It was still hard to get past the fact that he was my best friend.

"Lex." He chuckled and drew my hands away. "Just good morning. This is weird for me too. But it's nice." He tilted his groin toward me again, and a soft growl rumbled low and deep in his throat. "Mmm . . . very nice. Like I said to you at your mom's, I'm going to prove to you we're good together. Trust me."

"I do." I cupped his face. "But some lines are hard to cross."

"You think?" A hint of mischief shimmered in his eyes. "We've had sex and I went down on you at your mom's house. We've already crossed a few."

I pursed my lips as fire crept up my neck. At Mom's party, we'd pretended nothing had happened between us while we mingled with the guests, but every brush of his arm against mine, every stolen glance, every conversation had stirred the embers we'd ignited. Mom had continually glared at us and had shaken her head. Avery had kept giggling and winking at me. Aunt Nora's big smile had turned into a frown when I'd fumbled my way through telling her Hayden was no longer single and wouldn't give her any details.

Hayden was mine, at least temporarily. My head hadn't stopped spinning with excitement, fear, doubt, and hope. I really didn't want to fuck this up.

He kissed the tip of my nose. "We're going to have fun. I promise. My first plan of attack is to buy your affections."

"What?" I slapped his shoulder. "I don't want anything, and besides . . . you already have them."

"Good, then this is a bonus. Stay here. I'll grab your Christmas present."

"You want yours, too?"

"Hell, yeah."

Hayden dashed into his bedroom. I zipped to the bathroom to relieve myself, then grabbed his present from my closet and jumped back into bed. As I drew the quilt over my lap, my eyes widened when he walked in carrying a huge rectangular present wrapped in Christmas paper. Like Lionel Richie, my heart danced on the ceiling. I knew the shape of a boot box when I saw one.

I glanced at my twenty-inch-long gift box for him. I winced and held out the slender present tied with a red ribbon. "Does size matter?"

"Nope." He jumped on the bed, crossed his legs, and placed my present beside him. His beaming grin lit the room as he flicked his gorgeous brown hair off his face.

I eyed my present. "What have you done?"

"I kept my promise."

Oh! The night of the Everhide's concert. The night he kissed me. He'd promised to buy me boots.

Hayden rubbed his hands together. "Who's first?"

"Maybe we should open our presents at the same time."

"Deal."

He placed the big box in my lap, and I handed over his. "On the count of three . . . one, two, three."

Ribbons were untied and paper was ripped.

The Jimmy Choo logo shimmered gold across the top of my box. My heart skipped a beat. My hands trembled as I lifted the lid. The most gorgeous pair of black leather boots with a two-inch chunky heel lay nestled within the tissue paper. Tears welled in my eyes. The boots were perfect. "Oh my God, Hayds. You shouldn't have. These are too expensive."

"True, but you're worth it. Luckily Everhide paid me."

I picked up one boot and glided my hand over the long gold zipper, then smelled the gorgeous, soft leather. *So divine.* I leaned forward and kissed him. *Hmm. Definitely good.* "They're gorgeous. Thank you."

"You needed something you could walk in. I don't want you killing yourself in your stilettos when I'm not around."

Shuffling around on the bed, I pulled the boots on as he lifted the lid off his present. Crinkles formed at the edge of his eyes as he smiled and stared into the box. Lifting out the set of drumsticks, he chuckled and read the etching. "Lexster and Haydster." One name on each.

"We're a pair, no matter what happens." I had to believe that.

"I love 'em." He winked as he spun the sticks around in his fingers. "Now I get to play with you every day." Pushing the wrapping paper and boxes aside, he crawled over me. As he kissed me, I fell back onto the mattress. "So?" He murmured against my mouth. "Do the boots fit?"

I wrapped my ankles around his waist. "Perfectly." I threaded my fingers through his hair and kissed him. *Hmm. Definitely nice.* He lowered his weight onto me. His roaming hands ventured down my side. Our kisses grew heavier. Hotter. *Yeah . . . okay. This was better than good.* "Want another present?" I asked.

"Does it involve you naked?" He kissed his way down my neck.

I eased off his shirt. "Yeah."

"Awesome. Leave your boots on."

But just as we'd gotten rid of our pajamas, Hayden's cell phone rang with Kilt's ringtone.

"Ignore it." He kissed and played with my boobs. His touch was soft and ticklish . . . and a hot turn-on.

But Kilt kept ringing.

"Shit. I better answer it." Hayden reached over and grabbed

his cell phone off the nightstand. He swiped the screen.

Kilt's voice screeched through the speaker. "Merry Christmas, motherfucker!"

Hayden wiped his hand down his face. "Dude, it's ten a.m. What the hell do you want?"

"Me and the boys, we've been thinking and drinking."

I rolled my eyes. By the slur in Kilt's voice, he'd definitely been drinking. At this hour? Or was he still on a roll from last night?

Kilt hollered even louder. "We want to have a huuuge party at my house for New Year's. You in?"

"Sure. Now fuck off. Oh . . . Merry Christmas." Hayden ended the call and tossed his phone aside. Flicking the bedsheets high, he shifted over me. Skin on skin. Heart to heart. Connected.

"Hmm." He swept his lips over mine. "We did not need that interruption."

"Wait?" My hand shot up to stop his kisses. "New Year's? At his house?"

He kissed my fingertips and drew my hand away. "You're included. No questions."

"But . . . I thought . . . we're not telling our friends about us yet, right?" New Year's was less than a week away. I wouldn't be ready to tell everyone about our relationship by then. Lewis would be cool, but Kilt and Reg would act like jerks. I didn't get along well with them at the best of times. I didn't want to deal with our friends, or Boston, or our future—I wanted to stay locked in this bubble with Hayden and never leave.

"Lex." He ran his hand down my thigh, grabbed my knee, and drew it up by his side. "I'm sure we can have a good time without them finding out. We've done the friends thing for years."

Worry spiked through my veins. "So you'll be able to keep your hands off me all night?" Maybe he could, but if this kept going the way it was, I was worried I wouldn't.

He dipped his head, kissed my lips, my neck, my shoulder. Goosebumps darted across my skin. A smoldering smile full of way too much sexiness curled the corners of his mouth. "If it's just my hands, I'll be fine."

Tease. I could play this game too.

Wrapping my booted feet around his hips, I wriggled beneath him, teasing his cock against my pussy. I glided my hands over his shoulders and scraped my fingers down every ridge of his muscled back. "That means no touching, no flirting, no midnight kiss?"

"Hmm." His eyes darkened. "If I have to go to a party and can't do those things, I better get my fill of you before then."

"Okay."

He grabbed a condom from the nightstand and put it on in record time, then buried himself inside me. As his body moved against mine, a wave of warmth coursed through my veins. My nerves dissipated. Lost in the moment, our souls connected. We were on a path I'd never expected. I had no idea where this road would take us. It excited and terrified me. Filled me with elation and doubt, happiness, and fear. But there was one thing I was certain about . . .

I fucking loved my new boots.

***

After visiting Mom's for Christmas lunch and Hayden's mom for afternoon tea, I used the heavy snowfall as the excuse to stay indoors for the next two days. Hayden and I hardly left the bedroom. But by the time New Year's came around, I still couldn't put a label on my feelings for Hayden. I didn't want to, because the word that had filtered through my mind scared me.

Being with Hayden felt as natural as morning sunshine. But our trial-run relationship was nearing an end. Soon, we'd have to face reality, deal with Boston, long-distance, lonely nights, and commitment.

Was this thing between us worth continuing when he left?

Was it love or just some crazy fun?

I needed something inside my brain to click and produce a Polaroid that revealed the answer. I had ten days until he left.

The New Year's party at Kilt's house in Williamsburg was as wild as Woodstock. Friends and family danced and ate and drank enough alcohol to sink Brooklyn into the East River. People filled every inch of the tiny kitchen, small living and dining rooms, and overflowed into the courtyard. The upstairs bedrooms were occupied as well, but I didn't want to think about that. Not when I had to keep my hands off Hayden and vice versa. With a few too many champagnes under my belt, I couldn't wait to take him home and have my way with him.

By two-thirty a.m., the party had died. A few stragglers—Reg, Kilt, Basil, and a couple of other partygoers—had disappeared into the basement to smoke pot. The sickly stench drifted into the living room. Hayden was quick to jump off the sofa, shut the door and light some vanilla-scented candles.

"Do you wanna go home?" I ruffled my fingers through my curls.

"Soon." Hayden returned to sitting behind me on the sofa and drew me against his chest. "It's nice just chilling, listening to music, holding you."

Nestled between his legs, I tugged the quilt over us and let my head fall back onto his shoulder. Cuddling like this pushed the boundaries of our just-friends pretense, but it was cold, Hayden was warm and I was just too damn tired and comfortable to contemplate moving.

The gas fire flickered brightly. Video clips played quietly on the flat-screen TV. Kilt's grandpa snored in the corner on his rocking chair. Lewis and his boyfriend Emilio were wrapped up in a blanket, asleep on the other sofa.

As Hayden draped one of his arms over my shoulder and across my chest, and the other one low on my stomach, my eyes fluttered closed. If I wasn't careful, I'd fall asleep too.

He slipped his hand underneath my sweater and stroked his thumb against my skin. His touch was like a sedative, calming and relaxing.

With my curls hooked out of the way, he kissed the soft spot beneath my lobe and made his way up to my ear. "I love you in my arms."

I smiled and cuddled his arm. The scent of his sandalwood

cologne filled my head. "Yeah. It's nice."

"Wanna know what I love more?" His fingertips glided across my stomach, drawing tiny circles in their wake. Then he stopped, fumbled with the top button of my jeans, and popped it open.

I grabbed his wrist, but he drew my hand away with his free one and pinned it to my chest. "Shh. Sit still. We don't wanna wake Grandpa."

Grandpa's head lolled forward, and he continued to snore.

"Grandpa's not the one I'm worried about," I whispered. "But Lewis and Emilio are right there." I jutted my chin toward them.

"Then don't move and no one will notice anything." Hayden's voice lowered to a dangerous level of sweet seduction that ignited my insides. He licked and nipped at the rim of my ear. "I wanna touch you."

"What?" Just his words, and his hot breath rushing down my neck, sent jolts of electricity straight between my legs.

"I've wanted to be with you all night. Please?" He lowered my zipper ever so slowly and cupped my pussy.

"Hayden. Stop." I squeezed my knees together, capturing his hand.

"Lex, let's have some fun. Let me make you feel good. Trust me."

Fuck! He knew me better than anyone else. We'd always had a great time together. I trusted him. There was no facade. And he'd fucking turned me on.

I was game.

The quilt tented over our knees. If I didn't move, no one could see he had his hands down my pants. Could I do this in a room with other people? They were asleep. Right?

"I've got you. I promise." He grazed his teeth over my earlobe.

"I know." I melted against his chest. He'd never do anything to hurt or embarrass me. I could do this. I wanted his touch.

I wriggled my butt to loosen my jeans and to give him more access.

He smiled against my hair as he dipped his hands into my Levis and rubbed his fingers over my silky panties. Doing this . . .

in Kilt's living room . . . was hot. *Damn hot.*

"That's my angel. Now relax."

"It's hard with Grandpa over there," I whispered.

"Close your eyes." He fumbled with the top edge of my panties and slid his hand inside them. My whole body was on fire, and he hadn't even touched me yet. "Pretend you're asleep." Slipping his finger into my slit, he stroked me up and down. He growled low into my ear. "Fuck, I love it when you're wet."

Holy fuckity fuck, alright.

So hot.

I wouldn't need much fingering; it wouldn't take me long to come. I'd pop just from his panty-dropping voice rasping in my ear. This was insane. Scrunching my nose, needing more of his touch, I let my knees fall wider.

"Don't screw up your face." He chuckled against my hair.

Panicked, I glanced around the room, but no eyes were on us. Pulling the quilt tight under my chin, I turned my head toward his chest. His thudding heart and heavy breaths charged every nerve in my system. Slipping his other hand underneath my sweater, he cupped my boob. Played with it. Teased my nipple. I was losing my mind. This was crazy. Anyone could walk out of the basement at any moment. Lewis and Emilio could wake at any second. Grandpa, too.

"You feel so good." Hayden stroked my clit in slow, torturous circles. Dipping his fingers inside me, a moan rumbled deep in his throat. "And fucking turn me on."

He tilted his hips and pressed his hard-on against my lower back. I bit my lip. I liked having that effect on him. Maybe I could reach behind me and touch him? But when I shifted forward, he pinned me to his chest.

"Stay still."

"I can't."

"Yes, you can. If you don't . . . I'll stop." He stopped moving his hand with two fingers buried inside me.

Oh wow. My insides clenched around him, greedy for more of his touch. I wanted to rock my hips and pulse against his palm. Get friction. Get off. "Fuck. Don't stop."

"Then be good." His voice was soft velvet in my ear.

Oh . . . I liked him taking control.

I ran my hand down his leg and clutched onto his jeans. Taking a deep breath, I sank into his chest. I was at his complete mercy. "This better?"

"Much." He kissed my neck as he thrust his fingers deep inside me, then dragged them toward my clit and rubbed it. He did it again. On repeat. *Oh my god. So good.* My arousal soaked his fingers and my panties. His other hand tugged the cup of my bra aside and teased my bare nipple.

Fire ripped through my veins. My breath quickened. I curled my fingers around his thigh and dug them into his muscle. My knees fell wider. Slowly, with the smallest of hip pulses, I fucked his hand.

"Mmm . . . there," fell from my lips.

Hayden's heart hammered against my back. His breath was hot and heavy in my ear. He rubbed me harder. Drove into me deeper. Stroked me faster. Each touch wound the tension in my muscles tighter and tighter, like a fuse about to blow. I tried not to move too much. My breath shuddered. My chest ached. My hips twitched.

"Fuck, you do it for me." He nipped and kissed the small of my neck as he rubbed my clit harder and faster.

"Oh, wow." A jolt of electricity shocked my body. My orgasm ripped through me, shuddering through every cell, coiling up my spine and tingling my toes.

"Hayds?" Lewis's sleepy voice drifted from the sofa. "What time are we practicing on Friday?"

Fuck!

I couldn't breathe. My heart had lodged in my throat. My orgasm still coursed through my entire body.

Fuck. Fuck. Fuck.

Terrified of being busted, I pretended to sleep.

Hayden chuckled into my neck, held me tight and took a steady breath. "Um . . . not until after lunch. Two, I think."

"Are you okay, man?" Lewis quizzed Hayden.

"Yeah. I've just got a dead leg. Lex is asleep, and I don't want to wake her."

Like hell I was. The heat in my cheeks was hotter than coals in a fire. I gripped Hayden's thigh tighter to let him know I was in agony.

"Okay." Lewis lowered his voice. "We're going to go home."

I took a quick peek. Lewis dragged Emilio to his feet, and they grabbed their coats. Before they turned, I snapped my eyelids shut. My insides still pulsed and throbbed against Hayden's hand stuck down my panties. *Shit.*

His chest vibrated as if he chuckled, enjoying my torture too much.

"You wanna share an Uber?" Lewis said quietly.

"No, we're good." Hayden rested his head against mine. "I'll see you on Friday. Night guys."

"Night," Lewis said.

Once Lewis and Emilio left, Hayden removed his hand from my panties and nuzzled against my ear. "Oh my God. How fucking hot was that?"

I slapped him on the arm. "We nearly got caught . . . but yeah, it was hot."

"Would you like me to do that to you every night while we watch TV?"

"Or we could do this?" I turned around onto my knees and shuffled beneath the quilt. I unzipped his jeans and freed his rock-hard cock.

"Lex. Shit." But he didn't stop me—he just adjusted the quilt and wriggled his ass so I could pull his jeans lower.

Taking him into my mouth, I licked and kissed and sucked him. I pumped and stroked his smooth, velvety cock and massaged his balls. He buried his hands in my hair. His heavy moans and pulsing hips urged me on. It took him less than thirty seconds to blow his load.

"Fuck." He slumped against the sofa arm. "You truly are an angel."

I flicked off the quilt, rinsed my mouth with the remains of my champagne sitting on the coffee table and did up my jeans. I couldn't stop smiling as I stole a kiss from his lips. "We're even."

"For now." He zipped up his fly.

"Let's go home."

"Sure." He called an Uber and grabbed our coats off the floor.

Walking past the rocking chair, Grandpa chuckled, his head still drooping forward. "You sly dogs, you."

Oh shit. Grandpa had been watching.

Laughing, we raced outside and into the Uber.

Hayden's eyes glinted as he hooked his arm around my shoulders. "We just gave Grandpa the best thrill he's probably had in years."

"How embarrassing." I buried my face in my hands. "I'll never be able to go there again."

"Good thing you won't have to. We won't be here."

That was a low blow to my stomach.

As the car headed toward Manhattan, Hayden's looming move to Boston pressed heavily against my chest. My feelings for him were still as unsettled as boiling water. Love hadn't smacked me over the head and dragged me into a cave like it had when I'd met Quintin. Insta-love had been so quick, easy, and undeniable. But with Hayden, I'd known him for so long I didn't know how to distinguish friendship from love.

For my peace of mind, I needed certainty, stability, clarity. I had none of those things.

But sleeping with him had changed me.

It had made me question everything about my life. My work. Taking care of Mom. What I wanted for the future. I'd been stuck going nowhere since Quintin had left. I'd given up on my photography. I'd avoided close relationships for too long. They were things Hayden had been telling me for years, but I'd been too shut off to notice and had ignored him.

But now I was aware of everything. I had so many decisions to make. Once I sorted out what to do with my career and Mom, I was certain my future direction with Hayden would become clear.

As we crossed the bridge, the car wheels thudded against the road.

He entwined his fingers with mine and kissed me on the temple. "I love you," he whispered.

I squeezed his hand and nuzzled my cheek against his shoulder. "I know you do."

He chuckled and held me tight.

When I was with him, he made anything and everything seem possible.

I eased my hand beneath his coat and rested my palm over his heart. The steady beat soothed my troubled mind. I didn't want to worry about what lay ahead. I wanted to savor the moment. Be present. Because right now, in his arms, everything felt perfect.

And perfect never lasted.

But maybe, just maybe, this time would be different.

Chapter 21

LEXI

I jumped off the subway at East 23rd Street and rushed up Madison Avenue toward Everhide's office. Running ten minutes late—thanks to Hayden distracting me in bed this morning—I picked up my pace, dodging dawdling pedestrians, dashing across busy streets, and skipping over piles of snow sludge. Gemma and the guys were back from their travels and had called me in for a meeting. They'd been vague about the agenda, only hinting that it had something to do with my photography.

That had escalated my nerves. Had something gone wrong with the photos I'd taken at the concert two and a half weeks ago? I'd been monitoring the number of hits and comments on their social media accounts. The results had seemed great. Surely they would've told me by now if there had been a problem. Had I missed something? If there was an issue, I'd do my best to fix it.

Sweat beaded underneath my thick curls as I waited for the traffic lights to change at a crossing. Now that my friends were home, I had to be careful. They'd no doubt ask what I'd been up to. I had to remain elusive about Hayden. But Gemma was often too perceptive. I didn't want her to grill me for more information in the middle of our meeting. I didn't want to lie. Hayden and I were having a lot of fun, in and out of the bedroom. But I still didn't know what label to put on my feelings. With only a couple of days left until he moved to Boston, he'd be expecting an answer about whether or not to continue our relationship. My blood ran hot and cold with every yes and no outcome.

Maybe I should just flip a coin. Let it decide.

No, I needed to be brutally honest with myself. After this meeting, when my nerves weren't on edge, I'd find a nice, quiet bar, order a wine—maybe a bottle—and sort out my head and my heart once and for all.

By the time I walked into the lobby and took the elevator up to Everhide's office, my stomach was tied in more twists and knots than a pretzel. I had to put on my best poker face and make it through this meeting. I could do that. *Easy.*

Pulling off my coat and scarf, I followed the receptionist to the meeting room and stepped inside. Gemma, Kyle, and Hunter were already sitting at the round mahogany table, talking to Bec, Kate and Sophie. Folders and documents, laptops, and tablets were scattered before them. *Hmm . . . planning day.*

"Hey." I dumped my purse on a leather office chair. "Sorry I'm late. Subway was a bitch. How was Japan?"

"Awesome." Gemma jumped up and gave me a quick hug. "The shows were huge."

"It's so good to see you." I rubbed her arms. "I've missed everyone." After I rushed around the table, hugging and kissing everyone hello, I sank into the chair beside Gemma.

"How was New Year's?" Gemma asked. "Did you and Hayds do anything fun? We've been so crazy busy. I haven't heard much from you."

Shit! I smoothed my hands over my dress pants and summoned a cool smile. *Just breathe.* "Um, I've been busy too. And no . . . nope . . . we didn't do much. We went to Kilt's for New Year's. That's it." *And we'd gotten each other off on the sofa. And we've had copious amounts of sex in every room in our apartment since then, multiple times a day.*

Fuck. Was it hot in here?

"Fair enough." Gemma shrugged and hooked her hair behind

her ear. But her gaze remained glued to me. The hair on my arms stood on end.

Was Gemma onto me? *Damn it!* I hadn't said anything.

I swallowed hard. My hands trembled as I grabbed the jug of water and poured myself a glass. "So, what's up? Why did you call me in for a meeting?"

Seriousness set on everyone's faces. My pulse jumped even more.

Kyle leaned forward and flicked his dark blond bangs off his face. "What's happened with your job at *Gourmet Reviewer*? Do you still like it there?"

Wait. What? "Um ... No, it's been awful since the incident with Chase. The promotion was canceled thanks to him. So I'm stuck doing the same old thing—blogging, reviewing, racing across the boroughs." I glanced around the table. "Why? What does that have to do with anything?

"Maybe everything." Hunter leaned back in his chair and threw me a lopsided grin. "We've run into an issue that needs fixing." He waved his pen at Bec, Sophie and Kate. "These three can't keep up anymore."

"Why? Are you too much of a diva? And constantly give them grief?" I slapped him with my usual dose of sarcasm.

"Me? A diva?" His fake shock morphed into a humble grin. "Okay. But only sometimes. You know me too well, Lexster."

"So true." Gemma laughed and nudged her elbow against my arm. "Lex, our popularity has grown, and the behind-the-scenes workload has gone into overdrive. We've reached the point where we need to expand our team. And we wondered if you'd be interested?"

My heartbeat rocketed skyward, hit the space station, and hurtled back to Earth. *Holy shit.* This was not what I'd been expecting. Not at all. "What? Me? Work for you? Doing what?"

"Photography and marketing. We'd like you to be our full-time photographer, help Kate with our publicity and socials, and work with our creative team for shoots and video clips, and on the documentary Sophie just roped us into doing."

Oh. My. God! My heartbeat thundered in my ears. I placed my hand over my somersaulting stomach to stop it from cartwheeling down Madison Avenue. Tingles shivered across every inch of my skin. Tears welled in my eyes. After my work dramas, I couldn't believe what I was hearing. But doubts slammed into my head. "Marketing? I don't know anything about marketing."

"Yes, you do." Kyle jerked his chin back. "It's what you do now. Kate needs help writing articles and press releases. If you make us sound as amazing as the food in your reviews, we'll be super happy. We'd love you to come work for us."

I stared at the table and blinked. *Wow.* But . . .

"Lexi, your photography is stunning." Kate opened a folder with printouts of some shots I'd taken of Everhide and sifted through them. "Your talent has grown over the years. You've got a great eye for detail. Your pictures are raw, sexy, and fun. We need this type of material for socials. Every time these guys go somewhere, get dressed, perform, or tour, we need to post something online. Bec and I are so busy, we often forget. And we're not professional photographers like you. We'd love you to join us."

The breath shot from my lungs. Praise from someone other than my friends made my head spin. Kate had given my confidence a massive, much-needed boost. Hayden had always said I was good; maybe I should believe it.

Before I could say a word, Kyle added, "All travel, accommodation and expenses are covered in addition to your salary. We'll be writing and recording our new album over the next few months, so that will give you time to settle in, work with us and our creative team to come up with our new image, look and feel, before we release singles, go on promo and prepare for our next tour."

"Tour?" I closed my eyes. A deep throb erupted inside my head. "Like . . . go with you around the world?"

"Um . . . yeah." Hunter chuckled. "It's what we do."

"For months on end?" *Travel?* My stomach sank like a rock in quicksand. I'd desperately wanted to see the world, but could never afford it. I'd only been overseas once. To Belize. With Kyle and Gemma for their wedding. Visiting different countries would be a dream come true. London was at the top of my list. It had been my number-one place to visit with Hayden. *Oh . . . Hayden. No, don't think about him right now*. I had too many responsibilities, bills to pay, and an apartment to maintain. I couldn't leave New York for months on end. I had to keep an eye on Mom. "I'd love to, but my mom—"

"Lex?" Gemma clutched my hand on the table. "I know you care for your mom, but you've always wanted to travel. It's not like you'd never see her. We have a few breaks during those long months away. You can come home and visit her. You can call her every fucking day if you have to."

I pulled my hand free and wiped my clammy palms on my dress pants. Could I do this? Leave my boring but stable job and follow my dreams? This was an opportunity of a lifetime. I burned for it. Craved it. Nothing I'd done to date had advanced my career. Nothing I'd done with my life had pleased my parents. It was time to do something radical. Something for me. Hanging out and working with my friends would be a dream come true. I always missed them when they traveled. I'd be doing photography, learning something new, doing something exciting, something I loved, but . . . I'd never see Hayden. *Oh . . . shit . . .* Traveling around the world would put more distance between us than between New York and Boston.

Shit! Pain stabbed my chest. What was I going to do?

This changed everything.

I pressed my hands against my cheeks and wiped tears from my eyes. "Gem, guys, this is incredible. I'm in shock. I don't know what to say."

"You don't have to answer right away, Lex," Kyle said. "Sleep on it, take a couple days. But we'd like to know before we head to LA next week."

"Okay. I can do that."

"We'd love to have you come on board, Lexi." Sophie gave me an encouraging smile. "Maybe this will help you decide." She handed me an employment contract.

I flipped through the pages.

Holy fuck! . . . The salary was four times the amount I earned at my current job, plus an expense account, health insurance and benefits. A tear slid down my face. I felt like I'd won the lottery.

But Hayden . . . when would I see him?

Bec grabbed the box of tissues off the shelf behind her and handed them to me. "Lexi, you're already part of this family. You'd be a true asset to the team."

"Thank you." I dabbed my eyes and blew my nose.

But Gemma swiveled toward me. She narrowed her eyes and stared at me. My skin prickled from my head down to my toes. She leaned closer. "Guys, can I talk to Lex alone for a few minutes, please?"

"Sure." Kyle stretched his hands above his head and stood. "We'll go grab coffee. Want one, Lex?"

"Yeah. With cream and sweetener, please. Oh . . . " My hand shot over my chest. "Will I have to get you coffee if I take the job?"

Hunter laughed and slapped Bec on the shoulder. "Nope, that's Bec's job."

Bec smirked and punched him in the arm. "I'm just your bitch, aren't I?"

"Yeah, but we love you." He ruffled her hair as they left the office. Kyle, Kate, and Sophie followed them.

The second the door closed, and the latch clicked, Gemma pounced. "What the hell is going on? Why are you not jumping at this job? It's not about your work or your mom; there are solutions for those two things. So it's Hayden, isn't it?"

A shudder ripped through my body, and my heart hid behind my ribs. My tears turned to acid. "No." *Liar.*

Gemma turned my chair to face her, and she grabbed my hands. "We love Hayds, so much. But he's decided to move to Boston."

"I know." I sobbed, trying to pull myself together. *Boston is so far away. Why does he have to move?*

Gemma straightened and her eyes widened. "Oh my God. You slept with him."

"What? No. How did—?" Did I have it stamped on my forehead?

"Because you're a blubbering mess. You won't look at me. Your cheeks flushed at the mention of his name. Maybe I've just had too much media training. I know when you're fucking lying."

"I'm not." There wasn't an ounce of conviction in my voice. *Pathetic.*

"You. So. Did." Gemma gaped and swatted my knee. At the top of her voice, she shrieked, "You slept with Hayden and didn't tell me?"

Kyle and Hunter fell through the door.

"You *what?*" Kyle's eyes bulged to the size of donuts.

"About fucking time," Hunter cheered, placing my coffee on the table.

"Get. Out." Gemma pointed to the door. "Now!"

"But we need the details." Hunter grinned, nudging me on the shoulder.

"Out." Gemma pointed to the door again.

Kyle pouted and Hunter protested, but they reluctantly obeyed and headed toward the door.

"Oh, we're so calling him." Hunter patted the front of his leather jacket and ripped out his cell phone.

"No!" I screeched, half-standing. "Please don't. Please let me talk to him first."

Hunter halted. He slipped his cell phone back into his pocket and winked at me. "Spoilsport. You've got until this evening. Then we're onto him." He chuckled and closed the door behind them.

I lowered back into my chair and deflated like a balloon. So much for keeping our relationship a secret. *Shit.*

Gemma clasped my hands again. Intrigue shimmered in her eyes. "So, are you two a thing now?"

"No. We're . . . not." I lowered my chin. I cared for Hayden, loved being with him, but this job offer was my dream. Was there any way to continue seeing him and take on this role when I'd rarely be at home? A shudder coursed through my bones. I was crushed by the answer. "We're just having some fun before he leaves."

"What are you doing?" Gemma shook my hands. "He really loves you."

Thanks Gem. Now you're making me feel like shit. "I know. But he knows the deal."

Wait. That was right.

We had a deal.

A deal I could walk away from, no questions asked. We'd gone past the point of fun and games. But this job was life-altering; the career I'd craved for so long. I couldn't turn my back on this. Just as my relationship with Hayden had evolved, this would bring it to a skidding halt.

"Are you sure it's nothing more?" Gemma quizzed with concern. "It's okay if it is. We still want you to work for us. When we return home after traveling, we'll ensure we get you to Boston to see him. That's easily done."

Job, Hayden, job, Hayden, ping-ponged through my mind like a ball ricocheting between the bumpers of a pinball machine.

Then the ball dropped.

It hurt like fucking hell.

I clutched at my chest. Regardless of how strong my feelings for Hayden had grown, this was about chasing dreams—Hayden's dreams and mine. We'd worked so hard and had wanted to make something of our lives. Hayden had wonderful opportunities ahead of him. So did I. The light was finally shining on us, but it would tear us in different directions. I never wanted to stand in the way of his music. He lived and breathed it. I didn't want to tie him down or hold him back. He needed to be focused. Be dedicated. And not worry about me.

Taking this job was a no-brainer. But the travel put dating Hayden into the realm of impossible.

Before we grew more serious, before we hurt each other, before our feelings turned into resentment and died, I had to let him go. I wanted the best for him, always. "Gem, I assure you. There is nothing serious between Hayden and me. We're just awesome friends." A knife twisted in my heart, dug in deep and cut it in two as the words left my mouth. "But I will miss him like crazy."

"We miss both of you when we're away." Gemma stroked my hair. "But don't worry. You will see him. You can catch up with him every couple weeks or months. It'll be fine."

I blinked away my tears. "You're right. " *Wrong.*

Worry darkened Gemma's eyes. "Are you positive you're *just* friends?"

Nodding rapidly, I straightened my shoulders. "Yeah . . . just friends."

Fuuuuck! No.

We were so much more than that . . . No.

No, we aren't. No.

We're just friends.

If I wanted this job, there was no other option.

I had to end things with Hayden.

Lucky I was sitting down, otherwise I'd collapse onto the floor.

"Well then . . ." Excitement jumped through Gemma's voice. "Stop hesitating and fucking come and work for us."

I flung my arms around her. "Yes. Yes, I will. Thank you. I love you so much. You have me. Two hundred thousand percent."

"Yay!" Gemma shot back and clapped.

"I can't wait." I trembled all over."

This will be amazing.

It would be.

But how the hell was I going to tell Hayden?

Deep down, I'd wanted to give our relationship a chance, do the long-distance thing, but this was a life-changing opportunity. I stared at the employment agreement. The ache in my chest twisted and throbbed. This was my dream job. But Hayden wouldn't be around to share it with. He'd been the one who'd encouraged me, supported me, slipped those initial photos to Gemma. He'd opened the door I would've never stepped through otherwise. He'd made this happen. How would I ever thank him? He'd made my dreams come true.

Now I had to help him with his.

There was only one way to do that. I just hoped we were both strong enough to survive it.

Being together wouldn't be fair on either of us.

My job needed commitment. Devotion. Dedication.

So did his.

I needed to give Everhide my all. I wouldn't let my friends down.

No holding back.

My heart looked to the heavens and cried. Before I took on the role of a lifetime, I had to face my toughest assignment yet.

I had to call it quits with Hayden. End it. End one of the best things in my life to pursue another.

It was time. Time to say goodbye.

Chapter 22

HAYDEN

Towel-drying my hair, I walked out of my bathroom dressed in my best jeans and white sweatshirt. My muscles thanked me for the hot shower. Practice this morning had been brutal. Prepping a surprise for Lexi had been a rush. I'd never done anything romantic; I wasn't the romantic type. But I was about to give it a shot. The weather had turned sleety, so indoor activities—movies, massage, and good food—were on the agenda. And over some fine champagne, we'd plan to see each other when I moved to Boston.

Fuck. Two days to go.

I glanced around our transformed small living room. I'd draped Lexi's favorite twinkle lights over the big photo hanging on the brick wall of the two of us on the Brooklyn Bridge. Vanilla-scented candles flickered on the bookshelf, spilling an ambient light across the darkened room. I'd ransacked our closets, beds, and the sofa to create a comfy pile of scattered cushions, pillows, and quilts on the floor in front of the TV. Her favorite Bollinger champagne chilled in the fridge. The plate full of her go-to chips, cheeses, crackers, and chocolate was ready and waiting on the kitchen counter. Rom-com movies on Netflix were set to play. All going well, I'd be licking her favorite mango ice cream off her body for dessert.

I rubbed my hands together. Our date was on. This afternoon would be perfect.

Keys jingled in the door lock, and my pulse jumped.

Lexi walked in, glanced toward my setup on the floor, and froze with her keys still stuck in the lock. Her red-rimmed eyes filled with tears. Her chin trembled, and she sobbed.

My heart slammed against my ribs as I rushed to her side. "Lex?" I shut the door, took her purse, and helped her shrug off her damp coat.

She pursed her lips, scanned the rest of the room, and shook her head. "Oh, Hayds. What have you done?" Her tone was full of overwhelming sadness, not happy delight.

That wasn't the response I'd been expecting. "I planned a romantic afternoon. But it can wait." I wrapped my arms around her. As she pressed her cold cheek against my shoulder, she shivered like a kitten in the rain. I rubbed and stroked the back of her head. "Angel, what's happened? What's wrong?"

Her hands clutched the waistband of my jeans. The tension contorting her body planted fear in the pit of my stomach. I held her tighter. Whatever it was, we'd get through it.

She eased out of my embrace and placed her trembling hand on my chest. Her face warped from happy to sad and back again. "Gem and the guys offered me a job."

"What?" My chest swelled. My heart leaped toward the ceiling. "So why are you crying? That's incredible, isn't it? What do they want you to do? Just another show?"

She sniffled and wiped her eyes with her palm. "No. It's full-time. Doing photography and marketing."

"That's brilliant." My voice pitched high.

"I know. It's totally mind-blowing. They want me to start as soon as possible. I've got so much to learn. So much to sort out with Mom. And get up to speed on their projects."

Stepping in close, I smoothed my hands over her hair and braced her face. "Angel, I'm so happy for you." I was beyond ecstatic. But I didn't like the distance darkening her eyes.

The reality of working for Everhide smacked into me like a

car crash. The travel, the long hours, the time away from home. They'd offered Lexi her dream job. But *Fuuuuck.* Where did that leave us?

I closed my eyes and took a steady breath. "This doesn't change anything. We can still be together. We'll make it work."

Just when I was certain she loved me and would commit to a long-distance relationship, had my best friends ripped her from my fingertips? *God, I hoped not.*

She drew my hands away from her cheeks, lowered them and held them between us. She pursed her lips and shook her head. "There's nothing to work out."

"Yes, there is." I gave her hands a gentle shake. "We're a good thing. We'll come up with a plan."

She lowered her chin and let go of me. "Hayden, don't make this harder than it has to be. You need to focus on your music. I need to focus on my new role. We have to be realistic." Her tone, full of resignation, hit me like a ton of bricks. "Long-distance never works. If I was here all the time, we might've had a slim shot, but not now. Not when I'll be away so much."

I wouldn't accept this. "Can we at least try?"

She half-turned toward the wall. "Don't you understand? I'll be gone for months on end. You'll be in Boston, doing gigs, recording, and hopefully touring. We'll never see each other."

She snipped at my heartstrings, one at a time. I spun her around to face me. She wasn't going to hide from me. Not ever. I caught her arms. "We'll make the effort, Lex. We'll fly to see each other. Call each other. Catch up whenever you're home."

"It's not that simple." Her voice quivered above a whisper.

"It is. I would spend every dime in my pocket to come see you. You know that."

Tears welled in her eyes. Her shoulders slumped. "You're moving to save money. We'd see each other for a while, then it would become too much of an effort. The excuses would start. You'd end up hating me. I couldn't handle that. I don't want to go down that path again."

I wasn't having a bar of this. "I won't give up on you like Quintin did. You know me better than that. He didn't love you like I do."

She edged back a foot, and pain rippled across her face. "Please don't say that."

I'd say it a million times if it got through to her. I shot forward and cupped the back of her neck. "We're meant to be together."

"No, we're not." She swayed on her feet. "Our circumstances have changed. You don't need to worry about me. In Boston, you will have girls falling over you. There will be temptation all around. I don't want you to miss out on having fun."

What the hell? This wasn't about trust. She could trust me with her life. Drawing her closer, I inhaled the sweet scent of her perfume, let it consume me, and poured my heart into my words. "I don't want anyone else but you. Don't walk away from what we have."

The nearby candle flickered and caught the anguish in her eyes, but she blinked and it disappeared. "What we've had has been great, but let's end this before we get hurt."

Too late for that. My heart splintered into a million pieces and spilled across the floor. The pain was unbearable. "No."

"We need to be sensible."

Her shields had gone up. *Fuck.* Was there any way I could knock them down? "I don't want to be sensible. I want you." I'd fallen for her hard. I was in over my head. I couldn't crawl out of this ocean in one piece. "Why can't you admit you want me too? What are you afraid of?"

"I'm not afraid." She clasped my arms.

Then why was she trembling?

"We've had some fun." Her tone remained flat and cold, full of steely resolve. "But it's time to go back to being just friends."

This wasn't Lexi. None of this was making sense.

"Friends?" I tilted my head back, hating how the word left a bitter taste in my mouth. Why was she pushing me away? I adored her. I was her rock. I did everything I could for her. But maybe my mother was right. I just wasn't good enough for someone like Lexi. Someone so talented, adorable, and ambitious. She'd finally gotten her break and was going after what she wanted. I'd never stop her from doing that. I was her biggest supporter. We didn't have to end our relationship because we'd be in different cities. I pinned her with my gaze and fought the tears burning my eyes. "Don't do this, Lex. I fucking love you. And you love me."

She winced and slowly shook her head. "I love you . . . as a friend . . . " She closed her eyes. Deep grooves furrowed her brow. "But I'm not in love with you. I don't love you. Not the way you want me to." Her voice slashed and sliced my heart.

A ringing in my ears erupted like a tuning fork being hit with a hammer. I couldn't breathe. My knees buckled. She'd just ripped my heart from my body and tossed it out the window. It went *splat* on the sidewalk below. "That's bullshit, and you know it."

"It's the truth." The tears pooling in her eyes told a different story.

Why was she lying?

"I don't believe you." My whole body shuddered. "Look me in the eye and tell me you don't love me."

She straightened her shoulders and sucked in a deep breath. Her gaze set on me, but her focus was distant, like she looked through me, not at me. Her jaw tensed. "I don't love you, Hayden."

Bull. Fucking. Shit.

"You do," I rasped, breathless and fatigued.

She shook her head. "No. I don't."

"Fuck you, Lexi." My voice cracked with a chilling tone. "Fuck you. You keep telling yourself that, but I don't believe you. What happened to always being honest? What we had was a good thing. But you just killed it. I hope you're happy now." I ripped my fingers through my hair. "Fuck, I should've known you'd tap out. It was stupid of me to think otherwise. I've gotta get out of here before I say something I'll regret."

I rushed into my room, grabbed my coat and cell phone, and charged toward the door. I left Lexi crying near the kitchen and headed out of the apartment. I had no idea where I was going. I just needed to get out of there before I broke something. I wanted to rip the photos of us off the walls and burn them. I wanted to smash my drum kit into a million pieces. I wanted to punch every door. But most of all, I wanted to grab Lexi and kiss her. Kiss some sense into her.

But it would've been a lost cause. Ice had set around her heart.

She'd used her new job as an excuse to end things. But I knew her better than that. She was afraid to admit she loved me. Afraid to give us a chance. I'd tried to win her heart but had failed.

I reached for the door handle to exit our building and stopped. I closed my eyes and took a deep breath. Every bone in my body ached. My eyes stung. If Lexi was too scared to give long-distance a shot, there was nothing I could do to change her mind. I had nothing else to offer. I loved her, but I was done. So done.

I walked outside and stormed down the street. I picked my heart off the sidewalk, threw it into a trash can and left it there to rot. It was broken, damaged, and useless. I didn't need it anymore.

***

Surrounded by boxes, bags, and a suitcase full of clothes, I was packed, ready to go. Only one item remained: my drum kit. I sat on the stool, headphones on, pummeling out a tune. Not my band's songs, but Everhide's. I wanted one last session here in my apartment to bid farewell to these walls. I needed the beat to help me find the words and strength to say goodbye to Lexi.

The past two days had been hard. We'd barely said a word to each other. Now, I was hours away from leaving, and my brain had entered panic mode. Trying to find the right thing to say seemed impossible. It didn't help that I had a hangover from hell. Hunter, Kyle, and Gemma had thrown me a farewell party last night. I'd drunk too much beer and whiskey. Now, each thud of my drums split my head like a lumberjack's axe.

What could I say to the person I'd spent seven years of my life with, had fallen in love with, and now had to leave?

I had no idea. Words were not enough.

Packing had been awful. Deciding what was Lexi's and mine had been a nightmare. We'd bought everything together—the sofa, the flat-screen TV, the kitchenware, the dining table, the rug.

In the end, I hadn't wanted any of it. It would only remind me of her. So I'd left everything in its place. I only needed my belongings from my room and my drums.

As I played another track, the air in the room prickled. The hair on my arms bristled. I looked up. Lexi stood in her bedroom doorway, dressed in sweatpants and a hoodie, and leaned against the jamb. Her gorgeous curls were pulled back into a messy ponytail. *Picture perfect.*

My heart ached just looking at her.

"Sorry," I said, taking off my headphones. "I hope I didn't wake you."

"No. You didn't." She rubbed her hands down her face. "Ugh, I feel like shit. I drank way too much last night."

"Me too."

"I didn't sleep well either." She lowered her voice so much I could barely hear.

"Same." We hadn't shared a bed since she'd gotten the job. Yep, we were well and truly over.

She pointed at the drums. "You're really good. You know that?"

"Time to make something of it." I eased off my stool, ready to pack the kit away into equipment cases. "Boston, here I come."

"Want some help?" She waved toward the drums.

"Yeah. That'd be nice."

She ambled over to my drums, undid a cymbal and glanced at me sideways. "You look like shit."

"Feel it too. JD always gives me a hangover from hell."

"You want me to make you something to eat? A breakfast sandwich?"

"No, thanks." Bile gurgled up my throat. "I can't face food yet."

She giggled. "You must be bad."

God, I'd miss her laugh. "Yeah. I am."

We worked in sync, dismantling my kit and packing it into cases. After stacking the last box by the door, a heaviness washed over me. I headed into the kitchen with Lexi for one last coffee.

I glanced at the clock.

The minutes were ticking by too fast.

My heart didn't want to face life without her, but it had to. "So, our first big gig outside our in-house stint is in four weeks, on Saturday, the eighth of February. You gonna come?"

"I'll be there. I promise."

"Won't you have to check with your new bosses?"

"Nope. It's already on our schedule."

I took a seat opposite her at the small dining table and sipped my steaming coffee. My chest ached. This would be our last morning having coffee together for weeks . . . maybe even longer. Something we'd done for years had come to an end.

She stared into her cup. "The house Kilt's dad found you looks nice. Total bachelor pad."

I'd had nothing to do with it. But it had four bedrooms and was close to our new gig. That was a bonus.

I pinched my eyebrows together. "I've never lived with guys before. Is that weird?" I'd spent most of my school years and the first six months of college with foster families. Once I'd gotten a part-time job, I'd moved in with Lexi. That seemed like a lifetime ago.

"No." Lexi blew into her cup. "You'll have loads of fun."

"It won't be the same without you." The truth hurt.

The buzzer rang. *Shit.* I jumped up and pressed the intercom.

"Heeeey! What's up, motherfucker?" Kilt's voice crackled through the speaker. "You ready to roll?"

Crap. Kilt was early. I glanced at Lexi, and my heart screamed. I didn't want to say goodbye. I wanted to reach out and never let her go. I closed my eyes. "Yeah, man. Come on up." I pressed the button.

Moments later, Kilt, Reg, and Lewis slammed through the door.

"Lexi, baby." Reg held out his arms. "Give me a goodbye hug."

She gave everyone a quick embrace, but she was quiet. She kept glancing at me. Fuck, this was harder than I'd thought.

"Let's move." Kilt clapped his hands. "Let's get your shit in the truck and hit the road."

The guys grabbed cases, boxes, and bags and headed out the door. After a few trips, my gear was crammed into the removal truck. Standing on the sidewalk as cars zipped down the narrow street, I dusted my hands off on my jeans. "Guys, I need a few minutes to say goodbye to Lex." Nausea pooled in my gut. My chest ached. Fuck, I didn't want to do this.

"No worries, man." Kilt lit a cigarette. "We'll wait here. Don't be too fucking long."

I dashed up the stairs into my apartment. I stood in the middle of the living room and took in my home one last time. *Fuck.* My empty bedroom, visible through the open door, looked weird without my bed. The living room looked twice the size without my drums filling the corner. Even my towel was gone from the hook on the bathroom wall.

Lexi ambled out of the kitchen, head down, hands stuffed into the pockets of her hoodie.

My heart cried. Tears threatened to fall. "So . . . this is it. This is goodbye."

She nodded and cried. I stepped forward and wiped the dampness from her cheeks. "We're going to be okay. You know that." Our friendship would survive, but my heart had been broken. It needed time to heal.

She sniffled. "I'm gonna miss you."

"Me too." I whispered. "More than you'll ever know."

"Come here, goose." She held out her arms, and I fell into her embrace.

Closing my eyes, I held her tight against my chest. I just stood there. Breathing her in. Unable to let her go.

She sobbed against my shoulder. Fuck, she was killing me. Breaking my heart again and again.

"You'd better go." She tapped my back.

"Yeah." I eased out of her arms and stroked her perfect curls. I glided my fingertips down the side of her face, taking every detail in—her lips, her gorgeous skin, her smile. But before I turned into an utter mess, I had to get out of there. "See you in a month." I spun on my heels and headed toward the door.

"Hayden," she called out, her voice a croaky whisper.

I stopped and stared at the old floorboards. Fuck, my heart

couldn't handle this.

"I'm going to miss you. So much," she wept.

My vision blurred. She still couldn't say what I wanted to hear. I wanted her to tell me she loved me. Tell me to stay. Tell me to be hers. But . . . no such luck.

It killed me because I still loved her. So fucking much it hurt.

So this was it. This was goodbye.

I turned and took one last glance at her. I wanted to rush over to her, to kiss her, hold her, touch and taste her, one last time. But no . . . too much damage had been done. "Bye, Lex."

I turned and rushed out the door. I left my heart behind on the floor.

Lexi was right.

Love hurt. Love killed you inside.

Love. Totally. Sucked.

Chapter 23

LEXI

My cell phone buzzed and beeped. *What the . . . ?* Fumbling in the dark, I grabbed it off the nightstand. As I rubbed my eyes to focus, Hayden's name lit the screen. *Finally.* But at three a.m.?

I'd heard from him only once since he'd left for Boston a week ago. He'd sent a text to say he'd arrived, but that was it. He hadn't replied to any of my dozens of messages or calls. *That hurt.* I missed him like crazy, hadn't slept well, and worried about him constantly. The gut-wrenching look on his face when we'd said goodbye still burned in my brain.

I'd nearly caved. I'd wanted him to stay and to be mine. The words had hovered on my tongue. My feelings had threatened to escape. But letting him go was for the best. So our lives could flourish, we could chase our dreams and our friendship could survive.

I opened his message.

HAYDEN: I MISS YOU.

I replied.

ME: MISS YOU TOO.

Seconds later, he video-called.

"What are you doing?" I whispered. *Why?* There was no one to wake. Just me. In my bed. Alone.

"Aaaangel." His face filled the screen as he hollered through the speaker. *Oh my God, he was drunk.* "I miss you. So fucking much."

The noise in the background was deafening—music and laughter and cheering.

"What's going on?" I tugged and straightened the pillow beneath my head. "Are you having a party? At this hour?"

A lopsided, drunk grin inched across his mouth. "It's been one big fucking party since we got here. It's insane."

Glass shattered behind him, and he burst into raucous laughter. "Reg, you dick."

"Fuck you, Hayds." Reg's voice slurred somewhere off-screen.

I rubbed my forehead, ignoring the party chaos. "Hayds, why haven't you texted or called?"

"Wait. What?" He tapped his ear. "I can't hear you. Hold on."

The party noise drifted into the distance as he ran upstairs, down a hallway and into a bedroom. He closed the door behind him, cutting off the music. "Sorry, what was that?" His voice, louder and clearer without the rage going on around him, sounded like he was right next to me. I wished he was.

"Why haven't you called?" I repeated.

He sank onto his bed and placed his beer on the nightstand. He swayed as he rubbed his fingers over his scruffy chin. "Because just thinking about you fucking hurts, Lex. I don't think I've been sober since I left."

I clutched at my chest and fought the sting in my eyes. "I never wanted to hurt you."

"Yeah, well. You did."

"I'm sorry." I touched the screen, and stroked my finger over the image of his hair, wishing I could erase the worry lines embedded in his brow.

He closed his eyes. A muscle in his jaw ticked. "I want us to work, Lex."

"We work. As friends."

"Fuck being friends. I want more."

My heart constricted like a boa crushing its prey. This

heartache would pass. It would. "I can't give you more."

"You did." His voice, back-loaded with anguish, punched me in the guts. "For two and a half weeks I had all of you. And you had me. We were so fucking happy." His eyes reddened as he raked his fingers through his hair. "Why give up on us?"

"I told you why." Love . . . I didn't love him. I didn't want to risk falling in love to only watch it die. Like all love does. Our friendship meant too much.

"It's bullshit. Complete bullshit." He grabbed his beer and guzzled what was left in the bottle. He waved it toward the phone. "I need another drink."

"Hayden, wait," I called out before he stood. Shaking my head, the pillow rustled beneath my curls. "Don't shut me out. Please don't be angry. You're my best friend."

He closed his eyes, winced, and dipped his chin. "Yeah. I am. But I guess I need more time to get over you."

"How much time?" *Stupid question.*

"I don't know."

"Okay." My chin trembled. "I'm here for you. Always."

He shot me a *not-in-the-way-I-want-you* glare.

I quickly changed the subject. "I start at Everhide's office on Monday."

"That's . . . awesome." He tilted his head to one side and narrowed his eyes. "Everything you ever wanted, right?"

The chill in his tone slid through the air like a puck on ice and struck me hard in the chest. I'd hurt him more than I'd thought. I hated that I'd done that. "Yeah, it is."

"Look, I've gotta go." He stood and headed for the door. "You still gonna come to our first big gig?"

"Absolutely. I wouldn't miss it."

"Cool." He stumbled and hit the doorjamb. "I'll see you then."

He hung up. My screen turned black. Darkness flooded the room. I hadn't expected a call like that. Sniffling and rubbing my nose, I hugged my phone against my aching chest. I cared about Hayden so much. How long was he going to be upset with me? Fear of losing him raised its ugly head in the back of my mind. *No.*

Don't go there. Friends were supposed to forgive each other. He just needed more time to do that.

But the next few weeks didn't improve.

I texted him, but his responses were rarely more than an emoji. I called him, but he cut me off as he was often drunk or distracted by his band. My new job had kept me flat-out busy—writing articles, doing my first studio photo shoot of Everhide, and flying to LA with them for the Grammys. They'd won 'Song of the Year'. I had so much fun hanging out and working with them. But every day, I'd missed Hayden. I missed our long talks about work, and colleagues and friends. I wanted to share all the exciting details about my new role. I hated I couldn't just *pop out* to see him.

I counted down the days until Boston.

Three days before seeing Hayden, he group-texted Everhide and me with an invitation to a party at his house on the night before their show. No message of *'Can't wait to see you'*—just the time and his new address. I dropped my cell phone on my desk at work. I couldn't believe we hadn't had a decent conversation in weeks.

On the afternoon of Hayden's party, I traveled to Boston with Gemma, Kara, the guys, and their security team. By eight o'clock in the evening, we'd checked into our hotel near Hayden's place. We freshened up and headed to his house. Uncertainty about what to expect sat like a lump of lard in my gut. I just prayed Hayden would talk to me . . . and be my friend again.

As our driver pulled onto Hayden's street and stopped by the curb opposite his house, I gaped. "Holy shit!" At least twenty partygoers overflowed onto the snow-ridden street. Heavy *doof-doof* music blared from the crowded home. Lights flashed through the windows. "I thought this party was just for the band and a few friends, not a gazillion people."

"Same." Gemma stepped out of our Mercedes passenger van after Kara. Chester and Giles, their bodyguards, zipped up their puffer jackets and tugged on their beanies as they scoped out the place. Concern darkened their eyes.

"Stay together," Chester warned Gemma. "I don't like this."

"Absolutely," she said, linking her arm with mine.

Hunter, Kyle, and their security, Sam and Mick, jumped out behind us.

Kyle stuffed his hands into the pockets of his leather jacket and winced. "I can smell pot from here. Reminds me of our old parties."

A chill as cold as the night air coursed through my blood. What was Hayden doing?

As we walked toward the house, eyes widened on the faces of party-goers once they'd recognized my famous friends. Inside was like a college party on crack. The stench of alcohol and drugs wafted through the smoky haze. The dining table was covered with bottles of liquor. Broken dining chairs lay on the floor in the corner. Takeaway pizza boxes littered the kitchen counter. People clustered in groups, laughed, shrieked, and downed their drinks.

I dragged off my beanie and stuffed it into my coat pocket with my gloves. I glanced around the place. It looked like it hadn't been cleaned in weeks. Hayden wouldn't handle that.

Gemma slipped her trembling arm around mine. "I'm all for parties. But this is insane."

I tugged her closer to my side. "Let's just find Hayden, say hello, and get out of here."

"It smells like skunks threw up in here." Kara screwed up her nose.

This definitely wasn't her usual Upper East Side party scene.

"Come on." Kyle led us toward the living room at the back of the house.

We wove through the crowded hallway and stepped over random people sitting on the floor.

But when we entered the room, my heart stopped.

Hayden was lying face down on a sofa and didn't move.

I rushed to his side and shook him. "Hayden, it's me. I'm here."

He didn't stir.

I shook him harder. "Hayden."

Still nothing.

The air prickled, and I spun around. Gemma's face had turned ghostly white. She stood frozen, staring at the smorgasbord of drugs on the coffee table—party pills, pot, pipes, cocaine, and crystal meth. She wasn't naïve. She'd had her fair share of dabbling in drugs and wild highs in her earlier days. But after this shit had twisted one of our friends into a psychopathic stalker who'd drugged and kidnapped her, and had been hell-bent on killing her, this would be freaking her out.

Fuck. I needed to wake Hayden. And get Gemma out of here.

"Lex . . . is he okay?" Gemma's voice came out jagged. She clutched her chest as if she were hyperventilating.

I turned back to Hayden. "Hayden." I nudged him hard on the shoulder, then tapped his cheek. But still, there was no response. Panic seized my heart. "I don't know. He won't wake up."

"Shit." Gemma flapped her hands in front of her face. "Lex . . . I don't think I can do this. I can't be here. I'm sorry."

"Don't be sorry. Go. It's okay." I spoke over my shoulder as tears loomed in my eyes. "Kyle, get her out of here."

"Abso-fucking-lutely." Kyle caught Gemma around the waist, Kara did the same from the other side, and they led her toward the front of the house.

Hunter and Mick rushed over to the sofa. While Mick checked Hayden's pulse and vitals, fear held my breath hostage. I gripped onto Hunter's arm for support, praying for Hayden to be okay.

"He's breathing fine. Pulse is good," Mick said. "I can't tell whether he's taken any drugs or if he's just drunk. He stinks like he swallowed a bottle of whiskey."

"I'd vouch he's just drunk." Some relief washed over me. "He doesn't touch drugs . . . or didn't when he lived with me." I didn't know what he was doing anymore.

Kilt sauntered into the room, holding his arms wide. "Lexi, baby. You made it." Then he flicked his upturned nose at Hunter. "What are you doing here, asshole?"

I jumped between them and pointed at Kilt. "What's wrong with Hayden?" My voice sliced through my clenched teeth.

Kilt tilted his head back and laughed. "Nothing's wrong with him. We just popped a couple Xanax into his whiskey to chill him out. He'll be fine."

Hunter grabbed Kilt by the front of his shirt and slammed him up against the wall. "You fucking did what?" Hunter's eyes flared with blue fire. "You drugged him? You asshole. He hates that shit. Why would you do that?"

"Because he's lame." Kilt hissed with contempt. "We want to smoke weed, and pop some pills, and he hates it. Mr. Fucking Goody-two-shoes. It's my house. We wanted to have some fun."

Trembling all over, I fell to my knees beside Hayden. I stroked his hair, which was so much longer and shaggier than before. Scruffy stubble covered his face. He was usually so well-groomed. "Hayden, wake up." I sniffled through my tears, but he didn't move.

Other people had gathered around. Giles and Sam were quick to snatch cell phones from onlookers' hands. They didn't need Hunter roughing up Kilt to hit TMZ's headlines, no matter how much Kilt deserved it.

"You're such an asshole." Hunter shoved Kilt against the wall again. Kilt's head hit the plaster with a dull thud. "Have you been with him to see his mom lately? You want the rehab bed beside her, assfuck? I'm sure that can be arranged."

"Get your hands off me." Kilt shoved Hunter hard on the chest. But Hunter held his ground. Kilt sneered and flicked his hand toward Hayden. "He's fine. He just needs to sleep it off."

Hayden stirred. "Lex, is that you?"

"Oh, Hayds. I'm here." I rubbed his back and kissed the top of his head. But he collapsed into nothing but dead weight against the cushions.

Fear gripped my heart. "Hunt, we need to get him out of here. Can we take him back to our hotel?"

"Sure. Let's go." Hunter charged over, leaving Kilt to slump against the wall like a sack of rotten potatoes.

I grabbed Hayden's coat and cell phone. Mick and Hunter hauled Hayden to his feet. I followed them down the hallway. Sam and Giles cleared a path through the crowd and shielded us as much as possible, but with every step, cell phones flashed and clicked in our direction. I'm sure we'd make the headlines, but all I cared about was Hayden. I had to make sure he was safe. I'd help deal with any publicity nightmare later.

At the hotel, Mick and Hunter dumped Hayden onto my bed. He was still in la-la land as Hunter and Kara helped me take off Hayden's boots, jeans, and hoodie, and tucked him into bed.

"I've called a doctor," Kara said as she folded his clothes and placed them on the desk. "He'll be here soon."

"Thanks," I sat beside Hayden, stroking his hair. I glanced at Hunter sitting at the end of the bed. "Is Gem okay?"

"Yeah, Kyle's with her." Hunter thumbed toward the door. "She's shaken after walking into a shitfest like that."

So was I, but not as bad as Gemma had been. "Thanks for your help. You can go if you like. I'll be okay with Hayden." I gazed down at him, taking in his gorgeous face, wishing he'd open his eyes.

But Hunter and Kara stayed with me. I loved my friends. They were concerned about him as much as I was. Not being around Hayden twisted my stomach. I missed hanging out and taking care of him.

Twenty minutes later, after Dr. Evans had examined Hayden and given him the all clear, he gave us a stern lecture about partying too hard, said goodnight, and left.

Hunter and Kara headed to their room shortly after.

I locked the door behind them. I leaned against the cool surface. Exhaustion deadened my bones. It was only ten-thirty but felt like three in the morning. Wandering toward the bed, I gazed at Hayden sprawled out across the mattress. His hair was a tousled mess. His chest rose and fell as he breathed. His long eyelashes brushed his cheeks. My heart fluttered and flopped like a butterfly that wanted to take flight but couldn't.

I missed him in *my* bed.

No . . . don't go there.

I tossed the thought aside. The pain in my chest morphed into disappointment. I'd longed to see him this weekend. I wanted to spend time with him and have fun like we used to do. Reset our friendship. Why did nothing ever go to plan?

I changed into my pajamas and curled in beside him. Maybe tomorrow, we could start afresh. I drew the quilt up to my chin and snuggled a spare pillow to my chest. It had been a long, emotional day. My eyelids grew heavy. Sleep slowly lured me under.

Hayden lay on top of me.
His gorgeous steel-gray eyes darkened like he wanted to eat me for breakfast.
I threaded my hands through his hair and drew his lips against mine.
I flicked my tongue into his mouth to taste him. Devour him. Savor him.
Murmurs escaped me as I raked my fingers over every muscle on his sculpted back, his shoulders, his arms.
My body moved in time with his, rocking, pulsing, craving.
His fingertips were cool against my burning flesh as he explored every inch of my naked body. Over my legs, my hips, my stomach, and headed between my legs.
Yes. Touch me.
Yes. Yes. Yes!

"Angel?" Hayden's soft voice pulled me from my slumber. "You okay?"

Shit! My eyes popped open and stared straight into his chiseled face. My heart thundered against my ribs. My pussy throbbed and ached. *Oh my . . . it was just a dream.*

Rubbing the sleep from my eyes, I cast my fluster aside. Rolling toward him, I tucked my hands underneath my cheek. "I'm fine. How are you?"

"Perfect." A delicious grin slid across his lips. His eyes twinkled in the dim nightlight spilling softly from the bathroom. "I'm with you."

It happened so fast I barely had time to draw breath. He hooked his arm over my hip, edged his knee between mine and rolled on top of me. Then . . . he kissed me.

My eyes widened. Planting my hands on his shoulders, I

shoved him backward. "Whoa there. What the hell are you doing?" Did he think this was a make-out session? *Fuck no.*

"Um . . . I'm kissing you."

There was way too much sexiness in his voice. But I wouldn't be distracted by it. "No. You're not. You stink." Morning breath and stale whiskey weren't a good combination. I shoved him off of me and shimmied sideways. Sitting upright, I crushed a pillow to my chest. "Don't you remember anything from last night?"

He dragged himself upright and leaned back against the headboard. Confusion furrowed his brow. "Not exactly. But I'm here with you"—he half smiled—"so it must've turned out all right."

He leaned forward to kiss me again, but I held up my hand to block him. "No. Stop. Last night was shit. I don't know what you're thinking, but we *did not* get back together."

"You mean we didn't . . . " He stared at the messed-up bed. Happiness drained from his face like water from a bathtub, sucking my heart along with it. "Nothing's changed? You still don't . . . fuck!"

"You're here because our friends and I saved your life." Exasperation snapped in my voice.

"What?" Scraping his fingers through his way-too-sexy bed hair, he grimaced like I was delusional.

"When we arrived at your house, we found you passed out on the sofa thanks to Kilt slipping Xanax into your whiskey." Anger swelled in my blood like a rising tide. Kilt's juvenile behavior had been cruel, stupid, and dangerous. I clenched my hands. Oh, how I'd love to fucking punch the shit out of that idiot. "Then things turned ugly." I counted on my fingers as I spoke at one hundred miles per hour. "Gemma freaked out at the buffet of drugs littered across the coffee table. Hunter wanted to kill Kilt. People went camera-happy over the commotion. Security had to get us out of there. We couldn't rouse you, so we brought you back with us. We called the doctor. He checked you out. Then—"

"Whoa." He slammed his eyes shut and held up his hand. "Slow down. My head's hurting."

"So it fucking should." I flicked my hand at him. "You wanna tell me what the hell is going on with you?"

"Nothing's going on." He shrugged, but the crack in his voice suggested otherwise. "We had a party. That's it."

"With all those drugs? What the hell?" We'd been to enough parties with drugs present. Hell, I'd even tried a few when I'd first left home, but I'd never touched them after I met his mom and he'd told me countless horror stories surrounding his parents' addiction. I'd never expected to see so many drugs in his home. Not ever.

He stared off into the distance. "I told Kilt not to bring that shit home, Lex. I swear. Even Reg and Lewis told him off."

I wanted to wrap my arms around him, hold him close, and make everything right. But I jabbed my finger against his thigh. "Kilt's supposed to be your friend. But he's a fucking dickhead."

He puffed through his nose. "No, he's not. He's fine."

"Fine?" My blood simmered like a kettle about to boil. "Are you kidding me? You're going to defend him? Kilt *drugged* you."

Hayden lowered his head like it was too heavy to hold up. "He's a good guy. Things just got out of control."

I clutched his hand. "Do you know how scared I was when I saw you on the sofa? It was like finding my mom in one of her down moods. It was like seeing your mother drugged off her head. It was like watching Gemma in the hospital, fighting for her life after being drugged and kidnapped. I don't want to add you to that list."

Losing him would be unbearable.

"You won't have to." He tensed his jaw and looked at me with hard eyes. "You don't have to worry about me anymore, Lex." He swung his legs off the bed and reached for his clothes. "I'm not yours to worry about. Remember?"

Ouch. "Don't say that. I care about you. Always will."

"Well, maybe you should stop." He tugged on his jeans, zipped them up, and pulled on his sweatshirt.

"What? No. Don't say things like that." I crawled across the bed and grabbed his hand. "Where are you going?"

"Home." He yanked free of my hold, pulled on his boots, and laced them up. "I don't need rescuing, Lex."

"You did last night." Why was he being cold toward me? I'd done nothing wrong.

"Clearly, I'm all right."

"Clearly, you're not." I sat back on my haunches. "Every time I've called and you've actually answered me, you've been drinking. Have you been getting wasted every night? That's not you. You're going to fuck up your opportunities here if you keep doing that." I winced at how motherly I sounded. Shit, I'd turned into Kara.

He straightened and glared at me. His eyes swirled with so many emotions I found it impossible to work out what was going through his mind. But then a muscle ticked in his jaw. "It's good here. I've got my band. My music. I'm having fun. Okay?"

I was all for having a good time, but not if it altered your personality. "Why are you acting like this? We're supposed to spend the weekend together. Please don't leave."

He grabbed and shrugged on his coat. "I have a gig tonight. I need to go."

My shoulders slumped. My heart sank. "Fine. But don't shut me out."

He took a step toward the door and froze. "Maybe that's exactly what I have to do."

His voice splintered my ribs and speared my heart. "Hayden. No. What's going on?"

A shallow chuckle burst from deep within his chest. "You don't get it, do you? You came all this way, say you miss me, did everything last night to make sure I'm okay, but you still can't admit you love me."

Love him? No. "I was worried about you. Any decent friend would do the same."

He lifted his chin and glared at me with bloodshot eyes. He clenched his fists by his sides. Every muscle on his face tensed. It was as if every breath would break his ribs. "I have to go. I'll catch up with Hunter, Kyle, and the girls later." The veins in his neck bulged and throbbed. "But Lex, you shouldn't have brought me here. Waking up next to you, I thought my prayers had been answered. I thought we were back together. But I was a fool. Nothing but a fool. The truth is, I'm not over you. I thought I was, but it still fucking hurts too much. I need more time."

He turned and headed for the door.

"Hayden, stop," I cried. I splayed my hand across my chest. "How long are you going to avoid me? We're best friends. Not seeing you or talking to you is killing me."

"Then don't come to the show tonight. Go home."

He charged out the door and didn't look back.

I flopped back on the bed and sobbed into the pillow. This was ridiculous. I wanted to grab the cushion and hit him over the head with it until I knocked sense into him. I wanted to run after him and tell him everything would be okay. I wanted to hold him in my arms until he forgave me for not loving him back.

My heart bled onto the sheets. I'd let him go so he could follow his dreams. I didn't want him to screw everything up by getting wasted all the time. He wasn't like that. He was better than that. Living with Kilt, Reg, and Lewis wasn't healthy for him. I cared for him too much to see him self-destruct.

But if time away from me was what he needed, so be it.

I clutched the pillow to my chest. Tears slipped down my face. I'd do anything for Hayden . . . even back off.

I searched my foggy brain for other ways to fix things between us, but nothing came to mind.

Nothing.

Time apart . . . with no contact . . . was the only option.

I closed my eyes. Fear rattled my heart.

Love died, but not friendship. I had to keep telling myself that. I had to believe we'd be okay soon.

Or had I already lost him? Was it too late?

Chapter 24

HAYDEN

I placed my hands on the kitchen counter and stared at the toaster. Curls of smoke spiraled into the air. The scent of burning bread filled the room. I didn't care. The toast could burn, like the gaping hole in my chest. Lexi hadn't come to my gig last night. I couldn't blame her. I'd pushed her away. Kyle and my other friends had been there, but not the person I cared about the most. I'd struggled through the entire show, but I had only myself to blame.

Even after a month apart, I hadn't moved on.

I missed Lexi every fucking day.

Nothing had gone right since moving to Boston. My band's in-house job hadn't drawn the crowds we'd expected. Our booking agent hadn't secured us as many gigs as promised. Sharing a house with the guys was a nightmare. The partying was out of control. Reg and Kilt were filthy pigs, and Lewis kept disappearing back to New York to see his boyfriend. Any attempt to discuss my grievances had fallen on deaf ears. When I'd lived with Lexi, I'd had a life outside the band. Now, I had none.

She'd been my angel, and now she was gone.

I'd never been this broken before, not even after dealing with my drug-addict parents. I'd never loved a girl so much. I'd put every effort into my music, made something of myself, and had fallen for the one person who had seen me through the worst and best of times. It'd crushed me she didn't feel the same way.

Ugh! I needed to get her out of my head. She'd invaded my every waking moment for long enough. I wanted to feel good again. Be happy. Stop fucking hurting.

Stop the pain.

Stop the chaos in my mind.

I glanced at Kilt's jacket lying on the table. I closed my eyes and swallowed hard.

There was a way.

I tossed the burned toast into the trash, grabbed Kilt's jacket, and headed down to our practice room in the basement. I sank onto the old sofa and dug around inside Kilt's pockets. *Bingo!* I pulled out the silver tin and opened the lid. My fingers trembled as I picked up the small glass vial and thin plastic tube. I blinked away the sting in my eyes.

This had to work.

I shoved aside the pile of music magazines on the coffee table and tipped a quarter of the white powder onto the glass surface. I took the old credit card out of the tin. Shuddering, I cut and sliced the powder, forming two perfectly even, perfectly straight white lines. My gut twisted like rope. Cutting coke was the only thing Dad had ever taught me.

I'd thought it was cool when I was six. My parents had only tolerated my existence when I prepared their drugs. Ignoring the shake in my hand, I tapped the card on the table.

The lines were a runway that promised to take me to a better place.

A better place where I didn't have to think about Lexi.

Where I didn't have to hurt.

Was this what went through Mom's mind every time she snorted a line or injected shit into her veins? She wanted to stop the pain, the ache, and take away the loneliness when Dad was gone for weeks on end driving long-haul trucks. Or was it the need for the high? To feel good, to be happy, to have fun.

I fucking needed all those things.

I rolled the plastic tube between my fingers and peered down the barrel.

As I stared at the cocaine, my vision blurred.

I can do this. I can do this. I can do this.

I need this.

My heart stampeded, pounding like a brute against my ribs. I leaned forward and hovered the tube an inch above the first line.

One hit. Feel better.

Shuddering, I closed my eyes. Childhood memories flooded my mind. I'd been so excited to go to a friend's tenth birthday party. I'd rushed out of my bedroom ready to go, but I'd found Mom passed out on the sofa. Blood had trickled from her nose, vomit had dribbled from her mouth, and her glassy eyes had stared into space. That had been her second OD and trip to the emergency room.

That had been the first time she'd screamed, '*I hate you.*'

My heart lurched against my ribs. For years, I'd watched Mom deteriorate from an attractive woman to the gaunt skeleton she was now. I shuddered, recalling the countless police visits to our house. Being dragged off to foster care. Visiting her in the hospital. Her stints in rehab. Dad was just as bad. My parents had never gotten better. They'd never loved me.

Neither had Lexi.

Lexi didn't love me.

Arrrrgghhh!

Tears sprang from my eyes. The tube slipped from my fingertips, hit the table, and rolled onto the floor.

I couldn't do this. I couldn't go down this path. If I started, I was sure I wouldn't stop. I refused to end up like my parents. I had to fight this, get over this pain—not be tempted by a quick fix. I might not be good enough for Lexi, but I was certainly better than this.

Slumping back, I rubbed my eyes and stared at the ceiling. *Fuck. This. Shit.*

There was only one thing that always made me feel good.

Music.

My drums.

I jumped to my feet and sat behind my practice kit. I picked up my sticks and ran my fingers over "Lexster" carved into one of them. I wanted to snap it, burn it, toss it away . . . but couldn't. I spun it around in my hand and struck the snare hard. I'd hidden my heartache from my bandmates and had tried to drown it out with alcohol. That hadn't worked. So I had to thrash it out of my system.

My life was here now. Without Lexi.

Pumping my foot on the bass pedal, I played around with the tempo. Fast, then slow. Loud, then soft. I didn't care if I woke the guys upstairs. Lexi bombarded my mind. Her contagious laugh when we'd danced at a club. Her cheering when I played. Her infectious smile over morning coffee. The feel of her in my arms and in my bed. *Fuck!* I slammed my sticks against the snares, the tom-toms, and the cymbals. *Bang. Crash. Bang . . . boom. Boom. Boom. Boom. Bang.*

I needed to find the right beat to erase the pain spearing the center of my chest.

Clutching my sticks and digging deep, I drummed out my pent-up emotions. Loss flowed through my fingertips and escaped through each strike. Every single cell in my body screamed.

As I clenched my jaw, I tightened my grip on my drumsticks. I closed my eyes, rattled by the words that formed in my head. Sucking in a deep breath, I swallowed hard. The beat morphed from angry to sad to slow and heavy. Words fell from my lips.

> *I'm staring at the moon*
> *Do you see it too?*
> *Are you missing me as much as I'm missing you?*
> *I'm watching the sea*
> *Hear it calling to me*
> *Are you feeling the same ocean breeze?*
> *I didn't think leaving would hurt*
> *As much as it did*
> *Didn't think I'd miss your laugh*

And everything you'd ever said

Every strike burned my muscles, my bones, my chest. It wasn't enough to release the hurt, so I drummed harder. Faster. Louder.

> *Where are you now?*
> *Where are you now?*
> *Are you thinking about me?*
> *Are you dreaming of me?*
> *Can't you see*
> *I'm lost without you*
> *I'm drowning without you*
> *I'm nothing . . . without you*
>
> *I'm staring at my phone*
> *Wishing you'd call*
> *Did you get my message*
> *And know I'm sorry for it all?*
> *I wish you were here*
> *Lying in my arms*
> *I'm broken without you*
> *'Cause you own my heart.*
>
> *Where are you now?*
> *Where are you now?*
> *Are you thinking about me?*
> *Are you dreaming of me?*
> *Can't you see*
> *I'm lost without you*
> *I'm drowning without you*
> *I'm nothing . . . without you*

Clapping filled the air. My eyes shot open. Kyle and Hunter stood at the bottom of the steps. Thank God it hadn't been Kilt or Reg. They'd fucking laugh their heads off at the emotionally fueled song I'd just played. These guys . . . they'd get it. Understand it. Respect it. No question.

"That. Was. Awesome," Kyle said, stepping toward me. "I thought you didn't write songs."

"I've been tinkering." I shrugged as I sucked in air to regain my breath. "Nothing serious. That shit just came out."

"Good thing I recorded it." Hunter waved his cell phone.

"Please delete it." Grimacing, I grabbed my towel off the floor and wiped the sweat from my brow.

"Nope. Posting it to TikTok right now."

"Don't!" I stood and charged around the front of my drum kit, reaching for Hunter's cell phone.

"Dude." Hunter pulled it away. "Chill. I won't."

"Fuck." I tossed my towel aside, staggered back a couple of steps and slumped onto the sofa. Hunter took a seat beside me while Kyle grabbed the old office chair by the rack of guitars, swung it around and plonked his ass on it.

Hunter spotted the cocaine. His eyes grew to the size of golf balls. "Holy shit." He pointed toward the coffee table. "You didn't, did you?"

"No." I shook my head. *Idiot for even being tempted.* They didn't need to know how close I'd come. "It's Kilt's."

A wicked grin slid across Hunter's mouth. "May I?"

"You?" My heart screamed at Hunter to stop. "Please don't. You haven't touched that shit for years."

"I know." Hunter poured the rest of the vial onto the table and picked up the tube off the floor. His eyes glinted with mischievousness.

I grimaced. I didn't want my friends to go down that path again. "Hunt, don't . . ."

He sucked in a deep breath, smiled, then blew through the tube, sending cocaine into the air. The cloud loomed like a puff of smoke and slowly sank into the carpet. He erupted in a fit of laughter.

"Holy shit!" I joined him. Kyle too. "You just blew an eight-ball away. Kilt will fucking kill you."

"Nah." Hunter put the tube and vial back into the tin and threw it onto the table. "He was so wasted at the after-party last night he won't fucking remember if he took it or not."

"You're ballsy, man." Kyle chuckled as he leaned back in the chair, swiveling it from side to side.

"I know." Hunter bobbed his head and grinned.

I couldn't erase his smile even if I tried. I didn't want to. Getting rid of that shit was for the best.

Kyle crossed his ankles and arms and jerked his chin at Hunter. "You just get off tormenting Kilt, don't you?"

"Yep." Hunter wiped his hands on his jeans and leaned back on the sofa.

"Enough about Kilt." Kyle turned to me. "We're here for you. How are you doing? It's been a bit of a crazy weekend."

"Tell me about it." My voice swung with cynicism. "Nothing's gone according to plan." I'd gotten drunk and drugged on Friday night. I'd driven Lexi away. I'd fought with my band before our gig. And hit an all-time low. "Sorry we haven't hung out."

"Don't sweat it," Kyle said, picking up Reg's guitar. "You played really well last night. You held the show together. Without you and Lewis, it would've been shit. Reg and Kilt were too wasted."

"Yeah. After soundcheck, they'd downed tequila like it was water." I hated it when the guys got drunk or high before a show. That was what we'd fought about. My band and I had to pull our shit together, or venues wouldn't want us to play.

Kyle struck the strings, turned the tuning pegs.

I held out my hand. "Kyle, don't fuck with that."

"I'm not. I'm tuning it. Reg is fucking tone deaf."

Exactly what I'd thought. Kyle strummed the strings. Tweaked the pegs until it sounded better.

Thank God. I'd wanted to do that for weeks.

"Where are the girls? Are they here?" My gaze lingered on the stairs, wishing Lexi would appear. I needed to say sorry for being a jerk. But I didn't want any more conversations to turn into arguments. We needed time apart.

"They headed home." Kyle placed the guitar back on the rack. "Lex wanted to see her mom before we fly to Miami."

"Why didn't she come to the show?" I rubbed at the ache in

my chest. I knew the answer, but wanted to make sure she was alright. "Is she okay?"

"What are you talking about?" Hunter jerked his chin back. "She was there, taking photos and at the bar."

The knife in my heart dug deeper. She hadn't come to see me before the show. Hadn't joined us for a drink after. She'd left without saying goodbye. *Fuck!* She'd avoided me. I'd deserved that.

"Did you two have a fight?" Concern lodged in Kyle's tone.

"You could say that. I'm not handling the way things ended between us. But I'll get over it. I'll be fine." I was counting on it anyway.

But enough talk about Lexi. It wrecked me too much. "Are you guys heading home soon or do you wanna grab some lunch somewhere?"

Kyle glanced at his watch. "We have to take off. But before we go, can we talk business?"

"Why?" My voice turned lackluster. "Are you going to lecture me about fucking up my chances too?"

"Nope." Hunter rested his arm on the back of the sofa. "Quite the opposite. We wanted to wait until after the gig. We didn't want to mess with your headspace."

I lowered my chin and rubbed the back of my neck. "Yeah, I'm not sure my headspace could get any worse. It isn't in a good place right now." I couldn't feel any crappier than I already did.

Kyle chuckled as he tugged on the collar of his leather jacket. "Well, we want to change that. We want to throw something on the table for you to consider."

"Shoot." I flicked my hand half-heartedly through the air.

"Slade gave notice last week." Kyle leaned forward, resting his elbows on his knees. "He wants to be released from his contract on medical grounds. His shoulder is fucked and has to have surgery. Plus, with a new baby, he wants to stay at home. So . . . we need a new drummer. We want you. Are you interested?"

What the fuck?

My heart faltered. My blood pressure skyrocketed as I

replayed every word Kyle had said in my mind. *Slade. Released. Need Drummer.* My pulse whooshed in my ears.

"Me?" I clenched my fist and jabbed it against my thigh. This was not happening. This was such bad timing. If they'd asked me three months ago, I would've jumped at the opportunity. I would've had a chance with Lexi.

But life was different now.

I'd moved cities. I had a new job. I'd given up everything to be here for my band.

The girl I loved didn't want me.

"Yes, you." Hunter slapped me on the knee. "You're a brilliant drummer. We'd love you to join us."

"Fuck." My mind hurtled like a satellite through space. Working for them would be insane. I'd get to travel, record albums, play in front of stadiums full of fans. It would be a dream come true. But Lexi would be there. She wasn't mine. Nothing would ever be the same.

"Fuck what?" Kyle tilted his head. A deep divot formed between his eyebrows.

I jutted my chin toward the staircase. Irritation itched my veins. "I've just moved here. I have a band. Are you doing this because you feel sorry for me? After what happened at the party?"

"Nope. But what Kilt did was fucked." Hunter shuffled around on the sofa to face me. "I know you guys have been together for years, and you're friends. But sometimes you have to look out for yourself."

"I am." Anger twisted through my veins. "This is what we all wanted."

"Hayds, we get that. We know what you're going through." Hunter nodded slowly. "We know what it's like to give up everything to pursue your dreams. The buzz, the high of finally being on the right path. We've been through the phase you guys are in now. We've done the drugs, the parties, the women. You can stay here and keep chasing the end game. We'll always support you, no matter what. But fuck . . . come home. Play for us."

"We want you, Hayds." Kyle fidgeted with his wedding ring.

"You're family. You're part of our lives. It gutted us when you said you were moving. We couldn't do anything about it. We couldn't just fire Slade for no reason. He'd sue our asses off. But things have changed. Slade's injured. There's only one person who can fill that legend's shoes, and that's you."

The corner of Hunter's mouth quirked. "While it would give me nothing but great pleasure to steal you away from Kilt, it's more than that, Hayds." His tone softened, exuding sincerity. "Kyle's right. You're one of us. You're family."

Family. That was all I'd ever wanted. A family to love me and to belong to. To have a place to call home. I'd had that with Lexi, but not anymore. I loved these guys more than my fellow bandmates, but their world involved Lexi. Seeing her every day, being around her and not having her would make it impossible to breathe. "What you're offering is incredible. But . . . I can't. I'm committed to these guys. I can't just pack my bags, come home, and move back in with Lex." My heart hit the floor with a *thud*. "I couldn't live with her again. Not after what happened." My old life was over.

"Then don't." Hunter shrugged his shoulder. "Move into my place until you find somewhere to live."

They weren't making it easy. My dream job of playing at the top butted heads with my heart. I was too broken, too messed up, too lost. "Thanks, Hunt, but it won't be necessary."

Kyle smoothed his hands down his jeans. "I'm sorry it didn't work out between you and Lex. She was so cut up about you leaving. She still is. I think she ended things with you out of love, not because of no love."

I wished I could believe that. But I knew her. She'd never wanted to get close to anyone. I should've known better than to fall for her, but I did. And I'd gotten burned badly. "You're not making me feel any better. I forgot you're a philosophical son of a bitch."

"Always." Kyle grinned. "Can I give you some advice?"

I sank deeper into the sofa and folded my arms. "Knock yourself out. You're on a roll."

"Don't make this decision based on Lexi." Kyle's gaze drilled into me. "Make it about yourself. About music. What do *you* want?

If you live and breathe music with your band, and trust each other with your lives, great. But if you don't, you won't survive. You need to be united on every front. Can you honestly say you are?"

"We're not perfect, but we're good." I lowered my chin. I didn't get along with my band all the time, but we wanted the same things. That was true.

"Hayds, you're our best friend." Hunter leaned forward. "When we're home, you hang out with us more than with your band. You jam with us. You fit into our world. We want you to become a permanent part of it."

I dug my fingernails into my palm. Why couldn't I just say yes? "You don't understand. You're asking me to leave my band." I couldn't quit on them. We hadn't made a mark on Boston. We hadn't done what we'd set out to do. Ever since I'd played for Everhide in D.C., I'd had a new hunger for success. That drive would rub off on the guys. I'd keep them on track. If I walked away, I'd regret not giving this my best shot. I'd feel like a quitter, a failure.

"I understand loyalty better than anyone," Kyle added. "Gem, Hunt, and I have been through hell and back and come out stronger. We've worked our asses off to get where we are. We want you to be a part of our future. I'm sorry we couldn't offer you anything sooner. But please, take some time to think about our offer. We've got a couple months before we have to find someone. Before we record our next album."

Record an album? Fuck, I so wanted to do that. I craved it. "Does Lex know about this?"

"No." Kyle shook his head. "Gem isn't going to tell her either. You need to make this decision on your own. You need to want this."

My heart pulled in opposite directions like a tug-of-war. These two guys were my brothers. But I'd rather stay here with my band than be tortured by seeing Lexi every day. I didn't need to be reminded of everything I'd lost. Resolve set into my jaw. "What you're offering is truly amazing. But I'm committed to staying here. I need to give this a shot. So, thank you, but it's a no."

"What?" Disbelief rocked Kyle's voice. "I know this is about

Lexi—not your band. You'll get over her . . . or work things out."

Would I? Could we? That was doubtful.

Hunter's gaze turned stony. He wasn't used to not getting his way either. "Hayds, you're not thinking straight. Go out. Get laid. Get your shit together. Then come play for us. I'm gonna get Sophie to email you through a contract. You call us with any questions. Okay?"

I shook my head and puffed out a short breath. "Whatever."

Kyle and Hunter had done so much for me. I hated letting them down. I loved these guys. The opportunity to work for them was mind-blowing. But without Lexi, New York held no place in my heart. It meant nothing to me anymore. Not even Everhide could change my mind.

Lexi had her dream job. I was even more determined to make mine come true.

Without her. Without Everhide.

It was time to focus on nothing but the music.

Here. In Boston.

This was where I belonged.

Chapter 25

LEXI

After two busy weeks traveling for work, I'd arrived home on Friday night and hadn't gone out anywhere since. For two days, I curled underneath my quilt on the floor in Hayden's empty room. It still smelled of him. The pillow he used to sleep on in my bed still held his scent. Working long hours had kept my mind occupied. But now I was home, loneliness consumed me like a thick, black cloud. It took all my willpower not to call or text him. He'd been gone for six weeks and two days. My heart was dying without him. Was this how hurt he'd felt when I'd needed space? When I'd wanted to run away from my problems, not face them? I'd been such a fool.

I cuddled Hayden's pillow against my chest and inhaled his lingering scent. How much time had to pass before we could be friends again? Time without him was cruel.

I grabbed my cell phone. The time flashed 9:21 a.m.

Would one text hurt?

Swiping the screen, I opened my messages and clicked on Hayden's name. Still nothing from him. Not a word since our fight in Boston two weeks ago. My fingers twitched, angry that he hadn't contacted me. Gliding my fingers over the screen, I typed '*Miss you*'. My thumb hovered over the send button. Tears pricked my eyes.

What is the point of sending him a message?

He obviously doesn't want to talk to me.

I deleted the text and tossed my cell phone aside.

It pinged. An Instagram notification.

I opened the app and stared at the image. My heart skipped a beat. It was The Saylors—the four of them in a studio, hashtagged with #RecordingNewSingle. My hand shot over my mouth and muffled my sob. The guys were recording! *Hayden, this . . . this is why I let you go. This is what you're meant to do!*

But the emptiness in my chest grew heavier. He'd moved on. Didn't care about me anymore. The chill from the floorboards seeped through the quilt and into my heart. I'd never been this lonely. Not ever. When Dad had left when I was thirteen and I didn't see him for months, I'd had my brothers to look after me. When Quintin had left, Hayden had comforted me. But now Hayden was gone, I had no one. I had my close friends, but it wasn't the same.

On days like this, I couldn't get out of bed . . . or off the floor.

Curling into a ball, I let my tears soak into my pillow.

I conceded to my fate.

I'd fallen ill. Just like my mother.

My cell phone sprang to life with the ringtone "I'm Just A Gigolo" by David Lee Roth. *Dad.*

I hit the answer button. "Hey Dad."

"Hey, sweetie. How are you this fine Monday morning? You free?" His voice sounded tinny through his car's Bluetooth connection. "I'm down your end of the city. Can we have a quick coffee before I head to work?"

"Um . . ." The thought of getting up, dressed and organized to walk out my door on my day off drained me. It'd take too much effort. My batteries were flat. "How about tomorrow?"

"No can do. I'm onsite doing a new client install for the next few weeks."

Dad's tech talk about SAP ERP software implementations often went over my head. He was a total computer geek. But if I didn't catch up with him now, I had no idea when I'd have the opportunity again. Gemma and the guys had hinted at spending time in LA to record their new album, and I'd be based there with them.

Even further away from Hayden.

Crap.

I hadn't seen Dad for months. I'd better go. "Fine. Pick me up in thirty minutes."

"I'm nearly at your place. Make it fifteen. See you soon."

Shit. Now I had to rush. Shower. Dress. Do something with my hair.

Ugh!

At least this gave me a reason to get out of bed.

***

Waiting on the curb outside my apartment, I rubbed my hands together and jostled my knees back and forth to stay warm in the bitter cold. Snow lingered on the sidewalks and turned to slush on the streets as cars drove by. Dad was late. I checked my cell phone again. *Where was he?*

Squealing car tires caught my attention. A racy red convertible BMW M4 veered around the corner, sped up the street and pulled to a halt in front of me. The window lowered, and Dad leaned across from the driver's seat. "Hiya, Lex."

I gaped, taking in the car. In a daze, I opened the door and slid inside. "Dad, what the fuck? Whose car is this?"

"Mine. My Christmas present to myself. You like?"

"Like? Are you crazy? A sports car?"

"I've always wanted one. So I thought, what the hell?"

"What the hell, all right." Midlife crisis 101. But *ohhh*, I melted against the heated seat. The leather was so warm and soft. The smell of new car filled my senses. My fingers twitched, wanting to play with every button on the dash, just like I'd done when I'd bought my new camera.

As we headed over to my favorite coffee shop near Tompkins Square, I glanced sideways at Dad. He'd changed since I'd seen him four months ago. His face had thinned, he'd dyed the gray out of his hair, and he'd slimmed down. Tina probably had him on some fad diet. But even I had to admit he looked better, younger, fitter.

Maybe I needed some of whatever he was on.

After parking and ordering coffees, we took a seat at a table by the front windows.

"How's my girl doing?" Dad asked.

I wanted to shrug, but my shoulders were lead weights. "I'm fine." *Not.*

"What's new?"

Staring at the sugar packets, my vision blurred. "My job with Everhide is great." As I prattled on to Dad about my work, the ache in my chest flared. I missed sharing all my exciting news with Hayden. I'd wanted to hear about his recording, and Boston, and his gigs. I missed my best friend.

"I'm so glad you're finally using that university degree in photography I paid for." The cynical edge in his tone wasn't lost. He'd been disappointed in me and frustrated ever since I'd taken the job at *The Gourmet Reviewer*. But I'd learned after a gazillion job applications and interviews that finding work as a photographer was too hard and competitive. I'd been happy to keep it as my hobby. Pursuing my dream back then would've been too arduous, too costly, too challenging.

Was that my problem? I'd given up too easily when things had gotten tough. I'd found it easier to run away than fight for what I'd wanted. Like I'd done with Hayden and our relationship. Short-term pain for long-term gain.

No . . . That wasn't the case. Letting Hayden go had been one of the hardest things I'd ever done. "Yeah, Dad . . . I'm finally doing what I love." I just needed to feel good about it.

The waitress interrupted our conversation as she placed our coffees on the table, gave us a warm smile, and disappeared.

"How's your mom doing?" Dad grabbed a sugar packet, tore it open and tipped it into his latte. He was way too chipper for my liking. He wanted something from me.

"Do you care?" I grimaced, reeling in my sharp tongue.

"Yes. Of course, I do."

I doubted it. He was just being polite.

I stirred my cappuccino, then tapped my spoon on the side of the cup. "Fine. Mom went off her meds before Christmas." I retold the events of Mom's birthday, finding her in the dark, depressed again, and stumbling across her smashed pottery. I puffed air through my nose. Sitting alone in the dark, feeling down . . . that had been me for the past two days. Like mother, like daughter. *Great . . . not!* "I've hired a home nurse to check on her twice a week. Hank and Billy are chipping in to cover the cost. Aunt Nora is a fucking waste of oxygen."

"Watch your language . . . but you're right." An understanding grin curled across Dad's mouth. "I never got along with her."

No, neither did I.

"So what's new with you?" I scooped the froth off my cappuccino and licked it from my spoon.

Dad shook and tore open a second sugar for his latte. "I'd like to talk to you about the wedding." As he stirred his drink, the teaspoon tinkled against the sides of the ceramic cup. "Oh . . . but first, let me show you some pictures of Niagara at Christmas."

His face lit up as he flicked through endless photos on his cell phone. My heart twanged at each shot of him and Tina smiling, laughing, covered in snow, drinking wine by the fire, and having dinner. I hadn't been on a vacation with Dad since I was twelve. Mom had never taken me anywhere either. Most of the holidays I'd had were with Hayden—summers at Kyle's beach house, camping at the lakes, or snowboarding in the mountains.

"Are you really going to marry Tina?" I couldn't keep the bitterness out of my tone. "You're sixty and she's thirty-three. She's the same age as Billy."

My brother would probably try to bang her.

"Yes. I love her." Dad stared at a photo of the two of them. The love in his eyes made me want to vomit. "She makes me happy."

I picked up my cup and blew across the rim. "What? Like Mom did? Like Helen did? And who was it before that . . . Veronica?"

"I loved your mother." His whiskey-colored eyes softened.

His voice remained calm, flat, monotone. "Very much. Helen and Veronica were lovely women, but we didn't connect."

"So why Tina?"

"Because it feels right." Deep furrows formed on his brow. "Where's this coming from?"

I sucked in a deep breath, hoping the aroma of coffee and freshly baked pastries would lift my spirits. But it just reminded me of morning coffee with Hayden. The backs of my eyes stung. "Because relationships fall apart. Love dies. Why marry her when you know it's going to end?"

He took a sip of his latte and placed the cup back on the saucer. "Because I believe it won't. Lex, you can't think about the end. You have to focus on the here and now, on loving each other and building a life together. In a relationship, if you don't do that, you'll never be happy."

Happy? I'd been happy. *When?* I sifted through my mind to find a time I'd truly felt that way—when I was a kid, when Dad had taken me and my brothers to football games and had always bought us mango-flavored ice-cream, when I was with Quintin, when I was having fun with my friends, when I'd lived with Hayden . . . and was *with* him. *Shit* . . . The Jingle Ball . . . Christmas . . . New Year's.

Stop. Thinking. About. Him.

My shoulders slumped. "What happens when it all goes to shit?"

"I hope it doesn't. But we'll cross that bridge if it does." He leaned forward, resting his arms on the table. "Lexi, there are no guarantees in life. But I'd sooner take another chance at being happy again than not. It took me a long time to get over your mom. She was my *one* for many years. But we grew apart, and it didn't end well. It's taken me ages to truly love someone again. No matter what you think, I love Tina. She's my *one* for now and hopefully for the rest of my days."

I sank an inch in my chair. "Do you hear yourself? You're only saying 'for now'. Why invest months or years into a relationship when one day you've had enough and walk away?"

"Sweetie, where's all this coming from?" Concern darkened his eyes. "I understand if you don't like Tina. But I do."

I glanced around the café. Other patrons huddled at tables, laughing and chatting. I shouldn't have come here. This place reminded me of *him.*

"I'm sorry. It's not Tina." I fidgeted with my hands in my lap. "It's Hayden. He moved to Boston." My heart compressed to the size of a pea. His post this morning on Instagram throbbed in my skull. Soon, he'll forget I ever existed. "We promised to be friends forever, but he won't even talk to me."

Dad half-smirked, puffed air through his nose, and shook his head. "Come on, Lex. Grow up. You're not twelve anymore. People change. I like Hayden. I don't want to be stereotypical, but he's a guy, moved cities, got a new life, found new friends. He's on a new adventure. Let him enjoy it. Be happy for him. You should be happy too. You've got a fabulous job and exciting times ahead."

Not what I wanted to hear.

I'd made another mistake thinking my friendship with Hayden could survive anything. Mom was right. Hayden was just like Dad and had moved on to something shiny and new . . . in the form of Boston. "He was my best friend."

My dad looked at me through hooded eyes. "Did you love him? Is that the problem?"

I shook my head. My heart didn't want to beat. "As a friend."

"Okay then." He patted my hand resting on the table. "If he's a true friend, he'll come around. If not, you'll just have to accept he's moved on."

I don't want to do that. I can't.

Dad pushed his empty cup into the middle of the table. "Let me cheer you up. Let's talk about the wedding."

I gave him a snarky look. He was kidding, right? There was no way wedding talk would cheer me up. But the sooner I got it out of the way, the better. Then I could go home to bed.

Undeterred by my less-than-enthusiastic presence, excitement shimmered in his eyes as he rubbed his hands together. "We're booked in for the second weekend in May at Pratt Mansion. Will you be our photographer?"

"May? Um . . . Let me check." I skimmed through the calendar on my cell phone. "I'm in LA, but I'm sure Gem and the guys will give me a few days off."

"Excellent. I assumed Hayden would've been your plus-one. That changing now?"

"Yeah, I guess. If Gem and Kara can swing it, they might come with me. Put me down for plus two."

"Will do." Dad typed something into his cell phone, then threw me a sympathetic smile. "If it's any consolation, I always thought you and Hayden would end up together."

"Why does everyone keep saying that?" I twisted my napkin in my hands. "We were friends. Roommates. That's it."

"Are you sure about that?"

"Yes." *No.*

"Okay. Got it."

I stared out the window at the park across the road. *Shit!* Hayden had been more than my roommate, and I'd killed our relationship. The biggest mistake of my life. "It doesn't matter if we were more." My voice came out as a pained breath. "He's gone."

Dad raised an eyebrow. "Boston is not that far away."

"It's miles away. If . . . and only if . . . we were together, we wouldn't see each other regularly, and it'd be too costly to do so."

"You have a good job. So does he."

"Hayden? He's a musician. His income has always been irregular. When we lived together, some months he struggled to cover the rent and pay the bills. The next month, he'd be living the high life."

"So?"

"So . . . what?"

"Money isn't everything, Lex. Your friends have it. They have nice homes, charter planes, and dressed in designer clothes. But is that what makes them happy? Or is it each other? Friends, family . . . love? Isn't it more important to have someone in your life who makes you happy, goes everywhere with you, puts up with your idiosyncrasies, stands by you through thick and thin, and loves you just the way you are?"

"I don't need anyone, Dad. I can take care of myself."

"You sound just like your mother. Don't let her taint you. You've got a beautiful soul. Having a great career and being independent is one thing, but don't deny yourself the chance of being with someone who genuinely loves you. It doesn't matter if they're a fisherman, a congressman . . . or a musician. If they make you happy, treat you right, and adore you, putting effort into the relationship will be worth it."

I pulled my hand away. "Until it ends."

"Then you start again."

Dad lived in dreamland. Always had. "Thanks, Dad, but I'm good."

If I kept telling myself that, I might believe it.

But right now, all I wanted to do was head home, put my pajamas on and go back to bed.

Chapter 26

LEXI

Dinner was on at Hunter and Kara's place. Kyle and Gemma had offered to cook ramen for everyone. Who was I to say no to a home-cooked meal? I'd been living on takeout for weeks. It wasn't fun cooking for one. I was often too tired to eat. But I'd brought the wine. I poured everyone a glass, grabbed a cushion off the sofa, and sat on the floor in front of the TV. I took one sip of my drink and struggled to swallow it. Not even wine went down well anymore. Tomorrow, we'd fly out to London. It'd be my first overseas trip with Everhide. I should be excited. I'd never been to London before. I'd be ticking off one of my big bucket-list items. But my adrenaline wouldn't kick in. It didn't feel right going without Hayden. I'd be so busy though, I'm sure I'd survive.

"Dinner will be ready in five minutes," Gemma hollered from the kitchen.

Finally. Kyle and Gemma had been laughing and giggling and smooching while they'd prepared our meal for over half an hour. My stomach had been grumbling since I'd arrived. But the thought of eating anything made me nauseous.

"You okay, Lex?" Kara tilted her head toward me. Curled up in Hunter's arms on the sofa, she looked way too comfortable. Stretched out and spooning her from behind, Hunter kept stroking and playing with her hair, and kissing her on the neck.

Just like Hayden used to do to me.

I closed my eyes. No, I wouldn't let him invade my thoughts. Not tonight. But the ache in my chest worsened. Each breath tore my lungs. *Stop. Breathe. That's it.* "Yeah, I'm fine. Thanks."

"Beef ramen is served." Kyle headed over to us and placed bowls of steaming noodles on the coffee table.

Gemma sat beside him on the adjacent sofa and handed out chopsticks. "Dig in."

"Wow. This looks amazing." I dipped and stirred my chopsticks through my dish. Hayden loved Ramen. It was one of his favorites. *Shit.* I took one mouthful and slurped a noodle. It was delicious. But it didn't sit well in my stomach. After a couple of mouthfuls, I couldn't eat anymore.

"You all set to fly to London tomorrow night, Lex?" Gemma asked before popping a slice of beef into her mouth.

"I sure am." My suitcase was packed. So was my photography gear. I'd left my bags in my living room—right where Hayden's drums used to be.

Ow! Wincing, I keeled forward a fraction and rubbed the burn in my chest. *What was wrong with me? Fuck.* If this ache got any worse, I'd have to go to the doctor. Something wasn't right. I'd first noticed it after Boston a couple of weeks ago . . . No . . . It had started when Hayden had left.

I prayed it was nothing serious.

"You ready to work with Clinton on our documentary?" Kyle waved his chopsticks at me, then shoveled a huge pile of noodles into his mouth.

I pushed my ramen aside. "Yeah. I can't wait." I tried to inject some enthusiasm into my voice but failed. I really was excited to work with Clinton. He was an incredibly talented creative director. He was fun, full of energy and filled with so many ideas that some days I found it hard to keep up. "He's given me access to a ton of footage to edit."

Hunter drained his bowl of its contents and pointed at my dinner. "You gonna eat that, or can I have it?"

"Knock yourself out." I pushed the dish toward him.

He picked it up and dug into it with his chopsticks. "It's going to be crazy watching old videos of us. Eight years captured in a doco will be so cool."

"It certainly will be." I nodded. "From teenage geeks to rockstars." I'd met them when they'd first moved to New York. They'd moved into the apartment next door. I'd been living with Hayden for a couple of months. I ran into them at the café downstairs, where I used to work. They'd invited Hayden and me to a party the following night . . . the first of many. It had been the start of an amazing friendship. History . . . we had so much history.

Hayden and Gemma. Hunter and me. Gemma and Hunter. Gemma and Kyle and . . . Hayden and me.

For so long, it had always been . . . Hayden and me.

Shit. Crap. My lungs seized. I couldn't breathe. My chest heaved, and stars appeared before my eyes. *Breathe. I can't breathe.*

"Let's put a movie on." Hunter grabbed and clicked several remotes. Electric blinds shut, apartment lights dimmed, and the surround-sound system kicked in.

Fire burned in my chest. *I can't do this.* I thumped my chest. Did I have indigestion? No, I'd hardly had anything to eat. Nausea pooled in my stomach. A cold sweat broke out on my brow. I wanted to throw up. I wanted to cry. I wanted to get out of there.

Fuck!

As I touched my forehead, my hand trembled. "Kar, do you mind if I go lie down in the spare room? I'm not feeling well."

"Sure." She jumped to her feet and helped me to stand. "Go lie down. I'll bring you some water."

"Thanks."

Four sets of eyes followed me as I staggered down the hallway and entered the room. I collapsed onto the bed and drew the throw over me. I burst into tears. Everything I did reminded me of Hayden. It had to stop. I had a great job. I was with my friends. I had so much to live for. But why did I feel so lost? Lonely? Lethargic?

Hayden used to take care of me when I didn't feel well. He'd always been there for me. Now, he wasn't.

I scrunched my eyes shut and curled into a ball. We'd never fought until he first kissed me. We liked the same things and going to the same places. Hell, I'd loved living with a drummer, loved his music. If that wasn't a sign we were perfect together, what was? We'd had a great life together. *What have I done?*

My heart clawed at my ribs. I should've given us a chance. Longing to see him would have kept me excited and would've given me something to live for. Now I had nothing. Every day he didn't talk to me was another day he slipped away.

I'd fucked up.

I was so afraid of being hurt again, but here I was.

I'd broken his heart.

I'd broken *my* heart.

My tears dampened the pillow. I clutched my chest.

Oh. My. God.

I loved him.

I loved him so hard, and I'd destroyed what we'd had.

I'd denied myself the opportunity to truly love him for fear of losing him. I'd lied to myself for too long. I'd wanted to protect him. But it had backfired like an old beetle Volkswagen.

He'd moved on.

Kara and Gemma slipped into the room. Gemma eased onto the end of the bed. Kara sat beside my head and stroked my hair, just like Hayden used to do when I wasn't well. "Hey, what's going on?"

"Nothing," I whispered. "Food didn't sit right." I knew food; there was nothing wrong with Kyle's noodles. They were scrumptious. I just couldn't eat anything.

"Lex, you've been like this for weeks." Gemma rubbed my leg. "We know it's not the food."

"Maybe I'm bipolar, like my mom."

"That's the biggest load of bull crap." Gemma slapped me on the thigh. "Get over yourself. There's only one reason you're like this, and it's about time you stopped denying it."

"Deny what?" I sniffled.

"That this is all about Hayden." Gemma jabbed me on the leg.

"And you're heartbroken." Kara rubbed my shoulder, her voice soft with sympathy. "And it's okay. We've all been there, done that. Remember when Gem broke up with Ben, and oh my God, the tears we endured when Hunt screwed her over? The nights we sat on your sofa, eating mango ice cream and listening to her bawl?"

"Hey." Gemma giggled and flicked her hand at Kara. "You can't talk. Remember Conrad? *'Oh, he's the one. I'm going to marry him. Have his babies. Be happy forever.'*"

I remembered.

But now, when I looked at my friends, they were so fucking happy. They'd survived broken hearts. Both had found love again. It was better to take a chance on love, be happy for however long it lasts, even though it may not last forever.

I'd ruined what I had with Hayden before it'd evolved.

Kara smoothed her hand over my hair. "See? We know what it's like. You don't want to eat. You can't sleep. You just want to cry. And listen to Kelly Clarkson's *'Already Gone'* on repeat all day long.

Oh my God. I'd so done that. "But Hayden and I weren't even together."

"Yeah . . . you were." Kara kissed the top of my head.

"I pushed him away. Broke his heart. He doesn't want to talk to me."

Gemma rubbed my knee. "I don't think things are as bad as you say they are. Kyle talked to him the other day. He misses you. He doesn't like the song they've recorded. He's not himself without you."

What? He wasn't happy? "But Boston is so far away. How could we possibly make it work?"

"With commitment and effort," Gemma said.

"But . . ."

"No buts." Gemma slapped my thigh again. "Do you love him?"

I closed my eyes and sobbed. "Fuck, I hate you girls. You know I do. I love him so much it fucking hurts."

"Yay!" Kara cheered. "Finally. Now, don't you feel better?"

"No." I sniffled.

"Then do something about it." Gemma sat upright. "Find a way to make it work."

"Hunt and I can recommend a cool place near Harford for dirty weekends." Sauciness sifted through Kara's tone as she nudged her arm against my head. "That's half-way between here and Boston."

"But we're hoping you won't have to do that." Gemma said with a glint in her eye.

I raised my head half an inch off the pillow. "What do you mean?"

"Nothing . . ." Gemma pursed her lips and shrugged.

What was she downplaying? There was something going on I hadn't been privy to. "Gem?"

"What are you going to do about Hayds?" Gemma skirted back to the subject

A huge weight had lifted off my chest. I could breathe easier. But the next step scared me. It was easier to jump off a cliff. My head sank into the pillow. "Love sucks."

"Nah . . . " Gemma patted my leg. "It's awesome. It only sucks if it doesn't work out. But you've got someone. You just have to tell him how you feel."

I clutched the throw against my chest. "I love him so bad."

"We know." Kara stroked my curls.

If she kept that up, I'd be purring like a kitten soon. "Okay." I rubbed the tip of my nose. "I can do this. I can tell him. I'll call him when I get home."

Gemma shook her head. "Nah. Why don't you go see him?"

"What? I can't." I shook my head. "We leave for London tomorrow."

"We fly out at nine tomorrow night. If you're back, great. If not, we'll survive this trip without you." Gemma reassured me.

Kara gave my shoulder a gentle shake. "Go get your man."

I clambered to sit upright. My heart pounded at an erratic pace. "Really? Holy shit!" My mind geared into action. I had to rush home. Get my car. Get moving. I shuffled to the edge of the bed. "Wait . . . What if he's not there?"

"One sec." Gemma dashed out of the room and returned

moments later with her cell phone in her hand. She clicked and swiped the screen, then turned it to me. "He's at home. Tracking apps can be useful sometimes."

I'd forgotten we all had those apps installed by Everhide's security team. I'd never needed to use them. "You think I should do this? Drive to Boston?"

"Absolutely." Gemma shoved her cell phone into the back pocket of her jeans. "You've got nothing to lose. You'll either get him back or get closure on what happened. You can't mope around like this anymore. I'll be Tinder swiping for you otherwise."

God, I loved my girlfriends.

"Okay." My palms turned clammy. "I'm terrified, but I'm gonna go." I clambered to my feet and hugged them. "I love you girls. I don't know what I'd do without you."

"Me either." Kara's warm smile hit my heart.

"Same." Gemma slapped me on the ass. "Now get out of here."

I dashed out of the room and hurried over to the guys watching TV. Hunter tossed a piece of popcorn into his mouth. "You feeling better?"

"Yes. Um . . . " I picked up my purse and coat off the floor. "I gotta go. To Boston. To tell Hayden . . . shit."

"Finally." Hunter threw up his hands.

"Let's hope this works out for everyone." Kyle winked at me.

What was with him? There was something going on. I'd get to the bottom of it after Boston. I didn't have time to dig further now. I had to see Hayden.

"Wanna take my car?" Hunter's grin grew as wide as The Great Lakes. "It's fast. Save you going home to get yours."

I gaped. "You'll let me drive your car?" Hunter's Ford GT supercar was a half-a-million-dollar beast—his baby. He hated anyone touching it but him.

Hunter splayed his hand over his chest. "Maybe I'm just a romantic at heart." He tilted his head toward the sideboard. "Keys are in the top left drawer."

Wow! "Hunt, I can't afford to fix it if I break it."

"That's okay. It's time I got a new one, anyway. Go. Quick.

Before I change my mind."

I grabbed the keys and hugged the girls again. "Thank you. I love you. But if seeing Hayds doesn't work out, we'll be on my sofa tomorrow. Have the tissues and mango ice cream on standby."

"Okay." Kara nodded. "We'll be here no matter what."

Gemma waved me toward the door. "Go you good thing. Drive safe. Oh . . . Hunt's car is awesome at drifting."

"I do not want to know how you know that." Hunter threw a piece of popcorn at Gemma.

Gemma just giggled, feigned innocence, and pointed at Kyle.

I rushed down the hallway and pressed the elevator button. As I waited for it to arrive, I glanced at my friends in the living room. They were wrestling and laughing and throwing popcorn and cushions about. I loved them so much. I wanted what they had. Love. A relationship. I wanted those things and more with Hayden. No, wait . . . I'd *had* those things with Hayden. It was time to get him back.

My heart skittered and lurched. What if he didn't want to see me? Maybe I should call first?

No. He'd talk me out of going. I wanted to be with him. Our schedules would be hard to align. Neither of us worked a nine-to-five, Monday-to-Friday job. But with effort, we could be together. Now all I had to do was convince him.

I had to tell him I was sorry.

Tell him I loved him.

In the garage, I slipped into the driver's seat. Butterflies took flight in my tummy. Taking a deep breath, I pressed the ignition button. The dash lit up. Music boomed out of the speakers. The Ford GT supercar roared to life. The rev of the engine jump-started my heart. I inched out into the laneway, eased across Manhattan, and hit the freeway north. I put my foot down. No more denial. No more lying.

It was time to get my man.

Chapter 27

LEXI

I walked up the paved pathway to Hayden's house. My knees wobbled. My stomach bubbled like broth on the boil. A lone light filtered through the sheer curtain in the front kitchen window. Every scenario of what to say to Hayden had run through my head during the long drive here. But now, standing in front of his door, nothing was clear. I'd checked my tracking app before getting out of the car. Hayden was home . . . I hoped he was alone and didn't have a girl with him. *Fuck.* I didn't want to walk in on that. Holding my breath, I pulled off my glove and knocked.

No answer.

No noise.

It was worse than *The Night Before Christmas*. Nobody stirred in the house. I prayed I didn't see a mouse.

With no doorbell in sight, I rapped my knuckles on the glass panel as loud as I could.

My teeth chatted. In the frigid air, I wrapped my arms around myself. I jostled from foot to foot and rubbed my knees together.

I looked up at the bedroom windows. No lights. Hayden's room was on the other side of the house. These guys rarely went to bed before midnight. Maybe they were asleep . . . or out. *Shit. Shit. Shit.*

I'd come all this way. I had to see Hayden. Call him.

I dug into my purse and grabbed my cell phone. My fingers shivered and ached in the cold. I hit his number and held the cell phone to my ear. His ringtone played on the other side of the door, but it wasn't getting any closer, not getting any louder. Just as I went to knock again, the door opened.

Hayden.

My heart leaped into my throat.

Dressed in a gray hoodie, long pajama pants, and socks, he stood with his cell phone to his ear. His eyes widened. "Lex? I heard the knocking. I thought the guys had forgotten their keys. Then . . . you called." He lowered his hand and held his cell phone against his chest. "What the fuck are you doing here? It's nearly midnight." Concern wobbled in his voice. "Is everything okay?"

I held up my hand and softened my voice. "Everything's fine." Except my mind was a complete train wreck. "I . . . I came to see you."

"My God, get in here. It's freezing."

I dashed inside the toasty warm house and dumped my purse on the dining table. I screwed up my nose at the smell of pot overpowering the subtle hint of rosy air freshener.

"Are the guys home?" I pulled off my beanie and scarf.

He eased back a step, leaned against the kitchen counter, and folded his arms. The soft light behind him glowed golden on his olive skin. "No . . . They're out . . . Somewhere."

"Oh . . . Are you alone?" I grimaced, glancing at the staircase, expecting to see a long pair of bare legs appear.

"Yes. Why?" He puffed air through his nose. "You think I have some girl in my bed?"

My jaw tensed. "I wouldn't know." I unbuttoned my coat and tossed it onto a chair. "You haven't talked to me in weeks."

A deep ridge furrowed his brow. "Did you come here to fight?"

"No." I shook my curls. "Not at all."

Hardness set in his eyes. He stuffed his hands into his hoodie pockets. "Then why are you here?"

Nerves flitted through my stomach. I wrung my hands, trying

to find the right thing to say. "To apologize. I'm sorry for hurting you. Home isn't the same without you."

"What did you expect?"

I took a step forward to close the six-foot gap between us. "I miss you."

He held up his hand and flinched backward. "Yeah, well . . . I've been busy."

"I've seen your posts. You're recording. That's awesome."

But excitement didn't touch his eyes. If anything, he shut down even further.

"Isn't it?" Concern softened my tone.

"Not really." His shoulders slumped. "It's not coming together as planned."

"I'm sorry to hear that." I flattened my hand across my stomach to settle the unease. "I hate not knowing what's going on with you. Hate that you haven't called or texted and hate that we haven't seen each other."

"I told you." He hugged himself tighter. "I need more time."

I shook my head, not wanting to hear those words ever again. "No. Time is up. I miss you. I've fucked up on so many levels. Every day you've been gone has gotten harder, not better. There have been days I couldn't get out of bed. I thought I was ill like my mom. I don't work without you."

He lowered his chin and closed his eyes. "So? You didn't want me."

I ignored the sharp edge in his voice, inched another half-step closer and lowered my voice. "What if I do?"

"What?" Shock shot through his voice.

"I was so worried about all the things that could go wrong between us, I couldn't see what was right. Now I do. I want to try again. I want to give us another shot."

"Don't fuck with me, Lexi." He stormed down the short hallway toward the living room, his hand tugging on his hair. I followed in his footsteps. He switched on the light and turned as quick as a tornado to face me. "You just want to pick up where we left things? Go back to the day I moved out, or to the day you said you didn't love me?"

My heart struggled to beat under the weight of the anguish in his voice. I'd broken him into more pieces than a shattered pane of glass. "No. To when we were happy, like at Christmas and at New Year's and the couple weeks before you left." I swayed on my feet as the truth pummeled me from all angles. "When you told me how you felt before Thanksgiving, I'd panicked. I didn't want to analyze the depth of my feelings for you. But the universe kept forcing me to do so. It kept pulling us back together, like during your mom's relapse, my creepy boss incident, and at the Jingle Ball. We're each other's rock." I twisted my hands together, searching for the right things to say. "When you asked me to move here, I freaked out about quitting my job, losing my independence, and not having an income. I didn't want to be a burden. I didn't want you to have to look after me. But for over seven years, you always have. You've been the only truly stable thing in my life. You've been the only person I could always rely on."

He stood rigid by the sofa. A muscle in his jaw ticked. "Lex, I had no doubt you'd find a job. I wanted you to get into photography, to follow your dream. I wanted to be with you and look after you. I could support you financially. I may never be a millionaire, though. Is that what you want? Is that all you care about? Money?"

"No. Stability is. Unconditional support, love, and trust is. *We* had that. We balanced and complemented each other in every way." Fidgeting with the ends of my long sleeves, my hands trembled. "I was so afraid of losing you. I was scared we'd turn into my parents, who resent each other. I thought if we just stayed friends, we'd survive anything. But we'd grown into something more. Something amazing. And I didn't see that until I lost you."

He took two steps toward the gas heater and faced the wall. "You were the first person who made me feel like I was worth something. That I was loved. Belonged. Had a home. But you threw it all away." He lowered his chin. "I was willing to do anything for you, but whatever I did was never enough."

I caught his arm and turned him to face me. "You have always been more than enough. No one I've dated since Quintin has stacked up against you. No one believes in me like you do. I couldn't let anyone else get close . . . because I already had you."

"*Did* have me," he snapped. "You broke us, Lexi."

It was written in the dark storm in his eyes—the pain, the rejection, the hurt.

I'd done that to him. My heart cried. I felt every inch of his suffering in my bones. I needed to make this right. "I'm so, so sorry." I placed my hand on his chest. His heart struggled to beat. "I want to fix us. Put us back together." Tears welled in my eyes. "We can make long-distance work. I'm willing to give it my all if you are."

He fell back a step and swallowed hard. "Why . . . why would I do that?"

"Because I don't want to be away from you for another second more than I have to be."

He shook his head. Ice set in his steely gaze. "No. You want me when it suits you. You want me to be your wingman, to be a shoulder to cry on, to change a fucking light bulb. What if we fight, or disagree, or face another hurdle? You just gonna take off again? Shut me out? Push me away? Like you did when I first kissed you. Like you did when I told you how I felt. Like you did when you got a new job."

"No. Never again. No more running, I promise. Time apart hurts too much. I'm better at facing life with you, not without you."

"Not good enough."

"Yes, it is. Because you can trust me. I trust you with my life, and more importantly . . . my heart." I pressed my hands flat against my chest. "You've had it for a long time. I was too afraid to admit it."

"Lex, you're embedded in my soul." He spoke through gritted teeth. "I couldn't bear you leaving again."

"I'm not going anywhere." A tear escaped onto my cheek. My heart thundered against my ribs like one thousand war drums. "Because . . . I love you."

"W-what did you just . . . ?" His voice was a hoarse whisper. "You can't come in here after all this time, and say that."

"It's the truth. We belong together. You're my family."

He sucked in a hard breath, pinched his eyebrows together and closed his eyes.

"Hayden." I stepped toward him, cupped his cheek, and let all my feelings for him rule my heart. "I love you. When I look at you and think about you, I don't see an end. I see forever. I want you to be my forever."

He shuddered all over. The breath shot from his lungs. "Do you mean that?"

I nodded.

His eyes glistened with tears. "I've been so lost since I left. I've hit rock bottom. I can't breathe without you. It's like a piece of me is missing."

"It's been the same for me. I want to put us back together again."

"How?"

The defeat in his voice stabbed my heart. But I had to be strong. "What are you doing for the next few days?"

Confusion drifted across his face. "Playing at the hotel. Why?"

"Can you get time off? Come to London with me. It was always our plan to go there together."

He jerked his chin back. "I can't just drop everything and go overseas."

"Are you sure?" I searched his face for a sign of hope, but all I saw was doubt. "Everhide are playing at an awards show. I'm sure you'll fit on the chartered plane. If not, I'll buy you a ticket. I know it's a huge ask, but London wouldn't be the same without you. It was our dream. The first place in the world we wanted to see together. I don't want to do this without you. Please say yes."

He swayed on his feet. He clenched his jaw and shook his head.

Why wasn't anything I said getting through to him? Fire licked through my veins. "Stop fighting this." I placed my hands on his shoulders and gave him a gentle shake. "We've done enough of that lately. No more. I love you and want to be with you. So please . . . be mine."

In less than a heartbeat, he closed the distance between us. He clutched the back of my head and crushed his lips against mine. I wrapped my arms around him and held him tight. Our tongues lashed out to touch and taste each other. His kisses were like fire, hot, hungry, and hasty. His body warmth was like a snug blanket that fit just right. His roaming hands soothed my troubled mind. I'd missed him so much. He was my home. God, I'd been a fool to let him go.

"I haven't stopped being yours," he whispered over our kisses.

A happy sob escaped me. "I'm so sorry for everything. I'm so in love with you."

"Angel." He cupped my face. "You don't know how long I've waited to hear you say that."

"Too long." I kissed him hard. I'd never tire of his kisses. His touch. His taste. And *mmm . . .* his smell, so good, all sandalwood and vanilla. All Hayden.

Grabbing the front of his hoodie, I pushed him back against the wall. He thudded against it. A picture fell off its hook and smashed onto the floor. He slid sideways to step away from the broken glass, but his hip connected with the low bookshelf, and sent the lamp resting on top tumbling to the ground. The shade shattered.

I smiled against his mouth. "You goose."

He guided me backward. My butt connected with the back of the sofa. It slid forward and hit the coffee table.

I giggled, quite happy to destroy the house if that was what it took to show him— and for him to know, feel, and understand— how much I loved him. I wasn't going anywhere—not now, not ever. Distance had kept us apart physically, but not our hearts. We were too connected. As I slipped my hands underneath his hoodie, I sucked in a dizzying breath. I loved touching him again. *Hmm.* I definitely wanted to show him how much he meant to me.

He caught my head between his hands. He scanned my face as if making sure I was really here. "I don't want to be away from you anymore."

"Me either. I've been such a fool."

"No, you're my angel. You will always be my angel."

He slipped his hands around my waist and pulled me flush against his chest. His kisses grew hungrier, deeper, hotter. Every touch of his lips, and every stroke of his fingertips, sent tingles from the top of my scalp down to the tips of my toes. Nothing had ever felt so good. Oh wait . . . yes, it had. Him . . . naked. That was much better.

I lifted his hoodie to rip it off. The grin that lit his face when he pulled it and his shirt free slammed into my heart. I glided my fingertips down his cheek, over his bare chest and across the hard plane of his stomach. "I love you."

His lips found mine. Moaning against my mouth, he crushed me against the sofa. His hands roamed over my hips, my ass, and the bare flesh underneath my sweater. Panting, he dragged his lips away from mine. "God, I want you. But not here. Let's go up to my room. Just in case the guys come home." The most delicious, devilish grin slid across his face. How could I say no?

"Okay."

He entwined our fingers and led me toward the stairs.

Chapter 28

LEXI

I followed Hayden into his bedroom. His king-size bed took up nearly every inch of the space. We had to shuffle between it and the wall to shut the door. The second it was closed, he pulled me into his arms, and touched his lips to mine. "I've dreamed about being with you again every night since I left."

"I tried not to, but failed too." I knotted my fingers in his silky hair and breathed him into my soul. "I'm tired of fighting how I feel for you. I don't want to do that any longer."

"Me either. I love you. I love you so fucking much."

The heat in his voice ignited an inferno inside me. "Same."

"Are we gonna keep talking . . . or get naked and make love?" The want in his tone coiled through my belly and struck my core.

I reached for the tie on his pajama bottoms. "Sex, then talk."

He caught my hands and shook his head. "No . . . Lex. This isn't sex. It's love. Make love to me."

I caught my bottom lip between my teeth. My heart raced as I dragged my fingernails across his stomach and eased his pants down to his feet. He stepped out of them. My eyebrow arched. God, I'd missed his cock. "Yeah. Let's make love."

His grin shone like the top of the Chrysler Building. Color touched his cheeks as I ran my hands up his legs, over his thighs, across his groin, and around his waist.

I kicked off my boots and discarded my clothes. Over fresh kisses, we crawled onto his bed. I hadn't touched the ground since he'd kissed me downstairs. I still floated on a high.

As he hovered over me, his breath entwined with mine. "I've missed you. So much. It took you way too long to realize we belong together."

"I know." I threaded my fingers through his hair and tugged him toward me.

His soft lips skimmed across my mouth, my throat, my breasts. His fingers rediscovered every inch of my body, tracing my legs, my stomach, chest, and face. He grabbed a condom from his nightstand, rolled it on, and buried himself inside me. Tilting his hips, he rocked into me. Hard and deep. Slow and steady.

Fire flooded through my veins, reigniting my heart. Shivers spiraled up my spine.

He smiled over our kisses. "Now that you're here, I'm never letting you go."

"Good. Don't."

Wrapping my legs around his waist, I pulsed my hips to meet his languid thrusts. My fingertips sizzled as I re-explored the ridges of his muscular back, his sculpted arms, the curve of his hips, the firmness of his ass. *Pure heaven.*

He caught one of my hands in his, threaded our fingers together and pinned it beside my head. He did the same on the other side. A cheeky smile lit his face as he drove, and rocked, and thrust into me. "You're mine, forever."

Oh, hell yes.

The tenderness of his touch, the tantalizing taste of his kisses, the intoxicating scent of his skin, and the feel of him inside me, sealed him into my heart. Where he'd always belonged. "Okay."

He drove into me again. A moan escaped me. "*Ohh.*"

"You like that?" He nibbled on my ear. His hot lips brushed softly against my skin.

"Yeah." My eyes fluttered closed as I dug my fingers into his back. Arching my chest, my hardened nipples tingled as they grazed against his torso. My pussy clenched around his dick, wanting more. And more. More friction. More rubbing. More fucking.

"Fuck, you feel incredible." His breathy voice teased my neck. With a hot groan, he picked up the pace. I rocked and met his every move. We were connected, mind, body, and soul. Skin on skin. Heart to heart. Warmth washed over me and filled my chest. It had taken me too long to admit how I felt. I'd made too many foolish errors along the road to getting here.

Now, there'd be no more mistakes.

This felt right.

I needed Hayden. Wanted him. Loved him.

Driving into me hard, he sent me over the edge. Sparks of electricity skipped across my skin and coiled through my insides. As I held him close, I shuddered and quaked. Every nerve sailed on the ultimate high. My Hayden high.

With a pounding thrust, he found his release. A sexy grin curled across his lips as his body convulsed. Jerked. Shuddered.

We kissed. Touched. Breathed each other in. My pussy throbbed around his thudding cock. *So good.*

"Fuck, I've missed you." He kissed my forehead, the tip of my nose, my lips, then fell beside me. He discarded the condom, drew me into his arms, and pulled the quilt over us. "I've missed this, too" He kissed my temple and hugged me tighter. "Holding you. Having you close."

"Yeah." I tickled the fine hairs on his chest. "I didn't know how good we were until you were gone."

"Never gone. Just temporarily misplaced . . . No, that's not right. I was totally fucked up."

"Me too." I kissed his hot flesh, hoping each touch of my lips eased his hurt, healed his heart, mended his wounds. "So, how are we gonna make this work?"

"I'm not sure yet." He stroked my hair. "There's a lot to think about. This changes everything."

"I know it does. I'll come visit as often as I can. We can rendezvous in Harford or somewhere along the coast. You can come home for the holidays."

He pulled his chin back and glanced down at me. Smugness shimmered in his eyes. "Did Kyle and the others have anything to do with this?"

"The guys didn't, but Kara and Gem certainly gave me a kick up the ass. They couldn't believe it had taken me so long to work out that I loved you. They told me to come and tell you face-to-face."

"Sooo, they didn't tell you about the job?"

Confusion swam through my brain. "What job?"

"The morning after the show you came to see, they asked me to drum for them."

I shot upright, swiveled toward him, and tucked the quilt under my armpits. "And you didn't jump at the opportunity? Are you insane?" Fuck! I stared out the window. "So this is what they were keeping from me."

Hayden propped himself up on his elbow. "They said I had to decide on my own, and not be influenced by you. But you were the main reason I couldn't take it." He slid his hand over my bare thigh. A half-serious, half-humorous grin quirked the corner of his mouth. "I was really screwed up."

Shit. I'd broken him so much that he hadn't taken the job of a lifetime. But his loyalty and faithfulness to The Saylors would've played a big part in his decision. "So where are you at now?"

"I owe so much to Kilt and the guys. We've been doing okay. Things have improved over the past couple weeks. They've agreed not to get so wasted before a show again. If it were just about the music, we'd be fine. When we play, and they're not bent, it's great. But it's all the other bullshit I struggle with."

"Like what?"

"I can't live with them. They're pigs. The drugs do my head in. I hate being in the same house as the pot and pills and God-only-knows what else they take. I like having a life outside the band. I miss that. I was gonna move out next payday."

"You weren't coming home?" That twisted a knife in my heart. "What about now things are different for us? We could both be in our dream jobs and be together."

"That is mind-blowing. But like I said to Kyle and Hunt, if I left, I'd feel like I haven't given here a real chance. I don't like giving up. It killed me giving up on you."

I threw him a sad smile as I swept his hair off his brow. "You gave up on me?"

"Yeah, Lex. I did . . . Well, I tried to." A glint shimmered in his eyes. He caught my hand and kissed my knuckles. "I loved you, but it wasn't enough."

"That's where you're wrong." I squeezed his hand in mine. "You are. I'm the one who screwed up—not you. If you took the job with Everhide, you wouldn't be giving up—you'd be moving forward, moving on to greater things. I know you're loyal to your band, but you've never had a synergy with them like you do with Hunt and Kyle. They're your best friends. Wouldn't playing with them be unreal?" I combed my fingers through his hair. "You've worked so hard. You're a brilliant drummer. Don't be a fool and miss out on such an amazing opportunity. Drumming for Everhide is the chance of a lifetime. You'll get to tour, and play, and shine on stage. And I'm gonna be right by your side . . . well, offstage, taking photos."

Sitting up, he rubbed the back of his neck. "The job has been playing on my mind for weeks. I wanted it, but I was so torn between you, my band and Everhide. I couldn't see anything clearly."

I softened my voice. "And what about now?"

"Everything is wild, and stormy, and traveling at sonic speed."

The torment in his eyes needed erasing. I touched his cheek, stroking my thumb over his soft stubble. "Then take a breath. Come to London with me. Take a few days to think things through. I want to be with you regardless, whether or not you join Everhide."

"Hmm . . ." He leaned forward and kissed my lips. "A trip to London sounds like bribery."

Warmth swirled inside my chest. "Maybe it is."

"It's not needed."

"So . . .?" Hope ignited in the pit of my stomach. "Does that mean you've decided? To come home and work for Everhide?"

"I have. There are a few details I need to discuss with Gem and the guys, but yes, I'll come home."

I shot forward and kissed him.

But he caught my shoulders and drew back a fraction. "But there is one thing that would make the decision even better. It's not a condition, but it would just make everything perfect?"

"And what's that?"

He took my hands in his, linked our fingers, and rested them against my lap. "Are you serious? About forever?"

"Yeah . . . I am. We belong together. You are my life."

Nodding, he inhaled deeply and let it out slowly. He looked up at me. The intense adoration in his gaze stole my breath. "Then marry me."

I blinked. My heart beat doubled in time. "What?"

"I mean it." He shuffled closer until his knees rested on top of mine. "You know me better than anyone else. We've lived together for seven years. We've slept together. We've survived through better and worse. All I've ever wanted was a home and someone to love . . . and someone who put up with my drumming. I had those things with you. I want that again. I've never stopped loving you. I can't. There's no question in my mind I want to spend forever with you. So . . . marry me."

A hot flush rushed across my skin and crept up my neck. This was happening too fast. Wasn't it? "But . . . but . . . we've only just gotten back together. How can you be sure that's what you want?"

"Because I know you." Sincerity set in his every word. "I want you. Please be my wife."

Tears prickled my eyes. "What if I get sick like my mom?"

"Then I'll be by your side to take care of you." He smoothed his hand over my hair and rubbed the back of my neck. "Will you still love me if I become an addict?"

"I promise I won't ever let you fall that far. But if you feel the need to be addicted to something . . . be addicted to me."

"I already am. You're definitely the only drug I need." Tears pooled on the rims of his eyes. He kissed the back of my hand, then held it against his heart. "I love you, Lex. Be mine. Forever."

My heart hammered against my ribs. My head spun. Stars swirled before my eyes. This was insane. This was crazy. But it felt oh so right. I lunged forward and kissed him. "Yes. Yes, I'll marry you."

He pulled me onto his lap. The sheets tangled between us. Pressing his forehead to mine, he swept his hand over my curls. "No more time apart. That shit nearly killed me."

"Me too." I cupped his face. "I love you, Hayds. So much."

"I don't want to wait." He glided his hands over my bare back. "Let's get married as soon as we get back from London."

"What? We can't organize a wedding that quickly."

"Yes, we can. We have Kara and Bec, the organizational queens. Just something small, simple—maybe a church."

I gnawed on my lower lip. His mom would be out of rehab. My brothers would be home. I'd try my best to track down his dad. A few friends and family were all I needed to share our special day . . . and Hayden. Hell, I'd elope if that was what he wanted.

"What do you say?" Hope flitted through his tone.

I linked my hands behind his neck. Tears blurred my vision. "I can't believe I'm about to say this . . . but . . . yes. It sounds perfect."

When he smiled, my heart filled with light. Best feeling ever.

He chuckled softly as he tucked my hair behind my ear. "I guess this means I've gotta break some hearts here in Boston."

"Whose?" I questioned, jerking my chin back. "All the girls you have to leave?"

"No. My band. I'm gonna have to tell them I'm leaving."

"Yeah. That'll be hard. Just remember, I love you. I want you to come home so we can live and breathe our dreams together."

"Home is wherever you are, Lex. It has been for a long time."

My chest swelled, intoxicated by his love. After all our hard work, heartbreak, and honing our true feelings, our dreams were coming true.

Hayden untangled our bodies from the twisted sheets. He pushed me back onto the pillows and after making love again, he drew me into his arms. Our hearts beat as one. I finally felt what everyone else had seen blossoming between us. Love. Chemistry. Magic. Together, we'd move onward and upward to bigger and brighter things.

Nothing would ever come between us again.

I believed our love would last, not die. We'd survived breaking each other's hearts, surely we could survive anything else life threw our way. I wanted to risk everything to be with him. Take a chance on love and be happy. *He* made me happy.

And . . . *holy shit* . . . the biggest grin slid across my mouth. Fireflies fluttered in my stomach.

We were engaged.

We're going to get married.

I cuddled into his chest. There was no end to my love for him.

Without a doubt, Hayden was my forever. My happily ever after.

Chapter 29

HAYDEN

I paced the floor of the small living room, waiting for my band members to grab their morning coffee and join me. My nerves were strung tighter than a guitar string. Last night, after making love to Lexi, I'd lain awake making firm decisions, solidifying plans, re-reading Everhide's contract, and jotting down questions to ask them. This morning, during an hour long conversation on the phone to Kyle, Gemma, and Hunter, and their lawyer, we'd tweaked, refined and finalized my terms and conditions to join them. Now I had to tell my band.

Footsteps clopped on the floorboards.

A cold sweat broke out on my brow. *Here goes nothing.*

Kilt walked in and took a seat on the sofa. His gaze jumped between Lexi and me while we waited for Reg and Lewis to get their asses into the room. My blood pressure rose with each passing second. Nerves gnawed at my stomach. But Lexi sat on the armchair beside me, sipping her coffee, calm as always. *She's my end game. Remember that.*

Kilt jutted his chin at her. "When did you get here? When I saw Hunter's car outside, I wasn't expecting to find you."

"I arrived around midnight." Lexi curled her legs up and rested her knees against the padded armchair. "Thought you'd prefer to see me rather than Hunt."

"Too fucking right." Kilt pointed at the broken lamp and picture resting on the floor. "What happened here? You two have a fight?"

I grinned and chuckled. "Something like that." My band had never known Lexi, and I had been together. They'd never known she was the reason for my mopey moods. I had to come clean about that too.

Dragging their feet, Reg, and Lewis piled into the room and sat next to Kilt. Reg rubbed sleep from his eyes, and Lewis scratched at his tangled bed-hair.

"What's so urgent you had to get us up before midday?" Lewis covered his yawn.

My heart jumped to an allegro beat. Taking a seat on the side of Lexi's armchair, I clutched my knees and took in each of the guys sitting before me. Kilt, the first guy I'd met at college. Reg, the party animal. Lewis, the most chillaxed dude I'd ever known. I sucked in a deep breath. Saying goodbye would be harder than I'd thought.

Where to start? With Lexi or the job?

Easiest one first.

"So, a couple things have happened. First . . . Lex and I are together."

Reg laughed like a hyena. "Are you fucking kidding? As in, you're hooking up? No way. You two are like brother and sister. That's just wrong, dude."

"Ew!" Lexi winced. "Good thing we're not."

I glided my hand across her shoulders as I filled the guys in on everything that had happened during the past couple of months.

"Wow!" Lewis's silver eyes widened as he bobbed his head. "So that's why you've been in a constant crappy mood. I'm so glad you're finally together. You two always had the weirdest relationship."

"Thanks, I think." I winced, smiled, and glanced at Lexi. Unable to look away, I spoke to the guys. "There's one more thing—we're also engaged."

Kilt snorted coffee. "Just like that, you're engaged. What the fuck?"

"So does that mean you're moving to Boston, Lex?" Intrigue swung through Lewis's voice as his eyebrows shot skyward.

"Actually, no." I jumped in before Lexi could say anything. "That brings me to the main reason I needed to talk to you . . . About . . . um—" My stomach swayed and lurched. I clutched at my hoodie and rubbed at the ache in my chest. *Crap. I can do this.*

"Hayds?" Lexi's voice was barely above a whisper. "You've got this."

"Yeah. I do." I sucked in a deep breath and lifted my chin. "Guys, I'm leaving."

"What!" they hollered in unison.

"You can't leave." Kilt snapped.

"Yes, I can. I've thought about this for weeks, and I've made my decision."

"So this is her fault?" Kilt flicked his hand toward Lexi. "You're leaving for some chick?"

"Hey!" Lexi protested, throwing Kilt a fuck-you glare.

I smoothed my hand over the back of Lexi's head and kissed the top of her crown. "Chill. It's okay." Straightening, I turned toward the guys. "Lex is more than that, and you know it. But I've also gotten a job offer I can't refuse."

The three of them gaped, then blinked. It took a second or two for them to comprehend what I'd said.

"Fuuuck." Reg sank deeper into the sofa. "Let me guess. Fucking Everhide."

I lowered my gaze and nodded. "Yeah. Slade's injured and wants out. The guys asked me to play for them a couple weeks back."

"Why would you want to join them?" Kilt hissed. "You'll never be in the frontline with them. You'll always just be the backup drummer. You won't ever be famous, or walk the red carpet. You'll always be in the background."

"See, Kilt? That's where you and I will always differ. I don't need to be in the spotlight. I'll be playing for one of the biggest bands on the planet, playing alongside some incredible musicians, right there on stage with my friends. I wanted us, The Saylors, to get more popular and hit the charts again. But things have changed. We've flatlined. We've struggled to record one track. We all wanted to go off on different tangents with the sound." I jutted my chin at Reg and Kilt. "You guys are more focused on partying than music. It's a constant battle to get you to focus on what we came here for. And it's been hard for me to put in my best efforts since I've missed New York and Lexi."

"What about the music with Everhide?" Lewis's brow furrowed. "You won't be on an album cover, or write songs, or get a cut of royalties. Are you happy just to earn a salary?"

I half-grinned. "I won't just be on salary. I'm not giving up creating music. Kyle, Gem, and Hunt are incredible songwriters and have an amazing chemistry and creative process I don't want to interfere with. But I will play on the next album and hit the recording studio with them. If I write or contribute or create something unique for them, they have the option of taking it onboard. I will get a cut. If things evolve, and we compose songs together, my contract is flexible to accommodate future changes."

A muscle ticked in Kilt's jaw. His nostrils flared. But then the tension in his shoulders deflated. "So?" He leaned forward and rested his elbows on his knees. "You think you're a big-time hotshot now?"

I shook my head. I wouldn't miss Kilt's jealousy over other people's success. "Kilt, I've been loyal to this band for years. I've worked damn hard to get where I am. Being headhunted by someone like Everhide is a huge achievement. Yes, they're my friends, but out of all the drummers they could approach, they chose me. Because I'm fucking good. I'm stoked, man. Be happy for me."

"Where does that leave us?" Reg scratched his fuzzy black beard.

"You have Basil." I shrugged my shoulder. I was certain Kilt's brother would jump at the chance to take my place. He'd wanted to play with Kilt for years. "I'm sure he'd love the opportunity to play with you guys."

"Fuck." Kilt rubbed the back of his neck. "Is there nothing we can do to get you to stay?"

Shaking my head, I smiled as Lexi rested her cheek against my arm. "Nope. Not a thing."

Reg drained his cup and placed it on the coffee table. "When do you want to leave?"

Now that I'd decided, I wanted to start my new life as quickly as possible. "Basil is already here, working with Kilt's dad at the hotel. You won't have any issues in replacing me. So, I'd like to call it quits today if that's alright? Lex and Everhide are heading to London tonight, and I want to go with them."

Kilt huffed. "Just like that. You want out."

"Yeah." I nodded. "Just like that."

"Kinda surprised it took this long, man." A bittersweet smile slid across Kilt's mouth. "To be honest, I've expected it for a while. You're so fucking good. I've hated the thought of you leaving. But you've earned it and deserve it. Go take on the world, asshole. We're gonna fucking miss you."

I splayed my hand across my chest. "Thanks, bro." Deep down, Kilt was a good guy—he was just more often a dick.

"You'd better invite us to the wedding." Lewis said. "Do you guys have a date in mind?"

"Yeah." I hooked my arm around Lexi's shoulders. "When we get back from London."

"Well, shit, dude. Go pack your bags." Kilt waved toward the staircase. "Get your ass moving. You can sort your drums out when you get back from overseas. Go, you crazy son of a bitch."

"And you." Lewis pointed at Lexi. A big, sad smile drew across his face. "You take care of this one. He needs you."

"I need him too." Lexi clutched my hand.

As she glanced up at me, the love in her eyes filled my heart with warmth, making it beat stronger. With her, I was a better man. The man I was meant to be.

I gave her a quick kiss on the lips, then flew upstairs and packed my clothes. After giving the guys farewell hugs and well-wishes, Lexi and I jumped in Hunter's car. With my head still spinning, Lexi drove us back to New York. She took me home . . . to where I belonged.

***

In the green room at the Eventim Apollo in London, I rolled my sticks against my thighs. My legs jiggled. As I sat next to Adam, Joey, and Link, the rest of Everhide's backup band, my nerves swirled in my stomach, like a swarm of locusts. I hadn't expected to drum on this trip. Playing live at the Global Awards, three days after arriving in London, was totally surreal. Totally. Freaking. Awesome.

Slade excused himself from talking to Sophie and came over to sit beside me. "Hey bud, thanks for stepping in at the last minute." He tucked his long, blond hair behind his ear. "My shoulder's hurting like a bitch. Saves me needing more physiotherapy, painkillers, and another cortisone shot to make it through the song."

"I'm freaking out." I clutched my sticks tighter.

Slade leaned back and chuckled. He had that whole Taylor Hawkins from Foo Fighter's cool air about him. "You'll be fine. Sorry we haven't had much of a chance to talk since we got here. I've been at the doctor's and you've been at rehearsals. I'm so stoked you're taking the seat behind the drums for Everhide. You've got true talent and a raw edge, man. Keep at it and you'll become a legend in this game. I wish you every success. It's gonna be tough hanging up my sticks."

"Thanks." I scratched my chest, chuffed by Slade's commendation. "It still feels surreal. But I can't wait. I'm sorry-not-sorry you can't play for them anymore. What will you do after the surgery?"

"Look after my baby girl. She's so beautiful." Slade's eyes glistened as he gloated. "And . . . I hear there's an indie recording studio in Hell's Kitchen looking for a drummer."

"Are you shitting me?" My eyes widened as I stilled my sticks. "You wanna get a job at Cannon's where I used to work?" There was a strange twist of fate.

Stroking his beard, Slade dipped his head. "Maybe. I've put some feelers out. They're interested. I've gotta wait until my shoulder's healed after surgery. But yeah, I'd love it. I'd love the opportunity to work with different artists, and not have to travel anymore. For a worn-out, thirty-five-year-old man like me, it'd be awesome. Family comes first."

"So true." I smiled and tilted my chin toward Kyle, Gemma, and Hunter getting prepped and preened by their team for their performance. Dressed in leather pants and different shiny black button-downs, they were almost ready. "Good thing these guys are my family."

"Yeah. They are. They treat you like royalty. They're an incredible bunch of people. I've loved working for them. It truly sucks my body can't handle it anymore."

Fuck, I hope I never get injured. "Yeah, that does. You're a legend. Always will be."

"Thanks, bud. Now, go knock 'em dead." Slade slapped me on the thigh and stood. "While you rock up a storm, I'm gonna have another beer."

"Lucky you. Have one for me." But the thought of beer made me nauseous.

"Will do. Catch you later."

Slade headed to the bar. I sat fidgeting with my sticks as Everhide came over to join me and the rest of the backup band. My friends transformed when they were ready to perform. Their smiles doubled in size. Their energy tripled. It was hard not to be affected by them. They hovered around us, hyping us up for the show. Lexi darted back and forth, snapping photos of us. I jumped to my feet, weaved past my friends, and stole a kiss from her.

"Good luck," she tapped my chest. "Have fun."

"Always." I kissed her on the forehead. "You too."

Cary from the production team came into the room. "Everhide. You're on next. Let's go."

"Alright." Gemma clapped her hands. The backup band jumped to their feet. Laughing, Gemma yanked on the back of my shirt, dragging me away from Lexi. "Come on. It's showtime."

Kyle high-fived Adam, Joey and Link and then gave me a huge hug. "Welcome to your new world, dude."

Hunter threw his arms around both of us and jumped with excitement. "We're going to have the best fucking time. Let's rock."

"Hell, yeah." I hollered. It was only one song. *Easy, right? Yes . . . absolutely.*

I still wanted to throw up, though.

We were led backstage and cued to get into position.

Sitting behind the drum kit in darkness, I closed my eyes. The electric vibe in the auditorium zigzagged through my veins. I tried not to think about the award show being recorded, or about it being telecast live across the United Kingdom and Europe, or about the hundreds of fans and celebrities present. Nope. I focused on my drums. Luckily, Everhide were singing the hit I'd played at the Jingle Ball. I'd rehearsed it for the past couple of days, and knew it backward. I could play it perfectly. But that did nothing to settle my nerves. This was my first performance . . . as Everhide's new drummer.

I took a deep breath and let it out slowly.

I jiggled my foot. Stretched my neck from side to side.

The Global Awards host introduced Everhide and the crowd erupted with a roar. The energy hit me right in the center of my chest. That rush of adrenaline was what I lived for.

I stuffed in my ear monitors, muffling out the noise. My heartbeat, my breath, my pulse were amplified inside my head. Gripping onto my sticks tighter, I wriggled on my stool. I placed my feet on the pedals. With my eyes on the cue light on the monitor just offstage, I licked my lips and swallowed hard. The light turned green. The production director pointed at me.

Time to play.

I struck the bass drum. *One. Two. Three.* Boom! Unable to contain my grin, I hit the cymbals, the snares, and tom-toms. I pummeled out the beat. The back-up band joined in—guitar, bass, and keys. Music hummed through my bones and reverberated through the floor. Pyrotechnics popped, and blazing lights illuminated my friends at the front of the stage.

I took a quick glance toward the side of the stage. Lexi stood there with her lens in front of her face. My heart thudded louder than my drums. She lowered her camera and smiled. *Damn, she's so freaking perfect.*

Kyle, Gemma, and Hunter sang, and revved up the crowd. The entire audience was on their feet, dancing, clapping and singing along in time. I struck my drums, swept up in the rhythm and electric vibe. My skin sweated and tingled. This was magic. I hadn't had a buzz like this with The Saylors in so long. I'd missed this. I'd craved it. Now I had it back.

This was music. This was living. This was a dream come true.

At the end of Everhide's performance, I rushed off stage and caught Lexi in my arms. I swung her around, placed her back on her feet and kissed her. While my friends quickly changed and were ushered to their seats for the awards, I got to stay behind the scenes with Lexi. It was so much better than being the center of attention. This was where I belonged.

"You were amazing." She stroked my hot, sweaty cheek.

"Thanks. That was such a rush."

"I took some awesome photos of you."

"You're supposed to take them of Gem and the guys. Not me."

"Hmm . . . I did. But I can't help myself. I have a thing for drummers."

"Better not be all drummers." I grinned, rubbing my hands over her back.

"Definitely only one." She thumbed toward the green room. "You want to go have a drink? I've got about thirty minutes to kill before their category is announced."

"Sounds good. But after this." I hooked my finger through her belt loop, tugged her close, and pressed my lips to hers. I didn't think I'd ever get enough of kissing her. It felt so right. So good. She was my forever.

Taking her hand, I kissed the shiny diamond sparkling on her finger that we'd bought yesterday on Oxford Street. "I love you and can't wait to marry you."

"Same." She blushed, kissed me again, then led me toward the bar.

There would be no more regrets, doubts, or fears. With Lexi by my side, I'd finally found home. My dreams had come true.

Chapter 30

LEXI

Smoothing my hand over my long, silky cream skirt, I took a deep breath to steady my racing heart. The arched doorway of the St. Boniface Church in my hometown of Sea Cliff loomed before me. As I stood by the limousine, my head spun. The nerves skipping in my stomach upped their pace. "Holy shit. I can't believe this is happening."

Kara and Gemma, in their matching navy dresses, fussed over my skirt and veil, straightening them into place behind me.

"You look beautiful." Kara gave me a quick hug.

"Thanks to you." I hadn't wanted an elaborate dress. Just a simple floral-lace top with cap sleeves and a plain silk skirt. Kara had designed and delivered the perfect gown. "Thank you for making my dress. It's gorgeous."

"You're welcome." She dipped her chin, and her stunning smile lit her face.

Wade, the photographer Gemma had organized, darted around us, taking shots from different angles. The flashes blinded me, and my cheeks ached from all the smiling.

It felt weird not being behind the lens.

The last two weeks since the awards show in London had been another mind-blowing experience. When Hayden and I told our friends we'd gotten engaged and wanted to get married as soon as possible, Gemma, Kara, and the Everhide team had jumped into overdrive. They'd organized the whole wedding in a matter of days.

With a hint of spring afternoon sunshine touching my shoulders, I glanced toward the church. "I hope the guys didn't get too drunk last night and shave off Hayden's eyebrows, or his hair, or draw a mustache on his face in permanent marker."

"Who knows with those three? But it would be funny, though." Gemma's eyes glinted as she straightened her skirt.

I wasn't worried about Kyle, Hunter, and Hayden causing trouble. I worried about my brothers. They'd been with the guys, and things could have gotten messy. Real messy.

"I'm sure they're fine. Stop stressing." Gemma tapped my arm with her bouquet of pale pink peonies. "So, are you ready? Let's get this show on the road. Before the paparazzi track us down."

"Yeah. Okay." I exhaled slowly and fanned my hand in front of my face. *Shit. This is happening.* "Catch me if I pass out."

"You won't." Kara smoothed her hand over my veil. "You've got this."

Dad stepped over from where he'd been waiting patiently by the limousine. "Sweetie, shall we?"

"Yeah."

"I can't believe you beat me down the aisle." He beamed with an *I'm-so-proud-of-you* smile. "You look absolutely beautiful. Hayden is one lucky man."

"Thank you, Daddy."

He held out his hooked arm. I latched onto him for dear life and followed the girls across the paved pathway.

The church ushers opened the wooden doors, and the small congregation rose to their feet. Music filled the air. But I couldn't focus on anything other than my gorgeous man in a dashing black suit standing at the altar beside Kyle and Hunter. My eyes locked onto Hayden's, and my heart swelled to the size of the moon. Tears prickled my eyes. Loving him was effortless now. I wanted to rush down the aisle, say I do, get that ring on my finger and get this over and done with, but then . . . I wanted to take it slow, savor every moment, drink him in to my soul.

Gliding down the aisle behind Gemma and Kara, I smiled at my family and friends. I paused to kiss Hayden's mom on the cheek. Anita looked so much better, fresh out of rehab with her hair neatly set and color in her cheeks. Then, I turned to the opposite pew, and hugged and kissed my mom. She dabbed tears from her eyes. I wasn't convinced they were happy tears. Mom hadn't taken the wedding news well.

Tough!

I no longer let my past hold me back. My parents' divorce and past relationships had molded me into the fierce, independent, ambitious woman I am today. But I'd finally listened to my heart and not my head . . . or my mother. I'd let love into my heart, and I was deliriously happy. I had Hayden. Nothing else mattered.

Dad placed my hand in Hayden's and disappeared to the pews. The moment I connected with Hayden, I felt as light as cotton candy. I loved him so much it hurt. The pastor began the service, but all I saw was the man I was marrying.

At the pastor's cue, I handed my flowers to Gemma. *Time for vows.* Turning back to Hayden, my stomach fluttered with a million butterflies.

He took my trembling hands in his. His steel-gray eyes glistened as he smiled a soft smile. "Lex, my angel, my partner in crime. From the moment we met, I knew you were something special. We've been by each other's side through so many ups and downs I've lost count. You made the good times incredible. The trying times bearable. I couldn't have faced them without you. You've stood by me through thick and thin. Your support, your smile and your selflessness have made me a better person. Most of all, you've always believed in me, supported me, and encouraged me to follow my dreams. Today, every one of them has come true. I promise to love you forever."

I fought back my tears. *My turn.* "Hayden, my best friend,

my love. You are my strength, my guiding light, my undeniable soulmate. You've always stood by me, no matter what. I love that you challenge me and push me to face my fears. I was lost, but now I'm found because of you. You have opened my eyes and my heart. Our path hasn't been easy, but I want to take every step into the future with you. Because of you, every day is bright. With you, I see no end—only forever. I promise to love you for all time."

After we exchanged rings, the pastor pronounced us husband and wife. Hayden lifted my veil and kissed me, complete with a gravity-defying dip.

The flush never left my cheeks during the signing of the paperwork or while we had photos taken down by the harbor or throughout the limousine ride that whisked us and our friends back into the city to MoMA for the reception.

I took Hayden's arm, and we entered the MoMA lobby. My breath hitched at the gorgeous setting. Dotting the foyer were round tables elegantly draped in black cloths with centerpieces of my favorite pink peonies. Crystal glassware and white plates gleamed in the soft light. Panels of greenery and twinkle lights created a private space, blocking the street view and access to the museum halls. My favorite spot—the sculpture garden—provided a magical backdrop for all the guests.

But as we headed toward the bridal table, I stumbled a step in my white Saint Laurent stiletto boots and froze. My eyes widened. My hand shot over my heart. There, on the wall, was a huge black and white canvas of Hayden and me in Belize at Gemma and Kyle's wedding. My heart exploded, filling my chest with warmth. I'd taken the photo with the timer, testing the angle and setup of my tripod stand. In the shot, Hayden stood behind me as we leaned in opposite directions, our arms were held wide, huge smiles lit our faces, our hair blew in the wind, the ocean glistened in the background.

I tightened my hold on Hayden's arm. "Who . . . what . . . did you do that?"

"Yes, but Gemma helped organize it." Hayden tugged my arm,

dragging me from my daze, and guided me toward our table. He pulled out my chair, leaned forward and kissed me. "I had to make one of your dreams come true. Now you can say you've had artwork displayed at MoMA."

Oh, my. As I cupped his cheek, tears welled in my eyes. "That's incredible." He had made all my dreams come true. I'd never felt so loved, cherished, blessed. "Thank you."

Hayden settled into the chair beside me. Gemma and Kara sat on my right. Hunter and Kyle were on Hayden's left. Waiters rushed around, placing napkins on laps, filling water glasses and pouring champagne. I scanned our gathered guests. Hayden's former band and their partners sat toward the back and had already hooked into the drinks. Everhide's entourage filled a couple of tables in the middle of the room. Hayden's family and mine, including my brothers, sat in front of us. Only one chair remained empty.

I glanced at Sam, Everhide's head of security, and gave him a hopeful look. But he shook his head.

My stomach sank as I nodded. I wouldn't let one disappointment ruin the day. I glided my hand down Hayden's thigh and gave it a gentle squeeze. "This place is perfect."

He leaned in and kissed me. "So are you."

After appetizers and entrees, the night's speeches got underway. Gemma's heartfelt words about love and friendship brought tears to my eyes. Hunter had everyone in stitches with tales of our escapades at wild parties. Dad nearly sent everyone to sleep.

Hayden's mom trembled and stuttered in front of the mic before saying the only thing that was truthful. "Sometimes, your kids turn out to be much better people than you are. I don't think I'd be here if it weren't for Hayden and Lexi. Their friendship, love and support are a testament to their good spirits. I hope they survive whatever challenges come their way. I wish them all the best. Cheers." She downed a full-to-the-brim flute of orange juice and returned to her seat. I prayed her juice wasn't laced with vodka.

It was rare to see Anita clean and sober, and nice to hear some kind words for a change. But deep down, I knew it was temporary. Going by her track record, it would be three months tops before she was back to her old habits. And Hayden and I would be there to help her no matter how hard and heartbreaking it was. We were each other's strength.

We couldn't choose our real family, but our found family had become our world.

Kyle wrapped up the proceedings. "When two people are destined to be together, nothing can keep them apart. It's been incredible, sometimes frustrating, but totally awesome to see Lexi and Hayden come together." He turned to us. "Today, you married your best friend. Your love has stood the test of time and will only grow stronger over the years to come. The two of you have been part of our lives for so many years I'm honored to call you family. I'm even more stoked you are now part of Everhide. May music rock your souls forever. May your future be filled with happiness. Hayds, you've found one amazing woman. Don't ever let her go." He held up his glass. "Cheers. To the happy couple."

Hayden draped his arm around my shoulders and kissed me on the lips. "I'm not ever letting you get away."

I blushed. *So sweet.* "Me neither."

I clinked my flute against Hayden's. This getting married thing totally rocked.

As soft music from the DJ filled the room, guests chatted and dessert was served, Sam waved, catching my attention. My heart skipped a beat. He nodded.

Oh, shit. This would either go well or turn into a freaking nightmare.

I touched Hayden's arm. "I have a surprise for you. Come."

Following Sam, I led Hayden around to the entrance. I held my breath as I summoned a smile for the man standing by the revolving door. With his scruffy beard, hollow cheeks, and navy suit a touch baggy on his thin frame, he made The Rolling Stones' Keith Richards look like a young, handsome man.

Hayden's stride faltered. "No fucking way. Dad!" His voice rasped through the air. He rushed toward his father but stopped a few feet away. Their relationship was too fragile for welcoming hugs. "You came. How? I didn't even know where to find you. You didn't return my messages."

"I'm here, boy." Thomas tugged on his jacket lapels. "Some security firm tracked me down. Paid all my expenses. Here I am."

I twinkled my fingers at Sam standing nearby. "Thank you."

Thomas held his hands wide and stepped toward me. "Lexi, my girl. You look bangin' hot. Have I missed the reception?"

I gave him a quick hug, wrinkling my nose at the strong stench of alcohol on his breath. "Almost, but not quite."

As I eased back to Hayden's side, Thomas tilted his head back and whistled. His bloodshot eyes widened as he scanned the MoMA foyer. "Fuuuuck, this is a fancy joint, boy. I didn't even know you and Lexi were together. I didn't know you'd gotten engaged. Now you're married? That's fucking wild."

"You'd know if you'd been around." Hayden's voice slid through clenched teeth.

I wrapped my arm around his waist, hoping this didn't turn into an argument. But family was important to Hayden, even if his dad would never come close to qualifying for Father of the Year.

Thomas swayed on his feet, wiped his palm on the front of his shirt, and held out a shaky hand. "Guess congratulations are in order."

With jittery eyes and twitchy hands, Thomas was no doubt high and tipsy, but he was here. I just prayed that while he was in town, he didn't fuck Hayden's mom up again. That was wishful thinking.

Hayden sighed, relaxed his shoulders, and shook his father's hand. "Um . . . thanks. And yes, the engagement and wedding happened fast. We had no reason to drag things out."

"She's not pregnant, is she?" Thomas smirked, scanning me up and down.

Hayden hooked his arm behind me and drew my hip against

his. "No, Dad. She's not."

I stitched on a smile. *Thank fuck for that.*

"Oh . . . good. You want to enjoy the honeymoon, don't ya?" Thomas cackled and play-punched Hayden's bicep. "Now, where's your hospitality? It's a party, and I need a fucking drink. I'm headin' back tomorrow at noon."

"What? You're not staying longer?" Disappointment threaded through Hayden's voice.

My heart lurched. But when it came to Thomas, the shorter the stay, the better.

"Nope." Thomas grabbed his belt and tugged up his suit pants. They really were too big. "Gotta pick up the rig in Cleveland and drive to Bismarck."

"Oh. Okay." Hayden rubbed the back of his neck. "Well, we'll catch up before the night is over. But for now, we'd better get back to everyone."

As we headed toward the guests, Hayden's mom leaped from her chair. "Thomas?"

Thomas held his arms wide and quick-stepped toward her. "Well, who's this dashing young lady we have here?"

Anita blushed as pink as the peonies. "Oh, stop it."

"How you doing, darlin'?" He winked back at Hayden. "Enjoy your evening, boy. But if you'll excuse me, I've gotta reacquaint myself with this fine lass." He pranced toward Anita. She giggled like a schoolgirl.

As the room echoed with the clink of silverware against plates, and guests mingled, drank, talked, and polished off their tiramisu dessert, I drew Hayden to a halt behind our table.

"Hey?" I whispered and touched his cheek. "Is everything okay?"

"Yeah." His eyes lingered on Thomas. He was making a loud ruckus as he reunited with family and friends. "Dad hasn't changed a bit. Doubt if he ever will." He drew me into his embrace and rested his head against mine. "I don't know how you did it, but thank you. My parents are total fuck-ups. I love them and hate them so freaking much. But I'd never handle them if it wasn't for you. Thank you, my angel."

I glided my fingers down his chest and tugged on his silky black tie. "Our families are more dysfunctional than the Gallagher family in the TV show *Shameless*, but they're ours. And you are mine. I love you. Forever. I promise."

He touched lips to mine. "You are all I'll ever need."

Once the waiters cleared the dessert dishes, Gemma tapped me on the arm. "Gotta go."

"Where?" My gaze followed Gemma. She grabbed Kyle and Hunter and headed for the mic. The blood drained from my face. "Oh, no."

They weren't. Were they?

Kyle and Hunter grabbed guitars . . . *their guitars* . . . that had been stashed behind the DJ's table. They put them on, then strummed the strings softly.

Yep . . . they were.

Gemma winked at us and spoke into the mic. "Would Mr. and Mrs. Moore please take the dance floor?"

My pulse quickened. "What's this?" I lowered my voice as I leaned into Hayden and waggled my finger at our friends. I'd specifically asked them not to sing at our wedding. I loved them, but they deserved to enjoy the celebrations and not have to perform.

"It's my turn to deliver a surprise." Hayden held out his hand.

My stomach flipped. *For me?* Slowly, a huge grin swept across my face. I shook my head, blushed, and slid my hand into his. "Okay."

Hayden led me to the clearing in front of our friends. My skirt swirled around my legs as he spun me around. Stepping in close, he took me in his arms.

Overwhelmed and overcome by the amazing day, I melted against his chest. Swaying from side to side, I moved in time with his steps. My heart beat against his.

Gemma's beautiful voice filled the air.

Never knew the moon shined so bright
Never knew the stars held the light
Never knew I wanted to hold on tight
'Til I found you
'Til I found you

Never knew what a kiss could mean
Never knew how a touch should feel
Never knew how lost I'd been
'Til I found you
'Til I found you

Never knew what was at stake
Never knew what we could make
Never knew what my heart could take
'Til I found you
'Til I found you

Never knew how much I loved you so
Never knew I could never let you go
Never knew my love could grow
'Til I found you
'Til I found you

Never knew where I belonged
Never knew you made me strong
I've loved you, angel, for so long
With you, I've found home
With you, I've found home

As Hunter and Kyle played out the song on their guitars, I glided my fingertips over the lapels of Hayden's jacket. "Did you write that?"

"Yeah." Color touched his cheeks as he clutched my hand against his chest. "They helped with the music."

"It was beautiful." I waved and blew a kiss to our friends. Gemma flicked it aside with a huge smile plastered across her face. Linking my fingers behind Hayden's neck, I stepped slowly to the music and met his gaze. "You're right, though. *We've* found home. Together. I don't think I've ever been this happy. Ever. Life before you didn't exist."

His arm around my waist tightened, drawing my body flush with his. His warmth charged up my spine and settled in my cheeks. A subtle grin played across his lips. "You're stuck with me forever." Shards of silver flickered in the depths of his steel-gray eyes. His lips hovered an inch from mine. "You're my angel. Always. I love you."

I cupped his cheek. "And I love you. Forever."

As our lips met, the DJ took control. Disco lights flashed. Party music boomed across the room and rattled the windows. Guests joined us on the dance floor.

My head fell back, and I laughed. Hayden spun me around, drew me in close and twirled me across the dance floor. His laugh, his smile and being in his arms filled my heart with pure love, joy, and happiness.

After all our ups and downs, heartache, and pain, our lives had become one. As our friends and family danced around us, I absorbed Hayden's love into every cell of my body—his warmth, his tenderness, his kindness. I kissed him and closed my eyes. Images of us flickered through my mind—from our days at college, to living with each other, to being together. We'd been the best of friends. Now we were lovers . . . Husband and wife. Every captured moment, collected memory, and click of my camera had brought us to this point in time. The love embedded in my heart was now, and would always be, for no one else but Hayden.

***

Thank you for reading **REGRET – The Price of Truth.**
Lexi and Hayden finally joined the Everhide family and found their happily ever after. Yay!

But wait! Hunter and Kara's journey is not over yet! Be prepared for another emotional punch!

He had grand plans. Fate had other ideas. Was the past about to play on repeat?

Continue the series with Book 5 : **REWIND: The Price of Fate**.

AVAILABLE ON AMAZON and KINDLE UNLIMITED

P.S. If you enjoyed **REGRET – The Price of Truth**, would you kindly take a moment and leave a quick product review. They are music for an author's soul.

Thank you,
Tania Joyce.

BEFORE YOU GO.

Would you like a BONUS EBOOK for FREE?

Find out how my world of rockstars began with the Everhide Rockstar Romance series.

ROCKED – The Price of Dreams is the origin story to my bestselling Everhide Series. Find out how the band met in high school, experience their heartbreak and hardships, and follow their journey to stardom. It is the pre-romance to the adult relationships that develop, evolve, and change throughout the six books. (Three standalones, three follow-ons—all happily ever afters, no cliffhangers).

This series will have you falling in love, shedding tears, and laughing out loud.

Read the prequel, **ROCKED – The Price of DREAMS,** for **FREE** when you subscribe to my newsletter. I only send emails about once a month, so your inbox won't be inundated with my news. Please subscribe here: https://taniajoyce.com/subscribe.

NEWSLETTER

For information about my new releases, events, and special offers, please subscribe to my monthly newsletter.
Join at: https://taniajoyce.com/subscribe
REMEMBER: You get a BONUS BOOK if you join.

***

FOLLOW TANIA JOYCE

You can follow and find me on the following social media platforms.

Amazon: https://amazon.com/author/taniajoyce
BookBub: https://www.bookbub.com/authors/tania-joyce
Facebook: https://www.facebook.com/taniajoycebooks
Goodreads: https://www.goodreads.com/taniajoyce
Instagram: https://www.instagram.com/taniajoycebooks/
Pinterest: https://www.pinterest.com/taniajoycebooks
TikTok: https://www.tiktok.com/@taniajoyce
Web: http://taniajoyce.com

ABOUT TANIA JOYCE

Tania Joyce is an author of rockstar, contemporary and new adult romance novels. Her stories thread romance, drama and passion into beautiful locations ranging from the dazzling lights and glitter of New York to the rural countryside of the Hunter Valley.

She's widely traveled, has a diverse background in the corporate world and has a love for sparkles, shoes and shiraz.

Tania draws on her real-life experiences and combines them with her very vivid imagination to form the foundation of her novels. She likes to write about strong-minded, career-oriented heroes and heroines that go through drama-filled hell, have steamy encounters and risk everything as they endeavor to find their happy-ever-after.

Tania shuffles the hours in her day between part-time work, family life and writing. One day she hopes to find balance!

She loves to hear from her readers.

Visit: www.taniajoyce.com
or email her at: tania@taniajoyce.com

***

MORE BY TANIA JOYCE

Visit Tania Joyce on Amazon.Com